Goode Vibrations of

The Dead River Valley

Amy Safford

Saco River Books

Identifiers:

ISBN: 979-8-9903619-3-5 (paperback)

ISBN: 979-8-9903619-4-2 (e-book)

ISBN: 979-8-9903619-5-9 (hardcover)

Release Date: October 25, 2025

Book Cover Design and Title Page Illustration by Marissa Joly

Map Illustration by Dorette Amell

First edition 2025

Author's Note

THE DEAD RIVER VALLEY in northwestern Maine is a place of storied history, rich with courage and sacrifice. From Benedict Arnold's expedition at the beginning of the Revolutionary War to the flooding of riverside villages in the twentieth century, the historic tapestry of this fertile mountain valley is layered and spiritual.

In 1775 Benedict Arnold led over a thousand men through the wilderness of the Kennebec and Dead River Valleys on a little-known route to the Canadian border to take the British by surprise in Quebec. Although doomed from the outset, the expedition is nonetheless an epic story of sacrifice and bravery in the fight for America's freedom from oppression.

Later, in 1820, settlers moved into the Dead River Valley, nestled in the bosom of Mount Bigelow, to harness the rushing rivers and log the bountiful forests. Several generations and over 80 families settled in the villages of Bigelow, Flagstaff, and Dead River until 1950 when the power company built a dam at Long Falls and flooded the valley.

This novel is homage to the pioneers of our shared past—indigenous natives, hardy soldiers, and settlers who braved the Maine wilderness in the name of freedom. Apart from recorded historical facts, the names, characters, places, and incidents portrayed in this work are either the products of the author's imagination or, if real, are used fictitiously.

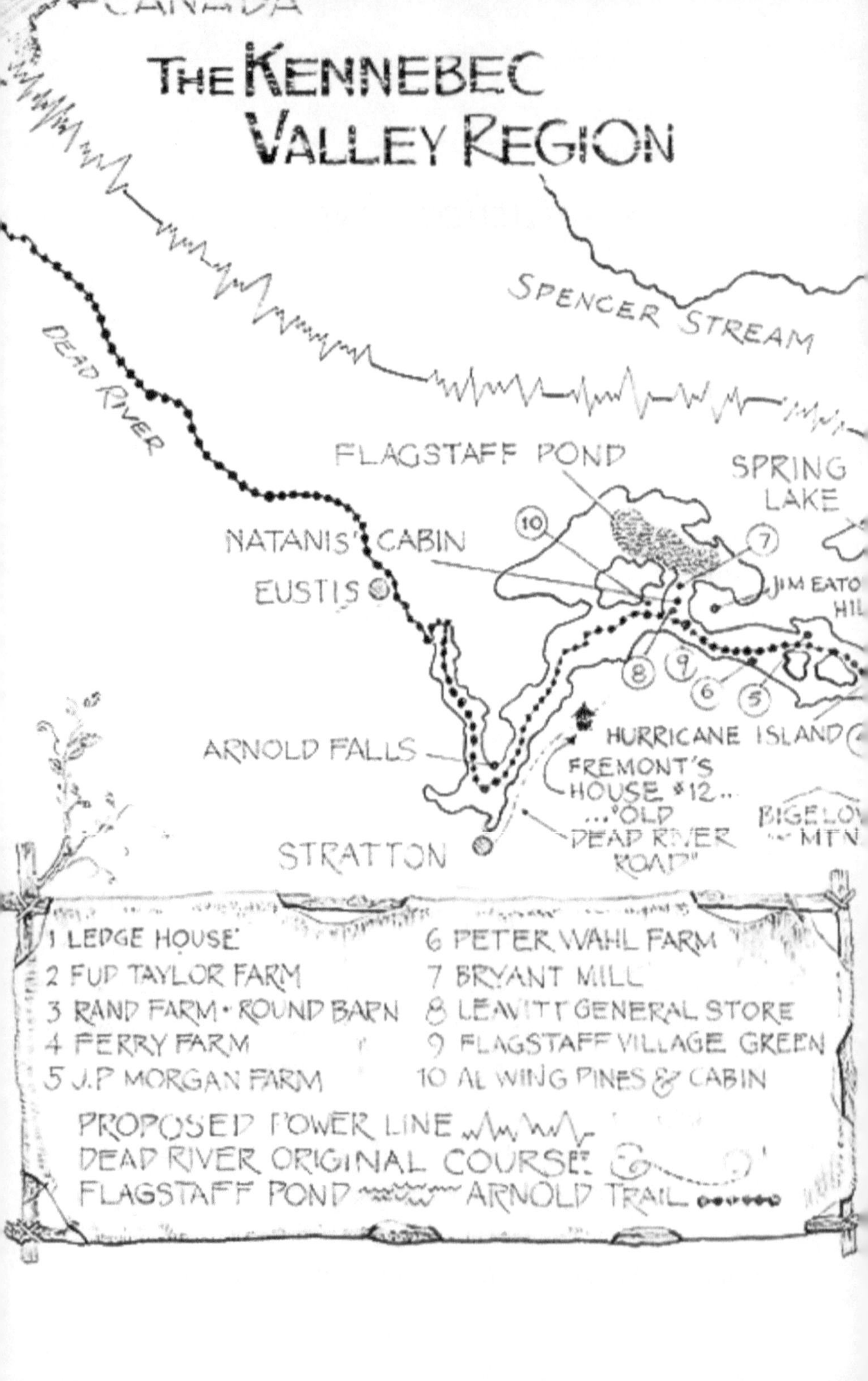
← CANADA
THE KENNEBEC VALLEY REGION
SPENCER STREAM
DEAD RIVER
FLAGSTAFF POND
SPRING LAKE
NATANIS' CABIN
10
7
EUSTIS
JIM EATON HILL
8
9
6
5
ARNOLD FALLS
HURRICANE ISLAND
FREMONT'S HOUSE #12 ...
... "OLD DEAD RIVER ROAD"
BIGELOW MTN
STRATTON
1 LEDGE HOUSE
2 FUD TAYLOR FARM
3 RAND FARM · ROUND BARN
4 FERRY FARM
5 J.P. MORGAN FARM
6 PETER WAHL FARM
7 BRYANT MILL
8 LEAVITT GENERAL STORE
9 FLAGSTAFF VILLAGE GREEN
10 AL WING PINES & CABIN
PROPOSED POWER LINE
DEAD RIVER ORIGINAL COURSE
FLAGSTAFF POND   ARNOLD TRAIL

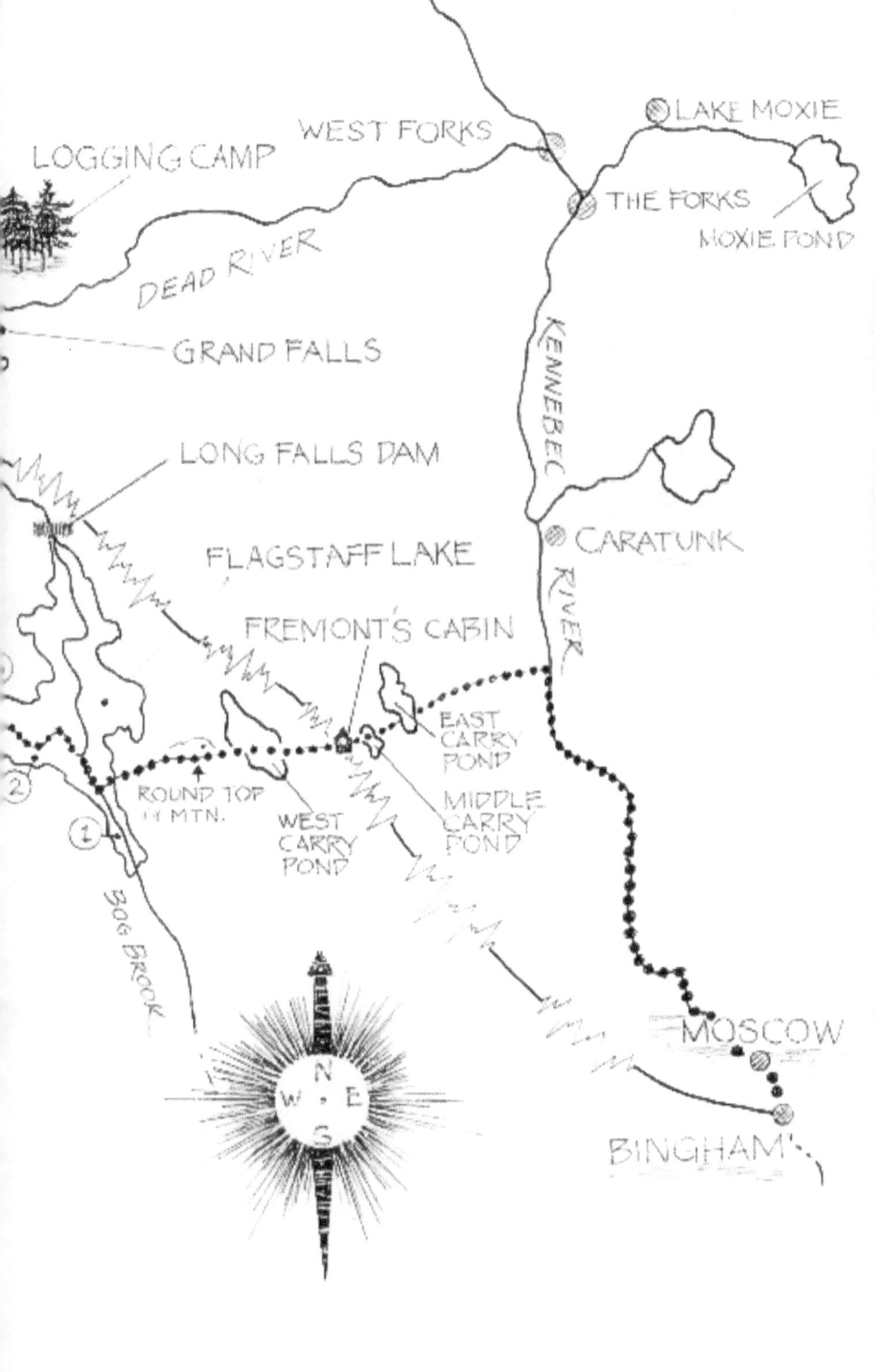

LOGGING CAMP
WEST FORKS
LAKE MOXIE
THE FORKS
MOXIE POND
DEAD RIVER
GRAND FALLS
KENNEBEC
LONG FALLS DAM
FLAGSTAFF LAKE
CARATUNK
RIVER
FREMONT'S CABIN
EAST CARRY POND
MIDDLE CARRY POND
ROUND TOP MTN.
WEST CARRY POND
BOG BROOK
MOSCOW
N
W E
S
BINGHAM

Foreword

GENERATIONS LIVING IN THE Dead River Valley

I am a fifth generation of this area. My grandparents moved to Dead River Township in the mid-1800s, and three generations of my family lived and worked in Flagstaff village on the winding Dead River for over a century before it was flooded in 1950. The Dead River Valley was a great place to live and raise families. Everyone was happy and contented, even though they never had any centralized electricity. Crank telephones were introduced during the turn of the twentieth century, so people were not isolated and cut off from the rest of the world.

My great-grandfather, Warren Wing, was a renowned bear trapper, bear hunter, and guide. My grandfather, Cliff Wing, was a boatbuilder, guide, log cabin builder, and woodsman. "Captain Wing" made good wages transporting woodsmen and supplies across the old Flagstaff Pond in his handmade boats. My father, Duluth Wing, was born in Flagstaff village and, immediately after graduating from the village high school, got a job as a forest fire watchman on Mount Bigelow where, incidentally, he also met my mother. Over his thirty-eight-year career as a state forest ranger, he watched over the woodlands of our valley and fought every one of the flowage fires in the late '40s when Central Maine Power was clearing the forests to make way for the reservoir.

My parents were forced to sell their property and move away for the creation of Flagstaff Lake. Their story is not unique around here. After giving up their homes, many took solace in the knowledge that the building of a new dam would better the lives of people living down-river—a decision made by the State of Maine back in 1927. Many relocated their families and homes to an area between the villages of Eustis and Stratton. This is where I grew up after our house was moved from Flagstaff village to what we refer to on this stretch of road as "New Flagstaff."

We have prospered and raised our families here just like those who once lived in the flooded Dead River Valley. The one singular feature we still have is the view of majestic Mount Bigelow, named after one of the officers in Benedict Arnold's expedition to Quebec City. People living in this area all know about Benedict Arnold and the hardships his men endured while passing through 250 years ago. Artifacts of that expedition have been found locally, many by my father, and are on display at our local museum.

As a lifelong resident of Eustis, growing up and living on the shores of Flagstaff Lake, I found a particular kinship in this story by Amy Safford. The history of Flagstaff Lake, the flooding of the villages of Flagstaff and Dead River, and the debate about the current transmission line and generation of electricity by wind on our nearby mountaintops, are very much alive in our community today. Needless to say, the story of this land, and Benedict Arnold's expedition through our mountains and valleys, are very near and dear to me and my family. I applaud Amy for learning our local history and bringing it to life.

—Kenny R. Wing, coauthor, *The Lost Villages of Flagstaff Lake*;
board member, Arnold Expedition Historical Society

The Arnold Expedition: An American Epoch

The Arnold Expedition of 1775 was a courageous military campaign across the wilderness of Maine to capture Quebec City from the British. The Continental Army traversed a footpath through the Maine wilderness—a little-known route used for hundreds of years by Native Americans, and later by trappers and Jesuit priests, between the Kennebec River and the St. Lawrence River.

Only a few months earlier, the Second Continental Congress had established the Continental Army and elected George Washington as commander-in-chief. Congress proposed a plan to capture Canada, believing the French might be willing to ally with the Americans against their common enemy and possibly become the fourteenth colony.

Another military force led by General Philip Schuyler moved along the traditional route up the Hudson River and across Lake Champlain toward Canada. The strategic attack would cut off the British from the waterways they needed to reinforce their troops already in the colonies by capturing Fort St. Johns [Fort Saint-Jean] and Montreal, and then Quebec City.

General Washington had heard of an alternative route to Quebec through the District of Maine by way of the Kennebec and Chaudière Rivers. An expedition like this would draw British troops away from Fort St. Johns to defend Quebec City, allowing Schuyler's army to seize Fort St. Johns and Montreal and then join forces with Arnold to capture Quebec.

Washington took command of approximately 16,000 troops of militiamen in Cambridge, Massachusetts, soldiers eager for duty but lacking direction and leadership. For the expedition to Quebec, he needed an officer who could motivate the men and make quick decisions to lead a fast-moving force with minimal equipment.

He chose Colonel Benedict Arnold. Although a controversial figure known to be stubborn and impulsive, Arnold had shown bravery and resourcefulness. Washington consulted with others familiar with the footpath through Maine and estimated it would take twenty days for the troops to reach Quebec City—an estimate that ultimately proved unrealistic and disastrous.

On September 11, just three months after Washington took command of the Continental Army, 1,150 soldiers boarded eleven sailing ships in Newburyport for a twenty-four-hour trip to the mouth of the Kennebec River in Maine. They continued upriver to the shipyard of Reuben Colburn, who had received a contract to build a fleet of two hundred bateaux for the expedition.

Now outfitted with heavy wooden boats to carry a hundred tons of supplies, they rowed and poled to Fort Western in the town known today as Augusta: the staging area for the incursion into Canada. On September 25, Daniel Morgan's division of three rifle companies was the first to leave the fort and clear the thirteen-mile Great Carrying Place Portage Trail between the Kennebec and Dead Rivers.

Over the next four days, the remaining three divisions followed, rowing, poling, and hauling 400-pound leaky bateaux up the fast-moving Kennebec River over rocks and ledges while the others marched along the riverbank. They portaged through the wilderness cleared by Morgan's men, crossing three ponds before they finally reached the long, winding Dead River.

Unbeknownst to Arnold, a division of about 400 men behind him had lost heart and returned to Cambridge with precious remaining food rations. But despite the hardships, Arnold's optimism and encouragement kept the rest of the haggard force pressing forward. The army faced raging floods, torrid whitewater, and a strenuous climb over the height of land before they finally escaped the wilderness to reach the St. Lawrence River.

An estimated 40 to 50 soldiers died from sickness, fatigue, or starvation. The original force of 1,150 men was down to nearly half after losses from desertion, disease, and starvation over 270 grueling miles through the Maine and Canada Wilderness in forty-five days.

When they arrived in Quebec, Arnold commanded a force of 600 men. The expedition was later joined by Schuyler's army of 300 led by General Richard Montgomery, outside the walls of the city. The two forces attacked the citadel on New Year's Eve of 1775 in a blinding snowstorm, but the doomed mission ultimately failed: 60 killed, 400 captured, and the remainder retreating from Canada.

Despite this, Arnold survived a leg injury and continued to prove his ingenuity. In the 1776 Battle of Valcour Island, his makeshift fleet of small boats delayed the British advance down the Hudson River by a year, and again at Saratoga his bravery, fueled by his impulsive nature, helped secure the defeat of General John Burgoyne's troops.

In the end, it was Arnold's oversized ego, sometimes questionable business dealings, and snubs from Congress over promotions that got the best of him. Benedict Arnold's biggest mistake was changing sides, believing the Americans would ultimately lose the war.

Although the attack on Quebec failed, the Arnold Expedition will always be remembered as one of the greatest adventure stories of a struggling nation fighting for self-determination and freedom. Two hundred and fifty years after the birth of our nation, America is still celebrating its independence.

—Norman R. Kalloch, Jr., Benedict Arnold expedition historian;
author of *A Long Way to Walk* and other historical Maine fiction

This book is dedicated to the families who settled in the villages of the Dead River Valley (1820-1950) and their descendants, and to the soldiers and Native Americans who marched and aided in the Arnold Expedition of 1775.

Contents

1. Romantic Redux — 1

2. Prickly Premonitions — 11

3. Witch Trials — 17

4. Greedy Gullet — 29

5. Wolf Tree — 47

6. Secret Wardrobe — 63

7. Great Carrying Place — 87

8. Dead River Valley — 119

9. Legend of Awasos — 139

10. The Hunt — 159

11. The Clearcut — 183

12. Logging Camp — 199

13. Scorched Earth — 215

14. Terrible Carrying Place — 229

15. Treasure Hunt — 245

16. Conjuring an Apport — 259

17. The White Owl — 273

18. Preservation — 279

19. Long Water Place   287

Afterword   293

Acknowledgements   295

Bibliography   297

Chapter 1

Romantic Redux

PENNIE SNUGGLED INTO HER comforter, into its darkness, the sounds of Aunt Maude and Uncle Charlie overhead, that low cadence of a settled couple, their quiet rumble of laughter spilling over now and again. From the gray light outside her shoebox windows, she guessed it was about two o'clock in the afternoon. Aunt Maude had insisted she move in and take the basement with its nether windows that offered glimmers of light. That's what she had to hold on to, that promise of light on the other side, before sleep pulled her into another dream of her mother on the bridge, calling for her, a silent scream in the shadows, the high beams coming for her, swerving at the last moment to crash through the steel girder.

Rolling over, Pennie remembered all the awful things Ward had done before he drove off that bridge. His lies about his wife, his accusations, his ties to Chloe's death. Another low rumble of pain grew inside her like a poisonous bulb until she groaned and screamed at herself. Was she responsible for Ward's death? Was her dead mother beckoning her on the other side of the bridge that night? Uncle Alfie's words came to her, how being there at that moment in time was some kind of alignment, a synchronicity. The only thing she really knew, deep inside, was that she would always, always try to save her mother.

The sound of the cellar door opening made her wince. She could feel Aunt Maude standing in the doorway above. "Pennie, are you okay? I thought I heard something."

She wiped her eyes and put on a smile in the dark. "I'm fine. Just watching a video on my phone. A...a horror movie." Pennie waited, praying her aunt would not flip the light switch.

"We're going to Aggie and Alfie's for dinner tonight. Why don't you join us?"

"I've got an early morning, but thanks anyway." Living in the basement, no one knew if she was there or not. As far as anyone was aware, she was still gainfully employed.

Her aunt's voice rose in a forced cheeriness. "Okay, but don't forget about our lunch reservation tomorrow for Tita's birthday."

She'd have to face the family. An invisible anxiousness closed in on her, but she mustered up her own false frequency. "Wouldn't miss it!" When her aunt finally closed the door, Pennie checked her phone. It was 2:10 p.m., and Dani had called her three times. She knew her best friend would want to get together tonight; it was Friday. Turning over her normal excuses about being tired or not feeling well, Pennie called back.

Dani picked up on the first ring. "It's about time. Been trying to reach you for three days."

"I know, I've been under the weather, I..."

"I don't want to hear your excuses, Pen. I haven't seen you in two weeks, and this is my first art opening tonight. I *need* you there."

"Oh, shit." She sat up and tried to grasp the details of the room, how long she'd been in bed, anything to get outside of her own head.

"Don't tell me you forgot. This is a big deal for me." Her voice was soft, a kindness that touched a nerve. If there was anyone who could make her feel guilty by applying even an ounce of pressure, it was Dani.

"Of course I'll be there. What time was it again?"

"You sure have a short-term memory these days. Cocktails start at five-thirty."

Pennie lamented her forgetfulness, hung up, and turned on the night-stand light. The basement, a hovel, looked like some awkward self-possessed teenager was living there, trying to figure out which end of life was up. Hours had turned into days that turned into weeks, especially after she was fired from her job at the vet clinic. It had only lasted two weeks. If she learned anything about herself, it was her abhorrence for desk duty. She knew she'd go completely mad if she answered one more phone call from an imbecile owner who did not know the first thing about raising a puppy. The tenth time she managed to improperly schedule an appointment, the manager asked her into her office and offered a comforting smile that told Pennie it was over and to pack her things.

Her black jeans and white smock, the last thing she'd worn to the clinic, lay on a heap of damp towels, rank socks, wrinkled leggings, and T-shirts. Dragging herself up, extracting her body from the quicksand mattress, she looked in the full-length mirror on the closet door. Her hair was a wild reddish tangle of snarls, her eyes sunk in dark shadows of depression, her long knobby legs as boney as an aged cadaver. And it wasn't even Halloween. She couldn't very well stay down here for the rest of her life, so she looked out at the evergreen holly bush scraping against her window and thought about the idea of bracing for the growing coldness, the inevitable ice and snow of winter.

Through the glass doors of the Portland Museum of Art near Longfellow Square, Pennie spied Dani and Mali talking with a stout bearded man wearing wire glasses. The Indigenous twins radiated a light all around them, brightening up the crowd of mostly well-fed white people filling the crowded lobby. She considered walking away into the mild September night to stroll around the Old Port and peer into the shops and restaurants, an invisible voyeur enjoying glimpses of camaraderie. A couple came up behind her, waiting to get in—two middle-aged women all rosy and smiley, as if they were the most content couple on the planet.

A familiar irritation grew inside her, a certain kind of jealousy at their open affection for one another, and she forced a smile, opening the door for them. Taking a deep breath, she walked inside and immediately spotted Tita in the drink line. What a relief. If Dani and Mali were preoccupied, at least Pennie had her cousin to talk to. As usual, she was put together, exuding coolness in her skinny jeans and high boots. Pennie drifted up beside her, poking her in the ribs.

"Well, well, well. Lucky Pennie, as I live and breathe." Tita ordered a champagne cocktail.

She chimed in for the same. "Been a little busy with, ah, the new job and all."

Tita held up the plastic flute with a knowing smile. "Right, the vet clinic. How's it going?"

"Oh, you know. Juggling appointments and answering phones and calming nervous dogs and cats." She looked around and took a sip of the overly sweet champagne.

"You can save the routine for Aggie and Alfie."

She twisted her hair, vexed. "What do you mean by that?"

"I know you got axed, that's what I mean."

Pennie pulled her away from the crowd and closer to a corner of the room to ask how the hell she found out.

"Lars. He said his mother went in and asked for you but, strangely, you no longer worked there."

"Fucking Lars." Pennie downed the rest of her champagne and stared at the painting of a river dam behind Tita, blue water foaming and frothing around the gray cement structure. The title of the painting was *Dammed If You Don't*.

Tita looked around the room, assessing the demure shabby-chic crowd of artists and philanthropists. "I feel the same way about him most days, but what can I do? We made a film together and we've got to sell this thing." It was their ski documentary starring the daredevil, irrepressible Tita, and now that it was complete, Lars was out in California trying to sell it to one of the big streaming services. Pennie egged Tita to talk about the project, to which Tita narrowed her eyes. "Stop trying to change the subject. What happened at work, and where the hell have you been?"

"Oh, you know, I keep busy." She grabbed a shrimp canape from a tray drifting by, her stomach flip-flopping from the bubbly.

"Sure." Tita eyed Pennie's wrinkled blouse and stretch pants. "Looks like you just rolled out of your aunt's basement." As usual, Tita made her feel self-conscious and as small as a gnat. Behind them came Dani and Mali with hugs, beaming in the energy of the evening, only to be interrupted by the event's sponsor, the bespectacled man asking for everyone's attention. All eyes moved to the front of the gallery.

He thanked everyone for coming to support the exhibition *Our Maine, Our Rivers: Art That Inspires the Freedom of Our Waterways*. All sales of the artwork, from drawings to paintings to glassware and mosaics, would raise funds to support their critical mission to remove dams on the Kennebec River to restore the native fish populations and free the waterways from centuries of impoundment. He introduced each artist and their work until finally pointing to the six fish paintings by Dani, explaining that Dani and Mali were recognized members of the Passamaquoddy and Maliseet tribes. Mali had to grab her shy twin by the elbow to get Dani to look up and acknowledge the soft clapping on her behalf.

When his speech came to an end, Pennie and Tita worked their way through the crowd of young, nervous artists, a colorful mix of hair and tattoos and piercings mingling with older, groomed men in tailored suitcoats and nicely coiffed ladies sporting bright lipstick and expensive leather handbags.

Dani's canvases hung on the wall by the front corner: six striking illustrations, fish outlined in bold, black swirling ink and painted with sublime watercolors, a signature of her style. From left to right, they lined the wall swimmingly: *American Shad*, its dark blue back and lower sides and belly covered in silvery scales, looking as if it were undulating inside the frame; *Alewife* with its gray-green back, pale serrations along its sides, a thick body; *Blueback Herring*, blue-green with big, dreamy eyes and a slender body; *Atlantic Sturgeon* inked with rows of bony scutes along the olive green body, a long snout and four barbels protruding from the mouth, and a shark-like tail; *American Eel*, snakelike, in blackish bronze, with its pointed snout and gaping mouth; and *American Salmon* with its deep body of brown and silver tones covered in tiny black spots, sporting a finely squared tail.

Tita gushed over them. "They're stunning, Dani. Wow, just wow."

"Mali did all the mounting, matting, and framing," said Dani. "She really brought them to another level."

Pennie jumped in. "Don't be so modest, Dani. These paintings are magnificent."

"Absolutely," said Mali. "This is all you. I just added the finishing touch."

"And entered my paintings in the show. You did all the heavy lifting, Mali."

"I know how much these prints will increase in value."

Said like a true entrepreneur. Their silk-screening business—making cards, posters, T-shirts, and other printed items—would showcase this art soon, Pennie knew. Up to this point, they'd mostly relied on orders for swag from schools and other clients, but business was growing, and they were beginning to sell more of their own designs.

Big, burly Max, Dani's husband and a fellow artist, came up behind her, hugging her around the waist. "Aren't these amazing?"

Pennie froze, stopped breathing for a moment. Behind Max was Peter, Mali's husband, and behind Peter was Kush. Her heart thudded as deep as a tribal drum when they locked eyes. He smiled at her like it was just yesterday they had been together, when it had actually been a full year since he had moved to Philly to start a new job and a new life with a new girlfriend—far, far away from this city where they had dated and dreamt up plans, possibly a future together, until things fell apart.

"Kush," said Tita, licking her lower lip. "Long time no see." She pinched Pennie in the waist, getting her to wake up from her impression of a statue.

Kush said something, but his face morphed into a swirl of dancing cheeks and eyes and teeth; the whole room blurred. It was as if the dim light of the gallery somehow brightened, intensified, and she could see a glimpse of life beyond her basement hovel, beyond the wall of refuge belowground that had sustained her existence over the last few months. Dani leaned toward her and whispered in her ear, "You okay?"

Shaking it off, she turned to face the crowd so that she didn't have to see his face, that olive-colored skin, that charming grin. She didn't realize how much she had missed him until this moment. Her body took control, and she made her way through the crowd, somehow managing to find another champagne before Dani caught up with her on the other end of the room near the door, her intense dark eyes pleading with Pennie to stay. "I should have told you he was coming, but I just found out tonight before we left."

Pennie looked out the door at the dusky brick walkway, the lantern lights squinting in the square, the leaves blowing aimlessly, early droppers tumbling in nonsensical circles. "I think I'd better go."

"No, no, you can't, Pen. We're going out to celebrate. Please, this night is so important to me, and it won't be the same without you here." Behind them came Mali and Peter, Max and Kush, followed by Tita, who was still mingling with people who knew her celebrity from the mountain and, now, her documentary. Her cousin was so good at this—this crowd glad-handing thing. Pennie was somehow buoyed by her friends, friends who'd been in her life for years now, and against her best instincts, felt herself being swept up with the comfort of the same old group, walking in a cozy huddle toward the dim sum lounge at Empire Chinese Kitchen, one of their favorite old haunts.

Inside, they were taken to a booth where they all squeezed in together. She moved down to the end of the bench, and to her dismay Kush sat directly opposite her, staring at her until she looked up and ordered a mai tai. He said, "Make it two," and then the whole table chimed in with the same all around, Kush's deep laughter rumbling under the high cadence of the rest of the table. "Pennie, how are you? God, it's been, what, three months since we talked?"

He was referring to a phone call, a call when she'd questioned him about taking a nude picture of her. She turned her attention out the window, watching cheerful couples walking arm in arm down the chaotic street, the last vestiges of summer fading. "Max told me about the photo of you circulating on Facebook," he said. "Sorry to hear about that, Pen."

She looked into his dark eyes outlined in heavy lashes and saw the caring man in there that she had lost. When she reached across the table to him, he covered her hand, squeezing in reassurance. Tears crept into her eyes, and she grabbed the napkin to pretend to blow her nose. The revelry around the table in celebration of Dani and the growing success of the silk-screening business, and of Lars and Tita's film, was infectious. They all drank at least three rounds, losing count along the way, eating dumplings and fried chicken and juicy, tender pork until they were satiated.

Buzzing with the revelry of the night, they ended up on the '70s lighted dance floor at Bubba's Sulky Lounge. Kush slurred, calling it the "sultry lounge," and Pennie found herself laughing like she hadn't laughed in a long while, inside the dark bar with its strange taxonomy of stuffed foxes, miniature lighted carousel, Betty Boop standing on the bar, creepy doll with possessed eyes riding in a roadster, paper mâché clown with bulbous red nose, and tall, hollow knight in silver armor. Movie posters of John Wayne and Jane Russell and Gregory Peck covered the walls. Caught up in the fever, she ended up on the dance floor with Kush, those old tunes of the eighties filling them with carefree exuberance—Culture Club and INXS, Spandau Ballet and Chaka Khan—and never once did Pennie ask him about his Philly girlfriend, and never once did he mention her.

They ended up in an Uber together, slipping through the wee hours of the morning until they reached the quiet house. As silent as clandestine

specters, stifling any laughter until they descended the stairs to her basement hovel, they fell into the quicksand mattress, groping for one another in hot passion, everything a hazy blur, knowing each other's bodies like
treasures that had been hidden, frozen in the earth, now rediscovered,
thawing. Time wound backward without any space whatsoever between
them in the past year, a simple continuation of the intimacy they'd shared
before he had left—the same intense longing that brought them together
from the beginning, something that felt like falling in love, a glimpse of
passion amid the chaos of their distant lives.

Her eyes leaked with tears of joyous release in the silence of the dark
room, the heat of their desire still smoldering. He sat up and put his head
in his hands. She caressed his bony back, that long, lean torso she had
missed. This moment, the first blush of morning barely visible through
the tiny windows, was a peace she hadn't experienced since he had left.

Into the quiet stillness of the basement refuge, he sighed long and
hard. "What am I doing here?" Pennie grew stiff, cold, as if someone had
thrown ice in her face, over her naked body, had flung a window wide
open to let in the cold fall air. He sighed again, like he was trying to lift
the heaviest deadweight from his chest. "Loralee and I had an argument
before I left, and here I am sleeping with you. There must be something
wrong with me."

He shifted his weight to the side of the bed and stood up to thrust his
jeans on, one leg at a time. "Sorry, I just got caught up in, you know, in
the night. I have to go." And without so much as a goodbye or a glimpse
back, he crept up the stairs and closed the door behind him, as quiet as a
silent, hot tear.

Outside, the holly bushes scraped the little windows, the dependable
angst, the mean bitterness of it all.

Chapter 2
Prickly Premonitions

THE SOUNDS OF MORNING Pro Musica came from the kitchen overhead. Aunt Maude's humming filled Pennie with a sense of peace until the memory of the previous night seeped into her like acrid smoke. Beside her, the impression on the mattress where Kush had lain with her, where he had left her, lingered.

The sticky cellar door popped open. "Coffee's on," Aunt Maude twittered, lightly as a bluebird.

Right. Today was Tita's birthday lunch, and she'd be *expected*. And wasn't it nice to be expected, to be wanted? To be appreciated by someone, *anyone*? She missed her Uncle Alfie and even the indomitable, self-righteous Aunt Aggie. Pennie wrapped herself in a thin, wrinkled terry cloth bathrobe that smelled like old socks, and ascended the stairs.

Aunt Maude sat at the table with two mugs of steaming coffee, peeling a bowl of apples. Pennie tried her best to smile, squinting at the sunlight coming through the double window over the sink. "Morning."

Her aunt smiled back with loving eyes, peeling the apples with the dexterity of someone who'd skinned thousands of apples over a lifetime, using nothing but a paring knife. A continuous, long, curved peeling of red and yellow dropped silently into a ceramic bowl that had been passed down from Grammy Goode's kitchen, from her own mother's mother. Pennie picked up a peeling and chewed on the deliciously tart little piece of Maine Cortland from a nearby orchard at least a hundred years old.

"Have a good time last night at Dani's art show?" Maude stuck a peeling in her mouth, chewing, working in a rhythm, her thick, knuckled fingers always moving.

Pennie blew on her coffee and sipped the bitterness of the strong pot. "Her paintings were amazing, like black illustrations of river fish. The insides were painted with watercolors. They looked as if they were literally swimming under the glass."

"I'll have to get Charlie to take me over to the museum." She lifted herself with some effort from her chair to get the cutting board. "You were out late last night."

Calming yellow morning light shimmered between the turning leaves of the red maple tree, the memories of the night swirling like a haunt: sitting across from Kush in the booth, their whispers to one another, lost in the crowd at Bubba's. "We went out dancing." She cleared her throat. "Sorry if I woke you."

"Oh, you know, I have the sharp hearing of an owl. Doesn't take much to wake me up." She winked at Pennie, who remembered the story about Chebellok the owl swooping down and taking Native maidens to his world high above, the story that Dani had shared with them over dinner last spring at Aggie and Alfie's house. That seemed like a lifetime ago. Maude tossed the sweet, sliced apple chunks with her fingers and said, "Nice that Kush came home for a visit."

Pennie sat up, embarrassed. "How did you—?"

"You can't get much by me. And neither could your mother."

"I'm sorry, Aunt Maude. That was a mistake, bringing him here." She put her chin in her hands to stop her jaw from quivering, looking down at the clean white linoleum.

"What's there to feel sorry about? You're a grown woman. I'm not judging you, and I know how lonely you've been lately. Sometimes what you need is a good romp in the sack." Her aunt's face turned jolly with the thought of it, then turned serious. "Just remember that you'll never find true happiness in love until you've found happiness inside yourself." Maude patted her arm. "I have a feeling you'll begin to see things more clearly very soon, Pen." She stared into her niece's eyes. "If there's anything we have in common, it's the ability to keenly sense things."

Since her skiing accident, she did indeed feel different. More vivid, alive, intense, *real*. Her haunting dreams took her to places, to different realms even, like Malaga Island where she'd seen the contented lives of the blended-race fishing community before they were forced out by the governor and the state. "You feel this, this ability to sense...and *see* things, too?"

"Certainly, I do. Not quite as intensely as your mother did, though. And you're just like her. But you must either start embracing these special gifts or they'll overtake you." Her aunt reached for the sugar and spices in the cupboard beside the stove and poured them into the bowl of apples without a measuring cup or a spoon. She just knew.

"How do you mean?"

"If you let your dreams and visions frighten you, the fear will control you." She stirred everything together with a wooden spoon while she contemplated. Moving to the sideboard, she sprinkled flour. "You must learn to trust in them and what they are trying to tell you."

Pennie poured another cup of bitter coffee. "Did my mother talk about her dreams?"

"Once in a while she would open up, and it was frightening to listen to her describe how her dreams would take her into the past. She told me stories about our relatives down in Salem, Massachusetts, that none of us had ever heard of."

"Salem?"

"Oh, sure. They were Goods—Good without the 'e'—and they were mixed up in those witch trials. She told me and Alfie all about how Sarah Good was prosecuted—saw it all in a dream—but of course we didn't believe her, not until Alfie looked everything up, even went down to Salem."

"Wait, are you saying we have a witch in the family?"

She chuckled dryly. "I don't believe in witches. I think some people just have more keen senses than others. And your mother swore she learned everything through her dreams." Maude absentmindedly wiped her hands on her apron. "I've had enough strange dreams myself to know that what we can see is more than what others consider normal. We just know things before others do."

"Like Uncle Alfie does."

"Yes, that's right, although you'll have a hard time getting him to admit that. He calls it *good instincts.*" She shook her head, rolling out the dough on the floured sideboard with the wooden rolling pin, blackened around the edges with age. "Alfie and I both knew your mother was pregnant with you before the medical tests could even tell us." She pressed the dough, using her shoulders for leverage, flattening it out. "And more recently, I had a prickly premonition that Alfie had a heart attack before he even had it."

Her pulse quickened. "Me, too! I just knew something was wrong the night before when Tita was on the phone with him."

"That's what you have to come to terms with, this knowing." Maude carefully lifted a circle of rolled-out dough and placed it in the pie plate, tucking it against the sides of the dish with soft, delicate motions.

"Did you ever feel vibrations? Like an energy in the ground?"

"Hmmm, sometimes I guess I feel spirits in an old place that's haunted or when I'm walking through the cemetery, but that's about it. I never communicated with anyone, if that's what you mean."

"I could feel these intense vibrations at the Fairview cemetery, when I was over there with Uncle Alfie, and later I dreamt about the people from Malaga Island buried there. These dreams were so real…I could not only see but *feel* the sadness and desperation of those people." She wrapped her arms around herself. "It's really scary."

"Your mother used to talk about her dreams like that. Mine just help me know things, like when a big storm is coming."

Pennie hesitated, looking out at the grand maple in the backyard, the tips of its leaves showing a hint of its magnificent transformation to scarlet before the snowfall. "Do you think a dream led her to, you know…"

"Well, she was only thirty-three when she died. And she'd only talked about having these dreams for a year or two before then. That's why I'm worried about you." She placed the second rolled-out circle over the lumpy apple slices and pinched the top and bottom crusts together around the pie plate in nimble, delicate motions. The sun filtered in and pooled on Aunt Maude's apron as she turned the pie plate around a few times on the sideboard before she laid her hand on Pennie's, just like Kush had done the night before. But these hands were weathered and thick and covered in flour, the hands of someone who truly understood her and loved her for who she was.

"You can be afraid of your visions, or you can accept what life brings to you and never be afraid of your gifts."

She squeezed her aunt's strong fingers and felt the hot tears filling her eyes again. Instinctively, she reached for the triskelion necklace she still wore, ever since Mrs. McCarthy had clasped it around her neck in remembrance of Chloe.

"Now you better get showered and dressed," Maude said, patting Pennie's shoulder. "We're due at the restaurant in an hour." She moved back to the sideboard to pick up the pie and place it in the hot oven. "And don't worry about a gift. I've got us covered."

Chapter 3
Witch Trials

PENNIE RODE WITH UNCLE Charlie and Aunt Maude to the Union Restaurant in the old Guy Gannett newspaper building. It was only a few blocks from Uncle's Alfie's law office where she'd worked alongside Tita for three months last spring. How she missed that, but her uncle had insisted she pursue her passion for the animal sciences. What a disaster that had turned out to be. Failed attempts were stacking up, weighing down one side of her emotional balance scale. She ran over ways to explain things, or avoid the inevitable questions, especially with Tita knowing about the axing from said job.

Inside the restaurant, the others were already seated at a long corner table. She immediately made her way to Aunt Aggie to give her a kiss and then to Alfie, who sat at the head of the table. Uncle Charlie invariably sat at the other end. The women sat facing one another, and they seemed like one big happy family, smiling and busily settling themselves. A brusque waiter showed up, seemingly perturbed by the size of their party, and asked for drink orders. While the others happily ordered cocktails, it being a birthday celebration and all, Pennie and Tita steered toward wine and away from anything resembling a mai tai.

"Happy birthday, Tita Bell," said Aunt Maude, her blue eyes twinkling.

Tita beamed. Uncle Alfie drummed his fingers on the white tablecloth. "What are you now, thirty-five this year?"

Tita threw her father an appalled look. "I'm only thirty-two, Pop. Don't you know how old your only daughter is?"

"Lost track after you graduated high school," he said, joking with her.

"You don't look a day over twenty-nine," said Uncle Charlie, quick to jump in, winking.

"Thanks, Uncle Charlie. The idea of getting old makes me nauseous."

Aunt Aggie beamed at her daughter. "You're just getting started, Christina. Now with the film launching, your new career is really taking off."

Tita looked especially proud of herself today, wearing a blue satin blouse, large gold hoop earrings that tossed in her bouncy brown curls, plum lipstick and matching nails. She was downright glowing. "I hope Lars can get the distribution we need to make this thing *real*." The waiter brought the drinks to the table while Tita expounded. "All we need is a large streaming house to pick it up. That's how we can make it big before getting to work on the next."

Pennie leaned in, taking a sip of her chardonnay. "The next? I didn't know you had another project in mind."

"Hopefully, if we can get the funding we need, Lars and I are launching a documentary company."

Uncle Alfie, wearing a button-down, dark green Scottish wool sweater, sipped his bourbon. "That's a big commitment. You getting married soon?"

Aunt Maude jumped in. "Alfie, don't be so old-fashioned. If she wants to go into business with a man, she doesn't have to marry him."

Aggie leaned in. "You're absolutely right, Maude. There's no reason Christina has to rush into anything. A woman has choices these days." She smoothed the arms of her boiled wool jacket and pursed her lips. All things considered, Pennie knew that Aggie did not think Lars was up to snuff.

"Anyway," Alfie said, "I'd think long and hard about your relationship before you go into any enterprise together. If your romance ends, things will get very sticky."

Tita looked straight at her father. "Pop, believe it or not, a woman can separate the head from the heart. We aren't all just weak little females looking for a savior."

He chuckled. "Christina, you're not exactly a meek little lady who needs saving. I'm more worried about him."

At this, Tita finally relaxed. The waiter came around to take their orders: halibut, roast duck, short ribs, and other choices around the table. The drinks did their magic and moved the family into the loose merriment of the day. Then Aunt Aggie half-smiled at Pennie in a way that made her squirm in her padded seat. "Christina tells me Kush showed up and surprised you at the exhibition last night."

Her cousin cocked her head to one side, enjoying the change of focus.

The evening scenes flashed around inside her head. His intense eyes, his bare back on her bedside before he left. She coughed. "Didn't know he was coming, but we made a night of it."

"That's what I *heard*," said Aunt Aggie.

Aunt Maude jumped in. "It was great to see him again last night. I was up reading late, as usual, and didn't mind him passing out on our couch. He's such a nice young man."

Uncle Charlie looked at his wife, perplexed. "So much happens under my own roof when I'm asleep. Glad we can be a stopping place for any out-of-town visitors that happen by in the night."

"Oh, Charlie," Aunt Maude said. "You could sleep through a freight train."

He raised his eyebrows and drank his scotch. Aunt Aggie surveyed the table, her suspicious meter on high alert. "And how's your job going, Pennie?" She stared through her, trying to pin her down.

"Oh, good, you know. Getting my legs under me."

"Is that so?" She twirled the olive in her martini.

Pennie knew that Tita had let the cat out of the bag. She took a large swig of her wine. "Actually, I shouldn't try to hide it." She faced Uncle Alfie. "I was fired from my job for making some stupid mistakes, and they had every right to let me go. It seems I'm not great at setting appointments, and the pet parents were not happy with me."

"That's too bad." He swirled his bourbon. "Maybe the wrong fit for you. Many more opportunities out there."

"And then there's the issue of getting good references," said Aunt Aggie. "*And* there was the unscrupulous picture of you on the internet. I hope that stuff doesn't follow you."

Pennie shot a look at Tita, who looked down at her lap. There was no way her cousin would confess about her film-director boyfriend circulating the photo. Pennie made an excuse about using the ladies' room and left the table. Making her way to the other side of the long bar, she checked to make sure no one was watching and grabbed the bartender's attention.

The fiftyish woman with fake eyelashes nodded to her. "What can I get for you?"

"It's my cousin's birthday, and I'd like to buy her a birthday cake shot."

The bartender looked across the restaurant at the celebratory table. "Sure thing."

"Oh, could you make it a double? She's celebrating a new business."

Pennie was careful to stay behind the patrons at the bar, hidden from view, watching the bartender mix the lovely concoction of chocolate liqueur, Irish cream, and vodka. She handed her cash before grabbing the shot from the bartender and walking around the corner to the ladies' room, where she dipped inside. Shot in hand, she downed it, lost her balance, and fell against the tampon machine, which shot a plastic-wrapped tube onto the floor at her feet. An uncontrollable laughter took hold of her, a crazy kind of hysterics, as she remembered that one time when she and Kush thought they were pregnant—how relieved they were when she wasn't, and how she immediately got the birth control shot. How glad she was now, that she had never become pregnant with *his* baby. And why, for Christ's sake, had today turned into her confession day at the table? *Whatever! That nude picture didn't even bother her anymore.* The double shot of liquid courage gave her a new sense of self. She checked her teeth, wiped the chocolate from the sides of her mouth, applied a fresh coat of pink lip balm, straightened up with a smile, and walked back to the table, where they were discussing Tita's legal formation of an LLC.

The food was set before them and, knives and forks clicking around the table as everyone dug in, Uncle Charlie shared that he'd been working on his family's genealogy and found lineage going back to the Scottish Highlands. Pennie remembered Aunt Maude's story about the family witch in Salem. "Uncle Alfie, I didn't know we had a relative who was in the witch trials."

Alfie glanced over at Aunt Maude and furrowed his brow. "Why, yes, that is true. There are generations of Goodes all over New England."

Aunt Aggie said, "Did you know that my grandfather's uncle was a barrister in Massachusetts?"

Pennie was confused. "What do you mean, that he may have been a judge during the witch trials?"

She sipped her martini. "Very possible. We have a long history of lawyers in my family."

The birthday cake shot magically took hold of her tongue. "I was talking about my mother's family, *not* yours."

"Oh, don't get so worked up, Pennie dear."

"I just wanted to know our connection to the Salem witch trials. When did this, suddenly, become about *you* and *your* relatives?"

Aggie tipped her head back and continued cutting her steak with her serrated knife. "Pennie, you have to learn to be a little more conservative and thoughtful in your rebuttal." She chewed slowly on her meat. "I simply stated a fact about my relations since you brought up the court system, that's all."

"Well, it seems like you're always trying to steer the conversation in another direction when it comes to my *mother*, and my *relatives*."

"How dare you turn this into a debate? I refuse to participate in this ridiculous argument."

Uncle Alfie sighed heavily, put his hand on Aggie's wrist, and turned to Pennie. "We haven't shared enough about our relatives. I can certainly understand how you'd be curious about your mother's family and our lineage. I've done some genealogy research that I should have shared with you."

She nodded, gulping her wine, hanging onto his words like they were a lifeline to sanity.

"Why don't you come to the office tomorrow and I'll show you what I've found."

"Thanks, I would like that." She was utterly exhausted.

"And you can help me file a stack of deeds," said Tita, to lighten the mood. "There's always work to be done at the office."

Aggie jumped in, "You can't keep depending on your uncle, Pennie. And I say that with all kindness, dear. You have to learn to stand on your own feet, take care of yourself."

"I'm sure she's well aware of that, Aggie," Alfie said, digging into his pot roast.

Aggie had her own strange and impatient way of seeing Pennie, not for who she was but for who Aggie thought she should become in the world, and had taken on the role of mother and mentor to her. But it was Aunt Maude beside her who squeezed her hand under the table, who knew that Pennie would figure out her place in the world, who would never try to push her into something, to be something, that she was not.

A five-layer chocolate birthday cake filled with raspberry cream arrived at the table, burning bright with candles. They all sang for Tita, who would always be the apple of her parents' eyes. They were all just trying to do their best in the Goode family. Tita's eyes flew open wide, the joy of blowing out the candles to their applause. She feigned surprise at the gifts that surfaced: a new video camera from her parents and a thick homemade wool sweater that Aunt Maude had knitted with the alpaca yarn Pennie had given her, from a farm up in Newcastle.

"Aunt Maude, it's gorgeous," Tita said.

"Pennie gave me the wool, and I finally found the perfect project for it."

Uncle Charlie said, "I thought you promised me a hat with that."

She slapped his hand. "You must be dreaming."

"Oh no," he said, pulling back the last of his scotch. "You can't pull the wool over my eyes."

IN THE DULL MORNING light, Pennie decided to walk to Uncle Alfie's office from Stevens Avenue, taking the route through congested Morrill's Corner to Baxter Boulevard and strolling along the Back Bay path, watching a gaggle of a dozen geese swimming in formation, a high frequency buzzing through her. She headed up the hill to Congress, where the wind picked up, and by the time she reached Exchange Street, she wished she had worn a heavier coat than her anorak. The old wooden sign for *Alfred Goode, Esquire* creaked in the wind. She looked up to the windows on the second floor and realized how much she had missed the office over the last few months. At the top of the stairs, the dogs barked, a wild ruckus until she bent down to greet them: the mild-mannered yellow lab, Cassie; the spitfire terrier, Fella; the blockhead rottweiler, Teddy; and the lazy bulldog, Daisy. The lab, Mama Cass, was her favorite, being the mother of her own dog, Boone, whose soul had left the earth but had not left Pennie.

Her cousin was nowhere in sight, so she peeked her head inside her uncle's door. As usual, he was on the phone, the *Tribune* open to a crossword puzzle on his desk. He was speaking to someone about an old deed with a right of way and the options to remove it, to keep new neighbors from infringing on their beach access. *Who ever heard of anything so ridiculous as owning a part of the beach?* she thought. He motioned her to sit in the chair where she'd sat so many times when they were working on the Heritage Acres Business Park development road. Her pulse quickened just thinking about the case.

He hung up the phone and asked her if she'd had any breakfast, which she hadn't and didn't want anyway, her stomach still flip-flopping from the day before. "Thanks for inviting me over today."

Fella sat at her uncle's feet under the desk. "You'll have to forgive your Aunt Aggie about yesterday. She gets very anxious when your mother comes up. When she died, it was a trying time for all of us."

Pennie fumed. "That doesn't mean she has to hijack the conversation."

"You're right, but she doesn't see it that way. Don't let your emotions get the best of you, Pen."

"I just want to know about my mother and her family. What's so hard to understand about that? And why does everything have to turn into an argument?"

"You sound like you want to argue right now." He scratched Fella's ears as the old clock ticked on the wall.

The last thing she wanted was to let her uncle down. "You're right. I guess I feel like it was never finished yesterday and I'm still boiling. Aunt Maude told me that we had a relative in the Salem witch trials. That's all I was asking about, really."

"What else did she tell you? Anything more about your mother you'd like to know?"

Always the attorney, wanting to get to the heart of the matter, curious about what might be behind this new turmoil building up inside of her. The truth was, she was wrung out and exhausted and not even sure why. "She told me that my mother had vivid dreams, just like I have. And that she was unusually, uncannily right, that she could see into your family's history."

"Yes, that's true. Brigid told us she dreamt about a woman, Sarah Solart Good, who was accused of being a witch. We had no idea about this family connection until Brigid told us about the dreams, so I began looking into it, and come to find out, Sarah was convicted of witchcraft. At the time, she was homeless with an infant daughter, Mercy, and a four-year-old daughter, Dorothy, so they all went to jail together. Sadly, Sarah was later executed."

Pennie drew in a sharp breath. "What happened to her daughters?"

He clasped his hands together and leaned forward on his elbows. "The infant died in prison, and Dorothy was released after seven months."

"That poor family. Are you sure we're related?"

"I've done quite a bit of research down in Boston and at the Salem Historical Society. Dorothy is your grandfather Goode's, my father's, great-grandmother."

"But our names are spelled differently."

"Yes, that's true. My grandfather changed it so we could distance ourselves legally from all that. And the family moved up to Maine, but that was the sticky part of the genealogy. I had to find that legal paperwork."

"I don't understand why we have to hide our history. Those witches were wrongly accused of crimes they never committed."

"Those things can follow you, Pennie. You know that from the Malaga Island research you did. Our descendants did not want that history following them. People are cruel, and old prejudices die hard. It's no different for people accused of witchcraft, superstitions held against them."

Pennie thought about her own dreams, the premonitions. "Aunt Maude told me she has premonitions like mine. And now hearing about my mother's dreams…"

He stood up. "Grab your coat. Let's go for a walk."

She followed him and the four dogs out to the front office when Tita breezed in with sunglasses on, coffee in hand, and not a worry in the world.

"Oh good, Tita Bell, you can answer the phone."

"Where are you headed?"

"A little field trip. We'll be back."

On the centuries-old brick sidewalks of Exchange Street, the foot traffic was light. The dogs trotted along behind them, down to the cobblestones of Wharf Street and across Commercial Street to the pier. They passed people clutching their coats around them, the wind blowing down the wharf toward the rough current of the harbor. He pointed to a sailboat, its mainsail switching in the gusts, and told her about working on a tuna boat when he was young, before he met Aunt Aggie, how he worked with many a sea captain who could make their way around Georges Bank, navigating only by instinct. A sixth sense, one could say. His father, Grampa Goode, had told him about an old captain who was the best navigator he had ever met in his life. The old seafarer could find his way through a storm without a compass or any mechanism to tell him which direction the storm was headed. He just knew where to go by his own intuition, the direction of the current, the smell in the air, and the location of the moon and the stars. It was just something he was born with. Maybe it was being a son of generations of ship's captains, just inherited, or maybe he was reincarnated from a former captain who had sailed the seas his entire life and knew every current and weather channel up and down the east coast. Whatever it was, he had an innate sense.

"You can ask me a million times over why you and I, and your Aunt Maude and your mother, have an innate sense of intuition, better than most, and I'd be lying if I told you I knew how or why. Your mother especially had an uncanny sense of everything around her. I don't know if she felt the vibrations like you did at the cemetery, but she did indeed have these uncanny dreams that would show her the past. Perhaps that's why she ended her life. Maybe she saw something that was too much for her. We will never know, and the last thing we would ever want is for that to happen to you."

The wind swept her nearly off the wooden planks. She clung to her uncle. "I don't want to live in fear. Aunt Maude told me to face my fears, learn to embrace them."

He whistled to the dogs and led her away from the ocean toward Jay's Oyster Bar for a cup of chowder. "I've got a little proposition for you. Something that will get you out of your aunt and uncle's basement for a while."

She tried to hold back her excitement. "I'll take anything at this point."

"I have a cousin who lives up in Eustis, and he called me last week about trouble they're having with the power company."

"I didn't know you had relatives up there."

"Yes, seems we have relatives everywhere. Anyhow," he said, "my cousin was served an eminent domain notice. Seems the power company is taking his family hunting camp."

"They can do that?"

"If it's for a power corridor, they sure can, but we have time to find out if there's anything we can do to stop it." He looked at her with renewed seriousness. "Are you interested in driving up there to get some pictures, maybe dig into this thing a little more?"

Even though a little signal of hope lit up inside her, she replayed Aunt Aggie's words over in her head. Was she relying too much on her uncle? He always knew the right things to say to help her move forward, though, and yes, she would take that lifeline. The only problem was, she did not have a car.

He, of course, had already thought of that, too.

Chapter 4
Greedy Gullet

A WEIGHT HAD LIFTED off Pennie, now that she'd finally shared her *un-gainfully* employed status with the family. She was sitting at the kitchen table having coffee and freshly baked apple pie with Maude and Charlie when they heard a car pull in to the driveway. She knew that sound anywhere: her old Karmann Ghia, the rattling engine. Outside, she met Uncle Alfie, hugging him until he protested. "Okay, okay. It's about time you had your wheels under you again."

"But I told you I'd pay for the repairs when I could. This must have cost a fortune."

"My mechanics take good care of me after all the business I've given them over the years."

Uncle Charlie looked over the car, duly impressed by the vintage model, still running. "Purring as rough as a VW," he said. He checked out the body, commenting on its mint condition, the three-speed semi-automatic transmission, and the leather seats with tears carefully stitched together in a few places. He thumped on the hood and congratulated Pennie on the luck of having such a fine car back in service. Aunt Maude yelled from the porch for him to grab Pennie's stuff.

He loaded Pennie's duffle, backpack, and camera bag into the trunk, slamming it shut with a satisfying thud. Alfie commanded her to get in, start 'er up. It was like reuniting with a long-lost friend, someone always there for her, and to her glee, it no longer took three tries to get her engine to ignite. The Karmann purred loudly and Pennie revved her a few times for good measure. Aunt Maude shuffled over to the car window to give her a kiss and a hug. "Tell Fremont I said hello, and don't do anything I wouldn't do," she said, winking. Uncle Alfie gave her the address to his cousin's house in Eustis. According to her GPS, it was three hours away.

"Daylight's burning," he said. "Call me when you get there. He's expecting you." Pennie backed out of the driveway as Alfie called out something about apple pie.

The day was sunny and bright, a few clouds moving like islands through the sky, and her mind hummed with the prospect of an adventure. As she rounded the on-ramp to I-295 through Portland, memories of the night on the bridge flooded her mind again. Her car stalling under the underpass, stumbling out in the rolling fog, walking along the sidewalk where she saw her mother on the other side of the bridge, calling for Pennie in the whipping wind off the harbor. Was it an illusion? She could feel herself leaping into the road and running to her, only to be startled by an oncoming light, the beams of Ward's BMW coming toward her before swerving.

A loud horn jolted her out of her musings, and she felt herself jerk the wheel, swerving back inside her lane, letting the irritated drivers move around her. *Oh, God, if I got into an accident, I'd never be able to face Uncle Alfie.* She whispered a thank-you to her trusted Karmann for being there for her and turned on the radio to the local university student station, WMPG. As Nina Simone sang, her thoughts drifted again, this time to the old man in the wine cellar, Mr. Snodgrass, who'd sold her this album the night she had seen Loralee and Kush together, the night she slept with Ward. What a mess she had made of things. How she hated herself, and now Kush, too.

When she passed the Falmouth exit, she pictured Mrs. McCarthy's stately home where Chloe's necklace had been found, the husky digging up the locket, how the dog had looked into her eyes, right through her. Why had Chloe's necklace come to her in a dream? She clutched the triskelion locket around her neck and the image of a child's jewelry box surfaced in her mind. She could hear Aunt Maude's voice telling her not to fear her dreams, her visions. As she passed the Fairview exit, she wondered if Stan Lewis was at the barn, if there was a horse show today. Ward's daughter, Winnie, flashed through her memory, riding in formation with the other high school girls, the ghost of Chloe alongside them, her image appearing and disappearing in the photograph, a phantom.

A few trees had turned already, it being the last day of September, little hints of red, gold, and orange popping up here and there until her journey north became constant splashes of color, all the way through Auburn then Jay and Farmington. A desperate hitchhiker waved, pleading, but she kept driving, sending a silent wish for safe travel, the clouds continuing their silent shift overhead. By the time she reached Kingfield, the foliage colors shimmered, flamboyant in all their late-September glory, the warm sun glinting off the steadily flowing Carrabassett River, a medley of autumn.

She drove past the Sugarloaf access road and into Stratton, the little village in Eustis. Only about five miles to go. Giant pickups and SUVs passed her, loud mufflers making it clear who owned the road marked *Route 27, the Arnold Trail*. Her heart leapt with the anticipation of meeting these relatives. What kind of people lived up here, in the middle of nowhere, year-round? Her VW sputtered loudly, turning down Old Dead River Road, a gravel lane. She passed A-frame camps, log cabins, and small ranches, smoke billowing from their chimneys. Finally, she came to a cute little red house with white trim, the mailbox marked *12*

Safford. She pulled in behind an aging Jeep Cherokee, Flagstaff Lake glimmering in the early afternoon sun at the back of the property and majestic Mount Bigelow in the distance. Finally, the home of Grampa Goode's oldest sister's son, Fremont.

A low vibration moved through Pennie when she stepped out of the car and contemplated the number on the house: 12. *One plus two is three. The number three again—synchronicity.* She shivered when the side door of the cabin opened and a young woman dressed in red flannel and blue jeans stepped out onto the porch, greeting her with a stunning smile full of youth and promise. "Hello, there. You must be Pennie?"

She waved. "That's me!"

"C'mon in, my grandfather's been expecting you." The young woman introduced herself as Brianna. Pennie was taken aback by her height: she looked close to six feet tall. They stepped inside a neat, homey kitchen that smelled like tobacco, with gray paneling on the walls, worn wooden cabinets with black iron pulls, a scuffed green linoleum floor, and small white appliances—everything as neat as a pin. "He ran out to get some coffee, didn't want to have nothing to offer you when you got here."

"He shouldn't have gone to that trouble." An oval table with a blue and white vinyl cover sat in the middle of the kitchen. The narrow refrigerator looked like it might hold a six-pack and a gallon of milk and not much else. The burners of the gas stove were haloed in black from things boiling over, and the scratched but spotless stainless-steel sink faced the glimmering lake. "Nothing extravagant here, but it's his home," she said, offering Pennie a seat in an old high-back kitchen chair.

"I think it's wonderful. There's nothing like a place on the lake." Out the window, she noticed a dock resting on a dark tumble of rocks, the water out of reach by four to five feet. "Wow, the lake is low."

"Yeah, our dock has never been this dry before."

The sound of a truck in the driveway made them turn. "Oh, good, he's back. He's so happy a relative has come to visit."

A wiry, grizzled man with gray whiskers and a wry grin stepped into the camp, slightly bent over with age, like a sturdy old tree bracing against the wind. "You must be Pennie," he said, reaching to shake her hand, smiling with his eyes. "Glad to meet one of my relatives from my mother's side. I haven't seen Alfie or Maude in a coon's age. And sorry to hear about your Ma. Birdie was a special person, from what I remember, smarter than most. She had a special kind of sixth sense."

Her heart filled with a surprise tenderness. "You knew my mother?"

"Well, o' course I did. Brigid, Alfie, and Maude used to come up here to stay with us when they were growing up. Your grandparents dragged them here to go hunting and fishing every year. Of course, this was after the power company dammed the Dead River and flooded it, made this valley into nothing more than a shallow lake and a reservoir." Waving toward the window, he lamented how the water had been drawn down lower than ever before.

Pennie said she'd like to go around the lake to take pictures, and he promptly offered up the services of his granddaughter. "She's training to be a Maine Guide, aren't you Bri?"

She flushed with embarrassment. "It'll take me a few years."

"Some training and more confidence." He arched backward in discomfort. "My back's not so good, but she'll take you on the back roads where you can get some good photos all around here. During drier autumns like this one, they draw down more water to create the flow they need to generate more power."

She followed him outside to the dock that sat on black rocks slick with dried dark green algae. The wind picked up and she shuddered with a sensation, the very vibrating spirit of the lake moving through her.

The secrets lying beneath its cold, dark surface washed over her like a slow-moving wave. She grabbed the dock's railing to keep from losing her balance. Fremont reached his gnarly hand out. "You okay?"

"Yes, sorry. That wind is strong."

Bri stood beside her, looking toward the grand mountain tapestry of autumn. "Comes down from Bigelow."

Fremont said, "I don't know if you know much about the history of this lake, but it was once home to at least ninety farms. Then the power company bought up all the property around it and forced the villagers out of their homes in '49 to make an impoundment to control the flow to the dams on the Kennebec. Our family lived on the Dead River for over a hundred years before the power company came in and took it all."

Another gust blew in, the water greedily lapping at the shore. "What happened to the families and their homes?"

"Oh, you know. They were booted out, had to move their homes or abandon them. Your uncle probably told you about the letter I received. This time, the power company wants to take my hunting camp over on Middle Carry. That camp and land's been in my family for over a hundred years."

Bri asked, "Can you and your uncle help us? You know, fight the power company?"

"I hope so. I'm here to find out as much as I can."

Fremont struck a match on his boot and lit a cigarette in his calloused fingers. "I should take you to the historical society. Show you all the photos of the farms, our relatives."

"I'd like that." The lake trembled under haunting, icy drafts. Fremont waved them inside with his long, crooked arms, and Bri helped her grab her bags from the car, telling Pennie how happy she was to have a cousin staying with them, how it could get lonely here in the winter, that all she did was work and take care of her grandfather when she wasn't with her boyfriend.

Inside, they walked through the sparse living room, thin brown curtains covering the windows, an old couch with a colorful but yellowed patchwork quilt, the stitching coming undone here and there, draped across the back. A scraggily orange cat lay stretched out on the quilt, his amber eyes watching her. A Defiant woodstove radiated warmth, burn holes dotting the worn, rust-colored carpet around it. Bri led her to the unfinished second-floor attic, where an old wooden dresser sat against the far wall under a window looking out toward the woods and lake. Twin beds—steel frames with creaking webs of springy wire holding up thin mattresses stuffed with cotton and covered in blue and white canvas ticking—sat nestled under the eaves on either side of the small room. Bri's bed, wrapped in a bright pink comforter, was home to stuffed teddy bears and lions and moose. Her head nearly hit the ceiling before she plunked herself on the squeaky springs. "It's not much, but I'm just happy my grandfather lets me stay here." She sighed like she was used to searching for the bright side of anything. "I don't think I've ever shared a room with anyone. I'm super psyched you're here."

Pennie set her things down next to the twin bed, the one with a green wool army blanket and flat, striped feather pillow. She sat on the hard mattress, the springs groaning with distress. "I'll only be here for a night or two to get some photos and find out more about the power corridor."

Bri leaned forward, giving Pennie her full attention, her deer eyes wide with wonder—of what, Pennie had no idea. "Oh, JD can tell you anything you want to know about the corridor. He keeps up on it."

"JD?"

Bri flipped her long, straight hair back behind her shoulder. "He's my boyfriend. His parents own the restaurant where I work. You should come over and eat there tonight." She pointed to Pennie's neck. "I love your necklace."

She felt for the triskelion. "Oh, thanks. It's a Celtic symbol, the symbol of three, representing birth, death, and rebirth."

"Oh, I love those ancient symbols. Just about anything to do with the sky and the stars. You might say that astrology is my thing. I'm a Gemini, which makes me a free spirit. What about you: when were you born?"

"March, Pisces."

"Ah, so you were born in the 12th house, representing eternity—you can see yesterday, today, and tomorrow all at once. Your necklace makes sense, because Pisces is associated with the number three and the Empress Card in tarot, meaning you're fearless and independent, and you also have incredible empathy toward others. Pisces is ruled by Neptune, the planet of dreams, intuition, and spirituality." Bri stopped herself and leaned forward. "Sorry, am I talking too much? I can go on and on sometimes, when I get talking about something that really rings my bell."

The number three again. "No, no, this is actually quite interesting." What a fountain of information she was, this newfound cousin.

"I'll have to introduce you to my psychic, Greta. She lives in town and does readings. I don't know what I'd do without her."

Pennie laughed. "A psychic. Not sure about that." She looked out of the attic window at the lake. "I'm here to gather information for my uncle, that's my main focus."

"Oh, sure, I get it." She looked disappointed and checked her phone. "Shit, I've got to be at work in ten minutes." Jumping up from the creaky mattress, she told Pennie to come over to the Greedy Gullet for dinner. "When I get off work, we can have a few drinks, and I'll introduce you to JD."

A whirlwind of kinetic energy, Brianna left the attic, her hair drifting behind her like an afterthought, before Pennie could ask where she'd find this fine local drinking hole. Maybe this was what she needed to get her out of her funk, keep her mind on other things, anything other than Kush. She fell back onto the musty pillow, cobwebs in the rafters overhead, and let her mind unravel, thinking about what Bri had said: *born in the 12th house...represents eternity...you can see yesterday, today, and tomorrow all at once.*

BRIGHT ORANGE FLAMES LEAPT and danced inside a dream. She wrestled herself out of it, her heart racing. *What on earth?* She sat up on the squeaky old twin bed, trying to slow her breathing. The vision remained, seared in her mind: the wall of fire down in the valley, surrounding her, trapped, the forest ablaze, trees exploding like firecrackers jumping toward her, a living, breathing heat.

The quiet inside the attic settled her mind, the dream fading away. Outside the window, darkness loomed, a night sky blacker than she'd ever seen, a cold, comforting darkness so unlike the night sky of Portland. She had fallen asleep. Pulling her phone from her sweatshirt, she was surprised to see it was already past seven. She crept downstairs, where a single lamp cast a soft yellow glow beside Fremont's gaunt figure on the couch, his mouth open and snoring quietly, his head sunk down between his humped shoulders. There was a thick hardcover book, *Arundel*, open and face down on his lap, the scruffy long-haired orange cat on his chest, its amber eyes staring at Pennie.

The room was chilly. She grabbed a mitt and lifted the heavy top of the woodstove to see only embers glowing on the bottom. She placed two logs of maple from the woodbox into the solid iron stove and closed it, making sure the damper along the bottom was turned down to keep it smoldering at a slow burn. Fremont snorted in his sleep and she jumped, looking at his face for any signs of waking. The cat never moved, only stared at Pennie with those penetrating eyes, snuggling into Fremont's slowly rising and lowering chest. This fragile old man lay fast asleep in his flannel shirt and jeans, crooked knees and saggy skin, soft wrinkles over a web of veins on his cheeks. The old quilt covered the back of the couch, the stitching stretched and broken in a few places but holding the cotton and wool squares of memory in place. The cat glared as if to say, *This house and everything in it is mine.*

Outside, the air was crisp, the night clear and cold and the stars and constellations stark and vibrant, twinkling and telling. No wonder Bri was so fascinated by astrology. This amazing sky without any light pollution to dim the dramatic display made her want to be one with land and sky. What was it that Bri had said about Pisces? Ruled by the planet Neptune, the number three. She groped in her backseat for her down jacket and looked up the Greedy Gullet on the GPS. It was only a couple miles down the road. The Karmann started right up, and she silently thanked Uncle Alfie again for giving her the gift of dependable wheels, her breath clouding inside the chilly car. On her phone were several text messages from Dani and a call from Uncle Alfie. *Right.* She was supposed to call him when she arrived.

He picked up on the second ring as she drove down the gravel buckboard road. "I assume you made it up there okay." She apologized and explained how tired she was from the drive. After meeting Fremont and his granddaughter, she had passed out cold.

"How's everyone doing?"

"Oh, good, but he has a bad back. Bri's a great help to him." Pennie kept her eyes on the dark paved road for any sign of the restaurant. "She promised to take me around Flagstaff to get some pictures. You can't believe how low the power company has drawn down the lake. Fremont is not happy."

The ice tinkled in his glass of bourbon on the other end of the line. "What about the eminent domain?"

"You didn't tell me about the power company kicking them out of their homes seventy years ago to make a reservoir, or all those families forced from their homes. I just can't believe they are using the same power to take Fremont's camp."

"I knew he'd fill you in."

She considered telling her uncle about the fire dream but instead promised to keep him posted. "I'll find out more about his camp." Bidding farewell, she pulled in to the restaurant parking lot full of pickup trucks. A spotlight over a giant wooden sign chiseled in the outline of a beer mug lit the walkway to a single-story building with a metal roof and a covered porch on the banks of Flagstaff.

Inside was warm as toast. Shoulder mounts of different game animals lined the walls—moose and bear and deer with enormous racks loomed over the diners. She walked directly to the bar near the front of the room, crowded with patrons happy to be out on a Friday night at one of the only places in town. The dining room behind the bar was full of loud chatter and laughter, a mix of families and couples huddled around wooden tables that gleamed under the dim lights. The smell of cornbread, baked beans, salt pork, and ribs filled the restaurant. Her stomach growled, and she eyed a seat at the far end of the bar.

Young and middle-aged bearded men quibbled loudly, drinking beer and watching the boxing match on the large-screen television. Either football or boxing or wrestling seemed to be the favorites on these bar screens. *What is it about men and violence?* She caught the eyes of a few who side-glanced in her direction, checking her out, knowing she was not from around here. She grabbed a stool and hid her face in the menu until the bartender, a guy about her age with long reddish hair tied in a ponytail and thick, black-framed glasses out of 1970, smiled kindly and said, "What's up?"

For some reason, this struck her as funny, this nonchalant greeting. "Not much, you?"

"Something to drink?"

She chuckled to herself, reading the menu. "I'll have the local Bigelow Cast Iron Bitch Pale Ale and a burger with fries."

"One Cast Iron Bitch coming your way." He was all business, pouring her ale from the tap, the foam crowning the top of the pint glass. It only took her a minute to spot Bri in the far corner of the room setting a tray on a stand and unloading plates for a family of five: a small mother with a dazed look in her eye, a paunchy father who kept his eyes on his plate of ribs, a teenager poking a younger brother who squirmed and whined, and a little girl tugging on her mother's arm. Bri looked flustered, eyeing the other tables around her, impatient patrons waving to get her attention. The place was jammed, at least fifteen tables of different sizes all serviced by three waitresses and a busboy.

Her burger came, and she inhaled it while taking in the black-and-white pictures behind the bar—houses halfway submerged in the lake, the flooding of the Dead River Valley. A Cape with two chimneys and a metal roof, a long farmhouse, a post-and-beam barn, and a general store—all flooded, the river rising to their second stories. A chill moved up her backside. These stark memories lining the restaurant walls told a story of tragedy. Again, hot flames surfaced in her mind, the wall of fire that engulfed her dream.

The bartender caught her eye, was about to speak to her, when a robust woman with a full head of brick red hair called to him from the other end of the bar. "Owen, a hot and dirty and a Guinness." He jumped into fixing the drinks with the rote smoothness of a skilled barkeep before his attention turned again to Pennie's end of the bar to ask if everything was okay. She took a gulp of beer and nodded, still looking at the old photos. "These are really sad."

He pondered the image of the barn slowly drowning. "People say we have a ghost town below us, but the truth is, there were only about seven buildings left in the valley when it was flooded. The next winter, when the lake was low and frozen, the power company burned them all. Most of the old buildings were moved before the flooding, like the Dead River schoolhouse. It's just down the road here."

"Sorry to say this, but these seem a bit...morose, for a restaurant."

He chuckled. "My mother's idea. She thought they'd be a good draw for tourists." He widened his eyes.

"Are you from here?" she asked.

"Born and raised." He rinsed a glass in the sink. "I'm Owen, by the way, nice to meet you."

"Same to you. I'm Pennie." She was about to ask him if he had any relatives from the flooded Dead River villages, but he took off down the bar to fill another drink order. Her plate now wiped clean, she waved to Bri, who finally looked up from her mad dash delivering food to wave back. The stout middle-aged woman with oxblood-colored hair and saggy jowls, apparently disgruntled with Bri for waving, pointed to a table that needed something.

Owen came back to refill her beer, telling her that his mother was the matron of the place, and before you could say Jack Rabbit, she landed at the other end of the bar again, motioning to him. Things grew louder as the boxing match came to a head, blood flowing from noses, the jabs more violent. Families and couples began to leave their tables, exiting the restaurant for nearby homes and camps. Every seat at the bar, on the other hand, was taken. A few women, in tight flannels open to show off their cleavage, sat beside their husbands or dates, who shouted at the screen. Bri came up beside her to clutch the bar, dropping her head between her arms. "I'm exhausted."

"You've really been running out there. This place is crazy."

"It's worth the tips if I can keep the orders straight."

Pennie followed Bri's glance across the room. The matron pointed to a table with two couples having coffee and dessert. Bri sighed, "I'll be right back." Her hair flew behind her in a ribbon of brunette as she rushed off. Owen joked with a handsome clean-cut guy who'd just arrived, pouring him a whiskey and Coke. Soon, other men gathered around this same stocky guy with the finely trimmed beard as if he had all the answers. Leggy Bri came up behind him to give him a hug. *Must be the boyfriend.* He turned and kissed her before nodding to the woman in charge, who was motioning Bri to keep working her tables.

As if reading her thoughts, Owen said, "My mother runs this place with an iron fist." He was so serious, Pennie wasn't sure if he was making a joke or not. She had the inclination to get up and help Bri clear the tables. Instead, she checked her phone: it was already almost nine o'clock. "Dining room closed already?"

He nodded, wiping the gleaming yellow, pine bar top. "We have two seatings, no more. Ma likes to get the place closed up tight by ten." He moved to the little sink to wash the glasses. "How do you know Bri?"

"My uncle and her grandfather are cousins."

"That's cool. She and my brother have been dating a few months. Nice girl."

"That's your brother?"

Owen stopped washing and lifted his chin slightly, batting his eyes. "Can't you see the resemblance?"

"Now that you mention it…" She laughed, liking his self-deprecation, making up for what he lacked in the looks department.

"Are you staying with Bri and Fremont?"

"Only for a few days, to get some pictures."

He motioned across the restaurant to the enormous window facing the lake, a black box reflecting the hanging metal lights inside. "Flagstaff is the fourth largest lake in Maine, about eighteen thousand acres. It's pretty shallow, though: only forty-eight feet at its deepest point."

The good-looking brother came up alongside the bar and sat down in the one empty seat beside her, thumping his glass. "What's the Walking Wikipedia talking about now?"

Owen turned away to take care of refills. The brother put out his hand. "Bri tells me you're a relative."

Pennie shook his confident grip. "I am, and you must be the boyfriend."

"That Fremont is a testy old codger, isn't he?"

"Seems like a nice enough old guy to me. Holding his own."

"Barely holding on is more like it. Bri's been taking care of him for a year now. I'm surprised they don't put him in a home."

Pennie wondered who "they" were. "Some of the *old-timers* prefer to live out their last days, or years, at home."

"And I'd like to live in a castle in Tuscany." He took the final swig of his whiskey and Coke as Bri came up behind them, bubbling with excitement. Pennie wasn't sure if it was because she was finally done work or if she was happy to show off her boyfriend. "Looks like you've met JD."

"She's met the whole damn family," Owen said, smiling.

"My *older* brother," said JD, nodding toward Owen. "He's the most dependable bartender you'll ever meet."

Pennie caught the sarcasm. "What about you, JD? What's your line of work?"

He leaned in toward her, more than happy to explain how he ran a Farmington car dealership and all the people who worked under him. Bri interrupted, leaning against him to ask if he wanted to do a tequila shot, which he did. She'd had a long night and needed a belt. He gave his brother the signal for a round, but Pennie refused. The birthday cake shot from Tita's birthday lunch was still burning a hole in her stomach. Just the thought of that day in the restaurant, after the crushing night with Kush, gave her a headache.

The matriarch walked behind the bar, asked Owen to open the drawer so she could cash out, and asked Bri if she'd made good tips. Bri nodded, saying she did alright. "You've got to hustle more, Brianna," she said, counting the money in her quick hands, the efficiency of a bank cashier. "I can't help you out every night. And I don't want to have to give some of your tables to Angela to pick up the slack."

"Yes, ma'am."

As soon as bossy-pants walked away with her fat stack of bills, her ample caboose bringing up the rear, Bri grabbed the shot in front of her and downed it. JD slapped her skinny ass and gave her an "Atta girl!" She kissed him and looked into his eyes like she'd like to get lost in them, making Pennie feel ill all over again. She turned away toward the wall beside her, where a giant old circular saw hung. She reached out to feel the curved spaces between the large saw teeth. "Those are called gullets," Owen said. "That saw is supposed to be from the original sawmill in Flagstaff village." A small tremor moved her, but instead of being afraid, she let the vibration course through her, a low, warming energy that seemed to come from the universe itself.

PENNIE LAY DOWN ON the squeaky twin bed in the dark, very happy she had left Bri at the bar with JD and the rest of the rowdy Stratton crew. On the attic wall beside her, someone had made a star pattern with thumbtacks on the wall. The bottom tack held a photo of Fremont, Bri when she was just a little girl, and a young woman who must have been Bri's mother. They sat in a canoe fishing, with little Bri in the middle. Pennie sat up and reached for her backpack, pulling out the picture of her own mother and her husky, Togo, to tack on the wall alongside the other picture. Her mother wore the sparkling cairngorm brooch pinned to her gold scarf, the Alaskan husky by her side. She let her head find the pillow, the heavy wool blankets piled high, and fell into the deep darkness of the valley, through the eyes of the husky...

Lying on the floor of the old mill, inside the body of the dog, she snoozed by the woodstove at the feet of men talking about how much birch they'd milled into squares, while outside, water moved through the penstock to the waterwheel, rolling patiently, making power. A lanky man in suspenders smoked a pipe, opened the stove to spit into the fire that cracked and hissed, remarking on the basketball game coming up that night at the school, how they'd have to shut off power to homes to ensure full, bright lights in the gymnasium during the game and turn it back on afterwards, lighting the path for folks to get back safe and sound to their farms in the belly of the valley. A heavyset man, as hairy as a bear, boasted of his wife's electric washing machine, her laundry on Monday, her ironing on Tuesday, their dependence on the old mill—the same saw and grist mill built by Myles Standish, Jr., a century earlier—still keeping them in flour for cooking and wood for building, and now in clean clothes, and bright lights for basketball games throughout the desolate winter.

She followed the tall man they called Harry outside, where a short, stocky Frenchman urged along the bristly old "hoss" Roger, hauling birch squares to the yard for stacking and drying, destined for spool stock, dowels for pencils, wooden toys, flag sticks, and flagpoles. In the springtime, old Roger hauled the long pine lumber, great logs that had made their way down from the northern logging camps to Flagstaff Pond, floating downstream to be milled into boards and planks and shingles. The man in suspenders, hauling on his black pipe, called to her: "Skidder dog. Let's go check the pump." They trudged through the snow, facing bitter wind along the mill-stream, following the power line from the mill to the pumphouse near the spring on Jim Eaton Hill, where he checked the silent motor and fiddled with it, cursing, cursing again, until it finally fired up, pumping water uphill to the reservoir and then down to the homes in the valley once again, filling him with delight at the ingenuity of their independence, their utter resilience in the deep river valley. He scratched her between the ears, looking out the window to the reservoir uphill, saying it was time to get home to Mama for lunch.

SHE OPENED HER EYES to the darkness of the attic. In her dream, inside the body of a dog, she considered the collective unconscious of those men living and working in the Dead River Valley. The dim light of the moon shone on the picture she'd tacked on the wall, of her mother with Togo. She smiled, accepting the duality of her wild spirit.

Chapter 5
Wolf Tree

THE SMELL OF COFFEE wafted up to the attic. An eerie glow shone through the old windowpane from the dismal gray sky. Pennie hugged the wool blankets, staring at the empty pink twin bed beside her. With substantial effort, she pulled herself from the cocoon and slipped on her sweatpants and wool socks before descending the stairs to the woodstove roaring in the living room. In the kitchen, Fremont sat at the table reading *The Rangeley Highlander*, the local rag. The coon cat owned his lap, tail swishing under the table, lost in his own devilish thoughts of the hunt. "Coffee's hot," Fremont said, sipping from a dingy tin cup that looked like it had been around since World War II.

She found a ceramic mug with a chipped-off handle in the cupboard and poured coffee from the cloudy glass carafe. Fremont looked over his reading glasses and launched into a wracking cough for a full minute before pulling a cigarette from his pack of Camel Lights, asking her if she didn't mind, which she didn't. "Good, because it is my house." He smiled with strong yellow teeth and winked at her. "How was the Gullet last night? Busy as usual?"

What was it about this genial old man, this cousin to Alfie and Maude and her own mother, that made her feel so comfortable, like she'd known him all her life? She sat down at the table and told him how hard Bri worked, waiting on tables. "That's Betsy." He lit his cigarette and set his elbows on the newspaper. "That battle-ax of a woman overworks her crew. She ought to hire more people. Controller-in-chief, that one."

"She does seem to have a tight grip on things."

"That's why Shep spends his time in the kitchen, cooking and drinking."

"Shep? Didn't meet him, but the food was good."

"He's the husband she keeps hidden away." He knocked his ash into a Hills Bros. coffee can that doubled as an ash tray. "How's Owen doing?"

"Running the bar. Seems like a nice guy."

"He's an odd stick, but a whole lot nicer than that other one, JD. That one thinks he's King Shit." He let out a long stream of smoke. "I wish she'd grow some common sense and see that ne'er-do-well for the con artist he is." Fremont thumped the newspaper with his knobby index finger. "He's part of this abomination, I'm sure." She strained to read the headline upside down: INDEPENDENCE CORRIDOR AP-PROVED BY TOWN COUNCIL. "They all ought to be shot for letting this thing go through."

"Aren't they building the corridor to bring hydroelectric power down from Canada?"

"All the power is going out of state. Instead of flooding our lands, this time the power company is buzzing a wide swath through our woods, the same woods Benedict Arnold and his men trekked through at the start of the Revolutionary War." He pointed his cigarette at her, pinched between his yellow fingers. "We'll have nothing but mile-high power poles through our woods. 'Independence Corridor,' my ass."

"Wait, are you saying that Benedict Arnold's army marched through here, the Dead River Valley?"

"That's exactly what I'm saying."

A vision of ragged men marching along the riverside surfaced in her mind. The cat's tail twitched, moving her thoughts to the conversation at hand. "What does JD have to do with this?"

"He's a selectman. I'm sure he's got his grubby little fingers involved."

She walked to the window above the sink and looked out to the lake. "Not to mention the drawdown here."

"That's what I mean." He started on a coughing fit again, hacking up a lung. "The power company scavengers come along to get what they want, leaving us with the aftermath."

His cup sat empty, so she filled it. Her dream came to her from the night before. "I heard there was once a sawmill that powered the towns."

He snubbed out his cigarette in the can. "Of course there was. That's how the settlement started. Myles Standish, eleventh generation descendent of the pilgrim, built the first gristmill and sawmill in the Flagstaff plantation." Hunched over, he joined her at the window, pointing up the lake to the northeast. "There was a millstream over there at the confluence of Flagstaff Pond and the Dead River. Perfect spot for a water-powered mill."

"And it later provided electricity?"

"That's right," he nodded, delighted in her interest. "Let me take you to the historical society today. Margaret's expecting us to stop by. That'll help you understand how our ancestors settled this land." He grabbed the package of individually wrapped Country Kitchen sugared donuts on the counter. "You like donuts?"

"What I'd really like is a hot shower."

Fremont showed her to the bathroom with its old clawfoot tub, a shower curtain hanging around it from a rusty oval-shaped rod. She grabbed her stuff upstairs, looked out the window at the end of the attic and envisioned the tattered band of soldiers trudging along the banks, through the wilderness, to attack Quebec City on a quest for liberty and freedom from the oppression of a king. This place, steeped in the history of the Revolutionary War and the settling of colonists on the Dead River, was like a window into the past.

With wet hair, she joined Fremont at the lakeside, the beauty of the mountain valley on the sunny morning, the first day of October, giving her pause. The foliage was vibrant and moving, its bursts of yellow, orange, red, and green, even pink, gold, and amber, shimmering and taking hold of her heart. He pointed out the mountains, their names like an ode to the generations who had come before—Veazy Ridge, Pickle Hill, Limestone Hill, Jim Eaton Hill, Flagstaff Mountain, Picked Chicken Hill, Blanchard Mountain, Hedgehog Mountain, Roundtop Mountain, Little Bigelow, and Mount Bigelow—one rise indistinguishable from another, yet he knew them like a mother of eleven knows the distinct cry of each child.

They rode in his rough-running black Ford pickup across town to the Dead River Area Historical Society to see Margaret. The gentle, frail woman waited for them outside the white Methodist church at the center of town. With slow, measured steps, she led them into the building, chilly for lack of heating, and pointed up toward the balcony overhead, encircling the room.

"The Dead River is on the left side up there, and Flagstaff on the right," she said. Fremont explained to Pennie that these were the two plantations of the valley before it was flooded, Flagstaff having about 145 residents at one time, and Dead River roughly 80. Bigelow was a third, smaller plantation that didn't last as long. She followed him up the stairs to the balcony, where he stretched his hand to a crude map on the wall. A thick line conveyed the snake-like Dead River before it was flooded, its path twisting and turning in the natural groove of the valley.

Flagstaff Pond fed into Mill Stream, which flowed into the Dead River in the village of Flagstaff, the site of Myles Standish's grist- and sawmill. Pennie's dream came to her again. "A guy named Harry later owned the mill, right?"

"Yes, that's right, Harry Bryant took it over after Arthur Rogers. Good to see you've done your homework." She pictured the men around the woodstove in her dream while Fremont pointed to the map where the homesteads, stores, boardinghouses, school, and church stood along the river, about seventy buildings on the Flagstaff side. He noted where a covered bridge once stood, torn down by a tremendous windstorm in 1922. His crooked finger moved to a dot that designated the Morgan Farm, owned by the well-known banker J.P. Morgan—11,000 acres that went all the way up to Spring Lake, a retreat he purchased for his employees to enjoy the famous hunting and fishing in the Maine woods. Locals like Warren Wing and Peter Wahl and Fud Taylor served as guides. Downriver, near the foot of Mount Bigelow, small dots designated about thirty homesteads, as well as the Mount Bigelow boardinghouse and the Ledge House.

Margaret called up from her post below, telling Fremont to make sure he showed Pennie the timeline. The History of Flagstaff was pinned on the wall with a thumbtack:

1775 B. Arnold and troops camp on Dead River and erect flagstaff.

1865 Flagstaff becomes organized township.

1909 Wyman develops plan to dam Dead River and create reservoir.

1911 The first bill is introduced to legislature regarding dam.

1916 The first electricity comes to Flagstaff, powered by mill.

1919 Power Company starts buying property in Dead River area.

1923 Bill to dam Dead River is passed and vetoed by Gov. Baxter.

1927 Revised bill is passed ensuring land & water rights are kept.

1932 Civilian Conservation Corp Camp set up on Jim Eaton Hill.

1948 Building of dam begins.

1950 Town floods with spring runoff.

1951 An act of legislature officially eradicates the town of Flagstaff.

Her mind whirred with so many questions. "Wyman was the guy who started the power company?"

"That's right. He built his first hydroelectric dam on Messalonskee Stream in the town of Oakland, then started buying other small dams and mills in central Maine. At some point, he figured he needed to harness the power of the northern Kennebec River, so he came up with the plan of creating a reservoir to hold back the water until it was needed during low-water times. This valley, with its healthy spring runoff, became the best prospect for a holding lake."

She noticed the years between the passage of the legislative bill in 1923 and the building of the dam in 1950. "What took so long for them to start building the dam?"

"It took about twenty years to buy up all the land. The townspeople went about their normal lives, almost forgetting about the plans for a dam until around 1937, when there was more talk in the newspapers about the project. Again, people tried to ignore it, but slowly the power company bought up the property. The final step was clear-cutting the area, so they moved cutting crews in with their families, who even sent their kids to the Flagstaff school."

"That must have been scary for the families, seeing their woods cleared around them."

He looked down at Margaret. "Would you call it scary, Margaret? Is that what it was like back then?"

She shook her head, peering up at them through her wire glasses, her fine white hair trembling in the cold of the old church. "I don't know if there is a word to describe the death of a town, is there?"

Pennie scanned the black-and-white images of the half-drowned houses and farms, the same ones hanging on the walls at the Greedy Gullet: images of Dutchie Leavitt's general store with its peaked roof, the Alvin Wing house with its sturdy metal roof and two chimneys, the J.P. Morgan farm with its fine, peaked dormers and large white barn—all half-submerged in the rising waters. Another photograph showed the Bryant Mill turbine and penstock remnants dormant in the mud, the rocks of the foundation piled up, like an old cemetery in the pooling water.

She thumbed through a large scrapbook with newspaper clippings, skimming the headlines: Flagstaff gets ready to quit, Flagstaff phone service bows out of picture, No more mail for Flagstaff, New Flagstaff rises as old bows to man-made lake, Fire destroys former Dead River post office, Flagstaff families leave as flames close In, Storm starts water rising behind new Dead River dam, Flood of memories.

Melancholy washed over her as she looked through the old photos. There was the mill owner she'd seen in her dream, Harry Bryant, and his wife, Alice, standing in a wildflower meadow on a hill overlooking a lake with Mount Bigelow in the distance. What must he be thinking in this picture, their lovely town at the foot of Bigelow soon to be a memory? Then there was Al Wing riding his chestnut Morgan, Budweiser, in front of the pool hall. A covered mail stage hitched to two workhorses in front of the Flagstaff Hotel. An old frontiersman, Bert Russell Horton, in front of his 1912 Brush Runabout motorcar. Three young, adventurous women huddled together on top of Mount Bigelow, perched high on a rock, the Dead River Valley in the background. Evelyn Leavitt in the general store bantering with a clothing salesman who displayed new checked shirts and trousers piled high. The 1938/39 girls basketball team in their uniforms, posing in front of the school with their coach. Flagstaff's 1924 student body: twenty students grade school to high school, many of them barefoot on the dusty ground. A young soldier with his wife and their toddler squinting in the sun beside a screen porch. A small Fourth of July parade through the village. Men smoking pipes standing outside a hunting camp, snow piled high, two bucks hanging between them. The wooden Dead River dam that the log-driving companies built to control the flow of water and move logs downriver. The rushing water of Long Falls before the power company built the dam there.

It was unfathomable to think that these settled places, home of open meadows, farmsteads, woods, and wild waterways, had disappeared under the unstoppable and insatiable power of progress.

BACK AT FREMONT'S HOUSE, Bri's Jeep sat in the driveway. Inside, the sound of the shower and the steam rolling under the bathroom door gave away her whereabouts. Fremont harrumphed about her free use of hot water, and Pennie walked upstairs to make a phone call. Dani picked up after four rings, sounding out of breath.

"Thought I'd lost you in the woods up there."

She was glad to hear Dani's familiar soft voice. Pennie launched into the view of the lake and mountains outside her attic window, the spectacular autumn display, wishing Dani could be up there to see it in all its glory.

"Well, you just might get your wish. Seems I have my first artist's commission."

"Your what?"

"You remember that philanthropist who spoke at the art exhibit? Well, he asked me and Mali to develop a kind of narrative to promote river restoration. I get to work on a series of paintings and drawings, and Mali will figure out the display or installation. Anyway, if I'm being honest, I'm feeling a little over my head."

"That's incredible, congratulations! Is Mali excited?"

"You know my sister. She's already got the whole thing planned. You should see the studio. She's hung giant maps of the Kennebec River everywhere for brainstorming. Turns out this guy Wyman started this whole hydroelectric power thing a long time ago on or near the Kennebec, so we thought we'd make our way up there."

Pennie's mind swirled and bubbled. "I just came from the historical society. Did you know that Walter Wyman decided to flood this area for a holding reservoir back in the 1920s? Families who'd lived in this valley for generations were forced to abandon their homes and farms after being here for over 100 years."

Dani pressed her. "What happened to their homes?"

"They had to move them or tear them down. Some refused, but the power company flooded the town anyway. It's so creepy."

"We knew it would be a great place to start—at the beginning of the movement to harness the rivers."

Pennie bid her friend farewell just as Bri came up the stairs, her hair dripping and long body wrapped in a polyester bathrobe covered in roses, right out of somebody's grandmother's closet. Her lanky cousin collapsed on the creaky twin bed, face down on her stuffed bears and lions. "No more tequila shots for me, ever." Pennie laughed at her, so young and vibrant despite her hangover. There was something about her that made Pennie feel exuberant about life. What was it?

Bri turned her wet head on the pillow to face Pennie. "Thanks for taking care of Grandpa. I usually sleep here so he's not alone, but since I knew you were here, I had a good excuse to stay at JD's place."

She held back her thoughts, careful with her words, keeping her judgy-ness in check. Bri was obviously gaga over this guy, the popular man about town. Mr. Charming. "I heard he's a selectman."

"He's a busy guy, that's for sure. Knows everybody." Without a hint of self-consciousness, she threw off her bathrobe to show her pink thong, her long, slender body curved from her small tummy to her generous erect nipples. Pennie turned away in embarrassment, looking out the window at the lake, then a knowing settled inside her. Bri was pregnant. She knew it with certainty, as if a blinking fluorescent message had appeared in her mind's eye.

Her cousin ducked her head to keep from hitting the eaves, zipping up her faded jeans. "He's so smart. He said he'd explain the drawdown to you so you could understand what's going on. It's got something to do with the whitewater rafting business and the power they need to generate downriver. It's a little over my head, but he says not to worry because this is just an unusually dry year. Things will get back to normal by next summer."

Rolling this over in her mind, she decided not to mention anything about the legal limits for any drawdown, regardless of the dry condition, not to mention its impacts on the water quality and the fish. Bri picked up her phone and sent Pennie JD's contact information. "He says to call him anytime." She wondered if Bri knew she was pregnant; she'd either be ecstatic or worried sick. It made her think of Kush again and how they had that worry once, how it turned out to be a false alarm. A wash of sadness fell over her.

Bri kicked Pennie's feet. "Hey, I promised to drive you around the lake. Ready?"

"Sure, if you have time." Jumping at the chance, she grabbed her camera, happy to move on. Downstairs, Fremont sat at the kitchen table looking at old photographs. He held one up for Pennie, of an old building with a truck and a horse out front. "Here's the Bryant Mill we were talking about. Harry bought this from Arthur back in 1926." Fremont coughed. "This is Harry's old Indiana truck and his hoss, Roger." She stared at it, her mind falling back inside her dream, the old horse hauling squares in the yard, hearing Harry talk in his calm voice, fixing the pump.

Bri hurried them outside where the air had warmed into the 40s, and they loaded into her Jeep. From the center console, her cousin picked up a half-smoked joint and started the engine. Taking a right onto the Arnold Trail, the sunlight streaming through the cab, she pushed in the lighter on the old Jeep. "I'll take us the back way on the other side of Flagstaff over to Jim Eaton Hill. It's really pretty back here." When the lighter popped, she pulled it out and lit the blackened tip before offering some to Pennie.

It occurred to her that it might be strange to ask Bri if she realized she was pregnant. *The hell with it*, she stuck the joint between her lips, sucking in. She tried to remember the last time she had smoked. Probably with Kush when he still lived in Portland. She rolled her window down, handed the joint back to Bri, and snapped some pictures of the shining water between the trees, feeling lucky for the bluebird day on a hastily planned adventure. Bri turned on to a dirt road, gunning the engine over the rolling terrain. Pennie gripped the roll bar and checked her seatbelt. Men and women in orange vests appeared alongside the road, dead turkeys, foxes, or partridges in the back of their parked pickups, their guns or bows propped up against their fenders. Pennie let her thoughts spill out. "I appreciate the hunters, but for myself, I could never shoot an animal."

"To be honest," said Bri, driving with one hand on the wheel, sucking on the roach. "I don't like hunting much myself. I just love to be outside, love to climb these mountains, love to camp in the woods under the stars. I love to fish, especially, something JD and I do together."

Her mind drifted to the baby. "You two seem pretty serious."

Bri scoffed. "My god, serious? No, we've only been dating a few months...but I will say, he's come on strong." Pennie had the urge to bring up Bri's birth control method, or lack thereof, but bit her lip and let her talk. "He's already asked me to move in with him, and of course I said no. I'm here for my grandfather, to help him as long as I can. He's done everything for me, especially with my mom—" Tears filled her eyes.

She reached across to squeeze her arm. "What happened?"

"Problem with drugs. It was drinking for a long time, which was hard enough, but now she's into some bad stuff. Half the time I don't know where she is. It's a miracle if I can get her on the phone. I never would have gotten through high school if it wasn't for Grandpa. He took me in when social workers got involved, and he tried to get her help but she won't take it. Refuses, really. But I don't want you to think she's a bad person. She can be very loving when she's sober."

Staring out the window at the tapestry of red maples, yellow birches, and purple ash, colors that could lighten even the darkest mood, Pennie said, "I lost mine to suicide when I was only three."

"Wow, that sucks." Bri put on a smile for her. "I feel so close to you already, Pennie, like we're sisters. I do miss having someone I can talk to. I mean, JD is a good guy, but we don't talk a lot about this kind of stuff, you know? Every time I bring up my mom, he changes the subject. Tells me to forget about her."

"You can never forget your own mother, and it does no good to sweep your emotions under the rug. You've got to face the pain." Sunlight filtered through the leaves like a gentle reminder of hope. Small fir trees grew down along the water's edge, and birches and aspens leaned over black rocks exposed from the drawdown, their yellow leaves twirling in the light breeze. Bri pulled over so they could relish the giant red maples, their leaves whispering, falling around them in a quiet crescendo.

Pennie snapped some photos of the lake, wondering how close they were to the lost Flagstaff village below. Bri said, "My Grandma Lena used to take a lot of pictures out here, too. She absolutely loved this land, would come out here for hours, sometimes days, to hike in the woods and fish, making my grandfather upset when she was gone too long." Another puff of smoke escaped her lips.

"Grandpa Fremont?"

She nodded, gazing at the lake, the yellow leaves of the birch reflected in her eyes. "From what I know, she was part Abenaki, along with some French and Irish, a little of all the early settlers around here. I guess she was quite a bow hunter."

"What happened to her?"

"Died of heart disease when she was only in her early forties. I wasn't even born yet."

"That must have been so hard on your grandfather."

"Yeah, I don't think he ever got over it, to tell you the truth. Had to raise my mother on his own. She was only five or six when Grandma Lena died." She let out a long, drawn-out sigh and smashed the roach in the ashtray. "Just like Grandpa, her family came from around here, but we've lost touch with them over the years. Not sure where anyone is anymore."

The water lay calm, the purple mountains in the background. Pennie turned to get a side profile of Bri, the innocence of a newly expecting, unsuspecting mother, a child herself of this valley, these woods cradled in the mountains, home of generations of fishers, hunters, seekers. "All the hopes and dreams people put into a place, to raise families in a remote land like this. Makes me sad to think all those dreams were submerged."

Bri hopped out of the truck. Pennie followed her to the water's edge, where Bri pointed to a distant midpoint. "You can just see some house foundations jutting up from the water." Pennie pointed her lens to capture the very top of a what looked like three or four cement foundation walls. Bri said, "If they draw down any more, they'll be completely exposed, something most people around here, especially the old-timers, would rather not see." The evidence of the lost village was there, a capsule underwater, homes that some holdouts had stayed inside, resolute, until the rising water gave them no choice but to leave, to abandon their family's history, their collective memories of perseverance and survival through the long, cold, isolating winters.

She followed Bri back to the truck to ride down the gravel road past logging operations with their skidders and giant, steel clear-cutting machines sitting still, waiting for the next operation. Bri pointed out Flagstaff Mountain before they took a turn onto Jim Eaton Hill Road, ascending the rise. She felt a strong vibration rumble through her and knew they were driving toward a place steeped in memory. Bri parked the truck at the top of the wooded hill, where they could see down to the lake on either side of them. "That's where the schoolhouse used to be." She pointed to the left. "And further down was the mill that Fremont showed you the picture of, where there used to be a stream that flowed from Flagstaff Pond. I think the main street ran along the bottom of the hill, following the Dead River." She motioned toward the lake below.

"Straight ahead was the town green where Benjamin Arnold erected his flagstaff. That's how the legend goes anyway."

"*Benedict* Arnold," said Pennie, stepping down the hill among the spindly birch trees, the whisps of pine branches and boughs against her face. Something pulled her toward the water. Bri's voice began to fall, far away, and she felt herself stumbling downhill before catching the low branch of a giant old maple to keep her balance. Out of nowhere, a large bird darted out, its yellow eyes looking through her, its immense wings brushing her face—a whisper from the sky reaching out to touch her, a chance encounter with something more immense than time and space.

Bri was there, calling her name, and she shook herself, struggling out of the trance. "I—I must have stumbled."

Above them, great branches spread from the immense ancient tree in a clearing in the dense forest. "This is a wolf tree," said Bri. She ran her hands along the thick, gnarly bark, its trunk maybe four feet in diameter. "Trees the settlers left when they cleared pastureland. For, you know, shade and acorns for the cows. These were like lone wolves, like the last great hunters of the forest."

The commanding branches created a canopy over them, crowding out the smaller trees. "I'm surprised the foresters never cut this down."

"I hope they never do." Bri's eyes grew distant, soft. "This tree offers so much to the animals. The squirrels and raccoons that live in the base of the tree, the spiders and other bugs that crawl in the deep grooves of the bark." She ran her long, thin fingers inside the deep, twisting channels. "The birds live in the hollows of this old tree."

Pennie looked up for the hole the giant bird had come from, and knew it most probably was an owl, could still feel the feather that brushed her face in its silent flight. "How old do you think it is?"

Bri grasped the branch overhead, assessing its girth. "I'm guessing at least three hundred years old—since the times the Native Americans lived in this forest, anyway." She looked down the hill toward the water. "They say hundreds of Abenaki once lived on this land, here on the Dead, and all the way to the Kennebec River." She let her fingers run along the papery bark of a sturdy gray birch.

"Your Grandma Lena's ancestors?"

"That's what my grandpa says, just one branch of our many ancestors. Like I said, I don't really know that side of the family." Her long legs carried her down toward the water, leaves and twigs crunching underfoot. "Down a little to the right is where the Flagstaff cemetery was."

"Cemetery?"

"Where the old settlers were buried. Of course, they had to dig them up and rebury them up in Eustis before they flooded the valley. I've heard strange stories about bones floating in the water after those first years of flooding. Who knows, maybe bones of animals, but some of the old-timers insist they were the bones of the dead buried here on this land for hundreds of years."

Under the sheltering maple, its comely orangey-yellow leaves hanging on for dear life, she breathed in deep to calm her heartbeat and steadied her hand to take some pictures of the downhill slope where the brush and spindly trees thickened on the riverbank. The old gravesite was now underwater. She sensed the mournful souls of the hundreds buried in these woods and pastures over a long-forgotten history, the vibrations of the spirits in this place still very much alive.

Chapter 6
Secret Wardrobe

WHEN HER UNCLE'S NUMBER appeared on her phone screen, Pennie pictured him driving his trusty Packard with one knee pressed against the steering wheel. "How's Eustis treating you?" he said.

"Getting stranger by the day."

He laughed and agreed, yes, that was the western hills of Maine for you. It would take the coldness of a corpse to be immune to the spirits rising out of the lake in the shadow of the great Bigelow. She filled him in on her trip to the historical society and the drive over to Jim Eaton Hill. "With the lake drawdown, some of the foundations of the old Flagstaff village are exposed."

"That's enough to keep you up at night."

She knew her uncle was referring to her dreams, maybe even wondering if she was having any visions. "The whole area is filled with strong vibrations of the Natives and pioneers. I still don't understand how they can draw down the lake like this."

"You remember a conservative governor took office last year, right? With that comes a relaxation of environmental regulations. But groups like Maine River Conservancy have filed suit."

A light went on in her head. "That's the nonprofit that commissioned Dani and Mali to do the art installation."

"No kidding? Well, good for them. Anything to spread the word about what's going on with these drawdowns. I wish someone at the state level would get their head out of their ass and put an end to restorations of these old dams. Most of them are decrepit and don't provide enough power to light a Christmas tree, let alone a city."

"Fremont told me all about the power corridor they're building through here."

"That's why they're pulling the eminent domain card."

She thought about Flagstaff and the settlement being forced out. "It's like history repeating itself."

"Has Fremont taken you to his camp on Middle Carry yet?"

She looked out the window at the lake. "Not yet."

"That's why you're there, Pennie. Let me know what you find out."

She hung up and walked downstairs to find the orange coon cat snuggled on the couch near the woodstove, staring at her with ochre eyes, almost pleading her to put more wood on the fire. Pennie loaded in three logs and looked around for Fremont, nowhere to be found. With a rumbling stomach, she checked the fridge to find a dozen eggs, OJ, and a half-eaten loaf of bread. What she needed was an early dinner at the Gullet.

It was already nearly five but still daylight when she pulled in to the dirt parking lot filled with trucks, a few station wagons, and a van. The building looked like an old lodge that had been renovated: new shingles, winter-ready windows and doors, and a metal roof overhead. Inside, the bar was crowded with laughing bearded men and take-no-shit women, orange vests slung over chairbacks, knit hunting caps on the bar top. Owen poured beer into a pilsner glass from the tap and nodded in her direction as she made her way to the far end where she'd sat before. A small, old bald man came through the double saloon doors of the kitchen and limped behind Owen to grab a bottle of whiskey from the shelf, looking like he'd sooner kill a person than speak to one. He mumbled under his breath to Owen, "Bring me a glass with ice."

So this was Owen's father, the infamous cook Fremont had mentioned, head of the Varney clan—one big, happy family running a restaurant in western Maine. Bri came up to the bar and asked Owen for two vodka tonics, waving to Pennie before whisking the drinks to a couple of middle-aged women with dark lipstick and coiffed dyed hair gossiping at a table in the corner. The black-and-white photographs of the submerged homes and stores she'd seen at the historical society surrounded her again. Owen brought her a menu and said, "What's up?"

She laughed at his greeting, his repeated refrain, making her instantly at ease. "Not much, you?"

He never cracked a smile. "What'll it be?"

She ordered a Lone Pine, and he asked if this was becoming her favorite spot.

"Is there another?"

"Not really, other than the Spotted Pig on the other side of Stratton. But they have terrible food."

"I guess you've got a patron, then. Until the money runs out. Then I'll have to hit the road back to Portland."

He considered her, maybe trying to figure out if she was serious or just kidding around. "We need help in the kitchen. Just lost our line cook. The guy hasn't shown up for two nights. Any interest?"

She mulled this opportunity over, wondering how long she'd be in Eustis, now that her fascination with the local lore was piqued. Kitchen work was not really her bag, but she did need money. And she had absolutely nothing else going on in her life. "Tempting, but I don't have any kitchen experience."

"Don't worry about that. He just needs a warm body to take orders and cut vegetables." Owen pulled a job application from a drawer and slid it across the bar top. She accused him of being pushy. He handed her a pen, unsmiling. "Not many options for jobs around here."

It occurred to her that he was trying to be helpful. Without any other prospects for money, she decided to humor him and fill it out. Under "employment," she wrote down "Library help desk, dog sitter, and visionary." Under "college," she wrote, "Dropout," and under "high school," "Barely passed." She slid it across the bar, sipping her IPA. He picked it up and nodded, raising his eyebrows. "Visionary? Well, well." Turning on his heels, he went into the kitchen and came back out with the skinny old man, two patches of white hair in tufts over each ear, a dirty, checked dishcloth tucked into his belt for an apron. He dragged his left leg and used his bulky right arm to support himself.

Pennie sat up straight in surprise. Owen left her, walking to the opposite end of the bar.

"You're kind of old to work as a line cook, ain't you?"

Did this old man just call her old? His sweet whiskey breath clouded the air between them. "I hardly call thirty old."

He moved his giant hand over his bulbous face and squeezed his red nose, looking at her in all earnestness, like he wanted to suss the truth out of her. "I've got a smock in the kitchen that will fit you, once you fill out the paperwork."

Before she knew what was happening, much less had agreed to any kind of job, bucket-faced Betsy was there behind the bar rummaging around in the same drawer where the application had come from. She pushed employment agreements and tax forms in front of her. "I don't know if you'll be more nuisance than help, but fill these out." She narrowed her eyes at Pennie. "Sometimes all he needs is company back there. Just fill these out, and don't get in his way."

Betsy marched to the dining room in her army boots and big bottom to check on Bri's activity. Pennie knew with utmost certainty that this was her worst employment offer by a long shot. Sipping her beer, she stared at Owen until he came back. "Now look what you've done. Your parents seem to think I need a job."

"Don't you?" Straight-faced, he waved to more hunters moving in to fill the remaining bar seats.

"That's beside the point. I'm not even sure how long I'll be staying here. Might not be more than a week at the most."

"Doesn't matter. We're in crisis mode. Just give it a try."

She contemplated the employment forms, looking up when Bri made her way over, as cheerful as Holly Golightly. "I heard you're joining us in the kitchen. That's awesome! You must have decided to stay a while."

"I'm not sure, really. Owen here volunteered my temporary services to the cantankerous cook."

"Oh, he's not that bad. He can be quite sweet if he's not too loaded." Bri knocked Pennie on the shoulder as she watched Betsy escort another family to a table. "We'll have so much fun working together!"

Unable to come up with any other excuses, and knowing that meals came with the job, she signed the forms, downed the last of her beer, and made her way behind the bar to Owen. He shook her hand a little too forcefully. "Welcome. Just yell if you need anything."

Regretfully, she opened the saloon doors to see Shep sitting on a stool with his glass of whiskey, listening to talk radio. The hosts were talking about the "Libtards" and "Antifas" and how the socialists wanted to tax the people out of their own state to make room for all the immigrants.

Before she could turn and run for her life, he stood up and offered her a drink. Tempting, but she declined, eyeing the bottle already a third gone.

"Smock's hanging on the door there. I'll get the vegetables."

He limped toward a giant refrigerator and took out bags of carrots, onions, peppers, and celery, asking her if she knew how to cut vegetables, which she did, growing up in Aunt Aggie's house. Handing her a knife, he ordered her to keep her fingers in the process and set her up with a cutting board. "I need a full bag of each chopped every day before four." He slurred his words. "I come in early morning to cook, then take a few hours off. Can you be here every afternoon to chop?"

She made a face that must have made it obvious that she had nothing to schedule around.

"Good, then. You can come in at three and work until close." Putting on the smock, she looked at the sharp knife on the wooden board, her stomach grumbling. He still hadn't told her when she'd be able to eat.

"Well, what are you waiting for?" He sat back on the stool and grabbed his drink. The dinner orders began to flood in, Betsy plowing through the saloon doors to clothespin slips to a makeshift line over the plating table. She eyed Pennie as if she were a wayward freeloader. Shep told Pennie to dish out the vegetables while he flipped steaks on the grill, manned the fryer for the fish-and-chips, and checked the heat in the oven for the covered dishes of lasagna and baked chicken. He did all of it with the ease of a man who knew his way around a kitchen and how to feed a mess of people. Despite his limp and the sweat pouring down his temples, he never stopped moving.

In between gulps of his whiskey, he barked orders at her, to take out the baked potatoes, to check the rice on the stovetop. "Too many goddamn options today," he said. "What happened to good 'ol meat and potatoes? Everybody's got to have gluten-free this and vegan that. I'm sick of this entitled bullshit." He flipped the tenderloin, and Pennie's mouth salivated. He took another mouthful of whiskey and asked her how long she lived around here.

"I'm staying with my Uncle Fremont and Bri for a while."

"You don't say. Fremont can be a real pain in the ass, but Bri's a nice kid. Works hard."

Pennie didn't know quite what to say, wanting to defend Fremont. Instead, she asked him what happened to his leg.

"None of your goddamned business. Now get those plates loaded before Betsy comes back in here and tans your ass."

Despite his crassness, she liked working with the old codger. Maybe it was the way he worked with his bare hands, scarred with burn blisters, stirring the bubbling-hot soup, dishing out the lasagna from the oven, working the fryolator and the open-flame grill without a mitt to speak of, never missing a beat. Pennie picked up on his hand gestures, directing her what to load on where before she brought the plates to the station where bossy Betsy picked them up. None of the waitresses were allowed in the kitchen.

"Shep, I asked for a *tenderloin*, not a T-bone."

"Get your order straight, or I'll get *this one* to take your job." He pointed at Pennie, who shrunk into her smock to avoid Betsy's glare. After she was gone, Pennie eyed the T-bone on the sideboard.

Shep slipped out to the bathroom, and she was about to dive into the steak when Owen stuck his head in the door. "How's it going back here?"

"I'm in the line of sniper fire between your parents."

He handed her a beer. "This will keep you going." Shep's thumping approach made him take notice and leave, smiling at her. Pennie raised the beer in thanks.

The next two hours flew by. The orders came one after another, until the magic nine o'clock hour, when the last slip finally dropped and the cook poured himself the remainder of the bottle, throwing his towel on the floor.

"I'll send Bri and Owen in to help you clean this place up." The kitchen lay in utter disarray, gravy splattered over the black iron stovetop, roasted potatoes and bits of lasagna on the floor, spaghetti left in the strainer by the sink, carrots and broccoli and lettuce covering the salad station, a film of grease over everything.

Clean up? This was not something she had signed up for, the mound of pots and pans staring at her from the sink. She was ready to quit when Owen whisked into the kitchen and offered to get started on the dishes, looking almost afraid she'd leave.

He told her to sit down and eat something, and when she finally cut into the tender T-bone that had been sent back, the juicy red meat melted away any bottled-up animosity. This was the best steak she had ever had, and she chewed with relish, mixing the au jus with the delicious pan-roasted potatoes, watching Owen stack the dishes in the dishwasher as he sang along to an Aerosmith song on the radio. Before she knew it, Bri had joined them in the kitchen, and they were all helping themselves to beer and wine or whatever they wanted to drink while they danced and dried pans and cleaned counters until well past midnight.

Pennie followed the erratic brake lights of Bri's Jeep back to the house. They crept in, and she loaded the woodstove while Bri wrapped Fremont in his quilt, the quilt with so many memories of lives lived, squares of old baby blankets and aprons and hunting jackets sewn together like a family album. Upstairs, they sank into their creaky twin mattresses, Bri complaining about her tables and the miserable, bitchy customers who were never satisfied with their food or their lives. "I'm never going to end up like that. The last place I want to end up is an unhappy marriage after twenty years. I'd rather be single the rest of my life."

Pennie mumbled, half asleep. "Who wants to get married, anyway." Bri said something about JD this or JD that and his crazy family, but Pennie had already drifted off to sleep…

Under a bright snow moon, the snake-like Dead River twisted and turned as if a giant's divine fingertip had drawn a deep impression in the rich mud lining the river valley. Through her husky's eyes, she sat high on a snowy clearing at Jim Eaton Hill, sentient Bigelow in the distance under the starry sky, children whizzing around her, their runner sleds like flying machines, some with toboggans or dented kitchen pans or lengths of cardboard, sliding in the crusty snow; some binding long skis to their boots with rubber canning bands, flying downhill between the birch trees, around the giant maple, toward iced-over Flagstaff Pond where more children skated near great bonfires lighting the black, wintry sky. She chased after them, barking and panting, clouds of warm breath disappearing, vibrations ringing, peals of joy in the clear cold night.

Then the darkness slowly lightened, bringing the awakening of spring, the snow melting and green grass emerging, small rivulets of water flowing down Jim Eaton Hill, twisting in different directions, all leading into a little stream at the base of the knoll, into the gully where children gathered, wading up to their knees in the bone-chilling spring runoff, squealing, pushing their tiny cedar-shake boats powered by mini water wheels or old cloth sails. The white and purple wildflowers swayed, a breezy dance in the meadow, down to the sheep's barn with the fresh smell of hay and warm, pure milk, of springtime and bleating new life. She followed the children inside the sturdy farmhouse built with lumber from the dependable mill, to sit by the woodstove burning in the kitchen, where a box on the floor held six tiny baby lambs and a small girl reached for a bottle to feed them, petting their newly woolen heads and looking into their dark shining eyes, inside their tender hearts.

DAYLIGHT SHONE ON THE old attic floor. The voices of Fremont and Bri vibrated from below, the smell of frying bacon and coffee filling the house. The dream, a slip into the memory of time, sat clear in her mind, and she relaxed into the reverie, knowing the window of her dreams reflected the story of this place.

Downstairs, Fremont poured her a cup of coffee. "We decided it was about time we made you a real breakfast."

His cat jumped onto her lap. "Oh, well hello, cat." Bri told Bartholomew to get down, but Pennie didn't mind. She felt the lumps in the old cat's skin and smoothed them with her fingertips, to which he purred and clawed her legs. Fremont was happy to hear she'd started a job as a line cook and would be staying awhile. Before Pennie could say that she wasn't sure how long she was staying, Bri jumped in to pronounce how well Pennie had done her first night and how Shep had taken a shine to her. Fremont raised his bushy eyebrows.

"That's an exaggeration," Pennie said, waving the compliment away. "Uncle Fremont, I talked to Alfie, and he was asking about your property the power company wants, on Middle Carry."

"They've offered to take it off my hands, as you can imagine. Those bastards have a fight coming their way." He opened *The Maine Atlas and Gazetteer* on the table and thumbed nimbly through its pages until he found the map he wanted. "Sit down, Pennie. I've got a little history lesson for you." Pulling up a stiff-backed chair, she sat down beside him, all ears. He pointed to the Kennebec River, running his yellow, knobby index finger from Augusta up to Waterville to Skowhegan to Bingham and west across the Great Carrying Place that led to the Dead River at Bog Brook. "This is the first half of the route that Arnold's battalion portaged. They left the Kennebec River here where there's a dam today, and portaged between East, Middle, and West Carry Ponds to reach Bog Brook and the Dead River before heading to Canada. This is the proposed electricity corridor"

The irony of it rose like the smell of skunk. "Why on earth would the power company choose this route—the same, exact route of Arnold's historic march—for a power corridor?"

"It's the most direct shot down from Canada. They'd rather destroy the woods here than pay to circumvent it. All in the name of 'clean energy' power for southern New England. Clean energy my ass. I see these power company guys sniffing around here, looking for support."

Bri jumped in, serving up the scrambled eggs and bacon. "JD is working with the other selectman to stop this. No one wants it except the out-a-staters and the power company."

Pennie felt her pulse quicken. "Any chance you could show me your camp?"

He flicked his cigarette into the Hills Bros. coffee can. "Bri can take you."

Her leggy cousin sat down, shaking salt and pepper on her eggs. "We should hike in. It's only about three miles."

Bartholomew still firmly planted on her lap, Pennie crunched on the well-done bacon, watching Fremont shovel eggs into his mouth, dip a donut in his coffee, and smoke from his constantly burning cigarette without skipping a beat. She was getting used to the cigarette smoke and the heat coming from the woodstove that constantly cracked and hissed, logs falling and shifting inside. The temperament of the place eased its way inside her soul, from the eeriness of the man-made lake to the woods where Jim Eaton Hill lay behind the trees, the place where the great wolf tree stood holding the history of this land like the inside of a tomb.

Fremont moved his plate out of the way and pulled the *Gazetteer* in front of him again. "Like I said, this is the same route Benedict Arnold took, but instead of running the corridor along the lake, of course, the power company plans to run it on the far side, the other side of Flagstaff Mountain and Spring Lake, and then down to cross the Dead River at Long Falls."

Pennie looked out the window, then at Bri. "It's where we were yesterday, right?"

"That's right, on the far side of Jim Eaton Hill."

"And the plan is to actually run a corridor of power lines across the Dead River?"

He pointed to small ponds on the map. "That's the best route to reach the Kennebec, running the corridor down between West and Middle Carry Ponds where my property is—right through the Great Carrying Place." He thumped the map at the shore of East Carry Pond with one hand and took a drag of his cigarette with the other. "Arnold was here for about four days in October 1775, while his army portaged their bateaux, food, and other supplies. He wrote updates to General Washington and ordered a makeshift hospital built for the sick or injured men, hoping they'd recover in time to meet the army in Quebec City for the siege. After he left camp, he passed through a swamp that took hours to cross before reaching Bog Brook *here*, where they washed off the caked, knee-high mud and launched their boats in the Dead River."

He ran his finger back to the area between Middle and West Carry Ponds. "This is where my land is, and I'll be goddamned if some power company is going to place a mile-wide corridor here." He stamped his fist. "Over my dead body."

Bri put her hand on her grandfather's arm. "Grandpa, don't worry. JD is not going to let that happen. He's already told me the selectmen voted it down."

He pointed at her. "Those townships up there above Spring Lake are under the *state's* control, and you have no idea how the *state* government can get its way, little girl."

She stiffened at his patronizing tone. "I know I don't know much about the ways of government, but I do know we can all chip in to help," she said.

Pennie squeezed Bri's knee. "No time like today. I'd love to go look at the property if we have time."

Bri stood up. "We'll just clean up these dishes—"

Fremont squashed his cigarette in the Hills Bros. can and collected the plates. "I've got these. You take Pennie over to see my property. Give her the lay of the land." Wagging his finger at Pennie, he said, "Your uncle told me you're good with a camera. I'd like some decent pictures. Been a while since I've been over there." Hunched over, he walked to the sink with the plates.

"I'll do my best."

ANOTHER BRIGHT DAY LAY before them, the trees flashing brilliant leaves still shimmering from an early morning frost. Bri drove down the Arnold Trail Road, going about ten miles over the speed limit, as was her normal habit.

"I wanna make a quick pit stop to see Greta, if you don't mind," she said. Pennie searched her memory for somebody by that name until Bri cleared up the mystery. "She's the psychic I was telling you about. I've been feeling really weird lately, and I just need to talk to her, if you don't mind. It's on the way."

Pennie didn't mind at all. The only so-called clairvoyants she'd ever met were the fortune tellers at the Cumberland Fair years ago—eccentric ladies dressed in long robes to cover their regular clothes, rubbing their pretend crystal balls. Bri drove through Stratton, passing A-frame camps and other small cabins that brought to Pennie's mind Uncle Alfie and Aunt Aggie's place over at Coos Canyon, where she and Tita would stay. She hadn't been there since her ski accident last winter. With any luck, Dani and Mali would be up this way any day to start their research for their art commission.

The gold and russets of the maples and beeches gave her a sense of peace and belonging. Bri pulled in to the dirt driveway of a small, white wooden building with a hip roof and single chimney, a covered front porch, and two simple front windows. Bri told her this was the old Dead River schoolhouse that had been moved before the flooding. They stepped onto the porch, and something made Pennie look up to see a bird's nest inside the eaves. She felt a chill come up inside her coat, a spine-tingling vibration.

In a moment, a small woman opened the door dressed in a long, dark green wool dress and black slippers on her small feet, her coarse salt-and-pepper hair pulled back in a bun, little wisps of hair flying around her delicate but serious face. "Brianna, I knew you were coming," she said.

Inside, her living room was lined with shelves of books, and every available side table was piled with more of them. There were baskets of half-finished knitting or polished stones, a few overstuffed chairs here and there, paintings of the valley before the flooding and of the peaks of

Bigelow covering the walls. A tiny potbellied stove glowed from the far corner, and the whole place smelled of woodsmoke and lavender.

"Been busy with work and, you know, *the boyfriend*." Bri shrugged like she wasn't sure why she'd brought him up. "This is my cousin, Pennie, from Portland."

Greta's green eyes rested on her like a warm hug. "Nice to meet you, Pennie. You've got an excellent local guide here. Brianna knows her way around, can take you anywhere." She motioned them to sit down at a large table where notebooks lay open, little drawings of birds between notes written in a delicate hand. She asked Pennie if she was any closer to her mission.

"Sorry...my mission?"

"You're here to discover something, is that right? Perhaps look deeper into the history that lies in the valley, under the lake?"

Another chill rose up her spine. The seer motioned to the oil paintings around her on the walls, different views of the valley with the Dead River twisting and turning in its original course. "My family lived on the Dead River plantation for generations until the power men came in to flood our valley. We need young questioners like yourself to help us preserve our liberty, isn't that right, Brianna?"

Her cousin took a deep breath. "I knew you'd feel it, too, Greta. From the moment Pennie arrived, I knew she was here as a kindred spirit."

Greta patted Bri's clenched fist. "Now let's talk about you. You're worried about something, I can tell." The clairvoyant turned her gaze to Pennie again, her eyes as shiny as marbles. "You know it, too, don't you? I can see it in your window. Let's get out the cards." She pulled a hand-hewn red oak box from a drawer in the table beside her. "This is a box that has been in my family for generations." She pulled out the deck, revealing an illustration of five chickadees, their black-capped heads and white breasts nesting in a pine tree on the backs of the cards. With her long, graceful fingers, she pushed the cards toward Bri, who hesitantly picked them up and began to shuffle.

The seer looked out the side window toward a bushy pine tree, as if going to a place beyond. "What's been going on?" Greta asked.

"I've been feeling out of sorts. Something is, I don't know, *off*. It's not my grandfather. He seems fine, tougher than ever, but I...I don't know. I'm anxious." Bri clumsily jostled the cards together a few times before sliding them back across the table to Greta, who fanned them and asked Bri to pick two. She took her time selecting the cards, then laid them face up between them, revealing 4, The Wardrobe—a drawing of an old clothing dresser with large paneled doors—and 3, Troll—an illustration of a crazed troll doll, its wild blue hair shooting straight up.

Greta said, "This is your past, Brianna. The Wardrobe signifies something that you are hiding that has happened, something you may need to shed some light on."

"Yes," she said, her breath catching. "I feel like there is something that I need to face, that needs to come to light, I just don't know what it is."

Greta turned up her palms. "Look inside your heart and trust your intuition, and the truth will come forth." She pointed to the Troll card. "You've been walking under this cloud of doubt, but you must not brush it off. If you do, the Troll will only feed upon your fears."

Bri breathed in deeply and nodded as Greta pointed to the deck. With hesitancy, she flipped over two more cards: 21, Partnership—silver salt and pepper shakers—and 13, The Lobster—a Maine lobster. Greta clasped her hands together in contemplation. "This is your current situation. A partnership is like a meeting of the minds, but you must work together." Then she picked up the Lobster card and crossed it over the salt and pepper shakers. "Lobsters are known for attacking one another in captivity. This could be someone in your life who may be trying to hold you back..."

Bri chewed on her hair and sunk down in her chair. "I'm wondering if the partnership is at the restaurant, you know working with the other waitresses and Betsy, who can be a real nag sometimes. I feel like that is the only thing that makes sense here."

Pennie thought about JD and the pregnancy and how these cards were trying to tell Bri about her personal situation, but she held back and remained silent while Greta encouraged Bri to look deep inside herself to understand her relationships and what she could do to thwart any selfishness or backlash from others. "Remember, all alliances require a give-and-take." She motioned to Bri to pick up two more cards.

Bri turned over 43, Poison—a drawing of a thorny vine—and 36, Well—an old crank well with a shingled roof and bucket resting on its edge.

"Ahh, of course." Her eyes glossed over. "The thorn apple bloom on the Poison card depicts a beautiful but dangerous warning, cautioning you to be careful. The Well, on the other hand, represents the deep, enduring strength of your family and friends to draw upon." Greta motioned toward Pennie and said, "You have come into Brianna's life at the right moment. You are more than a cousin and friend but a knower of things beyond."

Pennie quaked inside, a deep rumble of awareness. Bri reached over to Pennie. "I hope you stay with us for a while. Having you working at the restaurant means the world to me. You know how toxic it can be there."

Greta spread her arms toward Bri. "You have personal challenges to overcome, but Pennie is here to help guide you."

Bri whispered, "I know."

There was a knocking at the door. The slight woman stood up, coming out of her trance. "I'm sorry, but I have another appointment. I hope you can come back when I have time to do a reading for Pennie." They followed the seer to the door where an older gentleman stood stooped in the threshold, peering over his glasses at them. He looked oddly familiar.

"Herold, please come in."

Then it hit Pennie. He looked like Mr. Snodgrass, the wine seller, who worked at the local market on the West End of Portland, a strange resemblance. She said, "Herold, Herold Snodgrass?"

"Why, yes," he replied. "Have we met?"

"You look like someone who works in Portland, a wine seller."

He chuckled. "Oh, yes, that would be my brother. Haven't seen him in a while. Got to get down there one of these days."

Greta commented on the connectedness of things and explained that Herald was a dowser. "You see, I've run out of water in my well. Herald promised to help me find more."

The significance of the well grew deeper—the strength of relationships, past and present, of drawing on help from others. Pennie had never met a dowser before and was intrigued, especially because they were so close to the lake. How could she have run out of water? Bri was already out the door, so Pennie bid them goodbye, buoyed by the encounter, stepping outside into the open, blue skies of a crisp autumn day.

Driving along the road, Bri was strangely quiet until Pennie broke the silence. "Thanks for including me on your visit. Greta was amazing."

Clenching the steering wheel, Bri said, "I think I'm pregnant." Her shoulders, wracked with heavy sobs, tensed, and she swerved left, catching the shoulder of the road before swerving back to overcorrect.

Pennie held onto the roll bar and reached for Bri's arm, rubbing in consolation. "It's okay, Bri. Are you sure?" But Pennie already knew, sure as the snow would fall. "Why don't you pull over?"

"I'm okay, I'm okay." She took a deep breath and snuffed.

"Are you late?"

"Only a week or so, but I just have this feeling, deep down. I don't know. When Greta said, 'There may be something hiding,' I suddenly knew." She rubbed her stomach absentmindedly, crying. "What the hell am I going to do? We've been dating barely three, four months. I'm such a fuck-up."

"Don't say that. It was a mistake, an accident. It happens all the time. The important thing is to share it with JD, you know, if you are pregnant, and figure out what to do together."

"He's going to hate me for it. How could I be so irresponsible?"

"Were you on the pill?

"Yes, but my prescription ran out, so I used my old diaphragm instead. Obviously not a wise choice. Maybe I shouldn't tell him, just get rid of it."

"That's not going to fix anything. Remember what the cards said about partnership: you have to work on this together. You're not alone."

Tears streamed down Bri's face as she drove—well under the speed limit, to Pennie's relief. "I'm so lucky you came up here, Pen. What would I do if I were facing this alone?"

"Do you want to go back to Fremont's? We can do this another day."

"No, no, I want to show you the property. It will be good to get out in the fresh air."

They rode in silence, digesting the moment of truth, the stark awareness of a life unfolding inside a secret wardrobe. Bri followed Long Falls Dam Road until they came to a gravel logging road where a sign nailed to a tree read *Arnold Trail* and *Appalachian Trail,* arrows pointing toward the woods. Bri pulled over to the side and reached for a roll of paper towels in the back to wipe her face and dry her eyes. "This is the trail to Middle Carry. I'm so glad to be out here right now to clear my head. I hope you don't mind a hike."

Pennie was not exactly a hiker, but she was up for it on this fine day of clear mountain air. The well-trodden trail led to a beautiful wood of white spruce, scrub pine, mountain ash, eastern hemlock, and yellow birch. Thinking about the pregnancy while inside the cathedral of trees lulled them into a hikers' meditation, together yet alone with their thoughts. Bri, her fly rod hanging from the side of her backpack, followed the orange blazes on the trees, climbing over the hilly, rooted terrain, her long legs moving her at a steady clip. Pennie followed, out of breath after the first mile of stepping over rocks and fallen logs. When Bri asked her if she wanted to slow down, she pretended she was not tired in the least.

The granite outcroppings and mossy banks, the small streams of meandering clear water, the leaves sifting around them, bright yellow and red, drifting in the windless forest, left Pennie with a sense of stillness. Stumbling over the roots that crisscrossed the trail, over the moss-covered black rocks and piles of saturated moose-dung nuggets, she wondered if the moose were watching them from deep inside their forest. Chickadees welcomed them with melodic twittering. They crossed makeshift bridges over bogs and through thickets until they finally reached Arnold Point on the east shore of the pond, which was glimmering and sparkling under the cold, bright sun. The point was covered in a tangle of birches, hemlocks, and alders draped in green lichen. A wooden sign read *Great Carrying Place: 1775 Arnold Expedition Portage Route.*

She followed Bri in silence over a long bog bridge, logs strapped together over a swamp, ambling together until they came to a serpentine ridge. They followed a trickling stream covered in slippery rocks uphill, its banks a jumble of bushy willows and alders. She huffed and puffed, doing her best to keep up with Bri's steady pace, staying close behind her, up and over a low rise carved by glaciers millions of years ago. She felt the spirits of hundreds of soldiers marching alongside her, the heavy, flat-bottomed boats chaffing their shoulders as they stumbled on rocks, falling and managing to gain footing again, trudging the slow decent downhill. She felt herself trip on the flat, mossy rocks, the stream running underneath her careful steps through the woods of silver maple and paper birch as she ducked under half-fallen trees, bushwhacked her way through the thicket. Finally, they reached another long wooden bridge, logs halved and flat side up, crossing a dense cedar swamp with its sharp smells of the living forest.

The trail descended to a gravel road where they walked over streams running into Middle Carry. They finally came to an opening in the woods beside the pond. Bri pointed to a small log cabin hidden under a stand of pines, lovely against the dim sky, with black, shimmering water behind it.

"Here's our cabin. Haven't been out here in a while. Let's check it out." They entered the side door of the solid little lodge to the overwhelming smell of animal scat. Pennie held her nose.

Bri laughed. "It's a hunting camp. You never know who'll make themselves at home. We've had hermits living in here before." Outside, she pointed out the rise behind the cabin. "He owns this swath, about forty acres, between Middle and West Carry. I still can't believe they want to put a power line through here. This was a well-worn route the Abenaki tribes used, coming down from the St. Francis village in Canada, where they traded goods and kept clear of colonial violence. They portaged through here with their birchbark canoes for hundreds of years before Benedict Arnold trekked it with his men."

The spirits of the souls who'd traipsed through these boggy lands in search of food and freedom gave Pennie a feeling of interconnectedness, of one life moving seamlessly into another. She fiddled with the triskelion locket around her neck then took out her camera to snap some pictures of the pond, pines and spruces and hemlocks lining its shores, the sun coming down in glints between the bold colors of the hardwood trees up further on the ridge. A thousand tiny lights danced across the calm surface, rippling on the pond in merriment.

She walked back to the trail on the other side of the cabin to get an angle from each direction, almost hearing the marching of the tired, hungry men carrying their bateaux, the rustling of the Native Americans carrying their birchbark canoes. Bri sat on a giant granite boulder, her chestnut hair shining in the sun. "My grandfather has been coming here since he was a boy. Shot his first partridge here. Most everyone in this area still depends on wild game."

Through her camera lens, she focused on a deer in the woods, a mother doe with three fawn walking quietly, ears pricked, looking at her. She clicked a round of pictures, their soft brown eyes twinkling at her before they leaped softly, without a sound, in the opposite direction. Bri grew quiet, spotting a bald eagle, and Pennie turned her camera toward the sky, snapping images of the liberty bird soaring, its awesome wingspan and white undersides flying over paths well worn by the Abenaki, who knew the true meaning of freedom, of interdependence with nature.

The sound of engines broke their silence. Bri said it was ATVs. The rumble grew louder in the air and under their feet, until a line of three came through the woods.

Bri walked toward the first of them, and Pennie followed. The rider took off his helmet, opening his arms to her. "Didn't know you were coming out here today," he said. JD threw back his bulky shoulders and waved at Pennie as if she were a nuisance fly buzzing around his orbit.

"What are you doing here?" Bri said, full of surprise and hopeless innocence. "I thought you were working today."

"Taking the afternoon off." He turned to his friends behind him, who took their helmets off. "You remember Thad and Brett."

Bri waved to them, then turned somber, holding in a secret that was killing her to conceal. It was fear Pennie saw on her face. He took her hand. "You okay, Bri?"

"I'm fine. Never been better." She flipped her hair like she didn't have a care in the world, but her grimace gave her away. "You're not supposed to be on the trail with these machines."

"We're mostly off-trail or on the road." He turned to his buddies and smirked. "You're not going to turn us in, are you?" he winked at her, and she rolled her eyes.

"C'mon, I'll give you a ride back." Taking off his glove with his teeth, he checked his hefty platinum watch. "You need to be at work in a couple hours, anyway."

"No, no. This is Pennie's first time on the trail. We'll walk back together."

"She can ride back with Brett." He looked back. "You don't mind if she hops on, do you, bro?"

Overly friendly Brett wore a leather motorcycle jacket and wrap-around sunglasses. "I don't mind at all." He revved his engine and motioned to the seat behind him. "Hop on."

Pennie picked up her camera bag, gathering her equipment. "I'd much rather walk, but thanks anyway."

Bri turned toward Pennie, but JD grabbed her arm and pulled her back, standing up to kiss her on the cheek. "C'mon, baby. I've missed you this week." He patted the back of his seat. "I'll drive slowly, don't worry. You know I don't like it when you refuse me," he said sweetly.

Pennie zipped up her camera bag. Bri squirmed in discomfort, not wanting to make a scene. "Pennie, do you need help getting back?"

Part of her wanted to tell Bri to stay with her, but this was not her battle. "I can find my way back. Really, Bri, it's okay."

With her arm still in his grasp, Bri mounted the ATV behind him. He handed her his helmet. She dug in her pocket for her keys and threw them at Pennie. "You can take my Jeep back."

Without as much as a farewell, JD turned his ATV around, tossing up dirt and pine needles. Bri waved to her, yelling, "Call me if you get lost."

They sped away, Bri's backpack and fly rod swinging, ruts left in the earth from JD's big tires. Thad and Brett followed close behind, their engines loud, echoing, disturbing the quiet wood. She gathered up her pack and started on the trail, trekking back on the gravel road to the cedar swamp, where the bridge leading to the stream trickled up and over the ridge to the moss-covered forest of granite boulders and willows, of birch trees, black alder, and lichen. Despite her long hike alone in the damp forest, she felt the companions of the soldier's spirits all around her and fell into the hush of the warbler's warble, the stream's rush—the only sounds for miles and miles—thinking about the secret wardrobe and the doubting troll, the give-and-take of the salt and pepper, and the trap of the lobster, the poisonous flower of the ivy, and the depth of the well.

Chapter 7
Great Carrying Place

On her drive to the Gullet, Pennie was lost in thought about Bri and JD when Dani called. They were on their way and expected to arrive a little after eight. Finally, her friends were coming, the ones she trusted to help her sort through anything.

She turned into the restaurant parking lot. "Did you get my text about bringing me more clothes?"

"Done. And Aunt Maude sent a pie for you, too. She thought you might be starving up there."

"I would be if I didn't get a job at the local eatery."

"Wait, what? You're working in a restaurant?"

"Don't turn your nose up at me. A girl has to eat."

Dani laughed. "Don't take this the wrong way, but you don't seem like the waitress type. You know, remembering orders, being nice to ungrateful people."

She loved this about Dani, always with the reality check. "You have a point, but not to worry. I'm working in the kitchen, behind the scenes and well away from the thankless complainers."

"Ah, the culinary arts. *Still* a surprise. Name of this fine establishment?"

"The Greedy Gullet, in Stratton." On the far side of the parking lot, the dark surface of the lake rippled in the late-day sun.

"That's not too far from the mountain."

"Is that where you're staying? Sugarloaf?"

Dani was happy to report that Tita's friend from the US Ski Team had offered them a condo where they could stay for as long as they wanted to work on their project. Pennie told her about her newfound cousin, Brianna, who knew the area like the back of her hand. "She's like a personal guide. She can take us anywhere you want." Their excitement grew at the idea of exploring Flagstaff and even skiing if the snow came early enough.

Inside, she found the place empty. In the kitchen, a note was taped to the giant refrigerator door in block letters:

WASH YOUR HANDS. CHOP THE VEGETABLES IN THE STEEL TRAY. CUT THE CHICKEN BREASTS INTO STRIPS. MAKE A LARGE SALAD (DIRECTIONS AT THE CHOPPING STATION). —SHEP

Taking the pans from the fridge, she smelled the baked beans and pork in the oven and the homemade chicken noodle soup on the stovetop. She had just found a peeler and sharp knives beside the industrial wooden cutting board when she heard the front door shutting, then the sound of someone opening the drawer of the register, then Bri's voice. "Afternoon, Betsy."

The matron's booming response filled the place. "Afternoon, Missy. The condiments need filling." Pennie looked up to the vent overhead. When she moved to the sink to peel the carrots, she could hear nothing, but when she walked back to the chopping station, she could hear Betsy counting the money to herself, "twenty, forty, sixty..." Then Owen's voice. "What's the drink special tonight?"

"Let's do a mule and a blueberry martini. You got the stuff?"

"Let me check the blueberries."

He walked through the saloon doors into the kitchen and didn't see Pennie in the corner until she said hello.

"Jesus!" He stopped short and turned to her like a robot, all stiff arms and legs, saluting her. "What is up, Earthling?"

She chuckled. "Not much, you?"

He opened the fridge with the same stiff movements and punctuated each word in monotone. "On the hunt for edible berries of the genus *Vaccinium*, or the heath family." She directed him to the third shelf, back, where she'd seen them. She considered asking him if she could have a blueberry martini later but then thought better of it. What was the harm in keeping her eavesdropping to herself? Besides, she was happy she'd surprised him. He exited through the saloon doors, never leaving character.

She had the chicken breasts on the chopping block, wondering how she should slice these things when Bri came in, beaming and breathless, standing in the middle of the kitchen. "I told him."

Pennie moved to the sink to get out of the vent area, not knowing if the sound traveled both ways. "I thought you were going to wait until you got a test?"

"I couldn't help myself. I was a blubbering mess, but he was so sweet about it, Pennie. He told me he wanted to do a test right away, so we went to the drug store and did it together. Sure enough, it came up positive, and I wanted to die, waiting for his reaction, but he told me we would do this together." She took a deep beath. "We can do it *together*. He's being so supportive."

Pennie washed her red hands, running it over in her mind. "So, you both decided together you want to have a baby?"

"Yes, he definitely does. He says he's *in love* with me. How wonderful is *that*?"

Pennie looked into her innocent round eyes. "What about you, Bri?"

She chewed on her hair. "I don't know. Part of me is happy because JD is happy, but the other part of me is not ready to be a mother. My own mother had me at nineteen. I'm twenty-two, and I don't want to make the same mistakes she made. But JD says God has his plans and we should be thankful."

If there was one thing she wanted to make Bri understand, to get through to her sweet young soul, it was that God wanted her to make the best decision for *herself*, not for somebody she hardly knew. "This is a big decision to make, to bring a life into this world."

The matron interrupted them, poking her head in the kitchen. "We've got guests coming in, Brianna. Are you going to stand there gossiping all night, or are you going to wait tables?" Bri breezed out the door held open for her, hair whirling. Betsy scowled at Pennie and told her to finish her list before the cook arrived, or she could look for a job elsewhere.

She examined the chicken breasts again and made the executive decision to cut them widthwise into short, thin pieces. She had finished one and was admiring the uniformity of her work when the sound of Shep's limp came through the bar. He grunted his hello, stopping to grab a bottle of whiskey from the shelf before busting through the kitchen doors. He slammed the bottle on the counter and observed her work.

"Are you an imbecile? Have you never cut chicken strips before?"

How could he not appreciate her first attempt? He grabbed the knife from her hand and took out another chicken breast, slapped it on the cutting board, and with quick, fine motions, sliced the long way down the chicken until there were beautiful, equally thin fillets of chicken laying one over the other. "That is a strip. Got it?"

It seemed perfectly reasonable to ask him for one more demonstration, but she decided against it. "Got it." Holding the blade with one hand, pressing her knuckles against the breast with the other, she tried to create those seemingly uncomplicated uniform cuts. While she wrestled with the chicken, he switched on the radio, turning it to a football game. She strained to hear the goings-on out at the bar, the place already beginning to buzz on a Friday night. When she finally brought the chicken over to him, he shook his head, telling her to get busy making the salad. He stirred the soup and added spices, took sauces from the fridge to heat up, seasoned the steak, and checked the beans and pulled pork in the oven. It smelled heavenly. He ordered her to get the pans of corn bread that he'd made earlier and then stuck them in another oven, the whole time drinking his whiskey on ice, limping from one station to another, a marvel in the kitchen.

He tuned the radio to the news, and a story came on about the power corridor, also known as "the Independence Corridor." He muttered, "Money-grubbing assholes."

"Bri and I went out to Middle Carry Pond today, where they're proposing putting the line through. It's a shame they want a line right across Fremont's property and the Arnold Trail."

"You telling me something I don't already know? These power companies think they can come in here and take our land. Well, they ain't getting our approval for their New England power project. It's just like when they told us damming the Dead was going to generate power for the greater good. We won't see a red cent from the corridor, other than the land they're buying up dirt cheap."

"They're using eminent domain again to take it."

"They can shove their eminent domain up their money-grubbing assholes." He slammed his glass on the steel table and told her to get back to her job, to stop talking in the kitchen during working hours. Betsy brought the first orders in, and he fired up the grill for steaks while Pennie put the tossed salads in bowls and lined them up on the counter.

Under the kinetic whirl of a Friday night, she ran from one end of the kitchen to the next getting what Shep needed, helping spoon out baked beans, cutting the cornbread, dishing the soup, and learning how to operate the fryolator for the fish. If Uncle Alfie could see her right now, he would not believe his eyes. She never knew the satisfaction of working in a kitchen, the fast-paced timing of things to serve up hot, home-cooked food to your community in a gathering place. The images of the poison ivy and the well came to her mind. *Poisoning the well,* she thought, is that what Greta's cards were telling Bri? Was she being sabotaged by this family?

Betsy's slips began to slow their steady feed into the kitchen, the time nearing eight o'clock. Owen poked his head in the door. "You've got some friends out here asking for you." Without hesitation, she ran out the door. The twins sat at the end of the bar with Tita, beside JD and his buddies. Pennie wrapped her arms around Dani and Mali and turned to Tita. "Didn't expect to see you here."

Her cousin pursed her lips. "Don't be so excited to see me."

Dani told Pennie about the large condo they had at the base of Sugarloaf with three bedrooms, a spacious living room with a stone fireplace, and a jacuzzi on the deck. "I feel so spoiled," she said. "Tita knows the right people."

Pennie introduced Owen to the three of them, and he took their drink orders. Mali shook her head at Pennie. "Never thought I would see you in a kitchen. You're wearing half the menu." Pennie looked down at her apron covered with baked bean drippings, barbeque sauce, yellow breadcrumbs, and smears of butter.

"The need to eat is high on my priority list." Dani asked her if she could join them. Pennie let out a heavy sigh. "I have to finish my shift. What do you want? I'll put your orders in."

She raced back to the kitchen to give the order to Shep, who helped her dish out the baked beans and pulled pork, adding a plate for Pennie. "Get out there with your girlfriends. You're no good to me now. But get back here to clean up before you go." She touched him on the arm with a heartfelt thanks, only to be shrugged away.

Out at the bar, JD moved down to make room for Pennie to sit with her friends. His buddies from the trail, Brett and Thad, were checking them out when Bri came over. Dani wasted no time asking her if she'd show them around the Flagstaff area. "Pennie says you want to be a guide," said Dani. Bri beamed and looked at JD, who winked at her. Maybe this was his little way of encouraging her to keep pursuing her dreams, even with the baby coming?

Pennie scarfed down her beans and pork, catching up with the three of them for a few minutes. She couldn't remember the last time she had an appetite like this. When she got back to the kitchen for cleanup, Shep was already gone. Owen stayed at his post to serve the packed bar. Soon Bri joined her in the kitchen, rosy from serving on a busy night. They turned on the rock station, and Pennie took on the arduous task of washing the giant pots and pans, soaking herself in the process, while Bri loaded up the industrial dishwasher with the plates, glasses, silverware, and anything else that would fit, the whole time singing to the radio. The bar was getting boisterous, and Pennie could hear shouts about the Independence Corridor. How she wished she could hear what they were saying. Then, the unmistakable voice of Mali yelling something about damming the rivers.

She pretended to wipe down the countertop while making her way to the chopping station to listen through the vent. JD said, "We don't have enough dams in the state, if you ask me. You tree huggers come along trying to take them down. I thought you wanted clean energy. Can't you make up your minds?"

Mali shot back. "The dams are not as clean as you think they are. Most of them in Maine are over a hundred years old and take more greenhouse gas emissions to repair them, keep them running, than they're worth. Some are worse than natural gas plants."

Brett said, "If you environ-*mentalists* didn't get laws requiring things like million-dollar fish ladders that don't even work, the price wouldn't be so high."

Dani jumped in, softer than her sister, trying to make a point. "I thought you liked fish in your rivers and lakes? If you don't protect them, you'll have no fishery here to speak of."

JD's voice boomed. "You're living in the past. You Natives are still pissed about losing your land to the settlers and trying to take it out on us with your *regulations*."

Pennie knew this kind of talk was nothing new to the twins. Mali said, "You're right, we are still pissed about that, and we're not giving up on protecting our homeland, long before it was yours." Bri finished loading the dishwasher, singing to a Tom Petty song, oblivious to the argument in the restaurant. They wiped the counters and swept the floor to finish up.

At the bar, JD and his friends had moved to the far end, away from the three newcomers. Tita looked up at Pennie, rolling her eyes. "Those guys are assholes." Luckily, Bri had walked away toward her boyfriend, out of earshot.

Pennie said, "Have you tried the Cast Iron Bitch Pale Ale?"

Dani picked up her glass. "No, I'm sticking with iced tea. Somebody has to drive us home." Tita sipped on a blueberry martini. Under her breath, Mali recapped the highlights of the dam conversation. Pennie pretended she hadn't heard anything.

"Just try to ignore them. JD's parents, Betsy and Shep, own the place." She pointed to Owen. "He's the nice one."

Bri made her way back over to them, and Tita said she was glad to meet another member of the extended family, to which Bri hugged Tita, effusive as always. She turned her attention back to Pennie. "Do you mind staying with Fremont tonight? I hate to ask you, but JD really wants me to stay over at his place. Do you mind?"

Even though Pennie had looked forward to a sleepover at the condo with her girl tribe, she said she didn't mind but did have one favor to ask in exchange. "Will you take us over to the dam tomorrow so Dani and Mali can get some pictures?"

"Oh, I'd be happy to! There isn't much to see, but I'll take you." Bri thanked Pennie profusely with her dazzling smile and left them to their drinks.

"Are you serious?" said Tita. "You're taking care of her grandfather?"

"He's Alfie's cousin, Tita. Besides, she's in love. What can you do?"

"She can do better than that," said Mali, scowling. Before things could get testy again, Pennie thanked Owen and escorted them out.

She fell onto the creaky mattress, utterly exhausted, and slipped into a deep sleep...

Men poled bateaux through treacherous raging waters, Bumbazee's Rips and Caratunk Falls, phantom wooden boats crashing against rocks and boulders, splintering apart, leaving hollowed-out men crawling on riverbanks, legs broken and shoulders torn, weak from cold and disease. They hoisted the remaining boats up cleft ledges, their food ration barrels bloated, soaked from the leaky boats and incessant rain. Downeast Scotch-Irish farmers and wildcats, obstinate Yankees, faithful Dutchmen, and Virginia riflemen waded in the shallow and bitter-cold waters, pointing to a great mountain up the Kennebec River, calling it "sugar loaf."

Through the eyes of the husky, she trotted alongside Jacataqua, the lithe, tall Native American sachem of Swan Island who walked behind the comely rogue, Aaron Burr, trailing a line of men in fringed shirts and moccasins with heavy packs, sabers at their sides, laden with barrels of rotting salt pork, salt beef, and flour, traversing a steep ridge of tall spruce and cedar, through a primeval forest, to reach several bateaux waiting on the banks of a pond. They loaded them to paddle across the half-mile stretch while two soldiers drove poor, weary oxen around the ponds, over underbrush and through brambles, trudging on, the fate of slaughter in the beasts' eyes.

Unloading everything for a second carry to the next pond, the beaten men, a few accompanied by their wives, hoisted the heavy, flat-bottomed boats through sharp, slashing willow underbrush, falling and stumbling in the swamps, doubling back for their supplies and barrels of food, preserving their meager rations, weak and red-faced but trudging on. Jacataqua and Aaron followed with muskets over their shoulders, tomahawks in their belts, carrying their canoe over a path widened by the axes of scouts for several miles to reach the third pond. The men—covered in scrapes, their clothing torn from the wild, tangled forest, their shins bruised on cruel stumps—plunged deep into muddy black bogs soaked by the rain, their munitions sinking, lost to the deep, black mire of the carrying place.

An emaciated man gripping a musket stumbled out of the woods toward them with another smaller man behind, saying that he was Denis

Getchell—tall and wiry, of Maine stock and as wise as his Native brothers and teachers—that he'd come from scouting the height of land past the Dead River: "I found the cabin of the Abenaki Natanis at Jim Eaton Hill, where we found a birchbark map—the course to cross the height of land and through the chain of ponds." "God came to our rescue, helping us find that map and running moose right into our path," he insisted, heaving, catching his breath. Strong-minded Jacataqua knew he was mistaken, like so many white men who thanked their invisible, pious God for what her people gave them. It was the warrior, Natanis, who drove those moose, who left the map for them, she told Aaron.

Weary men, Liberty or Death *stitched into their hats, sabers hanging from their waists, gulped from the third pond, giddy with clear, clean water to drink while Jacataqua made a poultice from witch hazel bark to treat the men's gashes, the wounds from their fight for freedom, for independence, for the irrepressible leader, Colonel Arnold, urging them every step of the backbreaking march. They found sticks to fashion rudimentary fishing poles, some string, worms and bugs, and caught meaty, hook-jawed, square-tailed trout to roast on open fires, tearing the fish apart with their jaws, ravenously eating to quell their raw hunger before passing out from exhaustion under the darkest of skies, the stars shining upon them like twinkling consecrations, the smell of freedom in the forests, testing their will, questioning their right to survive. All the while, under Awasos, the Great Bear in the sky, Jacataqua lay beside Aaron, caring for his beaten body, whispering to the spirits of the forests for their guidance, to the moon and stars in the night sky, to the new life growing inside her.*

FREMONT SAT AT THE kitchen table with his usual donut and cigarette going when Pennie came into the kitchen. He held up a letter that he'd just received from the power company about his property on Middle Carry Pond. According to the Intent to Acquire letter, the acquisition under the power of eminent domain required an appraisal and review for "just compensation"—fair market value—for the property. The owner, Fremont in this case, had the right to accompany the appraiser during the property inspection.

"I heard it had been passed by the legislature, but I didn't believe they would allow this to happen." He hunched lower between his shoulders and blew out a long stream of smoke.

She read the letter over again. "I'll call Uncle Alfie. He'll know the next steps." Then Pennie wondered about the other property. "Did you hear anything more about the land they need for the corridor on the other side of Spring Lake?"

"Far as I know, they haven't voted on anything yet. But those are unorganized townships, so it would be up to the county commissioners to vote on it."

She squeezed his bony shoulder. "Uncle Alfie will find out what's going on. There has to be a way to stop this." Eyeing the coffeepot, she poured him more before heading upstairs to call her uncle with the latest news.

He picked up on the first ring. "Wondered when I'd be hearing from you. How's Fremont?"

His reassuring voice, and the sound of Fella barking in the background, made her relax. "Oh, he's good overall, but not happy about the letter he just received from the power company lawyers. They sent him an Intent to Acquire his property on Middle Carry. You were absolutely right. How can they do this, just take a man's property against his will?"

"They can only take it if it's considered a public benefit—*for the greater good* and all that other BS. I've been following the case. The legislature just granted eminent domain approval last week."

"Fremont says they want to clear the corridor above Spring Lake, on the other side of Flagstaff, which means it will cross the Dead River below Long Falls Dam at some point before dropping down to where Fremont's land is, between the Middle and West Carry." Out her window, the fiery colors of autumn burned around the lake, a final outburst like a last cry before the dormancy of winter. "This is so eerily like history repeating itself. How much of this land did the power company already buy up?"

"Far as I know, they've already purchased most of it, but if I remember correctly, a section of the Appalachian Trail goes through Fremont's property, right?"

"Yes, that's right. Bri and I hiked it yesterday." Pennie recalled her dream. It was the same area where they had walked to Middle Carry Pond, through the Great Carrying Place. "Did you know it's also the old Benedict Arnold route?"

He chuckled. "Fremont's told me all about it. He's quite a historian when it comes to that famous march through the wilderness. Of course, the power company is all over this, calling it the 'Independence Corridor.' Talk about taking something patriotic and turning into capital gain to line their pockets."

From below, she could hear the voices of the twins and Tita greeting Fremont. "Dani, Mali, and Tita arrived last night. The twins couldn't be more excited about their artist's commission. Thank you for everything you've done to help them."

"Oh, I just made some introductions. They did the rest. Those two are a real powerhouse." Pennie described their plans for driving over to

Long Falls Dam and promised she'd get some pictures. He asked her to get him a copy of the letter from the power company. Before hanging up, he cautioned her to "watch yourself out there." If there was anything she'd learned from her uncle, and their last experience in court, it was to proceed cautiously, with restraint.

Down in the kitchen, she was delighted to find Fremont showing his guests the path of the Arnold Trail in the *Gazetteer*, pointing out his property at the Great Carrying Place. When he shared the eminent domain plans, Mali said, "They can't just take a person's private property, can they?"

Fremont thumped his bony finger on the map at Flagstaff Lake. "Believe you me, young lady, they can, and they will. To flood this valley, they held the threat of eminent domain over everyone's head—the entire plantations of Flagstaff and Dead River—before people finally sold out and moved out."

Pennie's phone chirped: a text from Bri to pick her up at JD's place. "Speaking of," she said, seeing it was already nearly ten o'clock. "We're headed over to the dam now." When they stood to leave, Fremont offered to take the twins to the historical society to get the whole backstory. They were more than happy to take him up on it while they were in town. Tita hugged him on their way out, happy to meet another Goode family relative.

Outside, Tita's red VW bus, also known as the Jan Van, sat in the driveway, making Pennie nostalgic for skiing. This was the van they'd driven to Coos Canyon for years, the small mountain that offered the best backcountry and challenging slopes, the place where Pennie had fallen last winter. How drastically things had changed since then. Life had taken her in a new direction, enabling her to see beyond the everyday and into the dreams and memories of a sacred place, just like she'd experienced at the Heritage Acres graveyard where the Malaga settlers were buried, connecting her to that fishing community that had strived for their own independence, freedom on their own terms, only to be exiled.

Her cousin started up the VW bus. It rumbled loud and steady, just like always. Pennie gave directions to JD's place, explaining how he was the son of the owners of the Gullet. "Kind of a man-about-town, if you know what I mean."

"Oh, I know exactly what you mean," said Tita. "I've seen him around here before. I'm pretty sure he's made the rounds at the bars up at the mountain."

"Maybe," said Pennie. "But he's Bri's boyfriend, so let's play nice." She emphasized Bri's infatuation, leaving out the part about the baby, as Tita drove down the long dirt road lined with towering spruces and white pines leading to the Varneys' impressive log cabin in the woods.

When the garage door opened, they could see rifles of all sizes hanging on a far wall, including a few semi-automatic weapons. Dani said, "Why don't the guns surprise me? I hope they at least eat what they shoot."

Bri appeared in the garage with her backpack, net, and fly rod, walking toward them with a tenuous smile. They all greeted her eagerly when she jumped in the side door of the van. "Thanks for picking me up," she said, an air of unease filling the cab.

Pennie reached for her hand. "Everything okay?"

She looked around at the sympathetic faces. "Oh, I'm fine. Sometimes boyfriends can be so clingy, that's all." She brightened up. "I'm really excited for our girls' day out. This will be so much fun." She told Tita which way to turn, and soon they were driving down a windy, well-paved road that led to the far side of the lake, the dropping temperatures already beginning to dull the bright gold, fiery scarlet, and amber.

The twins, high-spirited from the adventure, told Bri how much they adored her grandfather. "What energy he has for his age," said Dani.

"He's pretty remarkable. Everyone keeps talking about how frail he's getting, but other than his back, he's full of vigor for eighty-six. I want to stay with him in his house as long as I can. He's everything to me." She grew misty-eyed and looked out the window at the vivid beeches, birches, and maples along the roadside, swaying in the wind between tall pines. She pointed out a road on the left that led to an old Dead River settlement house, one of the few that had survived the flood. "It's known as the Round Barn site. That's what it was always called, before the barn burned down."

Tita shifted and accelerated up a rise. "You lead us, Bri, and we will follow."

"That's right," said Mali. "You're our tour guide." The twins jumped into describing the details of their project and how they were funded by the Maine River Conservancy to spotlight the history of dams on the Kennebec. "Pennie told us how the valley was flooded by building the dam, to make a reservoir and control the flow of the Kennebec River. We knew we had to start here."

Bri wanted to know all about their work as artists. Dani took out her phone to show pictures of her paintings, along with Mali's descriptions of the river fish and habitat. Bri gushed over them and began to describe the fish in Flagstaff, the pickerel and perch, the stocked salmon and occasional brown trout. "It's not a great lake for fish, being so shallow and man-made, but the other natural streams and ponds and rivers in these woods are home to native brook trout and the only surviving Atlantic salmon. They love the cold, clear water."

Pennie said, "Bri's grandmother was from the Abenaki tribe."

The twins raised their eyebrows in unison, delighted. "Really?" said Mali.

"My Grandma Lena's family lived in the Carrabassett Valley. I think they were descended from the St. Francis tribes in Canada. But like I told Pennie, we're a real mixed bag, descended from French and Irish, too. Lena died before I was born...I never got to know her."

"Did your grandfather keep in touch with her family?" Dani asked.

"Not really. Her death was really hard on him, I guess. He had to raise my mother by himself, and I think he was just overwhelmed. One thing about my grandpa, he doesn't like to ask for help. When Lena died, I think they offered to take my mother from him, but he'd have none of it. I don't really know much other than that."

The van grew silent. Pennie thought about her own father and reached for Bri's hand. They squeezed in a tight grasp. "I don't even know who my own father is. He and my mother split when I was just a baby, and...well, he's never ever tried to contact me."

Bri nodded. "It seems hard to believe we could lose touch with our own families, our own flesh and blood." Dani and Mali agreed; their parents had divorced when they were young. "Even though our father tries to keep in touch, we only see him once or twice a year if we're lucky. He's a guide up on a Grand Lake Stream."

Bri's face brightened. "Oh, maybe I can meet him some day. Learn something from him."

Mali laughed. "If there's anything he likes to talk about, it's his job."

They arrived at the turnoff for the dam, a wooded, bumpy gravel road. Bri pointed them to another turn, toward the water, and they came to a chain across the road. The four of them hopped out to the warm mid-October day under skies growing cloudy and a light wind. Pennie had her camera equipment and was the first to head down the incline to the lake where the dam came into view. A long, low curved wall ran through the lake and joined with a tall metal structure that must have been the dam gates. Without much of a vantage point, she looked around for something to climb onto and spotted a few pieces of driftwood. She managed to get enough purchase to climb up the curved embankment, Dani and Mali following behind her, while Tita and Bri walked along the gravelly shore of Flagstaff.

With her trusty Canon, Pennie focused on shots of the giant iron dam above Long Falls, the water at least five feet deep, as calm as a millpond inside of the dam, while lively falls tumbled on the outside. She tried to imagine what it was like with the dam gates open, how those falls must rage with the rush of released water. The purple mountain range of Bigelow lay in the distance, an imposing backdrop to this man-made structure of control, the sky above covered in puffy clouds, streams of light shining down between them, dancing fingerprints of the sun.

Behind her, Dani and Mali took pictures with their phones. "I'm glad we came with the gates closed," said Dani, her eyes transfixed on Bigelow in all its glory, its hillside lined with the brilliant yellow needles of tamarack. Mali descended the wall to get better pictures of the rippling falls behind the dam. Pennie pictured the soldiers of her dreams, how they ascended the treacherous Kennebec falls on their way here, portaging three ponds and the leach- and bug-ridden swamps before reaching Bog Brook and the Dead River, risking life and limb in their epic quest across these wild Maine woods. How many Native warriors had traversed these waters, this ever-changing landscape of seasons, over the centuries to survive on this ragged edge of America?

Lost in thought, she was startled by a flock of ducks overhead before they descended, landing in the calm lake. She took some shots of the mallards in their iridescent green and yellow suits, the mothers in their modest plumage of brown and tan, their beaks bright yellow, eyes shining black. A cold wind picked up with the changing of the seasons. These hearty birds would overwinter here in this wilderness, finding sustenance by foraging for acorns, roots, and leaves along the riverbank.

One by one, the women made their way back to the Jan Van and jumped inside, rosy-cheeked. Bri told them how much she liked to fly-fish below the dam when the gates were open and the river raging. "There's nothing like it," she said, gushing with the memory before turning somber. "The power company plans to cross a little downstream from here for the corridor."

Pennie tried to picture the poles and wires over the falls, how it would forever alter this landscape already disrupted by the dam. Bri asked them if they were up for a hike to the Round Barn area, about three miles to the cabin. "If we take our time, it will only take us a few hours in and back, and there's plenty of daylight left." By now it was clear how much Bri was enjoying her time, how her mood had changed dramatically since they picked her up from JD's. They were all delighted with the idea.

It didn't take long to get to the trailhead where they felt grossly unprepared. But Tita, always armed with supplies for a ski trip, had a stash of refillable water bottles in the back. They each grabbed one to tuck into their packs for the hike; Bri knew of a spring to refill them near the cabin. With her backpack and fly rod swaying by her side, she led them around the chain fence that blocked vehicles from entering the old forlorn road leading into the woods at the base of Little Bigelow. The winds grew colder as they fell into pairs behind their tour guide—Pennie and Dani, Tita and Mali, walking briskly into the shelter of the small growth red oak and scrubby pine, paper birch and mountain ash.

The drum of a woodpecker broke the silence with its rat-a-tat-tat-tat-tat-tat-tat. "It's *pakahqaha*," said Dani, "the messenger of truth and prophecy." It made Pennie think about Greta, her hand-crafted deck of cards, how the pastel drawings on each one were beautifully rendered, mystical. "Bri—." She hesitated for a moment, wondering if Bri would even want to talk about her psychic. "Do you want to tell them about Greta?"

Their long-legged guide walked backward, facing them, without a stumble. "Of course. Greta's done some readings for me, but this last one was like a spirit reached inside of me and yanked at my soul. The wardrobe card came up first," she said, looking down. "It represents my need to shine a light on the truth. Then the partnership card came up, telling me to work on my relationships, and boy, do I know that. And finally, the well card, a message to draw upon the depths of my friends and family—and why, of course, you all came into my life right now. Greta could see it, clear as day." Bri turned around to keep leading them, as undaunted as the birches gently swaying around her. Pennie realized that, by leaving out the Troll, the Lobster, and the Poison, Bri was able to keep those rose-tinted glasses firmly in place.

Mali said she thought Greta sounded like a *m'téoulin*. "According to legend, *m'téoulins* can make themselves heard at any distance, can talk to one another secretly, miles away, or make themselves known."

"Sounds ghostly," said Tita.

"The Passamaquoddy believe that spirits lived in the natural world with us," Dani said. "Being in the woods here, I do feel so much more connected, like something almost supernatural."

Pennie wondered about her own dreams, and walking along in the quiet woods, a calm desire for openness awakened inside of her. "I know I've talked about this before, but I can see visions of the past in my dreams sometimes. I know that sounds strange but, when I visit a special place like this or a graveyard or any place with active spirits, I can feel a kind of spectral vibration."

Bri stopped and turned to her. "You're saying that just by being in a place you can look into the past, just conjure it up?"

Tita laughed. "Don't worry, Bri, she isn't always this crazy."

Pennie thought about her mother; how she'd been labeled *crazy*. "I can't conjure anything up," she said, holding back from sounding defensive. "I can only fall asleep with a certain place on my mind, a place I've recently visited or photographed, and dream about what happened there. Last night I had a dream about Benedict Arnold's army that marched through the Great Carrying Place where Fremont's cabin is, and could see how weary and broken they were, marching over that wild place so long ago."

Tita, always the pragmatist, said, "And you don't think it's just from what Fremont told you about that march?"

Dani said, "I believe in visions. The ability of clairvoyance is *Meelah bi give he*."

A raven squawked from deep inside the woods and, in a great clatter, flew out of the trees and over their heads. They all ducked to avoid the streak of black sailing over them, following the bird's long wingspan up into the gray sky until it disappeared into the mist. Pennie touched her own cheek, absentmindedly, remembering the brush with owl wings on Jim Eaton Hill.

Bri turned toward them, amazed. "I've never seen a bird just dart out of the woods like that, right at us."

"A raven come to call," Mali said. "The symbol of magic and transformation."

"A coincidence?" Dani asked. "Or is it our connection with the spiritual world?"

Tita stared up at the invisible path of the black bird. Pennie herself felt vindicated by the bird's presence, as if telling Tita that she may want to rethink her skepticism, keep an open mind to the spiritual universe. Grasping her triskelion, Pennie was sure they were all part of a great cosmos.

Bri stopped to crouch down, looking at something in the road. They crowded around her as she outlined a clear impression in the dirt with her finger without touching it: a triangular-shaped pad with five round toes and distinct claw marks. "A bear print. Must be living around here somewhere."

Tita put her hands on her hips, the same way Aunt Aggie did when vexed. "Okay. I'm all for an adventure, but I do not want to run into a hungry bear. Are we safe out here?"

Bri picked up a long, straight limb of deadwood beside the dirt path that seemed to appear out of nowhere. "Just find a walking stick, and if the bear comes toward you, wave it around. Believe me, that bear is more afraid of you."

They rummaged around on the edge of the woods until they'd all found something suitable—even if it was more crooked than straight, pecked by sapsuckers or woodpeckers—and followed the lead of their prescient guide. Deep inside their own thoughts, the air around them growing colder and the wind ruffling the trees, they rounded a bend, trudging along at a good pace. Bri told them about the forest they walked through, how the trees were like a superorganism, moderating their own temperature, storing water, protecting one another, sheltering each other from the wind and sun with their great canopies. She was pointing up to the yellow crest of a beautiful stand of paper birch trees when she suddenly stopped and put her finger to her mouth. Ahead of them, to the edge of the wood, stood a black bear with three young cubs toddling around her. The mother turned to them with her deep black, shining eyes and lifted her brown nose to catch their scent. None of them dared to move a muscle or breathe.

Sensing no danger, the sow corralled her three cubs, waving her snout, and they lumbered deeper into the dark woods toward Little Bigelow Mountain. The hikers clutched their sticks and breathed a collective sigh of relief. Bri turned to them like she was leading a Girl Scouts hike. "Like I said, they don't usually bother people if you leave them alone. They're gentle creatures unless the mother senses danger. I'm sure she's out looking for food, storing up for hibernation."

Tita laughed and said, "Wow. Just wow. My first bear sighting! Lead on, supreme guide, and we will follow."

Dani wondered aloud how long the cubs stayed with their mother, and Bri said she thought it was about a year and a half. Somehow, the near contact with the bear family made the four of them bolder, and they trotted behind Bri with renewed energy, wondering what else they might see in these woods, their handy walking sticks giving them pioneering courage. The reddish-brown leaves of the oak and purplish leaves of the witch hazel flew around them in magical song, enveloping them in a collective spirit of trailblazing, their ears filled with the songs of tufted titmice and chickadees, white-breasted nuthatch, and the piercing cry of a broad-winged hawk.

They finally came upon the site where the Round Barn once stood, back when the Dead River settlement was alive. Beyond this was a small cabin on the banks of Flagstaff, one of the few Dead River houses still standing, moved to higher ground to evade the rising waters. Bri pointed to the lake, the great Mount Bigelow cradling them. "The Safford Farm used to be down the hill from here. What a peaceful place to have a farm and raise a family, right?" She turned eastward. "The Bigelow Inn used to be up there. A man by the name of Fud Taylor moved his family here from Flagstaff and ran it as a boardinghouse for people who came to hunt and fish."

Bri led them to a clear-running spring beside the cabin to fill up their bottles. Pennie remembered seeing pictures of the Bigelow Inn, a large square place, two stories with a mansard roof and windows along the roofline. "What a beautiful spot at the foot of the mountain range."

The young guide lifted her face to the sun that had just peeked for a moment through the clouds. "This is like heaven here, isn't it? You can smell the earthy water and woods in the breeze. In the blink of an eye, a torrential storm can come down from the mountain and blow a gale through here." The wind picked up and rippled the lake in small, hilly currents. They looked toward the mountain, wondering what this valley had in store.

Tita asked about getting inside the cabin, and Bri followed her up the slope. "My grandfather says that anyone who's a descendent of the settlement is welcome inside, as long as we leave everything as we found it." She retrieved a key hidden in a plastic turtle on the porch and unlocked the door to the old cabin. They walked into a large living area with a stone fireplace of smooth river rocks bleached grayish white, the walls and floors planked in solid, dark red oak. Handmade wooden furniture made the place feel homey, old rockers and couches with flowered cushions. To one side of the room was a small galley kitchen with antique white appliances, and to the other side were a few small bedrooms with built-in bunks. Tita rubbed her hands together for warmth. "This is so charming."

"If you want, we can build a fire," Bri said. They all nodded as the cold of the cabin settled in. "We'll just warm up for an hour before heading back." She looked out to the lake. "It looks like a few clouds are gathering.

Might be a passing storm. I'd hate for us to get caught in anything." They followed her to the woodpile on the porch and brought in armfuls to fill the box inside.

Tita and Mali insisted on building the fire, crumpling the newspaper, arranging a crisscross pile of kindling. They lit it and watched it rage before setting a log on top. Bri made sure the damper was open while Dani took her sketch pad from her pack and went to sit outside, the wind swirling in and around the old cabin. Undaunted, Bri said, "I think I'll go out and see if anything's biting. The best time to fish is right before the rain." Pennie followed her outside with her camera, sitting beside Dani on the front porch in worn Adirondack chairs, the wind continuing its magical sweep around the lake as Bri assembled her trusty fly rod.

Inside of five minutes, she had strung her line and started flipping it out in big, easy loops, light sprinkles of rain dotting the water's surface. Pennie sat back and balanced the Canon to capture a portrait of Bri, the sweep of her arm, the quiet, settled moment when everything hushed to the faint patter of raindrops, the wind dying down, the harmony of breathing in the still air at the foot of the ever-present mountain. Pennie caught the moment Bri landed the fly, barely dropping it on the surface, her tip down, stripping it back, the line taut. The young guide concentrated on the catch, the tail of the fish flickering on the lake's surface as it swam in the opposite direction, the line buzzing out and running as she set the hook. The dance repeated itself a few times between woman and fish, pulling back, then letting it run, again and again in magical sweeps until the fish tired. Pennie and Dani watched with awe as Bri began to reel it in.

Soon Mali and Tita joined them on the porch. Pennie snapped pictures, a frame-by-frame story, and Dani's charcoal pencil never stopped moving, trying to capture the artistry, the gamesmanship, in this fertile valley. Bri continued to pull the line until there appeared on the surface a hook-mouthed brown trout, deep bodied and golden along its long belly. The fly-fisher reeled the fish up to the bank until she could grasp it, holding up her prize with shimmering scales, maybe sixteen inches long, wriggling in her firm grip. Her smile matched the magic of the moment, the heart of a fisherwoman.

With care, she laid the trout on the leaf-covered ground to remove the hook from its great jaw before bringing it down to the bank, where she let it wriggle from her hands into the water, back to its watery depths. They all stood and clapped as the rain turned from a drizzle to a steady shower. Bri ran back to the porch, breathless, and they moved inside, thankful for the fire that was now roaring. Tita added more split logs, and Mali found some blankets inside benches behind the couches. Bri found a towel in the bathroom and took her wet boots off, placing them on the hearth, now heated by the glowing flames.

The young guide's phone buzzed, interrupting the spell they were under. She pulled it from her side pocket. "It's JD again, wants to know when we'll be back." They all checked their phones. It was now two o'clock. Bri glanced out the window at the darkening sky. "Well, this should break in an hour, which still gives us plenty of daylight if we leave here around three."

Tita stretched out her short, strong legs toward the fire. "I, for one, am in no hurry to leave. I just wish we had thought to bring some food."

Dani and Mali grabbed their packs for granola bars and handed them out. Bri mentioned that people usually left nonperishables in the kitchen, so Pennie went out to check the supply and found a box of tea. Inside a large cookie tin, she found marshmallows, graham crackers, and chocolate bars to bring out to the others. Their eyes lit up when she displayed the surprise contents left by earlier visitors.

Bri said, "He is really beginning to annoy me with all of his questions."

"I don't know how you got this far in life without him," said Tita, laughing.

Dani hugged the blanket around herself, sitting on the rug before the fire. "Max is really supportive without being too clingy. Maybe that comes with time or marriage."

Bri looked into the fire, misty-eyed. "Maybe, but I'm feeling a little trapped right now. Like, what if he's not the one?"

Mali gathered her long raven hair over her shoulder and began braiding. "You're so young. Don't feel trapped in a relationship at this age."

Pennie wanted to rescue her but didn't know what to say. She waited for Bri to share. The fire popped and hissed until she finally said, "I just found out I'm pregnant, so feeling a little bit pressured, you could say." The cabin grew quiet.

Tita said, "Have you decided to keep it?"

"I wasn't sure until JD told me how excited he was about it. But, like I told Pennie, I don't know if I'm ready to be a mother yet. My own mother was only a teenager when she had us. We had it rough growing up, but she did her best." The rain pattered on the roof and she began to cry, her breath coming out in little shudders of heartbreak.

Pennie walked over to sit with her. "Don't worry, Bri. We're here for you. When life gets hard, you have friends to lean on. This is a big decision."

Bri's phone chirped again, and she looked at it only to toss it, the hard plastic thumping on the wooden floor, skidding over dirt and sand to land in a dark corner. Dani reached across to her. "We're all here for you."

The fire danced in her wide eyes as she wiped her nose on her arm, that same arm that captured the trout with the graceful ease of someone born with an innate sense, better than any lesson could teach. "I've never had girlfriends like you. Only boyfriends in high school. You don't know what this means to me."

Mali ran her hand along her braid. "You're a beautiful young woman, Bri. High school girls, being what they are, were jealous. But don't worry. As you get older, it gets easier."

They searched for answers to one of the most difficult questions any young woman can face under the emotional grip of fear. Meanwhile, Bri's phone continued to chirp in the corner. "He wants me to spend every night with him now. I can't just ignore my grandfather. I'm here to take care of him." She rocked in the old chair. "Pennie, you've been great, but it's wrong of me to depend on you."

"I really don't mind, Bri. You should decide what's best for you without feeling pressured."

"He can be a very sweet guy, you know. But now, especially working at the restaurant with his family, it feels like my world is closing in. I asked him not to tell his parents, and he promised me he wouldn't until I was ready. And what about my dream of becoming a Maine Guide? That takes years of training and coursework."

Tita, anxious for any kind of diversion, offered to go outside and find sticks to roast the marshmallows. The rain had let up. None of them knew quite what to say to Bri without bashing JD and his controlling behavior. Finally, Pennie said, "I had a dreadfully embarrassing situation a few weeks ago. My old boyfriend Kush turned up in Portland, and well, one thing led to another, and he came home with me. Before he left, the last thing he said was how he regretted cheating on his girlfriend...with me."

Bri said, "I would have killed this guy. *Kush*—and what kind of a name is that, anyway?"

Dani said, "Ugh, Pennie, why didn't you tell me?"

Of course she was embarrassed, but hadn't they all had experiences like this? Tita came in with a few long sticks, and they gathered closer to the fire to toast their marshmallows. One by one, they opened up, sharing personal stories of old wounds from past lovers, helping each other use graham crackers to remove the dripping charred marshmallows from sticks, sandwiching the melted chocolate to make s'mores, reliving stories of heartbreak and regret as the time melted away in the bittersweet darkness of the cabin.

Mali checked her phone. "Oh, it's already three fifteen."

Bri unfolded herself from her cocoon in front of the fire and looked out the screen door. "I'm so enjoying myself here. I don't want to leave."

"I'm not afraid to walk in the dark." Pennie looked out at the gloomy sky. "Let's enjoy the fire and stay a while longer." Bri ignored her phone, its incessant chirp in the corner. Tita shared how much she missed Lars but also distrusted him after his last time out in California. Dani and Mali, both married to good men, talked about the years it had taken to gain their mutual respect as artists. "That's why we're able to do this trip. They understand how much this means to Mali and me." When the fire slowly died down, they collected their things. Bri grabbed a bottle to douse the remaining embers.

They embarked on the trail before four o'clock, the light waning on the wet road, their clothes dry and their insides warm with friendship. After the first mile, Pennie felt a low humming on the ground. "Someone's coming," she said.

Bri stopped short to listen. "I don't hear anything."

They continued to walk, and Pennie felt the vibrations growing louder under her feet until they all heard the ATV in the distance. Soon, JD, full throttle on his red and white four-wheeler, came around the bend at full tilt, dirt flying, stopping short in front of Bri. He took off his helmet, fuming. "Where the hell have you been? Why haven't you answered my calls? It's almost dark."

"JD," she said, trembling. "It was raining, so we held up in the cabin for a few hours until it stopped. You know how it gets stormy at the base of the mountain."

"*Exactly*, that's why I've been worried about you."

She took a step back from him. Mali said, "We're grown women and can get back just fine on our own."

He took a deep breath, his harsh tone softening. "Listen, I know you are. I'm sorry, it's just the weather can be so unpredictable, and there are hunters around here all the time. I'm sorry, babe." He reached for her face. "Forgive me? I was just concerned."

She straightened. "As you can see, we're just fine."

"Yes, you certainly are." He patted the leather seat behind him. "Here, have a seat. I've got some chili cooking at home. Thought I'd cook for you on your night off."

With this small show of kindness, she began to bend like a branch under his windy words. "You cooked for me? Oh, that's so sweet." They all stood around her, her newfound friends, biting their tongues. She turned to them. "Can you find your way alright? There's still a little daylight. You just have to stay on the trail. It's less than two miles."

"No worries," said Pennie, offering her approval. "We all have headlamps in our packs. We'll make it back just fine."

Bri's face softened with relief, her eyes reflecting a girl trying to make sense of the situation, to do what was right, to put some trust in this man, the father of her child who was concerned about her well-being. JD revved his four-wheeler. "It's illegal to hunt after dusk, but if you hear any shots fired out here, just wave your phones and headlamps around so they know you're here. I wish I could take all of you."

"We'll be just fine." Tita looked like she'd sooner strangle him than take a ride from him. Bri took the seat he offered and waved weakly. Chunks of mud flew from his tires as they drove away.

The sky continued to darken, clouds quickening the night. They chatted loudly about what a controlling prick he was, for any nearby hunters to hear. A shot rang out in the woods, echoing in the darkness, and they ran the last mile, Tita leading the way with Pennie bringing up the rear, feeling utterly out of shape, her heart inside her mouth. At the van, safely inside, they slammed the door and stared at one another, heaving, out of breath, reflecting the primal fear that coursed through them, headlamps pointing into each other's faces and into their center of trust. Just like the forest all around them, the trees protecting one another, strength in unity. Pennie thought she could hear an ATV nearby in the woods, the sound of the engine slowly fading.

Chapter 8
Dead River Valley

FREMONT HAD FALLEN ASLEEP in front of the woodstove, the long-haired cat nestled on his rising and falling chest. Pennie filled the stove as the cat followed her with his amber eyes, squinting, almost happy to see her again. Upstairs, she crawled into long johns and wool socks before nestling onto the creaky springs with her laptop and camera, connected for download.

At first, she came across the pictures she'd taken at West Carry and Middle Carry Ponds. The burnt colors of autumn filled each frame, dancing before her in the darkness of her attic nook, the warmth from the fire downstairs filling the space. What a gorgeous day it had been, with soft sunshine filtering between the trees, the brambles of blackthorn and chokecherries lining the pathway around West Carry. Moss-covered roots and rocks under their footsteps, Bri's ever-present fly rod hanging from the side of her backpack. A shadow outlined her youthful silhouette and flickered a few times before it disappeared.

Then pictures of Fremont's small cabin on Middle Carry, broken steps and small, narrow windows winking in the afternoon sun, hiding a secret history inside. The long pond behind it lay nearly as pristine and isolated as it was when Arnold and his soldiers marched through these woods, its shoreline rimmed with gray rocks and pine trees, a bald eagle nesting on a far point, white plumage standing out like a searchlight. Inside the camp, cobwebs draped the corners of the single room, their intricate threads shining in silvery patterns. Bri stood by a window, her face drenched in yellow light, and again, she was outlined by a shadow that seemed to follow her like a constant companion, a whisper of the past.

The next frame showed the trail that led toward East Carry Pond, a set of bridges over a small marsh surrounded by spruce and hemlock. Other photos of Fremont's property behind the cabin, wooded and flat, the swath the power company needed for its Independence Corridor to cut through this wilderness and carry electricity down to other New England states, through this land that had already given so much in lumber for houses and barns, wagons and ships, pulp and paper. For warmth. Below her, the wood in the stove crackled and spit. Now, powers outside of Maine were asking for a roadway through its wilderness for a dubiously renewable hydroelectric-power strip.

She toggled to photos of earlier that day at Long Falls Dam. The gates controlled the water flow to the Forks, where it joined the Kennebec before flowing down to the Wyman Dam—the largest dam in the northeast when it was erected by Walter Wyman a hundred years ago. All this she'd learned since coming here to these western Maine hills, this place of alpine glaciers, rocks and ridges formed by ice and water tumbling down snaking rivers and streams, through pooling lakes and ponds, to reach the mighty Kennebec, the currents that sustained the Native peoples, families of woodsmen, river drivers and farmers.

From the man-made lake to the rushing falls below the dam, Mount Bigelow stood watch over the flooded valley. Meanwhile, the path of the hydroelectric corridor would slice through these woods and over these waterways in the shadow of this range. Images of the Round Barn site filled her screen, the striking reds and yellows of the woods lining their path, the giant granite formations, the pale gray sky, their pioneering spirits high. Then photos of the great bear's footprint, its outline in the dark mud jumping off the screen, then the lumbering black mother bear with three cubs toddling behind, the memory of the moment lingering, more thrilling than a picture could ever capture.

Pictures of the old log cabin filled the screen: Bri gazing out onto the lake for signs of fish before the rain, Tita peering in the cabin windows with anticipation, Mali inside lighting the fire in the stone fireplace, her face aglow, and Dani with her sketchpad, intent on the image taking shape under the spell of her mind's eye. And there was Bri again, at the water's edge, her fly rod back, the whip of the line in a perfect arc over her head, then her arm straight out, her line following, her fly barely touching the surface. A shadowy silhouette appeared again like a phantom.

She shut the laptop and closed her eyes, heavy with tiredness, falling into a deep sleep where she found herself on the shore of the lake again, the image of Bri fly-fishing against a cloudy pale sky...

THE OUTLINE OF HER graceful form, bending like a birch tree, began to transform into a man's silhouette, his long arm whipping straight out toward the lake that started to recede, one, two, three feet, then six, then ten feet, turning back the hands of time from a stagnant lake surface into a sweeping river that snaked its way through a valley of farmhouses and barns, fields and wooden fences. The man, standing tall in his mackinaw jacket, jerked the line and pulled back, his strength and determination hooking the fish, its tail below the surface flickering, fighting the pull of the line until the long gray- and white-spotted salmon rose out of the swift river, its wriggling body fighting for life.

Instinctively, she ran on all fours to sniff the slimy fish wriggling on shore. "Easy there, girl. This isn't for you." He scratched her between the ears. "Mama is going to like this for dinner." He pulled the hook from the mouth before sliding the beautiful silvery fish inside a basket, slinging the long leather strap over his shoulder, and reeling in the line. They walked along the riverbank, and he whistled for her to stay alongside him, chewing foul-smelling tobacco and spitting juice every now and again. A high-pitched voice came from behind them, and they turned to see a woman dressed in a green checked dress and apron and black wool stockings, her gray hair swept up, standing in front of her log cabin. "Good to see you out fishing, Horace," she sang.

"Howdy, Gladys!" He waved. "Salmon always biting around here."

Strolling along the winding bank, they came upon a farm with miles of wire fencing, a Cape with three chimneys in the distance. He mused, "You suppose Russell and Emma are ready for winter?" She wagged her tail, and they walked on, passing a small white shed with a building behind it—the schoolhouse with its hip roof and covered porch, trees and open pastureland in the distance. Making their way down the firmly packed dirt road, they came upon a great round barn with a domed shingled roof and cupola at the top as high as thirteen or more men, connected to a white farmhouse by a long extension. The buildings were enclosed by a simple wooden fence. He waved to a man on an old haying tractor. "Hey, Charles. Lovely evening."

They passed another rolling farm on a knoll with a house, barn, and outbuildings before reaching a gray, shingled, L-shaped barn and house in a field, two prominent chimneys sprouting from the rooftop. The man muttered to himself, "The old Ferry Farm." Out the front door came a little woman dressed in blue stripes, her apron trimmed in lace, waving and pointing toward the peaks of Bigelow. "There's a hurricane coming, Horace, you mark my words."

He smiled and tipped his hat. "Evening, Mrs. Goddard. I'll be looking out for it." Gentle clouds rolled along, languid in the sky, and he scratched his chin, contemplating.

A floating bridge took them to the other side of the river, where they strolled until reaching a series of tumbling falls. At the top, he knelt to take a drink, admiring the rolling dark water thundering over the rocks, and instinctively, she jumped into the charging river, sinking, slipping back in time, sucked into the churning torrents, fighting her way back to the surface until she found herself swimming beside a birchbark canoe with Jacataqua, dressed in deerskin, paddling in the bow, yelling to her. "Get back in the canoe, Adiak!" Aaron grabbed her by the neck and hauled her in, and she shook from head to tail, showering the two of them before lowering herself in the canoe rocking against the fast current, up and over the tumbling water, the paddlers missing the boulders on either side, maneuvering up and over rocks until the river ran calm.

Several bateaux poled ahead of them on the Dead River, barefoot soldiers in ragged clothing, scratched and bruised, emaciated, blue with cold. Jacataqua navigated around them on their way upriver, pointing to an empty cabin perched on a high rise of land. "Natanis has left here and moved to the height of land. He's waiting," she insisted, then they came to a bank where men had disembarked, their bateaux lined up along the riverbank, loaded with munitions and bloated barrels of flour and corn. A stout man in a tattered uniform ordered the men to empty out their cargo and waterlogged supplies. Soldiers saluted, addressing him as "Colonel Arnold," setting up camp on the hillside with small fires, more battered bateaux and weary, starving soldiers arriving by the minute, a few dropping at the bank, the swift river washing them back downstream.

Aaron pushed their canoe around the gasping men alongside the embankment and used his paddle to help himself up and out before he reached for Jacataqua's hand, but she was already on shore. "Aaron, we need to talk to the colonel." She followed him to the large, guarded tent, where he asked for permission to speak with their commander. A flap opened, and inside he found the colonel sitting at a wooden table covered with hand-drawn maps, a fine hunting sword with a silver hilt and ivory grip to the ready at his elbow, writing a letter with his fine nib pen, soaking his feet in a tub of steaming water smelling like rosemary.

"Sir, thank you for allowing Jacataqua and her dog to accompany me on this march." Arnold kept writing.

Finally, after an excruciating five minutes, the colonel looked up. "What have you to tell me about the whereabouts of Natanis?"

"Colonel, Jacataqua insists he is ahead of us, on the Height of Land, waiting to help our men through that treacherous climb and the swamps that follow." Arnold harrumphed, the sides of his mouth drawn down. "From everything I've heard, he and the other Natives are sabotaging our mission, working with the English, telling them our whereabouts."

Jacataqua peeked in the tent. "White chief, if I may speak?" She pulled on the sleeves of her deerskin shirt, stepping inside. "What they say is false. Natanis, Hobomok, and Paul Higgins, the half-white chief of the Norridgewock, are helping your soldiers find food." He eyed her, pointing to the birchbark map on his table with distinct Abenaki markings. "I was told that he left this map to help our men navigate their way." She nodded, her long braids swinging in agreement. "Yes, sir, I know the same."

"What do you know about this Natanis?"

"That he has been here in these woods, alone, since just a boy, ever since he watched his mother and father executed by those blood-thirsty Englishmen, Rogers's Rangers. He is on our side, White Chief."

He stood up, barely as tall as Jacataqua and twice as thick, waving them back outside his tent before he came out behind them, still barefoot.

The disheartened men continued to arrive on the banks, on the brink of death, hauling up their bateaux and unloading. Arnold looked toward the great mountain and spoke loudly, with earnestness, to the group of at least a hundred hungry, exhausted, slovenly men, of his plans to hold up there for the night, ordering them to bring all the supplies that they could manage into the tents. On an open, flat brown rise above the river, he spread his arms. "We will erect a flagstaff here to mark our journey for freedom and independence. I know you are weak and hungry. There are fish here, but please abstain from using your rifles for game. The Natives are everywhere, and we cannot be sure of their loyalty." He gave Jacataqua a sidewise glance, sharing his distrust once again. "After crossing the Height of Land further up this wretched river, we'll refresh our supplies at the French village on the Chaudière. Quebec is not far from our grasp." He shouted to a large man sitting on the bank of the river looking for fish. "You, Meigs, take some of your men and cut me a good, straight tall tree for a flagstaff."

The men jumped on command, a biting wind coming down the mountain in vengeful swirls. Soldiers huddled around the fire, whittling fishing poles from black alder and stringing lines for the trout or salmon or pickerel, anything that had not migrated downstream. Rain began to fall in giant drops that Jacataqua called "Glooscap's tears" while she and Aaron erected a small lean-to with nearby limbs and branches. Meigs's men came back from the woods, carrying a long spruce trunk horizontally between them, the icy rain falling steadily now, bouncing menacingly on the surface of the Dead River, the spirits angry with the invasion of their valley, which Jacataqua called Tewyongyadigt. The rain turned to snow, whipping in torrents while they huddled inside tents and makeshift shelters, the sky darkening, the men coughing from cold and sickness. Jacataqua made a tea of willow bark over a small fire, a new life growing inside her, holding on for survival. She offered ladles of the tea to the sick men, a few with wives by their sides, to lessen their fevers while calling out to Glooskap and the wind bird, Wuchoson, to quit their fighting. The wind howled and the thunder raged in great claps until sleep finally took them under, battered and bone-tired.

At first light, they rolled onto the soggy ground and woke to find the river had swollen nearly twelve feet, tents drowned by the great rains, trees uprooted and streaming by, bateaux laden with supplies of food, extra clothing, gunpowder, sabers, and rifles swept away, lost to the raging current. Men ran into the icy river to salvage what they could, and when the wind finally died down, Arnold called an emergency council of war. His lieutenants, captains, and majors gathered around the fire outside his tent to the drumbeat of men coughing in fits. Wet fires cracked and hissed around the camp. "This march is far worse than we expected. Our original maps were faulty, and I just received news that Captain Enos's division behind us, with rations, has turned back. Our food supplies are dwindling, and I do not know when we will get relief. But despite this, there has been only one death amongst us." His eyes flashed in the firelight. "Our soldiers are exhausted and hungry, but they are tough and resilient, fighters for liberty. I ask you now, given our present circumstances, whether we should continue with our quest for Quebec or turn back now?" One by one, in slow deliberation, the officers around the campfire raised hands, giving their consent and pledge to continue.

As the sun came out, the tents dried, Meigs's men dug a deep hole above the high-water mark to plant the spruce flagstaff, to which Colonel Arnold secured the Continental flag, a solid red standard with a single green pine tree on a white square in the canton—the first American flagstaff on the Dead River. "Onward," Arnold commanded, and they loaded what they had left in their remaining seven bateaux, Jacataqua and Aaron bringing their birchbark canoe down to the bank, where they jumped into the swift, angry river.

PENNIE WOKE UP TO frost on the window and a few inches of new snow covering the ground and black rocks on the edges of the lake. Downstairs, Fremont sat at the table with his newspaper, donut, cigarette, and coffee, stroking natty Bartholomew across his lap. How Pennie missed her uncle's dogs right now, how she missed home. He thumped his paper. "Get yourself some coffee. We've got some serious business brewing."

It was already eight, and he'd been up for hours. She shivered under her wool sweater and long johns. "Looks like a fair amount of snow."

"Just a dusting," he said. "More coming this week."

She sat down and stared at the orange cat, who purred loudly. "I don't think she likes me."

"Nope, doesn't like too many." He flicked his ashes. "Where's Bri anyways? I know she's got a boyfriend, but this is ridiculous. Haven't seen hide nor hair of that girl for three days."

Pennie shifted her weight at the table. "Young love, what can you do?"

"You can start by being smart about who you're dating. He's all about himself if you ask me, but no one's asking."

At a loss for what to say, she changed the subject. "What's going on in the news?"

"There's a public meeting coming up." He pushed the paper toward her. "The power company is holding a town hall tonight for anyone interested in the Independence Corridor. I'm sure they just want to blow more smoke up our ass, about how much they're doing for us poor country folk. At least I'll have a chance to speak."

"This should get interesting." She heard a car pull in, and soon Mali and Dani were at the front stoop. Fremont offered them coffee, and Pennie remembered the twins had made a date today at the historical society.

He continued on about the corridor. "From what I understand, the Land Use Planning Commission represents our unorganized townships here, and they have the final say on who has the rights through the townships and the Carrying Place—so, my land."

"Will the commissioners be there tonight?"

"Oh, I doubt it. They don't want to get involved directly with any disgruntled property owners like me. I think I'm the only holdout on Middle Carry anyway. The others have already been bought."

"I sent Uncle Alfie a picture of your letter from the power company."

Fremont slipped on his worn leather duck boots. "He says he'll drive up when they come to assess the property."

The twins couldn't contain their excitement about visiting the historical society, especially after their afternoon at the Round Barn area and in the old log cabin. Pennie remembered her dream from last night: the man she followed through Dead River, back when the homesteads and farms were still there almost seventy-five years ago.

They agreed to meet later for dinner. Pennie watched them drive away and texted Tita, who already had plans to help the US Ski Team set up a race at the mountain. Then she texted Bri, who was spending the day with JD doing who knows what; it didn't matter. Pennie had to think about her own life. Out the window, snow gently fell and disappeared into the lake, the accumulation on the banks hiding the recession of the water level. Her mind wandered back to her dreams about the Dead River Valley settlers, the children sliding on Jim Eaton Hill, then back even further to the soldiers, freezing and hungry, hunched by their small fires, planting their flagstaff on the rise near the banks of the Dead River before moving on to Quebec.

The Abenaki warrior, Natanis, had watched their movements the entire way, helping them with maps, leaving canoes on their route, and driving moose into their march. Then she remembered Greta and the prophecy she and her deck had given Bri. If there was anything Pennie needed right now, it was some guidance. She grabbed her backpack and coat and left.

The small schoolhouse down the road was exactly as she remembered it from her dream of the fly-fishing man walking along the valley with all its farms and homesteads, the building set back by the stand of trees in the pasture. On the porch, she looked up again to see a small nest inside the eaves. Greta, wisps of salt-and-pepper hair floating around her ethereal face, stood in the doorway, beckoning her to please come in. "Pennie, I've been expecting you."

The room was just as it was before, with its baskets of pebbles and knitting, its paintings of the valley before the flooding, of Bigelow looming large over the winding river. "This is the old Dead River schoolhouse, right?" asked Pennie.

"Certainly. Wonderful spirits inside this old building. You've seen it, have you?"

An uneasiness crept under Pennie's skin. "What do you mean?"

"You've seen the schoolhouse in your dreams of the valley, is that right?"

"Yes, but how—"

"Have a seat, Birdie. You don't mind if I call you, Birdie, do you?"

Pennie grew tense, rubbing her hands together. "That's what my uncle calls me, what they used to call my mother."

The old woman took the cards from the wooden box and laid them on the table. "Tell me about her." After an uncomfortable moment, Pennie let her guard down and shared how much she missed her mother. Sometimes she dreamt about her, could see her mother in the moments before she jumped off the bridge, had even run across the road to save her from her fate, only to cause a car to swerve off the road and through the steel girder into Casco Bay. She still had nightmares sometimes. The seer pushed the cards toward Pennie. She began to shuffle, her hands shaking with the memory of that night, trying to make sense of things. She placed the stack on the table, and Greta fanned them out in one long line, face down, the string of chickadees sitting on branches among the tassels of pine needles and clouds on the backs of the cards. "My hope is to give you a better understanding of yourself, Birdie. What is your question?"

"My question?"

"Yes, think very carefully. What would you like the cards to tell you?"

She looked deep inside at the pain that was settled there—the loss, the lack of attachment, feeling so alone. "I guess I would like to ask what my dreams are trying to tell me."

Greta pressed her palms flat on the oak table. "Choose a card, please. The one that calls to you."

She reached out and selected a card that seemed to almost jump out from the others. Turning it over, 14, Conscience, came up—the image of an eye in a pyramid against a backdrop of clouds and a pine tree. The seer said, "Ah, the Eye of Providence, or the all-seeing one, also referred to as God's benevolent oversight. I like to think of it as the universal eye that only some can see through. Birdie, do not fear your dreams, especially of your mother on the bridge. She is reaching out to you. Something tells me she had the power of vision, too."

"Some people said she went crazy because of her dreams, her power of intuition, seeing things." The psychic nodded and pointed to the fanned-out cards. The next one Pennie drew from the deck was 21, Partnership, with the drawing of old-fashioned salt and pepper shakers, the same card Bri had drawn, and this time it occurred to Pennie that number 21 is two plus one, or three. Greta said this was very interesting, rubbing her palms together in a sort of meditation before wondering aloud if Pennie knew the power of partnership, of how building alliances was critical to a fulfilled life, the give-and-take of relationships. Pennie said she was having a difficult time with any kind of relationship, and that she was doomed on the romantic front, that no matter how much she gave of herself, she ended up alone in the end.

Greta stared at her, looking through her. "Perhaps you are searching too hard for this romance in your life. And remember, there are more partnerships than just romance. You have bonds with family and friends, and even business partnerships."

Pennie thought about the twins and Tita, and Bri and Fremont, and Uncle Alfie. "I guess I can work on building those."

"You may find that working together you can accomplish so much more than working apart." She signaled Pennie to choose another card. The next was 9, The Right Track, with a picture of a train's bright beam heading down a train track. "Why, how splendid," she said. "You are indeed on the right track. You just need to follow your destiny and your intuition. Are you understanding the importance of this card?"

She thought about the recent dreams she'd had, of the lives lived in this valley of spirits and agreed that, yes indeed, she knew that the meaning of this card was about accepting her gift of vision, of seeing into the past, and listening to what it was trying to tell her. Her mind swam with the messages, contemplating the direction of her own compass, when another card jumped out at her, and she turned over 1, The Fish, a silver fish flying in the air. They sat quietly for a moment, absorbing the divination of this card. She thought about Dani's fish paintings and Mali's descriptions, about their quest to unharness the free-flowing rivers and bring back the fish that once swam up the Kennebec to the nearby streams and brooks to spawn. Then there was Bri's mythical talent for fly fishing that no one, not even JD, could take away from her. *We all have our own powers, if we know how to follow the call of what makes us different.*

"From your cards, I see a clear message. Use your moral compass and your alliances to stay on the right track and true to your destiny. Only by knowing your limits and your special powers will you be able to reach your highest calling." In a smooth, unfettered motion, she gathered up the cards, encouraging Pennie to remain undaunted. "From one seer to another, Birdie, you must learn to trust your visions."

For the first time, Pennie noticed a peculiar Y-shaped stick leaning against the far corner of the room. The seer knew what had caught her attention. "The dowser made that rod from a branch of an ancient yellow birch tree in my back woods," said the seer. "We believe *that* birch has been here for over two hundred years. It has special powers." Pennie pictured the funny little man, Herald Snodgrass, she'd met the last time she was here, a near twin to Mr. Snodgrass in Portland, the odd little wine seller in the cellar of her favorite store who also sold old albums and cassette tapes. What had he said to her that day? His voice came back to her in a whisper, *Sounds like the universe is telling you to follow your intuition. Keep going...*

THE GRUBBY MOOSE, ANOTHER eatery in Eustis popular with the locals, was abuzz with chatter about the power company taking over their woods to power lower New England. Practically the whole town was headed to the meeting after dinner. Dani and Mali sat across from Pennie and Fremont in a booth, animated by what they'd learned at the historical society. They recounted stories about Spring Lake and the sporting camps owned by J.P. Morgan for his employees and their families, who were led on hunting expeditions by Warren Wing, the infamous guide and hunter who had killed over fifty bears. About the CCC crews that came in during the Depression to build trails to fire towers on Mount Bigelow and strung miles of telephone lines for the forest service, constructing roads and bridges throughout the Dead River Valley. About Captain Cliff Wing, who transported livestock and supplies across Flagstaff Pond on his ferry pushed by a motorboat, and the boys who used to set off the old cannon on the Fourth of the July, supposedly a canon left there by Arnold's men.

Fremont said, "Old Bert Horton claimed he knew where there was a stash of Benedict Arnold's munitions buried."

Pennie's recent dream came to her again—Jacataqua and Aaron camping near Jim Eaton Hill, Arnold erecting the flagstaff there. "Have you ever heard of Jacataqua, a Native American guide on Benedict Arnold's march?"

Dani chewed on a french fry. "That's right. She was the sachem who met Aaron Burr near Swan Island in Pittston. Burr was supposedly quite a rogue, a young, dashing soldier who stole her heart."

Fremont drummed his yellow fingertips. "Burr sailed up with Arnold to Major Reuben Colburn's shipyard. Colburn had been commissioned to build two hundred bateaux, and from what I understand, those boats were heavy as shit, made of green pine, and leaked like a sieve."

Mali squirted mustard on her cheeseburger. "As the story goes, Jacataqua was Artemis of the Kennebec, the most skillful hunter of her tribe on Swan Island, and she showed Burr how to find a black bruin in the woods near a farmer's cornfield."

Dani continued. "When they all gathered that night for a grand feast of bear meat, venison, and pork, she raised her glass to Aaron, calling him her Chestnut Burr."

Freemont jumped in, remembering the story. "That's right, Burr pleaded with Arnold to let her join the expedition. He finally consented because she knew all the water routes and trails like the back of her hand and could hunt and fish better than any of them."

"And was unmatched in a canoe," said Dani.

Fremont chewed on his moose burger, ketchup on his sagging cheek. "I don't think they would have made it without Jacataqua, Natanis, and the other Natives."

Pennie asked, "Did she and Burr have a child?"

All three nodded in agreement.

"That's how the story goes," he said. "And from what Lena told me, her family was related to the Abenaki of Swan Island."

"Wait," said Mali. "Your late wife was related to the famous Jacataqua of Swan Island?"

"That's what she claimed," he said, wiping his mouth and taking and a swig of coffee. "Of course, she was also part French and god knows whatever else. We're all mixed breeds here in New England." Pennie thought about her dream and tried to bring up the memory of Jacataqua, a faint but insistent resemblance to Bri rising inside her imagination.

FREMONT FINISHED HIS CIGARETTE outside the town hall while Pennie, Mali, and Dani followed the townspeople, men and women of all ages, into the crowded meeting room. Chairs sat in long rows facing a table and a flip chart showing the path of the Independence Corridor. They took four open seats on the outside near the back. Bri and JD filed into a row on the opposite side of the room. When Bri turned around, Pennie waved to get her attention. She waved back enthusiastically with a huge smile. Pennie knew that, whatever had happened, she was a happy camper. JD snuggled up against her. Betsy and Shep sat in the row behind them, the room now a cacophony of heated discussion.

Fremont took a seat beside Pennie, coughing for a good two minutes. She offered him water, but he said he never touched the stuff. The entire town seemed to crowd into the room. A robust man with a dark mustache walked up to the lectern to review his notes while the company reps settled themselves at the long table, opening their laptops. A hush settled over the standing-room-only crowd.

The man at the podium introduced himself as Leon and then let the other men and one woman introduce themselves, all power company people. Leon pointed to the giant map of the state of Maine, the red line of the corridor running from the Canadian border south of Lac-Megantic through the Coburn Gore township, along the north side of the Chain of Ponds, through several townships above Flagstaff and Spring Lakes to cross the Dead River, then down between Middle and West Carry Ponds and through the Pleasant Ridge Plantation to reach the power station at the Wyman Dam in Moscow: 240 miles of corridor.

Arms open wide, he noted the same parallel route of the historic Arnold Expedition, the great march to Quebec City at the outset of the Revolutionary War in 1775. "Ladies and gentlemen, this was an important march for our nation's independence, just as this is an important undertaking today for independence from fossil fuels. This corridor will send clean, hydroelectric power from Canada through these mountains of western Maine to connect to a power station on the Kennebec River. From there, it connects to the existing corridor leading through New Hampshire to Massachusetts, Rhode Island, and New York." Murmurs rumbled. He raised his stout arms, the buttons on his white shirt straining to hold back his ample stomach. "My friends, this will provide fifteen hundred megawatts of energy, enough energy to power over a million homes, thereby reducing greenhouse gas significantly and our reliance on dirty fossil fuels—the power New England needs to sustain and stabilize the electrical grid for generations."

A flurry of hands raised. A few impatient men stood with questions, but Leon asked everyone to please hold them, that everyone would get a chance to speak. A large, rangy man walked to the podium and said he was head of the local sportsmen's club. "I've been hunting and fishing these woods since I was a kid. This area has been logged responsibly for generations. By putting this gullet through our woods, it's a permanent scar on our woodlands, and it won't stop there. Once you start, the proverbial flood gates will open and our way of life will be gone, given up for the rat-race life of the cities. All you care about is money and profits. You try this, and—I'll tell you what—you've got a mean fight on your hands."

He left the podium in a huff, and a balding man at the front table said that they were taking all the precautions to build environmentally responsible lines to keep the woods and waters pristine. One boisterous old man yelled, "How are the people of Maine being compensated for this power grab, if all the electricity's going to the flatlanders?" The coiffed woman from the power company stood up to address the question, saying they were investing over $200 million in Maine for heat pumps and electric vehicle–charging stations. Also, she wanted everyone to know that part of the deal was selling discounted energy to Maine, enough to run 70,000 homes.

An older woman with white hair and a long, lined face walked to the podium and asked, "Why is Maine becoming an extension cord for other states? This remote area is part of the largest forest in the Northeast. This corridor, one hundred feet wide, would cut through and fragment the forest, disturbing everything from moose yards to streams and rivers for our fish." In response, a beak-nosed man from the power company said the corridor would be no wider than sixty feet and that they would not cut trees taller than forty feet or use any herbicides in the corridor. They would also replace culverts that block fish passage and conserve acres of forests in the region. Dani leaned to Pennie. "That's what they said about fish ladders on dams, and most of them are not usable."

Fremont's name was finally called. He walked to the podium and pointed to the Maine map, running his gnarled finger along the route between Middle and West Carry Ponds. "This land has been in my family for at least five generations—forty acres on the Middle Carry, the same land that Benedict Arnold and his soldiers passed through with their heavy, leaky bateaux, nearly broken and starved to death from coming up the Kennebec without enough food." He pointed to the people seated at the long table, their somber faces staring ahead. "*This* power company took my family's farm and land in the Dead River Valley seventy-five years ago to build a dam and flood our valley. They lied to us back then, too, telling us that the dam would provide power for the greater good. Greater good, my ass. There was never any plan to produce electricity at this dam, and it never has." He turned to face them. "You power people have no respect for personal property. You want to control everything to line your own greedy pockets, and you'll do anything to get it, no matter how underhanded and illegal. Your corridor—what did that guy call it?—your *gullet* is a disgrace to this state, this country, and all the soldiers who fought for our freedom from bastards *just* like you."

He left the podium, and the audience grew quiet. Leon took his place back at the podium, looking down at his notes, his belly heaving. "Sir, I assure you that everything we have shared today is in complete good faith for this clean energy project. We're all working on this together. We have already invested nearly $300 million in construction costs. This is a tremendous investment in Maine's economy and workforce."

One man shouted out, "What about tomorrow? Are you creating any jobs for tomorrow?" Leon insisted that the construction work was invigorating the Maine economy. Pennie knew she had to add one more thing to the conversation before it was over. She raised her hand and felt the power of Greta's Conscience card behind her. "I read in the *Tribune* that your political action committees and supporters have spent nearly $50 million on the campaign over the last two years to push through the corridor and gain public favor. That's outspending the side against the corridor by nearly four times. If you're spending this much money to keep from failing, you must be making an outrageous profit. Everyone here in this room knows this is all about profits."

The room rumbled while Leon pressed his mustache and cleared his throat, saying he wasn't aware of that figure, and that both sides, not just the power company, had invested a tremendous amount of money, and that seeing it succeed would mean saving the environment, a tremendous step toward ending reliance on fossil fuels. He gave everyone a toll-free number to call if they had any other questions or concerns and put his hands in the air to tame any other banter, to quell any further questions, and thanked everyone for coming.

Chapter 9
Legend of Awasos

THE TWINS LEFT TOWN after the meeting, planning to head to Bingham the next day for more dam research. Pennie drove Fremont home and made some tea while he kept the ever-present fire alive in the woodstove, stoking the embers and loading in hot-burning sugar maple until it was chock-full. The fire now at a nice slow burn, he settled onto the couch with his quilt. She asked if he might not like to have his tea in the bedroom. "Oh, I can't leave the fire on a night like tonight. I'll sleep out here...keep the home fires burning."

She'd never seen Fremont sleep in his bedroom down the hall and knew that it must hold lingering memories of Lena. The draft coming in through the windowpanes crept around her like a lake mist. He curled his skinny legs under the blanket, showing holes in the heels of his wool socks. "Maybe you should turn the furnace up tonight. I mean, it's plenty warm upstairs, but the house could get cold."

"Are you kidding, with the oil prices the way they are? I'd rather heat with wood and save the oil in the tank. Don't want to fill that again too soon. Besides, it's only twenty tonight. You wait 'til it gets twenty below in January."

Already, the biting temperatures had descended on Eustis. She had no intention of still being around in January. Fremont lay still under his ragged quilt with patches of red and black plaid she recognized from her dream, the mackinaw worn by Horace, the man she followed through the Dead River Valley. When she asked Fremont about the quilt, he described each square like thumbing through an old family album: baby blankets, his grandmother's apron, his grandfather's hunting jacket, his flannel shirt as a boy, the wool blanket they used on sleigh rides, his mother's favorite tablecloth for picnics, his father's handkerchief with his initials, his sister's basketball uniform. All these layered memories, a patchwork of his life woven into this valley of dreams.

The fire crackled, and as she felt herself falling asleep her phone chimed. She pulled it from her pocket to see Bri had texted her. *Join us at JDs place for a few beers?* Fremont was already snoozing, Bartholomew curled on his stomach, amber eyes gleaming. She pulled her chair closer to the woodstove, the wind howling across the vast lake. Again, her phone chirped. Bri was quite insistent. Fremont wheezed and snored, and she found another wool blanket in the closet to put over his thin frame. Despite his age, he was still a fighter, she thought, still standing up for his property rights against the hands of control. Looking into her empty teacup, she saw a mini snow squall with an eye in the center. Here was her conscience, the reason she was here at this place and time.

She put on her coat and braved the bitter wind to drive to JD's place above Shep and Betsy's garage. Snow spit at her windshield as her tires rumbled down the long dirt drive. Several trucks sat in the driveway. The door beside the garage was unlocked, and she walked up the stairs to a roomful of laughter, mostly young men dressed in flannel and a few of the waitresses from the restaurant sitting around a large dining table playing cards. Bri stood with JD in the kitchen off to the side, talking with Owen. Pennie's gaze caught the glimmering gem on her finger.

She held her hand out for Pennie to see. "We're engaged! Can you believe it? Isn't it beautiful?"

So many conflicting emotions came at once, Pennie didn't know what to say, other than, "Congratulations, both of you!" She was trying to be happy for them, despite the rushed plans to get married, to start a family.

They exchanged hugs, and JD gave Pennie a stiff slap on the back. "Making an honest woman out of her," he said, his beer breath overpowering.

She wanted to say that maybe it was the other way around, but Owen rescued her. "The best-looking couple in town. And best of all, I'm going to be an uncle." He handed her a beer.

"We're just getting started," said JD. "We want to have lots of kids, a whole tribe, right babe?" For the first time, Pennie saw the iron cross on his forearm. Bri looked down at her glass of ginger ale and shrugged her shoulders, saying they had lots of time to figure that out.

They were certainly a stunning couple, Bri with her chestnut hair and wide smile and JD with his black hair and pale blue eyes. He was a smidge shorter than she was, thickly built next to her willowy frame. Owen stood a head taller than his brother. She said, "I bet your parents are excited."

There was a moment of hesitation before Owen said that they were, indeed, getting used to the idea of a grandchild. "Betsy always needs time to digest any change, you know, losing her favored son to a new woman and all."

JD smiled like a sly tomcat, pulling Bri closer to him, saying she was the only woman in his life. The dining table grew loud with a contentious game of spoons—react fast or be the one left with nothing. Was this Pennie's fate? The last one left, the old spinster? "Made any wedding plans yet?"

"We're getting married over at Spring Lake next summer, after the baby comes. It's a beautiful spot for a wedding, and if the weather's good, we'll have the reception outside under a tent," she said.

"You've really got this planned out already."

"I want my bride to have a fairy tale wedding," he said, kissing Bri on the cheek and laying his hand on her flat stomach. Her diamond glittered in the soft light of the kitchen. Pennie tried to picture Bri in a big white wedding dress, but the pretense of it seemed to go against the grain of her nature.

As if reading her thoughts, Owen said to Bri, "I hope you can get away to a fishing destination for your honeymoon."

She looked at JD with hope in her eyes, but he shrugged it off, saying he was hoping they could go to Hawaii or someplace exotic, to which she replied, "How about Alaska?"

He laughed. "Whoever heard of going to Alaska on a honeymoon?"

Pennie said, "I've heard they have an unbelievable cruise from Washington State to Alaska."

JD narrowed his eyes and took a swig of his beer. "You seem to know a lot about the campaign spending of the power company, Pennie. You been doing a little research on the side to help out Grampy Fremont?"

She shrugged. "I think we all owe it to our communities to get to the bottom of the corridor questions, don't you?"

"That's right, we all want what's right for *our* community," he said. "You don't live anywhere around here."

"No, but I care about Fremont and his property they're trying to take by eminent domain. Anything wrong with standing up to the power company, standing up for what is a blatant land grab?"

He took another swig of beer, flashing his iron cross. "Nope. We're all just wondering about your sudden interest in this land." His eyes flashed.

"Know your place around here." Turning away, he left the kitchen area to join the game of spoons, beckoning Owen to join him.

Pennie turned to Bri, mouthing *What the fuck?* Bri chewed her hair, twisting the ring on her finger, then asked Pennie if she didn't think it was the most beautiful ring she'd ever seen. Of course it was, she assured her, repeating how happy she was for the two of them. "You're starting a family. This is so exciting, Bri. Have you called your mother yet?"

She gazed out the window into the darkness, saying she'd tried but her mother's phone was no longer in service. "I'm worried about her." Tears filled her round eyes. "I'm so tired of being worried about her. All through middle school and high school when she didn't come home…" Bri shifted her gaze to JD. "I've been making my own decisions for a long time. I certainly don't need someone making them for me now. You know what I'm saying?" Pennie tried to smile, understanding exactly what she was saying.

JD called over to her, patting the chair beside him. "Come over here and join us, babe."

She puffed out her lips, letting out a long stream of air. Pennie set down her empty beer bottle. "You know, I've got to hit the hay. Get back to check on Fremont, asleep by the fire as usual."

"I miss him." She smoothed her hair. "Thank you for taking care of him. I owe you."

"You don't owe me a damn thing." She waved to JD and Owen, thanking them for the beer, and gave Bri a hug. Owen put on his coat and said he'd walk her out.

When the icy October wind hit them in the face outside, they shivered. He looked at his feet and said, "What's up?"

She laughed at his continued awkwardness. "Not much, you?"

"Wanna take some turns soon?" She saw this coming, this offer of a date. He hunkered in his down jacket, ears red, jaw quivering.

"Sure, I'd like that. I haven't been on skis since falling last March and slamming into a tree." She tried to smile in the flurry of light snow. "Be good to get back on the horse."

"You must be some tough cookie." He dug his hands in his jean pockets. "Don't take my brother too seriously. He gets easily riled. Just his personality."

"I'm beginning to wonder who's side he's on."

"He's on the side of the town, believe me. Doesn't want that corridor any more than the rest of us."

She thanked him, waved, and got inside her car. It started right up. Again, she thanked her uncle in the silent, bleak darkness, driving the streets of Stratton back to Fremont's cabin on the lake, the snowflakes like a splay of bullets against her windshield.

She found herself sitting outside a small schoolhouse, panting from running, her paws raw from the ice and snow. When the young brother and sister finally came out, she barked and wagged her tail in delight, Fremont and Fannie waving goodbye to their teacher, the lady with the long black skirt and thick wool sweater in the doorway, smelling like limestone, white powder on her fingertips. They ran all the way down the road to the farm, where Mama was waiting inside the kitchen with the woodstove roaring and biscuits rising for dinner, her hands red and raw from cooking and cleaning, the countless jars of pickles, berries, fruits, jellies, beans, tomatoes, and corn sitting up high on a shelf.

Mama sent the children out to the barn to feed the chickens and get the eggs. The old cow lowed in welcome, expecting they would relieve her and fill their pail, and soon enough Papa walked in chewing tobacco. Fremont asked him why he chewed, to which he gave a quick reply, "Won't catch the flu as long as I chew!" Brother and sister added grain to the chicken feeder, distracting the hens to check their boxes for eggs, while the whole barn filled with the smell of fresh, sweet milk, the sound of each gentle squirt against the tin pail, the yellow light dimming outside in the winter afternoon.

Fannie liked the baby goats in the stall beside the old cow, their coats soft like velvet. They wobbled on their new legs, curious and licking the buttons of her wool coat, nudging and butting against her, making her laugh way down to her belly. Fremont added more hay to the horse stalls for Dan and Polly with their furry, dusty coats, nudging him, munching away. They dreamed of springtime, taking the cows to the summer pasture to go blueberrying and picnicking on the Chain of Ponds. When Papa had a full pail, they followed him back to the house to the smell of baked beans, and Mama told Fannie to practice her piano. She gladly sat down to play for all of them to sing along, Mama with the best singing voice, her wistful melody filling the house.

Fremont groaned when Papa said he had to fill the woodbox in the kitchen if he wanted to go with them to the dance that night. Sitting down to a dinner of dried codfish, baked beans, hogs' head cheese, and pickled tripe, Papa said grace, thanking the good Lord for the bounty set before them, entertaining them with stories of working at the sawmill that day while Fannie and Fremont recounted what they had learned at school from Mrs. Taylor, how the other children had talked about the power company taking their homes, their land, to build a dam. Papa cast a weary look at Mama and told them not to worry about it. That was a long way away, and most likely wouldn't happen anyhow.

Soon enough, they all bundled up in fur and wool coats, and Papa hitched the sled to Dan and Polly to take them up the road to the dance in Peter Wahl's barn. Sitting on hay bales under a harvest moon, Papa sang loudly all the way to the farm, where people had come by automobile or shank's mare from both sides of the river to listen to the band of fiddlers and square-dance to the "Lady of the Lake," the "Boston Fancy," or the "Viriginia Reel" and sometimes do circle waltzes, the grown-ups teaching the kids the steps until the little ones eventually nestled by the fire under blankets and watched their parents thumping and skipping to the music on a wintery night inside a warm barn in the protected river valley.

The best part was the ride on the sleigh behind Dan and Polly along the winding river toward home under the black winking night, Papa smoking his pipe and pointing out Ursa Major, the Great Bear in the sky, and telling the legend of Awasos, the black bear who was chased every night by three hunters who killed him in the fall, turning the leaves brown.

SHE ROLLED OVER ON her creaky bed to see a text from Tita, asking her if she wanted to ski. Outside her window, the sun was bright over the snow covering the now-frozen lake. Yes, Pennie texted back, she'd be there in an hour. She didn't have to work at the Gullet until that afternoon. Tita texted back that she still had Pennie's ski equipment in the Jan Van.

Down in the smoky kitchen, she bid Fremont a good morning, and he shared the news that the appraiser was coming to his property that week; he had already called Alfie. His eyes reflected the sorrow of a thousand years, and Pennie knew he was losing hope. She stroked Bartholomew, who sat in a kitchen chair chewing on his claws. "Don't worry. I'm sure there's something Uncle Alfie can do to stop this." She poured herself some coffee. "Why can't they go around your property?"

"Not many options on the land between the ponds. My land runs all the way to Roundtop ridge." He flicked his cigarette into the Hills Bros.

can and coughed until the phlegm loosened. She wondered if he knew about Bri's engagement but decided it was better that Bri told him the big news. This was one family drama she did not need to be in the middle of. She gathered her parka and ski pants from the attic before making sure he was all set. He assured her it was just another day: the Grubby Moose for lunch, working on his woodpile, adding some weather stripping to the windows.

Driving to the mountain, she recalled her accident at Coos Canyon last year and how Tita had been there with her in the ambulance and later at the hospital. Her dog Boone, who'd died only a week before the accident, had come to her when she thought she was on the brink of death, as if their lives intertwined, one crossing into another. She followed the line of cars on the Sugarloaf access road and into the lot to find a parking spot as close to the main lodge as possible. At the base, Tita's van sat behind the ski repair shop. The mountain was busy with skiers swishing down the groomed, snow-packed trails, the glories of modern snowmaking. Pennie found Tita inside talking to the owner, Jed, who'd been there for as long as Tita had skied on the circuit. He handed Pennie her skis, freshly sharpened. "Thanks, what do I owe you?"

"On the house." He winked at her with a roguish smirk. She cringed. Why must older dudes always wink, as if men were in on some secret?

Tita led the way outside. "The mountain asked me to organize a fundraiser for them, to show the documentary."

"That's awesome. Did you talk to Lars about it?"

She looked up at the mountain, dropping her Ray-Bans over her eyes. The gleaming white trails between the fir trees rose up to the smoky mist covering the peaks. "He says it's fine as long as I do it before the end of the year."

"What happens at the end of the year?"

Tita's fluorescent yellow skis stood out at the end of the rack. "I guess he's working on a deal. Says we can sell the rights to the movie and make out big, but we have to sign the contract by the end of December."

The temperature on the giant disc thermostat read 26 degrees. Pennie sat on a nearby bench and buckled on her boots in the warming sun. "I don't understand. I thought he was out there to find a distributor for the film, not sell it."

"Yeah, that makes two of us." She shrugged, throwing her long boards down on the snowpack. "He says it's an offer we can't refuse. Says it will give us the money to begin another project, which is cool."

"But why would you sell the rights? Won't you lose all creative control?"

She pursed her lips together. "Sometimes you have to give a little to get a little, Pennie. Don't be so naive."

Somehow, this sounded exactly like something Lars might say. She held her arms up. "You and Lars know best about this whole movie business."

They latched on their skis and poled up to the chairlift where the lines were already ten or fifteen people deep, so unlike skiing Coos Canyon with its smaller crowds and more extreme conditions. But Sugarloaf had many more miles of trails, well-groomed slopes, and snowfields on the backside. When they reached the head of the line, a smiling young man in white sunglasses waved them through. The chair scooped them up, and they breathed in the crisp air, securing the goggles to their faces against the cold. Tita pointed out the trail off to the side where she'd been coaching a clinic for high school girls. "There's some real up-and-coming talent." Her voice fell against the hum of the chair.

"It must be strange being here, where you competed so much."

"Yeah, well, time to move on and figure out my next play."

Pennie knew she was thinking about her future with Lars. An unspoken question that floated in the air between them was something about trustworthiness. *Trust.* "When is Lars coming back?"

"Late November. He sounds excited about this opportunity to sell the film." It almost sounded as if Tita was trying to talk herself into it.

"Well, from what I saw, you have a beautiful documentary—a real testament to your rise in freeskiing."

"I don't need a pep talk, Pennie."

"I'm not—." She stopped herself. It was clear Tita was at odds with this whole proposition. They unloaded at the top, and Pennie felt that familiar adrenaline pumping through her veins, following her cousin down a blue intermediate trail—so unlike her for a warm-up run. Pennie felt freer than she ever had before, skiing in long, sweeping curves over the groomed hilly terrain, keeping her eye on her cousin's red helmet. The sun was high in the sky, the crust glimmering. She leaned in, turning from one side to another in the middle of the trail while Tita took the moguls on the side, showing off her artistry—still the athlete, just a little slower these days.

They skied for a few hours, taking several runs and working their way to the black diamond trails, where their sharp edges made all the difference. The memory of skiing too close to the edge of the slope at Coos Canyon and skidding into a snow gun flashed in her mind, her body like a ragdoll bouncing off the gun and hitting a tree. She faced the memory, working through her fear and embracing this ferocious desire to test her own limits. Maybe her cousin, the daredevil freeskier, was also thinking about her own limits on these mountains, these valleys that were a part of their very being, something Fremont and Bri felt as keenly as they did.

They skied their way down to the lower, easy terrain and finally to the base lodge to put their skis up. Pennie followed Tita to a seat on the deck for lunch where they enjoyed a beer and a plate of nachos in the sunshine, watching the skiers come down the mountain, families in tow, couples in tandem sporting the latest equipment and fashion-forward parkas, ski patrols roaming the slopes. Tita took a long swig. "How did it feel getting back on the boards?"

"Freeing, just like I remembered. Thanks for getting me back out here."

"Better than skiing alone." A young woman walked by Tita, thanking her for the clinic.

Pennie chewed on a cheesy nacho. "I'm sure you're not short on skiing partners."

"Yeah, but we needed to catch up." She held her beer up to cheers behind her Ray-Bans.

"I don't know if I ever thanked you for staying with me when I had my accident last year."

"I've had enough of my own close calls." Tita licked her fingers. "Besides, buying me lunch will be enough."

Pennie laughed, glad that she had her first paycheck in the bank. She shared her trials working in the kitchen with Shep, and the news about Bri's engagement. "Looks like she's all in."

Tita shook her head. "Not sure about that guy, but you never know when someone is ready to settle down." Pennie knew she was thinking about Lars. When he made it back from California again, he would have to make his intentions clear, that was certain.

Pennie still had not forgiven him for the nude picture of her that he had circulated. "Are you sure you trust Lars? I mean, he hasn't exactly been forthright with you."

Tita laughed. "You're not exactly a role model when it comes to healthy relationships."

"True," she said. "But I do think it's easier to see deceit from the outside looking—."

Tita waved and yelled to one of her apprentices, ignoring Pennie.

IN SHEP'S KITCHEN, SHE found his list on the giant fridge. The homey sweet smell of corn chowder on the stovetop and searing roast lamb in the oven filled the kitchen. Hopefully, those nachos would hold her until closing time. She brought the tray of vegetables to her chopping station. This job was not so bad, really. When Shep came in at the dinner hour, the night always flew by.

Her eyes smarted while she chopped the onions. She recalled Bri's eyes filling with tears the night before. Sounds of someone coming inside the restaurant traveled through the vent overhead. It was JD's low voice and the commanding voice of a woman. Their tones grew louder, a few chuckles, barstools scraping the floor. JD said something about Bri, the baby, and the wedding and how un-expected everything was. The woman spoke in clipped sentences, like a preacher. "This is God's will...you will be a wonderful father and husband...a man has to provide for his family...." Then JD said something she could barely hear, something about the power company corridor. Pennie tilted her ear toward the ceiling. "This corridor is the best thing for our future." Then the cadence of the preacher again: "God is showing the way." Again, the sound of stools scraping. She ran to peer over the swinging doors as a woman with short dark hair, dressed in a long tan overcoat, passed a stuffed manila envelope to JD. They shook hands, and she left the restaurant.

On the other side of the dining room, big Betsy came out of the office. "JD, there you are. Was that Pastor Laurel I just heard?"

"She came bearing gifts."

"Good, that should help grease the skids. Did you talk about the baby christening and wedding plans?"

Pennie ran back to her station and strained to hear their conversation.

The matron said, "I hope you told her you want a church wedding."

"I told you that Bri and I want an outdoor wedding over at Spring Lake."

"You can get married in a church like the Lord intended. You can do this one thing for your mother. Then we can go over to the lake for the dam reception and all the other nonsense."

He pushed his stool against the bar. "We'll talk about this later."

"And what about the lawyer? Did you get the prenup?" "Jesus, Ma, give me a few days. We only started planning this thing."

"That little money-grubber got knocked up because she wants a piece of this place. You can bet the farm on that."

"You're overreacting. She didn't even know if she wanted to keep it."

"Of course not, she's a little whore."

Heavy footsteps traveled away toward the front door. It closed with a thud. Betsy was behind the bar now, at the register, the bell chiming the opening of the cash drawer. The only thing this woman had on her mind was money, and who was trying to take it from her.

Pennie continued chopping the onions, the celery and carrots, the potatoes and squash. Betsy peeked over the swinging doors. "Oh, you're here. Good. You can slice up those brownies over there, too."

Everyone knew desserts were the waitress's responsibility, but she wasn't questioning the matron. She started on Shep's list and soon heard Owen at the bar, talking with Betsy about the drink specials. The sounds of the other waitresses filled the place: stamping boots, orders from Betsy, clinking silverware. Bri was the last to arrive, in a whirl of emotion, showing off her new engagement ring to the other waitresses before Betsy told them all to get busy or find another place to work. "You're one lucky little cookie that my son is so kind and understanding," she said to Bri. "But don't you think I don't have your number. Now earn your place here."

Bri busted through the swinging doors, rather scattered, asking Pennie if there was any ginger ale around. "That woman is really getting on my nerves. I'm so queasy lately. If this is what it feels like for nine months, I'm doomed." Inside the fridge, she found a can of soda. Washing her hands in the sink, her glittering carat as magnificent as ever, she said, "I'm afraid I'm going to lose this." She dried her hands on a dishcloth. "Would you mind holding on to it for me? I don't have any pockets."

"I can hardly hold on to a job, let alone a diamond." Pennie joined her at the sink to wash her own hands. "Why don't you put it in that mason jar?"

Bri grabbed the jar from the counter, unscrewed the top, and popped the ring inside. "Good idea." She placed the jar on top of the fridge.

Betsy glared at the two of them from over the swinging doors. "Are you two working tonight or having a tea party back here?" Bri took off, at the beck and call of the grand matron, while Pennie stirred the corn chowder on the stovetop. Shep's thumping step came in behind her. "How's the chowder coming?" He set the bottle of whiskey on the plating station.

"Smelling delicious."

"Good, now make those biscuits like I showed you last time."

She was happy to have a job and a sense of accomplishment, no matter how small. He snapped on the transistor radio over the stove, and the news came on about the corridor. "Hydropower is much more reliable," the reporter stated, an authority. "It's consistent generation of power, unlike solar and wind, which are weather dependent. As of today, the Department of Energy, Army Corps of Engineers, Maine Public Utilities Commission, and the Maine Department of Environmental Protection have all given their approval for the forty-five miles of new corridor through western Maine to connect at the existing power station on the Kennebec River. The Natural Resources Council of Maine has appealed the Maine DEP permit. If the permit stands, the final approval goes to the Land Use Planning Commission."

Shep shook his head. "If they let this happen, it's just the first step of outlanders taking our North Woods. You mark my words. We can say goodbye to 'Maine, the way life should be.' And hello to 'Maine, the way life used to be.'" He took a long haul of his whiskey on ice.

She sifted the flour into the giant bowl, thinking of her Aunt Maude making a pie. "Who's on the Land Use Commission?"

"A rep from every county." Shep limped his way over to the stove to take the roast lamb from the oven, lifting it out with his giant arms.

"Won't the county commissioner for this region vote against it?"

"Maybe, but there are six others on the board." He poured the drippings from the pan into a saucepan for the gravy.

"Seems like we should find out more about who they are and how they'll vote, you know, to find out if there are any conflicts of interest."

"Seems like you should get busy making those biscuits."

She added lard to the flour mixture, using a pastry blender to mix everything before adding water. Owen popped in to grab some lemon and lime wedges from the fridge. He leaned to Pennie on his way out. "What's up?"

She shook her head. "Not much, you?"

"How was the skiing today?" She wondered how he knew she was at the mountain but nodded, telling him it was excellent, kneading the dough.

As soon as he left, Shep said, "I don't need another *romance* starting up around here."

"Oh, don't be silly. We're just friends."

He whisked flour into the gravy. "That's what they all say."

It wasn't long before Betsy swept in with the first slips. Pennie put a batch of biscuits in the oven. She and Shep began their kitchen dance, mostly Pennie trying to stay out of his way. He sliced the lamb while she prepared the carrots and mashed potatoes on the hot stovetop. Her stomach growled. Bri came in to grab half-and-half and said it was busy for a Tuesday night. Shep grunted. "Nobody cooks at home anymore. Women are too busy with their *careers*, and men don't know what it means to work for a living. Our whole society's going to pot."

Bri rolled her eyes at Pennie on her way out, and Betsy steamrolled in with more orders, telling Shep not to be too stingy with the gravy, and he told her to stick it up her ass. "You want to run my kitchen now?"

If there was anything Pennie knew, it was to keep her comments about the meals to herself. At the fryolator by the chopping station, she plopped in frozen french fries and heard JD's voice through the vent, saying something to Bri about her ring. She stuttered. "I, I left it in the kitchen so I wouldn't lose it."

"I didn't buy that for you to keep it hidden somewhere."

"Do you want me to lose it?" she said, her voice trailing with resentment.

He laughed to lighten the mood. "Okay, have it your way...for *now*."

The flurry in the kitchen grew as the orders kept rolling in. Shep's brow glistened, and he asked Pennie to get him some ice from the freezer.

She filled his glass with cubes as Betsy strolled in with a hamburger on a plate, one bite out of it.

He roared at her. "What now?"

"Burger's not cooked enough." He looked at the slip. "Says medium rare here."

She put her hands on her hips. "I told Brianna to be more careful with these orders. I guess they wanted medium." He threw the cast-iron frying pan across the kitchen so hard it hit the giant fridge square, bouncing off the stainless steel. "Tell that little bitch to come in here so I can have a word with her." The glass mason jar wobbled and rolled toward the edge, falling off the top and crashing down to the floor, glass shattering in a grand fan of shards across the linoleum.

Betsy shouted, "Clean that up, Pennie. What the hell is that jar doing up there, anyway?"

The diamond ring glittered among the pieces of glass, and Pennie carefully plucked it out to stick in her apron pocket. She picked up the frying pan, stepping gingerly around the large pieces of glass, thinking, *What a big happy family Bri is joining*. Shep downed his whiskey, slapping another burger on the grill top, turning up the volume on conspiracy theory radio.

Bri came through the swinging doors, and Pennie raced over to catch her, grabbing her skinny arm to turn her around, taking her back out into the bar to secretly explain the hamburger incident. "I didn't take that order," Bri said. "Betsy did."

"Well, if I were you, I'd stay clear of the kitchen for the rest of the night."

"I need my ring," she said, annoyed.

Pennie took the ring from her pocket and placed it firmly in Bri's palm. She immediately slipped it back on her finger. "Somebody is ignoring me. Seems I was talking to one of the men at my tables too long."

There he sat, as big as Billy, at the bar, his friends hanging off his every word and Owen waiting on them hand and foot. Pennie went back to the kitchen to clean up the glass. It occurred to her that she could give her notice, walk out and leave this family dysfunction, but she knew that Bri needed her; that was the only thing that kept her there. Squatting down, she picked up the large shards one by one as Betsy came in and stepped around her, telling her to hurry it up before somebody cut themselves. Pennie rose above the calamity of the kitchen for a moment, could see herself on the floor cleaning up someone else's mess. But instead of hardening her heart, it opened a glimpse of pity for the lonely old man at the stove whose own anger blazed in the heat of the gas flame, in the bite of the whiskey, the constant pain of his bum leg, and possibly a past he had never reckoned with, that drew his ire like a leaping fire.

Chapter 10
The Hunt

THE CHILL OF EARLY winter settled into the mountain valley. Fremont drove them in his black Ford pickup and parked out front beside Alfie's trusty Packard. In the back of Pennie's mind, she tried to push away the worries of the heart attack her uncle had had just last spring. As far as she knew, he was fully recovered. But the truth was, she did not have any idea about his health. They found him inside the greasy spoon, in a corner booth near the front window, his profile kind and resolute. He stood to shake hands with his cousin Fremont, firmly and with a heartfelt hug, the two men embracing again after a long absence.

She tried to hold back her excitement, waiting for her turn to latch onto his bulk like a homesick child, thanking him for driving all the way from Portland. "How are the dogs?"

He adjusted his heavy frame in the booth. "I nearly brought Cassie with me but decided the whole trip would be less complicated without a dog in tow." Pennie couldn't hide her disappointment.

Coffees appeared, and they chitchatted about family before Fremont showed Alfie the Notice of Intent to Acquire from the power company. Her uncle blew on his coffee and scratched his chin, reading the entire letter before setting it carefully down on the table, flattening out the creases. "Well, they have every right to send this letter for an appraisal. The State and Public Utilities Commission gave the power company the go-ahead for the corridor route, so this is the next legal step. How was the town meeting?"

"Oh, you know, same old bullshit about the public good they're doing everyone. Isn't that nice of them to come in, cut a highway through our old forests for the good of us old Mainers? They've got quite a dog and pony show."

Alfie chuckled. "The energy business is a political dogfight, for sure. Not only do you have all the environmental groups in opposition, but the solar and wind farmers and the nuclear plants, too. Everyone knows this power line will dampen other investments in renewables. All for Massachusetts and Rhode Island and New York, and not so much for the people who live here."

Fremont fumbled with his napkin; he was all nervous energy without a cigarette in his hand. "It's a goddamn extension cord through the state of Maine is what it is. Not to mention the Flagstaff dam drawdown, leaving us with a giant nasty ring around the lake." Alfie explained how the commissioner of the DEP had dropped the ball on that. The paperwork had not been filed on time, so it was now out of the State's control.

The waitress came to take their orders of eggs and bacon, home fries and toast. Pennie handed back the menus and said to her uncle, "Most of these towns don't even want the corridor. What happened to the will of the people?"

"When there's this kind of money at stake, the people's will goes out the window." He clasped his hands together. "You know this is going to be a difficult fight. The argument about whether this corridor serves a public benefit has already been decided in favor of the power company, and the Public Utilities Commission has given the green light."

Pennie took a sip of her steaming coffee. "That's so shortsighted."

"That's politics," said Fremont.

Alfie set down his mug. "About the only thing we've got in our back pocket is the historical easement on your property."

"Damn straight," said Fremont, coughing. "This is probably one of the oldest portage trails the Abenakis used for thousands of years, before Arnold's march. I can't tell you what this property meant to my father and grandfather." He drummed his fingers, deep in thought. "Spirits of our ancestors are on that land."

The dream came back to her of Arnold's men carrying bateaux, the march from East to Middle to West Carry, tired, ragged souls on their earnest march for independence. "I still can't believe they have the gall to call it the Independence Corridor when they're actually taking away the very right of personal property." She grabbed her laptop from her backpack to share pictures of the property she had taken. Fremont pointed out the boundary of his property between the ponds. "It's only a couple miles from West Carry to my camp on Middle."

"Looks pretty swampy."

"Sure is." Fremont nodded. "There's a wooded ridge, too. I'm sure it's less expensive for them to set poles on my property than over that ridge." Their breakfast came, and Fremont wasted no time digging in to his greasy sunny-side eggs, bacon, and hash browns. Alfie talked more about the political schemes. As far as he knew, Fremont's property was the final lot needed to complete the corridor.

After they finished breakfast, they all hopped onto the bench front seat of Fremont's Ford pickup with Pennie in the middle. Fremont squinted in the morning sun. "There's a logging road takes us over to the gated road where the appraiser is supposed to meet us, if he shows up." He lit his cigarette and cranked his window down, the air clear and cold, snow covering the ground, tires crunching. Jostled on the rough logging road for miles, passing giant tree-clearing equipment and gravel pits with views of the mountain ranges around them, they reached the Mountain Road. He stopped at a gate blocking passage, and soon the appraiser pulled up behind them in a brand-new cherry red pickup, riding high.

An older woman sat behind the wheel, graying around the temples, with fat cheeks and the jowls of a hound. She lowered her window and got right down to business, introducing herself as Sandy and sizing them up like maybe she was assessing them along with the property. Fremont waved his lit cigarette, asking her where she was from. Turns out she hailed from North New Portland, had lived around here her entire life, and knew these parts well. Fremont said, "You know about the Arnold Trail, do you?"

"Oh sure. Everyone knows about the Benedict Arnold Trail."

"Those men sacrificed their lives for our freedom," he said, smiling at her amiably.

She nodded and told him to lead the way. Sandy was all business.

They drove along the wooded, snow-covered ridge around the edge of a large pond. Pennie's mind drifted to her dream of the soldiers climbing over a gravelly serpentine ridge to reach East Carry Pond, then portaging to West Carry. When Fremont reached a junction, he took a narrow gravel road to cross a small bridge over a stream before coming upon his hunting cabin. There it sat, desolate and lovely against the dim sky and black pond, shiny with new ice, embraced by the quiet woods. Pennie felt a low vibration move through her.

Fremont wasted no time hoisting himself from his truck. Sandy had barely set a foot on the ground when he said, "Well, this is it. You can see the property stake we just passed." With clipboard in hand, she turned to face west with her back to them. She waved her arms like she was bringing in an airplane. "So, your forty acres runs long this way, northwesterly, from here to West Carry?"

"That's right. Goes right to the ridge. This property's been in my family since my grandfather bought it in 1907. This cabin here used to belong to the Ledge House fishing camps over on the Dead River. That's where my grandfather worked as a guide before they flooded the Dead." They followed his gaze off into the vista toward the twin peaks of Bigelow to the southwest.

Sandy hoisted her belt and walked past them, asking Fremont if the camp was locked.

"We never lock this place. Got no bolts nor barriers around here, Sandy. This is wild country. If a person or animal wants to make a nest inside, well, that's okay in my book. Never done much harm in more than a hundred years."

They let her explore the old camp to her heart's content, not much more than four walls, a woodstove and few windows. He motioned to the old woodshed on the side of the camp, saying it was the only thing his grandfather added to the camp in all his years hunting and fishing out here. "Knew these woods like the back of his hand. He had an uncanny bird's-eye sense of these woods, knew every crest and valley, every stream and bog and rivulet from the Kennebec River to the far side of the Dead River Valley. If there was anyone to teach you the ways and means of the woods, it was him." He coughed and leaned against his pickup, watching Sandy take out her measuring tape to run it along the wooden foundation of the camp, very meticulous with her clipboard checklist. "He was kind of a philosopher at heart, you know. Never had a bad word to say about no one, and instead of fighting over anything, he was a fan of talking it out." He laughed and coughed up phlegm before spitting. "The man never shot down an idea that was brought to him, no matter how silly."

Uncle Alfie remembered him as a fair man by all accounts. "He took me out fishing for the first time, and I caught a sizable brown trout over on East Carry."

They fell into their friendly banter, trading childhood stories about the days when things were much slower, when a family only had themselves and their nearest neighbors to survive the long Maine winters. Fremont spit again. "Isn't that what freedom is all about? Being your own man, working your own way through life on your own grit and determination without being reliant on someone to give you a job or send you power? Growing up, we never had any central power, and we were perfectly happy."

As they talked, Pennie let the spirit from the earth move up through her legs, her arms, her fingertips. She could feel the presence of Fremont's grandfather at the woodbox under the hush of the great fir trees shading the camp that, despite the relentless rain and snow, stood sturdy to shelter generations of hunters and fishers bunking down, leaving a footprint in these woods, the same paths forged by near-broken men with bateaux and Abenaki Natives living on these shores, portaging their way to family hunting grounds.

Sandy came out, her copious notes in hand, and nodded to signal that she was done. She hoisted herself into her big truck, thanked them, and drove off. Uncle Alfie assured Fremont that he could get his case heard by a judge. "But before that," he said, "is the county commissioners' meeting. We'll see how that turns out, then come up with a plan." He looked toward the vista of Bigelow. "You never know, Fremont, they might give you an offer you can't refuse on this old place."

Fremont was not interested in "just compensation." She knew the land meant more to him than any amount of money. In the front seat of the old pickup, the weight of the world seemed to sit squarely on Alfie's shoulders. In the distance, Pennie heard the rumble of a familiar ATV, the vibration, an uneasiness, moving through her.

A MELANCHOLY SET IN as she watched her uncle drive his Packard south. Even though she had her differences with Aunt Aggie, she still missed her and Aunt Maude and wondered about their weekly bridge games with the ladies in the club. Her phone buzzed. In came a text from Bri asking Pennie to pick her up at JD's place. Something about the tone of the text made her apprehensive.

Fremont drove down the long Varney driveway, thick with white pines on either side. Ahead of them appeared to be a large dead animal hanging from a hunter's hitch mount. As they drew closer, the hulk of a black bear's limp carcass came into view, hanging from a chain around its neck, hind feet nearly touching the ground. The teats of a mother sow came into focus. Fremont said, "Son of a bitch." Bri stood outside the garage with her backpack, rod dangling from the side, her dark eyes red and downcast. She hopped into the front seat beside Pennie.

Her grandfather jammed the truck into reverse. "Haven't you grown any common sense yet, and dumped this asshole?"

She blurted out, "I can't, Grandpa! I'm pregnant!" Her shoulders heaved and shook in great spasms. This was not how Pennie had expected the news to come out; she reached around Bri's scrunched shoulders in an awkward embrace.

He rolled down his window and lit a cigarette, trying to disguise the faint tremble in his hands. "Hush, now. It's not as bad as all that."

She leaned forward like she might vomit. "I don't know if I can go through with this."

He took a long drag, blowing out a stream, clouding the cab. "We've got time to sort this all out. It only seems bad when you're first faced with a thing."

"I should have told you, Grandpa, that I'm *engaged*." She held up her strong hand, her fingers limp, the diamond dull. Instead of smiling, she cried again, her gut wrenching inside out.

"What kind of guy asks for a hand in marriage without asking a father or grandfather first?" He shook his head at the calamity of it all.

She ignored him and rolled down her window. "I can't believe he shot that mother bear." Silence engulfed the cab, a steady beat of uneasiness in their quickening pulses. *Was this the bear they had seen on the trail with the three cubs ambling behind?* Fremont waited for her to continue with the whole story. "He said she was attacking him." Bri thumped the dash. "I told him I'd seen the bear over on the Round Barn trail, and he went out and *tracked her*. I know he did, I just know it."

Pennie's heart came up inside her throat. "What about the cubs?"

"He said they ran off." She shouted out the window. "I could kill him!"

"I suppose he baited that bear, too. Nothing but a lazy, quasi-hunter on an ATV."

Fremont had a way of sizing up a person in a few words. A few excruciating minutes ensued without an utterance between them, and as soon as he pulled in to the driveway, Bri flung the door open and ran to the house. By the time they got inside, she was already upstairs in the attic. Fremont broke kindling into smaller pieces to catch the embers at the bottom of the stove. When he blew on it, a flame lit and grew at his coaxing until the fire was large enough for a small log to catch. The bags under his eyes sagged to a new low. He shuffled to the bottom of the stairs and called for his granddaughter.

The stove crackled, the dull light of day showing through the paper-thin brown curtains. She eventually slunk down and sat in front of the fire with them. Bartholomew appeared out of nowhere and sprang up, taking a seat on her lap to give some comfort. Bri talked in fits and starts. She knew, even though bear-hunting season was still open to residents, it was wrong when he came home with the kill. She'd pressed him until he confessed there were cubs with the mother. "He acted like it was no big deal, that the cubs were big enough to survive on their own." The cat's tail curled up as she ran her shaking hand over his lumpy coat. Bri said she hardly knew this man, the father of her child.

"It's okay, sweetheart. No matter what, we'll figure this out. Just know that you do *not* have to stay in a bad situation. *Ever.*" Pennie wondered if he was thinking about Bri's mother at that moment, that maybe she'd been in a similar situation once. His tired, sagging eyes reflected tender love in his soft heart for his granddaughter, this rugged, vulnerable girl who touched him to the very core of his soul, much like Lena must have.

PENNIE CONVINCED BRI TO call in sick at the Gullet that night. When she showed up for her own shift, big-bottomed Betsy was standing at the bar, figuring out the schedule.

"Your cousin down and out, is she?"

Pennie tried to smile. "Bit of a headache, maybe a stomach thing."

"Some women just have weak constitutions." This brute of a woman always seemed to have all the answers, never short of an opinion. Pennie walked into the kitchen to begin her normal routine. Somehow, she looked forward to Shep's note on the fridge, his chunky block letters. At her chopping station, she thought about the bear hanging from the crossbar, chained by her neck, the shining eyes telling them she meant no harm that day, corralling her cubs into the thick wood.

Chopping in smooth motions with her wrist, up and down, in a newfound rhythm, she heard the low voices of men through the vent. It was JD again, with another man, jabbering about the fall hunt, JD boasting about his bear. "What a beautiful sow she is. My fiancée told me where she'd spotted her, so me and the boys went out and set our bait. Didn't take long for her to come out for the honeypot. Took her down fast, pa-pow, pa-pow-pow-pow." The sound of palms slapping together. "Then three cubs in another round."

Pennie's ire grew.

The other fellow, in a low gravelly voice, said, "Damn straight. Man's got to have his bear meat for the winter. That hide'll fetch you a nice price."

"Oh, I don't eat bear meat. Hate the taste, but I'll be able to sell it, for sure. I just like the thrill of the kill, and the mount, of course." The man offered to buy the meat for the right price, and that's when JD began his negotiations. His voice lowered, and she heard bits and pieces: "...the power corridor...renewable hydro energy...the best thing for our community...that crazy Fremont character."

The low gravelly voice said, "If he was out of the way, you'd have a clear shot."

"Working on that," said JD. Then the sound of the stools scraping the floor, their voices rising again. "Good to see you, young man."

"It's at the butcher in Eustis. You can pick it up there. My fiancée is none too happy with me right now. Women never understand the thrill of the kill."

Pennie peeked over the saloon doors to see JD hand the man a manila envelope, just like the one that the pastor had given him. The man laughed. "Best thing to tame that spirit is a raft of kids."

She ran back to her station as the men left the restaurant and picked up the knife, thinking how good it must feel to kill. Angry and distracted, she sliced her thumb and nearly yelled in surprise, watching red stream onto the cutting board and over the potato wedges. At the sink she ran it under the cold water, wincing. The last thing she needed was Shep coming in to see blood.

The Band-Aids were in the cupboard, and she wrapped her thumb in a tight tourniquet to stop the bleeding. His thump, thump came through the doorway, whiskey in hand. He took one look at her hand and asked if she'd mastered the knife yet. She didn't bother to answer, keeping her distance as much as humanly possible at the plating station. Between the mason jar incident and JD's latest macho hunting spectacle, her animosity toward this family was growing like a barn burner. Around and around in her mind, she considered quitting that night, until calming herself down long enough to realize how much she was discovering about all of them, mainly the favored son.

BACK AT FREMONT'S CABIN, she crept in the dark, around the glow and sounds of the fire popping, his wheezing. She hoped Bri was still awake. Up the narrow stairs, she found the warm attic empty, the strong smell of weed still lingering. The middle of Bri's pink bed was still depressed from the imprint of her body, her polka-dotted pillow sunk in the middle. Thoughts of possible situations whirled through her mind. Did she just need to get some air? Did she have another friend she'd gone to see? Was she upset enough to do anything drastic?

Pennie pulled out her phone to text her and nearly immediately got a text back: *No worries, everything is fine! JD picked me up. He explained everything to me. Just a misunderstanding. Call you tomorrow!* She ended the chain with lots of hearts and smiley faces.

Pennie let a long sigh escape, but it did not relieve the stress of knowing Bri was still fooled by his lies. She took out her laptop to see the pictures she'd taken that day. There stood Fremont and Uncle Alfie under the shadows of bare oak tree branches and giant firs, leaning on the woodbox, their friendly banter alive on their lined faces. Then Sandy, surveyor of the lands, confident and detached by self-importance. Behind her, in the doorway of the camp, a ghostly image appeared, what looked like the shape of a man with a pipe. In the next frame, he stood outside the camp, a flickering image of a shape standing between Fremont and Uncle Alfie at the woodpile.

These ghostly vibrations inside the digital photos wouldn't last for long, she knew, from the ones she had taken in the past. As fast as they appeared, they vanished forever. Her eyes grew heavy, and she let herself drift and sway until she was back at the cabin on a winter day, the snow lightly falling, a small team of horses standing hitched to a wagon...

Two men loaded in bundles of supplies and guns, and a birchbark canoe, murmuring hopes of finding a bull at the end of the fall rut. Papa smoked a pipe and whistled to her, and she jumped into the wagon to sit behind him and another man he called Longtoe, the horses plodding down the well-trodden trail of Middle Carry, the hunters glad for the wind to sweep away their scent in the moose-calling season. The smell of ripe rabbit and fox and bear all around in the great forest, Papa ruffled her coat to calm her down, and Longtoe said, "Dogs are good luck on a moose hunt, if they know how to stay very quiet and respect the moose."

The wind picked up and the snow whirled around them gaily in the turn of early winter, the horses leading them over the hunting trail through old boreal woods, sure-footed, their coats gleaming and twitching under the bleak sun. Great pine trees creaked, sheltering them for a few miles before they reached an opening where Longtoe pointed to the old Abenaki hunting ground for moose. After riding through the brush and down toward the shore of West Carry as far as they could go before the thicket, they jumped down. Longtoe lithely drew the birchbark canoe from the wagon, over his head and onto his shoulders, positioning the weight with his lean arms before heading into the woods and water. She and Papa followed close behind with rifles.

On the shorefront, they dropped the canoe to let it balance on the black turbulent water, the snow still falling lightly, dissolving on the open pond, the temperature just above freezing. She jumped to the middle of the canoe, and the men paddled away, Longtoe steering in the stern, the scent of the ducks, beaver and badger, giant trout below the surface of the dark water, the landlocked salmon like silver serpents gliding under them, small pickerel and perch darting around the canoe. Papa warned her to be still, his voice low and kind.

The intense, gamey scent of the bull moose wafted around until they spotted him swimming toward the reedy opposite shore of the pond, his rack a massive crown. They paddled with long, quick strokes, patiently watching the bull climb onto the bank and take off into the woods for the chase, his great waddling snout dripping. At the shoreline, Papa guided the canoe onto the reeds to unload with their guns, searching for the tracks in the mud that she sniffed out, the footprints of the running massive bull wide apart. Into the woods they flew swiftly, tracking the moose, and sometimes doubling back and moving forward again to keep their scent hidden, the constant wind through the pines rustling and moaning, hiding the sounds of their movements and their smell.

They walked for a mile or more through the thick, gnarly woods until Longtoe stopped and peeled a large piece of bark from a birch tree and rolled it into a cone, pressing it to his mouth to let out a long bawling sound like a cow in mating season. They tread softly on the snow as he continued to bawl until, finally, they heard the moose moving toward them, thrashing in the bush, getting louder. Papa took out his rifle as the great moose, his giant antlers, came into sight within a hundred yards, through the tangle of branches and trees. He aimed and shot, the sound ringing for miles and miles, the heavy beast dropping vividly, branches cracking and snapping to his enormous frame, giving way to the sprawling palm of his antlers.

They ran between the birches and fir trees to the great bull lying on his side, his floppy ears, broad snout, and noble throat flap, the bullet hole through his breast, shot clean in the heart. Longtoe began his ceremonial chant, bowing to the moose for his offering to them and to the Great Spirit, revering the beast for his peaceful wild nature, thanking the pond and the woods and the Great Spirit for the bequest. With his sharpened knife in hand, he sliced off the head of the beast through the neck in one clean cut before carefully skinning the hide with the strong, easy strokes of his sharp knife, down the back and around the massive body. Together, they removed the rough, scarred hide in one piece, and Papa folded it, bundling it into his pack. Longtoe drew and quartered the animal, the soupy blood and guts falling over the boughs, removing the heart, kidney, liver, intestines, and entrails—every piece and part of the great animal of the northern forest kept for food or medicine—even the sinew for bow strings.

Papa loaded flour sacks with the meat and organs, the bones and hide, their work swift and without a word spoken between them in their ritual, making several trips back and forth to their birchbark canoe on the shore, carrying and loading all the remains of the great creature into the hull. Finally, Longtoe cut the great six-pronged antlers off the beast's head and left the enormous paddles with their twenty points on the floor of the woods, under a grandfather oak tree, as an offering to the Great Spirit, the giver of life.

The men paddled in haste to the shoreline, retracing their steps through the woods where the horses stood under the covered pine canopy, whinnying at their return. She barked to proclaim their success tracking and conquering the great moose, as Longtoe ran his strong, capable hand down her long, furry spine in gratitude and celebration for the gift they had been given, chanting to the spirit riding in the wind.

THE SUN SQUINTED THROUGH her attic window. Visions of the hunt moved around her mind, the bull moose falling among the trees in slow motion, offering up his life in sacrifice to the virtuous hunters. She heard her phone vibrate and hoped it was Bri, but instead, it was a text from Owen, asking her if she wanted to ski. Outside her window, fresh snow covered the lake.

Downstairs, the woodstove roared, but Fremont was nowhere to be found. Probably out for breakfast or maybe getting another load of wood to add to his never-ending pile. She'd kept her ski equipment in her car and so got herself dressed, thinking about Bri and what JD may have told her. What had he made up? Outside, the day was clear and bright. Skiing was not a date, she assured herself. The last thing she wanted to do was lead Owen on.

She wished Dani and Mali were close so she could see them, talk to them about the bear. They would know what to do, what to say to

Bri. And what about Fremont? Should she tell him the conversation she'd overheard between JD and that commissioner? What about the one before, the pastor? It seemed that she and the church were using JD to bribe this man to vote in favor of the corridor. And JD was lying about it to everyone, saying he was on the side of the town.

When she reached the ticket counter, Owen was already there waiting for her with a ticket in hand. "What's up?"

She was starting to get annoyed with this game but shook it off. "Not much, you? How much do I owe you?"

"Nothing. I get freebies from the mountain after working here so many years."

That uneasy feeling of owing someone something crept up on her, but she didn't want to be rude. "That's kind of you. At least I can buy lunch."

"Well, I kinda got that figured out, too." He pointed to the pack on his back saying he wanted to take her to the snowfields for the day. She looked up at the blanketed slope, thanks to snowmaking, and said she was up for anything that did not involve rocks or cliffs. He laughed at her with his goofy smile, his ridged nose like the small crest of a hill. One thing was for sure, he did not put on any pretense like his brother. Conversation easily moved between them, and she knew she was always getting the real Owen.

On the chairlift, they talked about the Gullet and how difficult it could be working with his parents. She told him about the frying pan incident in the kitchen, and he apologized, saying he had no idea that had happened. "Betsy and Shep have always fought like that. Neither would be happy in a peaceful, amicable relationship. You know what I mean? All they know is the fight."

"But you're not a fighter. You seem so chill, so unlike your brother."

"He can be a bit much, but he does have a way with people. We're kind of like polar opposites."

"Did you hear about the bear he killed?"

"Oh, yeah. Not surprised." He scraped the top of his skis with his poles as if deciding whether to go on. "When he was a kid, he was constantly killing rodents with his BB gun. But when he killed a neighbor's cat, well, that was the end of the BB gun."

Pennie's stomach churned. "So he's always been sadistic."

Owen gave her a resigned smile behind his thick, fogged glasses. "Seems that way, but he's not all that bad."

The image of JD at the bar with his chums, Owen waiting on them, came to her mind. "You must make good tips at the restaurant, keeps you around."

"I do okay, and I get to ski during the week. Don't know if I'd be happier in any other place." He talked about his camp over on the Carrabassett River, just below the bridge. "My grandfather's old camp. When Shep and Betsy built the new house, I took the camp over."

"That doesn't seem fair. JD living in the new house."

"I wanted to stay in the old place. Suits me just fine. Besides, I already spend way too much time with my family."

They unloaded at the top, and she followed him up the rise, over the knoll of the backside where it was ungroomed and wild, the snow swirling in great torrents. "A bit windy today, but the conditions are decent. Shouldn't be too many rocks." The vista of Burnt Mountain and other smaller peaks lay below the terrain of scrubby pines and rocks in the open snowfield. He strapped on his goggles over his thick glasses, smiling wide before pointing his boards downhill, and she followed his lead, skirting along the left side of the trail where the snow was deeper. It took her a few minutes to get her skis under her, around the grassy patches here and there in the early season. By the time he stopped five minutes later, she was winded. "What a workout," she breathed. The wind and gusts of snowy drift swept up under them.

Across the open slope to the woods on the right, tracks led down an open shaft between the great pines. She had to slow herself down to make the winding turns without plowing face first into a tree. He waited for her below, at the opening. Winded again, she laughed, trying to catch her breath. "Nothing like a challenge, Owen. *Jesus.*"

"I think Jesus would like this skiing, don't you? He was a bit of a rebel."

She pictured Betsy with her cross around her neck. He seemed to be making fun of it, like he never took himself, his family, and anything too seriously. And maybe that was the difference between him and his family. While his mother and brother were trying to prove their dominance in all things, he was trying to stay under the radar and sane, just by staying grounded, avoiding the silly power plays that took up so much energy, created so much havoc and anger. Owen was a realist like his stepfather, without the temper.

Out on the wild backside of the mountain, making tracks between the clusters of trees, he was at his very best. There was nothing like being with someone who was in their element, who wanted to show you their own version of happiness, of being at one with their environment. He followed a chute, taking a windy path down, crosscutting the mountain. They skied for nearly an hour before they reached the base, slipping toward a chairlift that would take them to the summit again.

Up at the top, the wind died down. He showed her another trail to the backside, between trees, that only a backcountry skier would know. Though the area was clearly off-limits, Owen waved to a ski patrol, and they were on their way over the knoll and down into the trees again, moving in smooth turns on fresh tracks that Owen had probably made the day before. Again, he led her across the backside, and they skied for a while out in the bright sun, making tracks on the windswept ridge until they reached a flat expanse. He stopped and nodded toward a giant flat rock. They were both starving.

Taking their skis off, they gained purchase on the indentations in the rock, climbing in their clumsy boots. He helped her to the top where the rock face was warm and the sun hit their faces. From his pack, he took out baggies of cheese and crackers, carrots and pear slices, lettuce and turkey wraps, setting everything on the space between them.

"I'm impressed," she said, waiting patiently as he took out two bottles of beer.

"Stole everything from the Gullet fridge."

"Why am I not surprised?"

"Want a beer?"

"Am I going to be able to make it down after this? I did tell you about my near-death experience last spring, right?"

"Don't worry, we'll take it slow from here, stay out of the trees."

From their vantage, he pointed out the direction of the great Mount Bigelow range to the north side of Sugarloaf, Flagstaff Lake on the other side. To his far right, he pointed in the direction of the Great Carrying Place and traced his finger along the imaginary line of the Arnold Expedition from Bog Brook to the Dead River and what was now the Long Falls Dam. Sweeping west with his imaginary line, he followed Flagstaff and what used to be the path of the winding Dead River, through the ghost towns to Arnold Falls on the other end of Flagstaff. "It's amazing to think they did this route half-starving to death and carrying those four-hundred-pound bateaux. Talk about perseverance."

Her dreams flashed in her mind. "All in the name of freedom from oppression, from having to live under some king's rule."

"I don't know how people can be so out of touch with that today." He stretched and lay back on the rock under a glowing sun. "That's what I love about living up here in these woods. We're so removed, like we're in a forest oasis from the rest of the world. Did you know that we're sitting in the largest contiguous temperate forest in the country?"

She lay back on the rock beside him and drank in the great expanse of Mount Bigelow. "That's what I've heard."

"Yeah, over ten million acres. We're almost ninety percent forested in Maine. From these North Woods rise our fourteen highest peaks, like the one we're sitting on."

"You sound like a real tree hugger."

He laughed. "Don't repeat that. My family thinks I'm gone in the head because I have all this useless information, especially when it comes to our woods and waters."

"I don't think it's useless."

He turned to her and put his hand on hers. She flinched, wishing he hadn't done that but not wanting to make him feel uncomfortable.

"I, um, am coming off a few bad relationships. Please don't take this the wrong way." He stretched his arms backward, awkward, as she tried to change the subject. "Have you ever studied this stuff, like in college? You'd be a great teacher."

Abruptly, he sat up on the rock and pulled his knees up, hugging them. "No, I was never much for the classroom. Couldn't concentrate. My home is here on the mountain. I can't imagine ever leaving here, for any reason."

She sat up beside him. "I could never finish school either, flunked out of veterinary school and couldn't even hold down a job as a vet technician. Now I'm here trying to help Fremont save his property, but I'm really just a lost soul." She reached for his hand in a kind gesture. "Thank you for asking me here today. This has been amazing, getting to ski with you."

A wave of something came over his face, and he locked eyes with her just for a second before darting away, out toward the vista again. Without a second thought, he stood on his long legs to strap on his skis, and she followed. More than anything, she wanted to remain his friend.

AT WORK THAT NIGHT, she barely had a chance to talk to Bri, who ran between tables, breathless, taking orders from her customers and Betsy. After the final dinners were served and Shep left, Pennie sat down on a stool at the plating station and surveyed the mess, utterly exhausted from the day on the mountain.

Bri showed up to look over the swinging doors, asking if everything was okay with Fremont. She never stepped foot in the kitchen, but spoke over the shoulder-high doors, winsomely, as if everything was just perfect in her life. JD was there, of course, and he had to get going, so she was leaving now, avoiding Pennie and any further conversation about the bear incident or her relationship with the father of her child.

Owen helped Pennie clean up the kitchen without much talk. Both exhausted, they bid each other a good night's sleep, and she found her way along the dark Eustis roads back to Fremont's cabin to fill the stove and tuck his memory quilt around him, his chest gurgling in his sleep, Bartholomew nestled in with him, tracking her in the dark. Feeling as weary as a warrior who had marched a hundred miles, she folded her legs under the woolen blanket, the glow of a full snow moon casting the long shadow of a tree branch on the floor, her mind drifting into a dream of flying over the Dead River, the water below raging in a torrent along its twisting and turning curves, its banks swollen with rain...

She dropped down into the little house, inside the body of the husky lying on the floor next to the bed of Papa and Mama, fast asleep, the only sounds the swift river outside, the lonely howl of a wolf, the familiar call of a long-eared owl, the snapping twigs of deer roaming. The first blue glow of morning came into Dead River, the night sounds fading away, replaced by buzz saws and chopping axes. Outside the window, the desecrated hills around them echoed, miles and miles of forestland cleared, nothing but hundreds of stumps, the chopping and sawing and felling of trees growing more distinct, agonizing, until Papa was up and out of bed. He dressed in his pants and flannels, his mackinaw, layers against the cold fall winds outside where a crew of at least twenty men cleared the great downed trees, the expanse around them growing wider and wider, removing their shelter of old-growth forest on the river valley all the way up to a red line in the distance, a blood red line that stretched all the way along the high ridge around the houses and barns of the settlement.

Mama was there in her wool coat with Fremont and Fannie, now grown half a foot taller, all with misty eyes at the destruction of their homeland. Papa drew them around him. "Never thought I'd see the day."

"What's the red line, Papa?"

"That's how far they're clearing for the water rise once the dam is built."

Mama began to cry as she desperately hugged Fannie, at the thought of losing the only home she'd ever known. "How can they do this to us? How can they just take our land, our homes, if we don't want to sell?"

"They don't care about us. But I'll tell you one thing, they ain't forcing us out without a fight." He turned to scan all the empty neighbors' houses

around them, those who had sold out and left town. "We're staying as long as we can. I will not have my family forced from our rightful land, the land our parents settled here to make a life for us, the generations of hard work and sacrifice they're trying to drown from our lives and our memories, to line their own godforsaken pockets."

Chapter 11
The Clearcut

WHEN SHE SAT UP on the creaky twin, all her joints hurt. She limped down the narrow stairway, one agonizing step at a time, to find Fremont sitting at the kitchen table, dressed and ready for the day. He blew out a long stream of smoke and eyed her curiously. "What ails *you*?"

She poured some coffee from the glass decanter, which seemed cloudier than ever. "It's the curse of the back snowfields." Bartholomew jumped on the counter, looking for a scratch as he rubbed his head against Pennie's arm.

"Didn't know you were a backcountry skier."

"I'm not. Owen talked me into it."

"That kid's quite a shredder from what I hear."

"He certainly knows his way around the snowfields."

Fremont's dazed expression told her that he was not thinking about their conversation but about his granddaughter, the young, effusive woman with so many dreams who seemed to have walked straight down a path of no return. Outside the kitchen window, the iced lake sat snow covered. "I had a dream last night about power company men clear cutting around the homes in the Dead River settlement."

"Remember it like it was yesterday. Looked like a war zone. My father was one of the holdouts, refused to move us, making a point that we would not be displaced, you know. It was a terrible time." Rheumy eyed, he took a long drag and brushed away the ashes that had fallen on the newspaper. He flicked his cigarette in the Hills Bros. can. "Anyhow, we have that transmission line public hearing coming up tonight in Farmington."

She'd nearly forgotten about it. The conspiratorial voices of JD and the commissioner ran through her mind. "I think JD knows one of the commissioners."

"Wouldn't surprise me."

"I guess I should get the night off from work."

Fremont chuckled. "Shep won't be too happy about that."

"Yeah, well he can deal with it for one night." She pictured him throwing the cast iron pan across the kitchen, wishing he had thrown it directly at his wife. "I need a break from that snakes' nest over there. You know what they say, too many cooks in the kitchen."

"You don't have to tell me."

She accompanied him to the local library to look through newspaper articles that had been written since the Battle of the Power Corridor began. Fremont had read all of them and seemed to be a virtual catalog of information. He made notes for his talking points while she skimmed article after article about the back-and-forth between the powers that be and the environmentalists. From what she could tell, about a year ago the giant hydroelectric company in Canada had made some kind of pact with the State's public advocate and governor's energy office for what they called a "benefits package" in exchange for allowing the corridor through the western woods. The backroom deal included EV charging stations, heat pumps, workforce development, and broadband expansion—a package supposedly worth over a quarter million dollars to Maine taxpayers. She recalled the woman from the power company detailing the savings at the town hall. Fremont called it "lipstick on a pig."

Reading about the history of the Public Utilities Commission, or PUC, she recalled the Fernald Law, which once prohibited export of the state's "white gold," or water power, to other states. Governor Bert Fernald and Representative (later Governor) Percival Baxter were conservationists behind the law to protect waterways like the Dead River from exploitation. But when a new governor, Frederick Plaisted, came into power, he formed the PUC for the expansion of private utilities to help along hydroelectric companies like those owned by Walter Wyman. Anyone who wanted to keep State control of the waterways was called a socialist.

Fast-forward to today. The PUC and Army Corp of Engineers had already issued permits on the corridor project, claiming Maine would see energy savings of up to $44 million each year. Other "benefits," they insisted, were better electricity transmission, an increase in local jobs, spending of nearly $1 million during construction, and no impact whatsoever on other renewable energy development. Pennie wondered how on earth they came up with these numbers, but what the hell did she know about pie-in-the-sky economic models? The more she read, the more the numbers seemed like nothing more than hopped-up promises.

Nearly 80 percent of the planned corridor was inside unorganized territories like Fremont's property. A high-voltage direct-current transmission line, with a capacity of 1,500 megawatts, would cross over a hundred acres of mostly undeveloped forestland between Canada and the Great Carrying Place.

Pennie glanced over to see Fremont fidgeting over his notes. Doodling, he drew a little red Revolutionary flag with a pine tree in the canton, just like the one Arnold's men raised along the Dead River in the fall of 1775. The Independence Corridor had ignited one of the most expensive battles over Maine's woods and waterways in the history of the state.

The power company had spent almost half a million dollars already on permitting, construction, and labor, not to mention the public ad campaigns.

She read they went so far as to threaten the people of Maine, warning of some supposed economic fallout if the corridor was killed. The truth was, only southern New England would benefit—densely populated states looking for greener, and more affordable, electricity. According to the giant hydropower company, with their five hundred dams and twenty reservoirs, electricity was "spilling over" their dams because they had too much capacity. Skimming an article about the history of hydroelectricity in the Northeast, Pennie read how Canada, like Maine, had flooded millions of acres of forests to build dams and how over time, as the forests decompose, greenhouse gases—carbon dioxide and methane—are released into the atmosphere, not to mention methylmercury, the poisonous mercury that collects in fish. She sent the article link to Dani and Mali.

THE HEARING THAT NIGHT was with the Maine Department of Environmental Protection and the Land Use Planning Commission for the unorganized territories, an hour's drive away in Farmington, at the University of Maine campus there. The rumble of the old Ford engine kept Pennie and Fremont grounded along the drive, nothing but snow-covered pine trees along the clear, dry roadway. The parking lot was nearly full, but Fremont found a spot in the back, and they followed a steady line of people into the Lincoln Auditorium.

Fremont added his name to the sign-up sheet before they found a seat near the front of the university lecture hall. A long, draped table ran parallel to the stage behind. He shook hands with several men and women he knew from town, all there to oppose the corridor. One man with a long gray beard leaned toward Fremont and said, "Give those fuckers hell."

The noise grew louder as a few hundred guests found seats in the lecture hall, mostly locals wearing jeans and flannels. Soon members of DEP and LUPC filed in to sit at the table up front. Just before the meeting began, JD walked in and up the aisle to stand in the back.

A DEP official sat in the middle of the red-skirted table and thanked everyone for coming. He wore a black suit jacket and black shirt against his shock of white hair. Speaking with congenial stiffness, he explained the permitting process for the Independence Corridor, welcoming public comments from anyone who wanted to address the region's character, wildlife habitat, fisheries, and recreation. Rumblings from the crowd, shifting feet, and coughing filled the room until the speaker asked everyone to settle. He called the first name on the list, Mr. Everett Wing.

A slight man with bushy gray hair and wire spectacles, dressed in a yellow chamois shirt and red suspenders, approached the microphone at the bottom of the stairs. He spoke hesitantly at first, stating his name and his address in the Wyman Township, not far from Long Falls Dam. "My family has had a camp on Halfway Brook since 1902, when my great-grandfather built it. The corridor you're planning is only a mile and half from my property and, to put it lightly, I'm concerned about the power lines traversing near our land and over the Dead." He adjusted his glasses, shifted his feet. "I wonder if the lease agreement between the power company and the Bureau of Parks and Rec is even legal." He looked around the room, disregarding his notes. "Like most everyone in this hall, I'm dead set against clear-cutting a swath through our woods. It's a threat to our deer and moose herds and black bears, not to mention the native brook trout. The hundred-forty-mile proposed line will cross no less than ninety-nine streams, two hundred wetlands, vernal pools, and deer wintering areas.

"I've been fly fishing all my life. If the woods around these ponds and streams are cleared, the water temperature will rise and the trout will die, not to mention the weed killers they use for clearing that destroy the wild fish and the insects they feed on, and contaminate our water supply. Around here, hikers come cross-country to enjoy the Bigelow mountains. Camping, fishing, canoeing, skiing, and snowmobiling. We have the largest forest east of the Mississippi. You talk about climate change. The power company wants to replace our trees, our natural carbon dioxide filters, with hundred-foot transmission towers, towers you'll see from almost every peak on Bigelow. Most of us live here because it's one of the last holdouts from industry. I ask this commission not to approve the permitting of our territories for this power corridor, a corridor that only benefits states to our south and the power corporations. Thank you."

The lean man in suspenders stepped away from the microphone. The audience rumbled. High vibrations in the room lent an air of positive charge. One by one, more opponents came to the microphone, from landowners to foresters to family sawmill operators, objecting to the damage the corridor would do.

A clean-shaven middle-aged man with slicked hair stood up to the microphone, introducing himself as Brett Townsend from Carrabassett Valley. Pennie recognized him immediately as one of JD's ATV buddies. He puffed out his chest. "As the owner of Spencer Rips Whitewater Rafting, we offer a hundred-twenty miles of class-four rafting in the wilderness, along with lodging and camping. As this commission is aware, my company has reached an agreement with the power company for donations and concessions if the corridor is approved. They've offered to donate eight million dollars or more for recreation and ecology programs to help our tourism and provide more opportunities for better access to recreation in western Maine.

"I would like to speak about the positive impacts the project will have on the scenic and recreational value of this area." He cleared his throat and straightened his back. "The power company has already addressed the environmental concerns, agreeing to buffer the power lines that cross the Dead River with ten-foot-high brush, and we believe this will maintain the quality of the experience for our customers. Many come from Massachusetts and are used to seeing the lines and dams where rafting trips begin and end. They understand that this development is necessary, and for their personal benefit."

The crowd rumbled in discontent again. Someone shouted, "Go back to your own state!"

The flatlander continued. "This forest they claim is *untouched* and *pristine* has actually been clear-cut for generations. And the power company is doing this in a reasonable way that will minimally impact our wilderness, while providing excellent routes for snowmobilers and ATV riders. We feel that this transmission line will help improve opportunities, increase economic development and eco-tourism. We ask that the commission and DEP grant the permits necessary for this green energy project. Thank you."

Fremont leaned into Pennie's ear. "Bought and paid for," he whispered.

Then a representative for a hydropower environmental group stood up to the mic and, tugging on her suit jacket and adjusting her black frames, introduced herself as Dr. Karoline Jennings. "As you know, there have been enormous climate disasters in the last decade, everything from monstrous forest fires to massive flooding and fatal heat waves. We are at a point in history where we must make some hard decisions to save our planet, and as a state who prides itself on ecotourism, we can make a huge difference for generations to come by allowing this hydro-connect corridor to move forward."

She looked down at her notes. "Along with the southern New England states, Maine has committed to net-zero carbon emissions by 2050. If Maine jumps on board, we can be a part of this solution. When we convert fossil fuel power to electricity supplied by hydro dams, we are supplying our electric grid with green decarbonization. Not only will we be moving toward a zero-greenhouse-gas future but increasing our electrical transmission capacity in Maine and lowering our own electricity costs. We can think of it as sharing the load with other New England states, working together to lower greenhouse gas emissions. Electricity from Canadian hydropower is a key driver to a renewable energy planet, complementing the development of solar and wind power. Thank you."

Finally, Fremont's name was called. He walked to the microphone and stood there for a few moments looking along the lengthy line of panelists seated facing them.

"Hello, ladies and gentlemen." He scratched his white beard and looked back at the few hundred people sitting behind him. "My name's Fremont Safford, and I've been living in the Dead River Valley area the entire eighty-six years of my brief young life." The audience chuckled. "I say brief and young because, in the grand scheme of things, that's exactly what it's been. When you consider the Native tribes who lived here for thousands of years before our ancestors, we white settlers have a very short history on this land. But we've certainly taken it over like we've been here forever, haven't we?" The crowd shuffled, a few coughs here and there. The panelists looked down at their notes.

"As most of you already know, the famous Arnold Expedition came through this area via the Kennebec River, across the Great Carrying Place, paddling the winding Dead River and up to cross the Height of Land at the Canadian border attempting to capture Quebec City. You also probably know that their mission was not successful, that roughly fifty men died, and another five hundred were wounded or turned back in starvation on the treacherous route, and that the Dead River they navigated in 1775 is now Flagstaff Lake, impounded by the power company in 1949. My parents and grandparents and great-grandparents helped settle the Dead River Valley. They were woodsmen and -women who worked their entire lives, only for the power company to come and force them out."

The vibration in the room began to rise.

"Now, today, we have the power company coming in again, threatening to slash a large swath through our woods from Canada down to Flagstaff to my family property at the Great Carrying Place, all in the name of progress. I've heard some interesting testimony tonight, and I'm willing to bet all the fine people who want to drive this swath through our woods don't have families who've been here for generations. The power company thinks in terms of dollars and cents, while we think in terms of hard work and common sense, a way of life you seem hell-bent on destroying."

He thumped the microphone and the enthusiastic crowd clapped loudly.

"This country has a short-term memory problem. We've forgotten those Revolutionary soldiers who fought and died for our freedom from the English despots who used the power of wealth to diminish any individual rights we had. It's a simple concept. Individual rights. That's what's at stake here. When did it become okay to take another person's property? Not only mine, but every person who lives in these unorganized territories covering half of the state of Maine. People have told you loud and clear that we overwhelmingly *do not want this corridor*. From what I can see, the governor is pushing it through."

He pointed to the panelists. "I tell you what the problem is about; it's about individual values. The people who live here value the property we have over—what did that lady call it?" He looked back at the audience until he spotted Dr. Jennings. "Our *shared environmental future*. Don't tell me how I"—he thumped his chest—"should *feel* about this, goddammit. Do you have God's measuring stick in your possession? Do you know what *my* values are? The power company is taking our land, and once they're in here with their destructive machines, their giant poles and wires, there's no going back. You all-knowing kings are taking it by force, totally disregarding our rights as residents in these territories, claiming your righteous reasons. All you're doing is rigging the system in your own favor for profit."

A few people whistled and clapped. The man on the panel in the black suit hit his gavel a few times before the crowd yelled for Fremont to continue.

"You've forgotten what our forefathers and the soldiers on the great march through these parts were fighting for. *Individual rights. Property rights.* Not some kind of *social welfare* project. Don't sit there and tell me I'll be better off, or my grandchildren will be better off, when you destroy our forest. You'll be lying just like the power company did when it told my father and grandfather that they were going to make electricity at that Flagstaff dam. All that lake is, all it has ever been, is a reservoir, an impounding pool, nothing more. Now you're putting a superhighway of power through our state to supply southern New England. I'm asking you, before it's too late, to give the people of Maine their power back. Once you let that slip away, it's gone forever."

A few people stood, and the swell grew like a cataract. At least three-quarters of the auditorium erupted with a standing ovation. He came back to sit beside Pennie and never cracked a smile but continued to look at the panelists for their reaction.

A man from the commission took the mic at the table and introduced himself as Geoff Skelton in a low gravelly voice. A small alarm bell went off in Pennie's head; she'd seen this man somewhere before, heard his deep voice. "Listen folks," he said, "we're all fighting the same demons of climate change and global warming in this room." She wracked her brain for a minute before she looked back at JD, who was in the back of the room standing and watching, his arms crossed. Geoff was the voice of the man she'd heard talking with JD at the restaurant about the bear, the stranger who'd taken the envelope.

Commissioner Skelton waited until the crowd settled down and said, "I can certainly understand how you feel, Fremont, and as commissioners, we're trying to weigh the rights of all our citizens against very real long-term consequences of climate change." He expounded more about saving the planet until he ended the public hearing, giving everyone a toll-free number to call with further comment. Men and women of all ages stood, rumbling with discontent, and slowly filed out of the auditorium. Fremont shook hands with at least ten people on their way out.

As soon as they were inside his pickup with the doors closed, Pennie said, "That guy, Commissioner Skelton, was in the restaurant meeting with JD about the corridor."

"Skelton met with JD? When was this?" "Just yesterday. I'm certain it was him. JD gave him an envelope."

He ran his hands over the steering wheel, watching trucks leave the parking lot. "Why doesn't this surprise me?"

She looked at her phone. It was almost nine, but she dialed her uncle's number anyway, picturing him in his recliner with his glass of bourbon, hoping he was still awake. He picked up on the second ring.

"I've been waiting to hear from you. How'd it go?"

Pennie told him all about the testimony, and the riveting speech Fremont gave that brought the auditorium to its feet. Then she described the commissioner's remarks and the conversation she overheard between him and JD, the manila envelope that Pastor Laurel had given to JD, that JD passed along to this guy. "I'm ninety-nine percent positive this is the same guy."

"Looks like you've got your work cut out for you. I'll do a little background check on Commissioner Skelton and give you a call tomorrow. Tell Fremont he'll need to hold on to his testimony for our day in court. I'm expecting it'll be sooner than later, the way the power company is pushing this through." Then Pennie remembered what she'd heard Skelton say about Fremont being the last thing in the way of the corridor, but instead of worrying Fremont about it, she kept it to herself. For now.

A fitful sleep overtook her as she fell into an agitated wash of anxiety and doom...sinking into the Dead River Valley through the eyes of the husky...

She sat in the bow of a canoe. Papa paddled down the winding Dead, swarms of men on either side clear-cutting the brush and the forests uphill to the red line. On the riverbank, the Viles Timber lumbermill, once stacked with millions of feet of lumber, was nothing more than a giant mound of wet sawdust, an afterthought. Past the bend of the river sat the Ledge House and Cabins, once a hunting and fishing lodge, now packed with trucks, cars, and logging machines, headquarters for the Hinman Highway construction crew hired by the power company for the demolition. A loud blast from downstream sent vibrations under the riverbed, shaking the canoe. She cried out in fear, the ringing from the explosion reverberating down the valley. "It's okay, girl. Those bastards are dynamiting a hellhole through that ledge for the dam."

Ahead sat the Fud Taylor farm, the grand hotel built in the 1800s, once the Bigelow House open year-round for vacationers, rusticators, sportsmen, and their guides, now a vacant and desolate windowless building ready for demolition. Papa paddled through the labyrinthine curves of the river that had carved out this passageway over thousands of years, a route for the Natives, for the hunters and fishers of generations. Houses sat high on blocks preparing to move, the pretty little farms once owned by the Daggetts and Withams, Saffords and Wymans, Taylors and Dexters and Beans, with their empty pastures and hollow barns, thousands of acres now cleared farmland.

Papa sunk his paddle in the crystal clear blue-black river, passing by the little schoolhouse with the hip roof, by Charles Rand's farm, its great round barn now abandoned, the sounds of family life but a memory. Further down, the Blackwell, Wing, and Parsons farms stood proud, silent and empty, windows open and curtains escaping in the breeze. Another blast from downriver ripped through the air and under the bedrock like an assault. They passed Ferry Farm, where people once crossed by floating bridge to get to Flagstaff and drifted up beside Captain Wing, the old ferryman and boatbuilder with his white hair and canvas hat, his shirt and pants rolled up, waving from his boat, the Grey Gosling. *"What I'd like to build is a boat like Noah built the Ark. And gather all these people and take 'em on and go out on this new lake and stay. There we could all be together. It's this separation that gets me." He peered into the distance, as if contemplating his own mortality. "And I can still build a good boat."*

Past the Durrell farm at Hurricane Falls, they disembarked. Papa dragged his canoe onto shore, not far from the grand J.P. Morgan farm, with its sturdy farmhouse and long, gleaming white barn, once housing the herd of Brown Swiss cattle, now sitting abandoned in the valley. The whine of saws and the constant chop of axes filled the air, men swarming the valley, their shanties and shacks popping up, housing the crewmen and their families while they cleared the vast flowage area, cutting and burning brush, their destructive little fires everywhere.

At the Big Bridge, memory cascaded in front of them: the bridge blowing over in the spring freshet of 1922, replaced by the floating bridge, then traded in for another permanent structure, only to be taken again by the hurricane of 1936, bringing forth a floating bridge once again until the new bridge was built. Papa waved to Perley Stevens, who strolled through his abandoned farmland, once Jim Eaton's place, saying goodbye to his green valley at the bottom of the hill. The ghosts of Natanis and a tribe of Abenaki hunted along the riverbank and paddled past in their birchbark canoes.

At an old cemetery behind the church, a tan-skinned man leaned out the window of an old pickup, wearing a banded hat, sleeveless T-shirt and suspenders, the dug-up hillside cemetery behind him, piles of dirt like an afterthought. Papa waved. "Hey Spider, where you headed with those remains?"

He scratched his head and nodded. "Moving them up to the Flagstaff Memorial Cemetery beside the new chapel the power company built." Stone markers sat piled behind him in the wagon alongside stacks of small wooden boxes not more than three feet long. "We packed the bones in there best we could, and marked them. Nearly 170 graves. One man, dead for nearly thirty years, still had on his wool socks." The gravedigger shrugged, turning around to look at the boxes behind him. "A little girl had a China doll, so I kept 'em together." Sadness sat as heavy as the smoky air from the brush fires. The only thing left of the cemetery was a tall white pine that stood amongst the gaping holes in the ground. Papa said, "Warren Wing planted that when he was a boy."

The little hollowed-out church built by Charles T. Rand in 1902 sat vacant, its pretty stained-glass windows, pews, and church bell now stacked on a flatbed truck with Glen Viles behind the wheel. He tipped his hat to Papa. "Taking this to the new chapel in Eustis." The bell had a small, widening crack at the base, a premonition. They strolled past the foundation of Walter Hinds's house, a dark hole in the ground, until they came upon the two-story Flagstaff school sitting on the other side of the hill, soon to be dismantled for salvage, the place where generations of kids attended kindergarten to high school, where basketball games took place every Saturday night in the basement all winter, the lights powered by the turbine.

Along Mill Stream, they came upon the stone pilings of the old Bryant Mill that sawed birch into squares, that once supplied lumber for all the houses, bridges, and fences, a memory obliterated now by the grinding noise of the power company's chainsaws. They passed the shadow of the place where "Old Bert" Horton's cabin once stood before it burned, his tales of hopping trains and riding with Buffalo Bill out west, of finding buried chests of gold and cannons from Arnold's Revolutionary march, all but the echo of memory in the disappearing lore.

In the center of the village, they came to the pool hall with its two-story covered porch, where Hazel Ames and his wife, Hilda, the schoolteacher, were loading their Studebaker full of remnants from their home and the old hall. He nodded to Papa. "I don't like it very well. I've always lived here in Flagstaff. It's hard to think of any other place to live." Hazel put his arm around Hilda's shoulders and pointed at his building. "We're moving the old pool hall on a flatbed to Eustis. Not sure what we'll do there, to tell you the truth." Across the street stood Dutchie Leavitt's Store, the place where goods came in weekly, everything from shirts to shoes to chewing tobacco to gun grease, a large two-story building with a covered front porch and gas pumps, a giant American flag draped on the side of the building like a badge of honor.

In the middle of the village green, the old flagstaff stood high and proud, painted white, the one that had replaced the one a trapper planted in place of the spruce tree erected by Benedict Arnold's men. In front of it, the World War II memorial monument was already dug up from the ground, preparing for its move away from this holy ground, the place where an encampment of starving, broken men fought for their nation's independence 174 years ago.

Chapter 12
Logging Camp

THE GULLET'S KITCHEN SMELLED of creamy fish chowder with onions and potatoes. Pennie chopped vegetables under the vent, listening for any signs of JD. Instead, Bri breezed in with a sing-song hello to Betsy. The matron tried to match Bri's cheerfulness with "Hello, dear," but it came off as condescending. "You and JD made that appointment with Pastor Laurel yet?"

"All lined up for tomorrow! She sounds super nice. I can't wait to meet her."

"You listen to her, and you'll find answers in the Lord. Our baby is a gift from God, don't you forget that."

Something about how Betsy took ownership of the unborn baby made Pennie's skin crawl. Bri came charging through the saloon doors, beaming with joy, a gold cross necklace just like Betsy's around her neck. "Pennie, so glad you're here! I haven't seen you for days!" She hugged her from behind. "I can't thank you enough for spending so much time with Grandpa and taking him to the public hearing yesterday." She gulped down a glass of water. "Sounds like he had a tough time getting through his speech last night."

Pennie turned to face her, square on. "Where did you hear that?"

"JD was there. Don't worry, though, we have his back on this thing. JD says that we'll continue to fight this corridor thing, whatever it takes. He knows how much the family property means to Fremont and me."

There were things Pennie was willing to dismiss to keep the peace, but slandering another person was not one of them. "Are you kidding me? Fremont was eloquent. He gave an unbelievably heartfelt speech about the history of your family property and the importance of *individual rights*. He brought the house down with a standing ovation."

A look of confusion crossed Bri's pretty face, and she shook her head, her tawny straight hair moving in waves, the gold cross glimmering around her neck. "Maybe JD just had a different interpretation than yours." She shook her wet hands, the diamond still firmly on her ring finger. "JD says there are many ways people can look at a thing, and we all come from our own personal perspectives. The Lord says that we should not judge."

Pennie wanted to ask who was judging whom, but she put her head down to chop the onions, her eyes smarting, holding back what she knew about JD for fear Bri would repeat something. "You know, your grandfather asks about you."

"I know, I know. I was just telling JD that. We're going to stop by tomorrow after we go see Pastor Laurel." She tucked her order pad in her apron pocket. "You're the best, Pen!" And she was gone again.

If there was one thing Pennie was sure of, it was that JD would be there to control whatever was said, to interpret for Bri whatever was said. Owen's head appeared over the swinging doors. "What's up?"

She wiped her eyes, still smarting from the onions, and dumped them in a pot. "Not much, you?"

"We missed you last night."

"Yeah, sorry about leaving you in the lurch."

"Lurch, that's funny." He made that forced smile of his. "We were left lurching." He pushed himself through the swinging doors, pitching forward in imitation.

"Ha, ha, Owen. Very funny." His silly awkwardness tickled her, despite her feigned annoyance.

He gave her a side glance. "Pastor Laurel has a brand-new white Cadillac Escalade V. *Brand*-new, Pennie. You should see its spinning rims."

She looked up from the chopped celery. "You don't say."

"No, I do say, Pennie. You should see it. Came from JD's dealership."

"You don't say."

"I do say, Pennie." He looked out toward the open restaurant like he might get caught.

She smiled and nodded. "You better get back out there before the matron comes looking for you." He made an about-face and headed back out to the bar.

Soon Shep limped in with his bottle of whiskey, slamming it on the plating station with relish. He seemed in a particularly cheery mood for some reason, something resembling a smile coming across his lined face. "Heard Fremont made quite a speech last night."

This is where her uncle's voice inside her head told her to tread lightly. "Yeah, he really got the place fired up."

"'Bout time someone grew some balls in this town. Those politicians will lie through their teeth to get a hand on our property." He clicked on his *Cult Wars* talk radio.

She thought about the irony of the moment. Who was lying to whom? "He's got an uphill battle with that commission." She waited for him to say something else as the podcast bloviator talked about the lib-tards and socialists putting smut into the hands of children at school libraries. "Do you know anyone on the commission?"

He limped to the refrigerator to take out steaks. "Geoff Skelton. Only one I know of."

"I wonder how he'll vote on this thing."

The bottle of whiskey glimmered on the stainless tabletop, and he poured himself two fingers and downed it. "He'll vote the way this town wants if he has any common sense, if he wants to keep his job and his friends in the church—people like my wife and son."

So, he was involved in the church... More pieces were falling together. *Perhaps JD was the buffer between the church and the commissioner?* Pennie thought about the bear that JD killed and gave to the commissioner as a bonus, to sweeten the deal. Something told her to stay clear of anything personal with Shep, now that she had him talking. "Do you like venison?"

"Best meat there is, in my opinion. Nothing like a venison stew. I'll make one this weekend for you."

This small offer of stew made Pennie stop to reconsider this man she had written off as nothing but an angry cripple. "How about bear meat? I hear it's tough."

Something turned in his face, a friendly ember turning to black smoke. "What is this, twenty questions? Get started on the damn biscuits. We don't pay you to stick your nose in where it don't belong." The bottle of whiskey gurgled as he poured himself a tall one, turning to stir the giant gray pot filled with homemade fish chowder, his back stiff, his wall firmly in place.

THE ATTIC WINDOW WAS frosted with ice crystals, a kaleidoscope she traced with her fingers, thinking about the empty, pink-covered bed beside her, the stuffed animals with their glassy eyes looking for Bri. She was supposed to stop by today after they met with the pastor about their nuptials in June. Pennie couldn't help but be excited by the thought of a new life coming into the world, coming into Bri and Fremont's world.

He hadn't shown much excitement about it but, she knew; there was so much wrapped up in the sad past of Bri's mother.

Downstairs, she found him standing at the sink looking out onto the lake. Bartholomew jumped on the counter and sniffed Pennie's hands before nudging his black nose against her cup, spilling coffee. Fremont blew on his own and stared at holes in the ice not far from shore, surrounded by piles of slush. "First ice is the best for catching perch," he said. "We've got a few inches of ice now, and those perch are still at those edges with the steep slope, looking for food." He'd drilled two circular holes in the ice only a few feet from the shoreline. She knew he was anticipating Bri's visit.

"Once I get my dead sticks set up with nightcrawlers, the fish'll bite early or late, or sometimes midday if its cloudy like this." He impatiently waited for Bri, lighting a cigarette. "Pretty mild day today, too." The arm of the giant round thermometer outside his window pointed to 26 degrees.

"You've only got two holes out there?" She recalled ice fishing with Uncle Alfie, at least half a dozen going at once.

"No, no, you don't want to be scaring the fish. And there's only about five feet of water there. You can't be stomping around on the ice tending too many holes."

They heard a car pull in to the driveway, and she eyed the clock: already almost ten. Fremont put on his jacket, and she followed suit, wrapping herself in a scarf and hat, putting on her boots. In the driveway, he greeted Bri with a hug like he hadn't seen her in months, although it had only been a week or two, asking her how she was feeling. He shook hands with JD, a stiff nod. "JD, I understand congratulations are in order."

"Fremont, good to see you. Yes, I've been meaning to get over here. Busy life these days." He smiled widely, showing all his bright white teeth, patting Fremont on the shoulder. Fremont shrugged away, stepped back. Pennie hugged Bri, who beamed, her cheeks rosy, blossoming.

Fremont said, "You been over to see the pastor, have you?"

"She's wicked nice, Grandpa. You know me, I've never been religious, but Pastor Laurel has so many good teachings." Bri looked down at the ice, unable to look her grandfather in the eye. "She told me to trust in the Lord and to trust in JD to provide for me."

JD beamed with pride, and Fremont pursed his lips. "Don't lose sight of who you are, Bri. You're a very special young woman with many talents."

"She sure is special," said JD, putting his arm around her. "You should see the baby blanket she's sewing." "Since when do you sew?" said Fremont.

Bri dug her rubber boots into the snow. "JD's mother is teaching me. She's been super."

A light snow began to fall under the cloudy skies. "Hey, I got some traps set up." He waved her to follow him, and they all walked through the crusty snow to the edge of the lake where Fremont had two buckets with small rods sticking up.

"Got your dead sticks ready, I see," she said.

"Damn right I have." He picked up the short poles and reeled in the line.

"Got some worms?" The light danced in her eyes.

His enthusiasm matched hers. "Sure do, you wanna bait one?"

JD looked at his phone. "I gotta make a call." He walked away toward the driveway in his black down jacket, his eyes fierce and darting.

Bri picked up a nightcrawler and grabbed the line from the rod that Fremont held out. In one quick motion, she threaded the worm. "I like your sinker set up with the swivel." She took the rod from him. "Drag is set nice and lose."

Fremont brought the two buckets down to the ice, and Bri followed, setting her rod into the side of the bucket beside the fishing hole, the worm dangling. He set the second line, and they continued to chat about the pan fish and dead sticks and hook setting power, when, inside a minute, the rod tip twitched. She picked it up to tug it, letting the line run, talking about the free spool, until she reeled it in and a big yellow perch came out of the hole like a sunburst from the depths.

"Just like that!" he said. Pennie moved in closer to get a better look at the mottled fish with prominent fins lining its back. She took a photo as the second rod began to twitch, and Fremont picked it up this time, tugging lightly. "She's running, alright." As he reeled in another fish, she dropped her perch in the hole and prepared to bait her hook again. JD walked back, asking what all the excitement was about.

Fremont said, "Bri here just got herself a big perch, the first catch."

He hugged her and rubbed her shoulders like a child. "Good job, Sweetie. You can catch those fish, can't you?"

The look between Fremont and Bri said everything. "You got real fishing talent, Bri. Remember to follow your dreams of becoming a Guide. Your Grandma Lena would be proud," he said.

JD pushed her lightly on the shoulder, egging her on to say something. She chewed on her hair. "Well, about that. JD and I have been talking, and we even talked about it this morning with Pastor Laurel. We think it's best if I concentrate on the baby for now. You know, I have to keep my priorities straight. There'll be time for that later." Her grimace turned to excitement when the rod twitched, and she picked it up to jig the line, let the line run, before reeling in another one. A beautiful long brook trout manifested from the hole in the ice. Their collective joy at seeing the magnificent creature from the cold depths shifted the energy, something like hope masking the controlling vibes of JD's presence. Fremont and Bri ogled over the trout, and Pennie got their attention long enough to snap a picture, a glimpse of pure gladness shared between kindred hearts.

THAT AFTERNOON, PENNIE WASTED no time riding over to the Northern United Freedom Church in Stratton, an enormous, prefabricated steel building with a pitched roof, brick facade, and large silver cross on the face, as tall as the two-story building, looking more like a sports arena than a church. Only two other cars sat in the parking lot. One was a church van, and the other a new white SUV.

She parked on the side of the road under the shadow of the building and crept to the parking lot in the back, running up to the front windshield of the Cadillac SUV to find the VIN plate on the driver's side. She snapped a few pictures before seeing a movement in one of the windows in the back of the church, what looked like a person looking out from behind blinds. In a panic, she ran back to her car and jumped in. Within a minute, she texted the pictures to Uncle Alfie, who immediately responded that he would start a trace. She had no idea if there was any time to do anything with the Land Use Planning Commission meeting coming up, but she had to try. Somehow, JD, Betsy, and the church were involved with the corridor development.

Her stomach rumbled, and her wallet was empty, so she found herself at the Greedy Gullet parking lot around lunchtime, knowing it was payday. When she walked into the restaurant, a shouting match was in full swing between JD and his father. Shep pointed to the black bear shoulder mount that hung on the wall above the bar. "Take that damn thing down before I take *you* down."

JD laughed at his stepfather. "Shep, what ails you about that bear? Never heard you complain before. You've got your deer and moose mounts on every corner of this restaurant." He motioned to the heads of beasts that surrounded them, his arms outstretched.

"I shot every one of them for food. And not one of them was a mother with cubs."

Betsy came out of the office, hands on her hips. "What the hell is going on out here?"

JD said, "Shep has got his knickers in a twist again. He doesn't like my bear here above the bar." The glassy-eyed black bear, dead and distant, hung on the wooden mount above the bottles of liquor, an empty spirit of the woods that once was.

She faced her husband, hands on hips. "What's the problem, Shep? We've got your mounts hanging all over this place."

"*You* are the problem. You've babied him his entire life. Now he's nothing but an entitled prick shooting mother bears with cubs for sport."

She turned to JD. "Is this true?"

He put his arms up like he'd been attacked for no apparent reason. "I didn't know when I shot her. The cubs were nowhere around."

"Do you think I'm some kind of an *idiot*?" Shep shouted. "It didn't take long for me to find the dead cubs in the sacks you hid around back of the house."

JD put his hands up in protest. "What? I don't know what you're talking about, Shep. You must be losing it." He looked at his mother. "I swear, I never shot no cubs."

Shep slammed his hand on the bar. "You're a damn liar. I know you disposed of them later that day, saw you loading them in the back of your pickup. Take that goddamned thing down now. If you don't, you can find yourself a new place to live."

Betsy sniffed. "You heard your father. Take it down."

The old cook hobbled to the kitchen. JD glowered at his father's back before grabbing a ladder behind the bar to take the bear's head mount off the wall. Coming down, he saw Pennie standing there by the doorway for the first time. He hefted his trophy, hissing at her, "You're always lurking around here. Looking for trouble, are you?"

To avoid the confrontation, she smiled at him sweetly. "Nice to see you, too, JD." Inside the kitchen, Shep fried chunks of meat on the grill top and turned on the radio, ignoring her. When she heard Owen out at the bar, she went out to ask him for Shep's bottle of whiskey and two glasses. He gladly handed them to her, feeling the lingering tension in the restaurant. Back in the kitchen, she poured the Kentucky whiskey into the two glasses with ice. Beef stew gurgled in the big pot, the smells of sweet onion, salty meat, and potato filling the kitchen. She handed him the golden liquid on ice, and he gladly accepted.

"You're welcome," she said.

"Since when do you drink whiskey?"

She laughed. "Oh, me and whiskey have a history. I try to stay away from it, but it keeps calling me back. One thing I really try to avoid are those dirty, rotten, no-good boilermakers. They tend to get me in lots of trouble." The vision of the night of her thirtieth birthday surfaced from last spring, her impulse to pick up the young ski patrol at the bar, her foggy goggles the next day. "I had a bad ski accident after one of those benders."

"You don't say." He took a long swig. "My love affair with whiskey came *after* an accident, not before." He limped to the fridge to grab some Worcestershire sauce for the stew. She listened as he unraveled his story, reminiscing about working as a river driver when he was only eighteen years old. "The problem was the sheer mass of logs that would pile up on rocks or banks—the kind of jam legends are made of." He jiggled the ice in the glass. "I fell into a center jam at the head of falls, a real boiler, the river roaring like a runaway train. I nearly drowned under the logs before it was calm enough to get out. My damn leg was crushed, but I was alive."

He downed his whiskey, so she poured him another glass with ice, marveling at his good humor. "That's when I became a camp cookie, feeding the men still able to river drive."

After all that, here Shep was, still feeding people night after night in a restaurant he owned despite a leg crushed in the springtime of his life. He jingled his ice. "Could have died on the river like so many log drivers back then, but for some reason, I was spared." His voice softened. "I guess I got that to be thankful for. All I've got left is this place and by God, nobody, and I mean *nobody*, is going to hang any animal trophy in here unless I give the say-so."

She found herself sitting on the deck of Captain Wing's Grey Gosling. *His coat and pant cuffs rolled up, smoking a pipe with Papa, he motored across Flagstaff Pond with other lumberjacks. They trekked miles through the deep woods to Spencer Stream, snow piled high in late fall, to reach the camp where men worked all day against the bitter cold inside the northern forest of pine and spruce, fir and hackmatack, maple, beech, cedar, and birch, chopping deep notches into bull pines with a double bit ax, chips flying like confetti, before bringing in the crosscut handsaw. The men worked in tandem, back and forth in harmony, until they yelled "Timber!" to warn the felling of the great, centuries-old trees. Papa set to trimming the butt nice and even before they sliced the tree into three 16-foot lengths with the same crosscut saw. She knew by instinct to keep low and away, the other men calling her "she-wolf" as she ran alongside the horse, Papa slapping the furry beast twitching the pine trees out of the woods to the yard, where they decked the logs into piles ten or more feet high on sleighs.*

The camp cookie appeared in the deep woods, laden with packs of canned beef, boiled ham, cookies, biscuits, and hot tea for the first and second lunches around a campfire in the snow, where they ate ravenously, efficiently, silently, a few men throwing pieces of biscuit or cookie her way before getting to work again behind teams of horses skidding great sleighs to the landing, the teamsters riding atop the logs piled ten feet high, steam rolling off the backs of the workhorses while Papa and the other men coaxed the logs down the bank of the cove with cant hooks.

The sunlight waned as the crew made it back to the wide log cabin of the main camp lit by kerosene lamps, gathering inside for supper around the tables, the camp cookie serving mounds of beef and pork and beans to feed the voracious hunger of logging men working in bone-chilling woods from dawn until dusk. The horses settled into the hovel next door, eating their own supper of grain and hay, bedding down for the night before another long day in the logging camp.

In her mind's eye, she could remember some earlier or later time when the ice was out in March, the men rolling the logs into the river, where they drove them down the North Branch of the Dead through the Ledge Falls, past Eustis, Flagstaff, and Dead River plantations, through the rapids and over Long Falls to the branch running north, all the way to the Forks to meet the great Kennebec, where the log drive headed swiftly downstream to the shipyards in Bath and Portland, where the great three-, four-, five-, and six-masted schooner barks were built; days when the ice and snow melted and the valley opened to the running spring freshet, the sound of rushing, rumbling, deep-throated water, of birds twittering and bees hiving in the deep river valley, beasts leaving the stench of tepid winter barns to revel in the green shoots and warm sun of pastures cleared by settlers inside the cradle of the great mountain range.

Lying in bed, images of the logging camp still on her mind, Pennie received a text from Bri, asking her to meet her over at Long Falls Dam. Pennie wondered what this was about, but was also happy to have a reason to talk to Bri about JD.

Along the way, the Carrabassett River rushed with life, its banks covered in snow. To the east, Sugarloaf sat in humble regard for the skiers driving up the access road to her base to seize the day. All the way over, she considered ways to talk to Bri about her lying fiancé. How much should she share?

At the gated gravel road where Pennie and Bri had been with Dani, Mali, and Tita back in October, Bri was sitting with her truck running, facing the dam down the slope. Pennie joined her inside the Jeep. It was clear she had been crying, her eyes red and desperate. There was nothing to do but empathize. Pennie reached for her arm, asking if everything was okay. Bri began to choke, just like she had when she told Fremont the news about her pregnancy. "You have to *promise* me you won't tell JD we talked." Bri kept her eyes focused on the dam that lay down the slope to the lake, her voice quavering like a girl scared of an abusive parent.

"Of course, of course, I won't repeat anything. What's this all about?"

Water rushed over the gate of the dam to the falls below, Little Bigelow in the far distance. "This is my favorite place to fly-fish in the springtime, right below these falls." She sighed, long and hard. "I like to stand in the rushing water with my hip waders on to see if I can make my fly just graze the surface."

"You caught a few nice ones in the ice the other day with Fremont."

She choked again and locked her long fingers together. Just below her sweatshirt cuff, Pennie could see a bruise on her wrist and asked what had happened. She pulled her sleeve down around it. Pennie asked her again. "What happened?"

"He's been so stressed out lately with work, he says. And he thinks…"

Pennie sat up in the seat, the Jeep still running, the heater warm on her feet. "He thinks what?" "He thinks you're trying to get Fremont's camp over on Middle Carry. That's why you're so interested in the whole power company corridor. He says he saw you and another man walking it with an appraiser."

"Bri, that was my Uncle Alfie, the real estate attorney. We're trying to help your grandfather keep his property, not take anything away." She tried to get Bri to look at her, but her gaze was fixed on the dam. She kept on, "That appraisal was ordered by the power company, not us. They're trying to take it by eminent domain."

Bri's thin shoulders rose and fell, a full body sigh. "That's what JD said you'd say. He says you'll make up anything to get the property, property that's rightfully my inheritance."

"Oh, Bri, just listen to me. I overheard JD talking to a commissioner at the restaurant. He gave him an envelope full of money to vote in favor of the corridor."

"That's just plain *crazy*." She turned to Pennie, angry now, her eyes brimming with tears. "JD doesn't want that corridor any more than any of us do. He loves this land. I think you're just jealous about me getting married and starting a family, while you're still single and…well, over thirty."

The idea was so ludicrous, Pennie wanted to laugh. How could she think this was about the baby? "Listen, Bri, I'm so happy for you, I truly am. This has nothing to do with me."

"Yeah, then why did you try to talk me out of having the baby?"

"Have you gone crazy? I've done no such thing." Pennie wanted to leave the truck but told herself to calm down, took deep breaths to get her heartbeat to subside. "Listen, I've only ever wanted what is best for you. You hardly know this man, Bri. He hasn't told you the truth about that bear he killed."

Bri turned toward her with wild, wide eyes. "That's exactly what he said you'd say! You're trying to drive us apart and take my grandfather's property from us!" Tears streamed down her red face, and Pennie reached for her arm. Bri pushed her away, resisting, until she finally let down her guard inside the warmth of the Jeep still running, the exhaust clouding the air outside around them, her bony shoulders rolling in long sobs.

"I know, I know how you feel." She could see Kush in her own mind, the echoes of his words, telling her that she was nothing but another mistake. "You want to trust him, but you're not sure. You're afraid. But don't worry, we can work through this together. I want you to call your grandfather and talk to him about everything. He'll tell you we're just doing what we can to save his Middle Carry property, *your* property, Bri." They stayed arm in arm, leaning against each other. Pennie wondered how she would talk to her about JD, how to break through, or if it was best just to let things lie for now. Out of desperation, Pennie asked her how she was feeling.

"Okay, you know, a little nauseous in the mornings." Her gaze lingered on the far mountain range. "I feel like my grandfather is so disappointed in me."

Pennie's own heart ached for her. "Your grandfather loves you, only wants the best for you." She reached for Bri's hands, the dull diamond twisted between her long fingers. "Promise me you'll talk to him."

Bri half-nodded, uncertain, gazing out to the rapids beyond the dam, the place of river drives, of guides hunting and fishing for centuries reflected in her eyes and vanishing, as slippery as a fish escaping her grasp.

Chapter 13
Scorched Earth

THEY SAT IN THE warm Jeep for a while, looking out at the cement dam, the gray November sky, the frozen perimeter of the lake. Somehow, Pennie was able to get Bri to talk about the valley she loved and the things she missed, things that made her who she was: wading in a cold brook as a child, swimming in a mountain lake under the constellations of a true dark sky, fishing in the river rapids, steadfast against nature's rush. Bri clipped on her seatbelt and backed the Jeep up. They talked about her favorite fishing spot on the lower Dead River and drove northward, following the winding Long Falls Dam Road until they turned onto gravel, heading through the remote western woods toward the Grand Falls, a cold-water spot for trout and salmon.

From their parking spot at the trailhead, Pennie jumped out to follow Bri. She noticed her cousin's packless back, a fisherwoman without her gear. "Where's your pack?"

Bri kept walking. "What do I need that for? It's too late in the season to fish."

A cold, biting wind swept through the dense pines and over the snow-covered trail packed down by snowshoes, the temperature just below freezing. The forest reminded Pennie of the logging camp in her dream, the tall white pines, red spruces, and oaks going on for miles in all directions, home to wintering herds of deer and moose, to beaver and porcupine, to hibernating bears in their dens. On the tip of her tongue was Shep's revelation about the cubs in the sack out back, but she couldn't find the right words that would fit the strange situation she found herself in, inside this community of generations of Maine woodsmen and -women.

She breathed in the soothing pine smell, the cold air cleansing her uneasy mind, keeping pace with her long-legged cousin who loped along with the ease of a deer. The sound of the rumbling falls filled the still air. At the opening on the riverbank, they looked up to Grand Falls cascading over black rock forty feet high across the entire span of the river, the saturated air alive, dancing. Their breath came out in cloud-like bursts and Bri's jaw trembled, as if the tumble of the rapids drew something out from deep inside her soul, driving her forward as she wiped her eyes. They walked up to a steel bridge with a wooden platform that crossed high above the river running swift beneath them, still unfrozen, its banks covered in icy crust. They took their time crossing the bridge, and Pennie sensed the vibration, the soul of the Dead River rumbling underneath, speaking to them. Memories of the Big Bridge over Flagstaff opened again.

On the other side, a rock stairway led up a steep embankment, at least twenty steps high and cleared of snow. They ascended the wet steps together, the mist of the river covering their faces, their eyelashes, their lips, tasting like organic life, of fish and stones, of hibernating toads and salamanders. They drank in their new perspective from high above, of the crashing falls tumbling in a reckless flow, icy water spraying in every direction, iridescent drops of fine mist a halo around the rushing water. "Isn't it spectacular?" Bri said.

"Extraordinary. This must be something to see in the springtime."

"Oh, I like it any time of year, but yes, when I come in the springtime, the fishing above and below the falls is the best there is around here." She seemed to drift away to another place in her mind, perhaps reminiscing about those warm fly-fishing days. Bri waved her long arm to the top of the falls. "Just above here is where the power company is planning to span the Dead River."

"Here? You're kidding me."

"JD says they have to stay clear of Spring Lake, and the area protected by the Bigelow Mountain range. I really hope it doesn't happen. Might ruin the peace."

The sound of the falls captured Pennie's mind, and she closed her eyes to store the memory for later when she needed strength. Bri said, "This is where the white-water rafters put in, just below the falls. From what JD told me, it's quite a wild ride when they open Long Falls Dam's gates in the springtime. The long raft trip goes all the way to the Forks where this branch of the Dead River meets the Kennebec." The thought of JD's ATV friend, Brett Townsend, speaking on behalf of the corridor flashed in her mind.

Bri pointed to the left. "Just up there on the other side of this bend is Spencer Rips, where Spencer Stream joins the Dead. My great-grandfather worked there."

Pennie's dream came to her again: the logging camp, horses skidding sixteen-foot logs on the snow, piling them on the banks of the Dead until the ice cleared enough to roll them into the lakes and rivers. "Shep was a river driver, did you know that?"

She laughed. "Oh, he's got a million stories. Just give him a bottle of whiskey."

His promise of venison stew came to her mind. "Not a bad old guy if you can get through his thick skin," said Pennie.

"He absolutely hates the power company."

The line of the corridor materialized in Pennie's mind, how it would cross the Canadian border, down through these great western woods, over Spencer Stream, then here above the falls and down between West and Middle Carry to meet with the power station at Wyman Lake. "Just the thought of cutting a swath through here, hanging high-voltage transmission wires over this place, makes me sick to my stomach."

Bri stared at something, far beyond the falls. "I'm sorry."

"What are you sorry about?"

"Accusing you of being on their side. I don't know why JD said that. I think he's just jealous of you. Doesn't like me having any other friends." Pennie bit her tongue again, holding back her dark thoughts about JD. Clearly, Bri still thought JD was on their side against the power company, despite what Pennie had shared about him bribing the commissioner. "No worries. Just know that my Uncle Alfie and I are doing everything we can to fight this thing and help Fremont keep his camp, your family camp. If there is any way to stop this thing, my uncle will figure it out."

They walked back down the steep rock stairway and across the steel bridge, watching the swift brown river below, its banks a crust of ice. They trudged through the wooded path, the sound of the falls lessening with each step until it was silent again. When they reached the Jeep, they checked the time and realized neither of them had had anything to eat. Bri wanted to know if Pennie had any lunch plans.

"Believe it or not, my schedule is wide open."

Bri smiled, all teeth. "Luckily, JD is off snowmobiling with his friends. Let's lunch, shall we?" It seemed she had come to terms with the situation, whatever it was, and they decided to drive to Kingfield where there was a good vegetarian place. She had read that a well-planned vegetarian diet could be good for the baby. Pennie wondered if this was about the bear, a way for Bri to come to terms with it.

When they arrived and walked in, she was pleased to find a jazzy little place with cute round café tables and windows on all sides trimmed with yellow and orange curtains. The waiter told them to sit anywhere, so they picked the sunniest table in the corner. A vase in the middle spilled over with daisies and asters. "Spring is such a long way away," Pennie said, looking at the menu.

"Oh, don't rush it. I love winter." The gold cross necklace around Bri's neck sparkled in the sunlight.

Fiddling with the silver triskelion around her own neck, she asked Bri what she and JD did with all their time together, and Bri was happy to fill her in about their weekly visits with Pastor Laurel, her Bible study, and how they were snowmobiling on the Arnold Trail, from West Carry Pond to Kennebago Lake, for ice-fishing trips.

"Sounds like you enjoy the same things," Pennie said, absentmindedly, her mouth salivating at the menu filled with berry and walnut salads, veggie chilis and lentil soups.

"Yeah, we do, when he lets me actually do things."

She tried not to sound too confrontational. "What do you mean?"

"Oh, he's overly concerned about the baby." She patted her flat stomach.

"What are you now, two months along?"

Bri nodded as the waiter came to fill their water glasses. "Ten weeks." Pennie asked if Bri didn't mind if she ordered wine, which she didn't. "You go ahead, get whatever you want. I'm good with hot tea, please." The waiter lingered on Bri, asking her what kind of tea, recommending at least five different kinds. Like most young men, he was smitten with her organic allure, her rosy face that exuded wholesomeness, her smile. He finally walked away, and Bri continued. "I spend most of the time watching him and his buddies ice-fish while I tend the fire."

"Seems like you could teach them a thing or two."

"Don't get me started." She broke off a piece of the homemade sourdough on the table and chewed, telling Pennie how the men misjudge where they drill the holes, how they're like girls when the flags go off, scaring the fish and pounding all over the ice like lunatics. "Might have something to do with the cases of beer they drink."

When the white wine came, Pennie took a delicious sip before ordering a bowl of the leek soup. Bri ordered the tofu chili, and the waiter had another million questions for her before he finally walked away from her infectious smile. "Do you ever get tired of it?" "Of what?"

"Of men fawning over you."

She laughed. "Very funny, Pennie. Are you making fun of me because I like to talk to people?"

Pennie realized that Bri really had no idea how attractive she was, and that probably made her even more endearing, especially to men like JD, who could take advantage of her innocence, could brainwash her into believing what they wanted her to believe. "I don't think JD realizes what a lucky guy he is."

The faraway look came across her eyes again, and she stared out the window to some unknown place where maybe life was less complicated, where maybe she could hike and canoe and fish all day long. She pulled off another hunk of bread. "He tells me how much he loves me and the baby every day, Pennie." Her defensive tone took on that uncomfortable edge again.

Gulping her wine, she weighed the risk of being perfectly frank with Bri again, of ruining their nice lunch. She thought about her own relationship with Kush, with Ward. Maybe she was being too critical because of her own failed romances. "He does seem to really care for you." She took another gulp of wine. "I just want you to be careful, that's all. In the past, I've put too much trust in men, and that hasn't worked out for the best."

Bri ripped off another chunk of soft bread, slathered it with butter. "Are you saying he's not trustworthy?"

Now she was in a corner. She couldn't lie about her feelings. "There are some things I've heard JD say that make me uncomfortable, that's all." She finished her wine as the waiter brought their food, taking his time setting the bowl of chili in front of Bri, asking if she needed anything, anything at all.

Pennie said, "I'll take another glass of wine." When he walked away, she took a deep breath. "Like I told you, I heard him bribing somebody on the commission."

"What commission are you talking about?" She took a big mouthful of chili and chewed, her brown eyes fixed on Pennie.

"The Planning Commission. He wants them to vote in favor of the corridor."

She shook her head. "I told you, that's crazy. He would never do that. I think you must have your wires crossed, Pennie. *Really*, you don't know him."

The smell of her creamy leek soup wafted up, and the first bite was heavenly, giving her pause to consider the best approach without making Bri upset. "You're right, I really do not know JD, and there is a chance that I got things mixed up when I heard them talking about the corridor." She wiped her mouth and picked up her wine glass to sip, trying to slow down. "Can we just hold off and see what happens before we make any judgments? Would you do that for me?"

"I'm not the one making judgments here, Pennie. You seem hell-bent on putting a wedge between us, and I don't understand why. I'm only trying to make the best of—to be happy with—my *situation*."

The obsequious waiter came back to check on Bri. She waved him away.

"*Absolutely*." Pennie picked up her wine glass like a lifeline. "Like I said, I could be completely wrong." Bri took great mouthfuls of chili and moved the conversation to her latest horoscope, which urged her to listen to her intuition and reflect. If there was anything Pennie knew, it was this.

Pennie managed a nap to sleep off the wine before her shift began, but her head still felt like it was inside a fishbowl. On the ride over, her phone rang and her uncle's number came up. Just what she was looking for, she hoped, some kind of confirmation. "Good afternoon, Lucky Pennie."

"I hope you have some information on that Cadillac SUV."

"Happens that I do. It's registered to the church as a donation from the car dealership where JD works."

Her mind squirmed at the thought of a donation. "What does that mean? They can get away with this bullshit?"

"Settle down there. Who put a bee in your bonnet?" She was in no mood for his little quips this afternoon. Her head throbbed. "I told Bri about our suspicions with JD and the commission. Now she thinks I'm jealous of her and her fiancé."

His tone grew impatient. "Now, why would you do that?"

She pictured him at his desk, furrowing his deep brow. "It's a long story. Let's just say that he's been feeding her lies about me because he knows I know too much. I'm pretty sure somebody at the church saw me snapping a picture of the VIN. If Bri finds out, she'll think I'm nothing but a lying interloper."

"What ails you today? Let's not get ahead of ourselves. The commission hearing is tomorrow afternoon in Augusta. I'll give you and Fremont a call afterward and let you know how it turns out."

She hung up feeling like they were swimming against the massive political force of the power company, a tsunami hitting the Maine woods with Fremont's camp in its path. At the dirt parking lot of the Gullet, JD's truck was parked behind Betsy's Volvo. Instead of going through the front door like she normally did, she decided to try the back door, where she'd seen Shep come in before. It was a long shot, but she walked surreptitiously to the back of the building, behind the dumpster, to the muddy path through the snow to the steel back door. She jiggled the knob, but it was locked.

Defeated, she turned around, and something caught her eye: a small plastic turtle sitting atop the outside kitchen vent. It looked just like the turtle on the porch of the camp by the Round Barn site. Sure enough, she found the key in the small slot on the bottom. *Finally, one tiny thing going my way.* The key slid into the silver doorknob, and she let herself in after restoring the key to its safe hiding place.

The kitchen was empty, Shep's rudimentary note tacked to the refrigerator like a welcome sign. She crept to the chopping station, the sounds of Betsy and JD's conversation coming through in hushed tones, her raspy voice saying something about playing it cool. "You're not going to win any battles with your father, especially over a stuffed bear mount. Now keep your head on straight." Then JD's low, urgent voice. "I've got this under control. The commission's voting tomorrow." Her raspy voice again. "If you play your cards right, you'll be on the church's board of directors. You just need this corridor to go through. They've got a lot of money invested in that Freedom Hedge Fund."

His armored voice: "Like I said, we're taking good care of Skelton." Her grating tone, growing insistent: "You haven't said anything about this to Bri, have you?" JD's voice, louder: "I told you, she doesn't know a thing about it, but I did tell her what a meddling bitch her cousin is. That girl has got to go."

Betsy's tongue clicking. "Don't worry, her days are numbered here." At the sound of scraping barstools, Pennie ran toward the fridge to grab the tray of vegetables and the butter for making biscuits, trying to stay as quiet as a mouse.

She began by sifting the flour and overheard Owen at the bar cleaning out the dishwasher, glasses clinking. Her heartbeat began to subside, digesting the conversation. Through the vent, she heard Betsy and Owen working on the drink specials: margaritas and cosmopolitans. He came back to check on the limes and hailed a bright, "What's up?"

Betsy's head bobbed just above the saloon doors. "When did you get here? Didn't see you come in."

"Oh, just a few minutes ago. I think you were in your office."

The overbearing matron wrinkled her nose like she smelled something foul. "Get the salt and pepper shakers filled then." Pennie twisted her mouth into a smile.

Owen said, "That's the waitress's job. Waitresses always fill the salt and pepper shakers."

"Yes, Owen, dear," she said, condescending. "That's right. But they're running a little late, so Pennie's going to help out. We all help each other when needed, just like a big family."

Under Betsy's watch, he carried a bowl full of limes out to the bar, and Pennie went out to gather the salt and pepper shakers. The other waitresses began to shuffle in: Angela and Jean and, finally, Bri. They brushed Pennie away from their station. She went back to the kitchen where Bri was washing her hands in the sink. "Hey, Pennie," she said brightly. "Thanks for having lunch today and going to the falls with me. I haven't done that in so long. Just wanted you to know what it means to me."

"It was nice to spend some time together." To make it sound sincere, she added, "I'm so happy for you." She couldn't make herself say, *and JD*. Just the thought of him made her want to punch something.

"JD was in such a foul mood as I was leaving the house. Not sure what his problem is."

Pennie began chopping onions. "I hope you didn't mention our conversation today."

"Oh, no, don't worry about it. That's girl talk. He doesn't need to know what I'm doing 24/7." A lonely look crossed her face. "I know I can be short-tempered. My hormones are getting the best of me, but I just want you to know how much I enjoyed our time and hope we can do it again soon."

The onions made her eyes water. She assured Bri they would get together more. The drag, thump, step of Shep coming into the bar area broke their conversation. Bri said, "Wow, you can really hear the sounds out there clearly from back here." Shep came into his kitchen, asking Bri if she didn't have better things to do than wash her hands for hours on end in his kitchen. She left promptly, and he shakily poured himself a large glass of whiskey. Something told her this was not the time to ask him if everything was alright. At his stove, he pulled out the pot roast from the oven and basted it, dripping the juices all over the stovetop, and turned on the burner to let it simmer. He fell against the plating table, swaying, reaching for his glass, telling her that he was going out for a cigarette, barking at her, his tongue thick. "Think ya can manage one measly second?"

He bumped and swayed his way out the back door, slamming it behind him. Her mind floated inside a vision of Shep losing his footing, falling in between the piles of enormous logs, sucked under the rips and currents, fighting for his life, then as the camp cookie out of Spencer Stream in the woods, limping around, welcoming the hungry men in from a long day in the woods, setting a bounty of venison and potatoes and beans and biscuits. The most revered man in camp at mealtime, giving them fuel for another dark night, another long day of hard labor making a sustenance living for their families, miles from their own homesteads, their wives taking care of their babies and their livestock until they could be together again come spring.

A red-hot flash caught the corner of her eye, the acrid smell of smoke, and she turned to see the stovetop on fire, a grease fire. The flame leaped and soon engulfed the stove. In a reflex, she ran to the small fire extinguisher on the wall beside the fridge, pulled the plastic plug and pointed it at the orange, dancing flame, squeezing the spray trigger with all she had, back and forth, up and down. Betsy's screaming came from behind, but she kept spraying, back and forth, dousing the stovetop with foam. The back door slammed open, and she nearly sprayed the drunken cook until he grabbed the fire extinguisher from her and threw it against the back wall with a deafening crash. "What is *wrong* with you?"

"I—there was a wall of fire! What else was I supposed to do? Let the place burn down?" She shook all over, her heart pulsating like a buzz saw.

"Look at this fucking mess," he slurred.

Betsy glared at her. "Get the bucket to clean up this mess."

She was paralyzed, could feel the blank, silent stares of Owen and the waitresses behind her. Shep's bloodshot eyes shot through the smoky haze, his giant scarred hands motioning to the pot roast pan filled with green foam. The smell of chemicals and smoke burned in the air. "You fucking whore. Ruined this roast. Get the fuck out of my kitchen!"

She grabbed her coat, pushing bucket-faced Betsy out of the way, past silent Owen, gaping Bri, and the other waitresses. Everyone seemed to be at a loss for words. All she could think to mutter was, "Go fuck yourself." She turned to Betsy before she left and poked her in the chest on her gold cross. "Especially *you*, you fucking hypocrite."

FREMONT LAY PEACEFULLY SNORING on the couch with Bartholomew on his chest, moving up and down to the gurgle of his lungs. The woodbox near the stove sat nearly empty, so she loaded it, making several trips to the woodpile out back. The stench of smoke and chemicals still clung to her hair and clothes. She sucked in the cold, clean air outside. Her arms overloaded, she threw logs onto the top of the woodbox by the stove before laying one on the embers. Slowly it caught fire, a low roar and menacing glow, the cat's amber eyes reflecting the flame that licked the smoked glass.

Wide awake after her kitchen firefighting catastrophe, she lay in bed thinking about the rushing water of the Grand Falls, the men working in the woods, the swift labyrinth of the Dead River. She breathed in, the smoke still in her lungs, clinging to her clothes, and finally settled, her shallow breathing slowing her heart as she drifted...

SHE LAY ON THE floor between the children when the smell of smoke woke her from an uneasy sleep to see flames jumping from one pile of brush to the next, approaching. Her low growl turned into a sharp bark, piercing the air in the small bedroom until the children sat up, screaming. Papa and Mama flew into the room, their faces aglow with the encroaching flames, and grabbed the children to take them outside into the cold chill of November, Papa ordering them to get in the truck while he went back inside. She barked and barked at the flames closing in until he finally came out, his arms laden with mattresses and blankets and clothes to pile into the truck bed, yelling for Mama to leave.

Arthur and Benny, Lee and Charles came running down the road with shovels. Papa demanded Mama drive to the other side of the river, again and again and again, until she stepped on the gas, her taillights falling away as the men, already busy with their shovels, piled up a dirt wall, the only thing between their house and the flames threatening everything they owned. Papa shoveled dirt as if felling a tree, fierce and desperate, the wall of flames roaring closer, racing down the hills, leaving only blackness and scorched earth behind.

Chapter 14
Terrible Carrying Place

Pennie awoke in the darkness of the attic to the sound of footsteps below, the glowing light of her phone: 4:35 a.m. It only took a moment to gain awareness of the early hour, the faint thumps of Fremont downstairs, the smell of coffee percolating. Maybe, like her, he could not sleep, the wind howling outside in low torment. In her long johns and sweater, she crept down the narrow, creaking stairway to the warm glow of a roaring fire, Fremont in the kitchen, only the single light over the sink illuminating the darkness of the early hour.

When her eyes adjusted, she realized he was cleaning something long and hefty, a rifle.

"Morning, hope I didn't wake you."

She poured him a cup, then one for herself, Bartholomew purring around her arms like a friendly ghost. "No, I was awake anyway. Had a nightmare." She sat down at the table to marvel at his dexterity with the old rag and canister of oil. "Hunting today?"

"You didn't just fall off the turnip truck. Your uncle told me you were a quick one."

The glint in his eyes struck her like a soft chord. She sipped the comfort of the coffee, asking him where he was headed, and he described his favorite spot over on Roundtop Mountain between Flagstaff and West Carry. "My father and grandfather taught me how to hunt over there." His eyes glistened. "Got to get my deer in. Don't know how much time

I have left." The weight of his words hummed low, bittersweet. "From what we know about JD and his bribe, well, let's just say I don't hold out much hope." He rubbed the battered silver-barreled shotgun, his thick knuckles lined with black grease. "Stevens 12-gauge single-shot," he said, "my grandfather's gun.'

She pictured Papa out hunting with the Indigenous man, Longtoe. "Did you ever hunt with your grandfather?"

"He taught me to hunt. Of course, I had to learn how to use a knife and hatchet and compass first, but that's all part of it." He wrapped the blackened rag around the top of a long metal rod that he thrust into the barrel of the gun. "Taught me how to find the tracks of a deer, to listen for them, to know the signs." He hefted the gun to his shoulder to look through the sights. "Once the hammer falls, there's no turning back. One, maybe two shots allowed, so you can't afford to be shooting reckless—that's a hunter's worse sin, wounding and wasting life." He stood up and drank the last drop of coffee before taking out his worn canvas hunting pack to load with supplies for the day.

She didn't want him to stop talking. The day was still under the shadow of complete darkness. "Can I go with you?"

He studied her for a moment. "You ever been hunting before?"

"No, but I promise to do whatever you tell me."

"It's mostly waiting around and doing nothing, in the cold."

"I can do that." Her pulse quickened. "I'll go grab my stuff."

"Bring enough for a couple days. Might not be lucky the first day out there."

She considered her cut ties at the Gullet, her newfound freedom.

THE HEADLIGHTS ILLUMINATED THEIR way down the Long Falls Dam Road, only a few other souls out, perhaps hunters or truck drivers. Pennie told Fremont about the grease fire at the Gullet and Shep's explosion over the ruined pot roast, how Betsy seemed to wallow in it.

"He's always had a hot head. Can't say as I'd be much better if I had my leg crushed, but still. He's a discontented old soul, always has been."

The moon was nearly full over the mountain range, high above them, a pale yellow against the black sky. Something about the early hour made her feel like she was ahead of the world, up and ready for the day that had yet to come, the possibilities. "I'm glad to be out of there, especially away from Betsy."

He coughed and gurgled. "She was a good-looking one in her day. I think they met when he was fifty and still a bachelor. You could tell she liked the idea of marrying a man with a restaurant. From what I know, she didn't have much of a family life growing up. Always in trouble and married a few times before she even met Shep. Lots of chatter about town when he took her and her little boys in, alright, when they were barely out of diapers. I think he liked a late chance at fatherhood."

"I didn't know you knew so much about them."

He laughed and choked, sucking on his thermos coffee. "It's a small town, so we don't have too many secrets around here. Just sad Bri got mixed up with that son of theirs."

The most difficult part of this mess was leaving Bri to work at the Gullet. "I told her our suspicions about JD, you know, working on the side of the power company."

Fremont widened his eyes. "That smells like trouble."

"She promised she wouldn't say anything to him." Her pulse quickened. "And I had to defend myself against all the lies he's been telling her, that I was on the side of the power company and trying to take your family camp."

"You know what they say about that brand of liar. They accuse their enemies of their own goddamn sins, turning the tables so to speak, to create suspicion, take the focus off them."

She remembered Ward, standing in his condo development in Portland when he accused her of taking advantage of his son, knowing Ward had seduced Chloe, a teenager. "You sure know a lot about human nature."

He turned onto the Boise dirt logging road, lit a cigarette with a wooden match, and rolled down the window. "Just know this about Bri. That girl can't keep a secret. Don't get sucked into the drama he's creating. I'm afraid she's going to have to figure this out the hard way."

They rode along to nothing but the rumbling of the gravel road, the woods stretching on for miles. He knew these roads like the back of his hand, like generations of settlers. She wanted to tell him about her dreams but knew it would seem too bizarre, would make him think she was crazy. The image of Fremont's father rushing into the house to grab anything he could, Fremont and Fannie and Mama driving from the encroaching flames, the men digging the dirt wall. He had survived it, and now the power company was taking his land once again.

The sky was still pitch-black, only the moon showing through gauzy clouds while he unloaded their packs and his hunting gear from the truck. Pennie followed him as he pointed in the direction of Roundtop Mountain. Bent over, laden with his heavy pack and rifle, he moved along at a good clip, never once complaining about the bitter cold, their breath frosty in the stark morning temperatures on the cusp of a deep winter freeze. They followed a path cleared by the logging company, crunching blowdown on the packed snow. She felt the soldiers there in the woods beside them, trudging in ragged moccasins.

At the base of a ridge, Fremont pointed to deer tracks in the snow. "Pocket of does."

They followed a cleared path over a frozen swamp, the hoofprints and black-pebble scat sprinkled here and there. "They're bedding near here, for sure." A ghostly aura hung in the early morning air, and she felt a chill up her backside as they climbed, envisioning the militias carrying their bateaux over this ridge, their shoulders sore and blistered, frames gaunt, through the swampy black mud on their way to Bog Brook and the snaking Dead River.

Fremont turned off the path to follow the base of a high cliff wall. Her footing slipped, and he turned to make sure she was alright. She urged him forward, adjusting to the downhill slant of the terrain, forging a new path through the brush. They came upon what looked like an outhouse made of pallets, balanced on the side of the ridge facing downhill. He cleared the snow and frozen leaves with his foot to open a small side door of the sturdy hovel, just big enough for two people. Folding chairs leaned against the wall inside; he took the seat closest to the door. A long rectangular hole facing downhill gave them a spectacular view over the expanse of evergreens amongst the skeleton branches of oaks, birches, and maples, the night still aglow under the dim light of the waxing moon.

He leaned his shotgun up against the corner and surveyed the view all around them, pointing out different spots where deer had bedded down, where the bucks might be searching during the rut. "I'll have to get within thirty yards to shoot," he said. "But this blind has worked out before. You never know." He unpacked the thermos of hot coffee, his hat and gloves and bullets from his satchel. The woods around them were completely still except for the occasional chatter of chipmunks, the crack of a twig from a fox or a porcupine, the hammer of a woodpecker busy at work, *rat-a-tat-tat-tat-tat-tat-tat-tat*.

They settled into their chairs and kept watch through the opening. The thought of power lines coming near these woods and through the Great Carrying Place made her sink into a dark pocket of despair, until the vibration of *hoo-hoo-hooo-hooo-hoooo* filled her with consolation, the great horned owl come to call. Dani's story about Chebellok soothed her, the owl spirit giving the Passamaquoddy maidens strength, special powers to ensure their freedom. She sent out a silent wish for the owl to bestow his power to Bri, to give her strength. Her eyes heavy, she settled in and slumped down, letting herself drift into sleep, moonlight filtering through the pallets...

SHE SAT IN THE birchbark canoe between Aaron and Jacataqua, leaving the stench of dying men on shore, great winds swirling through the valley as they paddled upstream over the raging rapids and falls at the end of the valley. The belly of Jacataqua grew with life itself as she yelled from the bow for Aaron to correct his course, to hang to one side of the river, to keep the nose of the canoe up as she fiercely fought the battle of the unrelenting rapids from the front, the canoe nearly capsizing in the tossing and turning of the icy washtub current. They paddled on, passing men poling bateaux, toiling in the roiling river until they finally entered calm waters, a short reprieve before heading straight into more falls, the violent, icy river a torrent of brown rapids testing any strength they had left. Jacataqua held her paddle high above her small bump, keeping her balance while they shot the falls, steering them to the calmer waters at the bottom of the winding passage until they reached a long oval pond with ice-encrusted banks, the first of a chain of ponds, a reprieve from the never-ending churn of the river's northern branch.

The sachem set out her line to catch fish for them, easily hooking giant brook trout swimming beneath the icy cold surface. They paddled for miles and miles before finally reaching the end of the third pond where other men had lugged their bateaux out and set up small camps, fires burning and hissing. She could smell the charred squirrel and frying fish, meager meals for the emaciated men. Their starving eyes were on her, calling out to her, "she-wolf." Jacataqua commanded her to walk by her side, passing by the body of Colonel Dearborn's black dog lying dead on the ground, the men sawing him up with their small knives. A half-dead, malnourished soldier, raised his pistol and aimed just as Jacataqua blocked him...

PENNIE WOKE WITH A jerk, fear nestled inside her gut. Fremont put his hand on hers. "Gunshot from another hunter," he whispered. It took a few minutes for her heart to settle, for the weight of the dream to loosen its grip. Sitting up, she adjusted to the yellow light of daybreak. The wind had settled down, and the hillside sat quiet and peaceful in solemn repose, the gunshot but a memory, the fading image of Jacataqua paddling the rapids with the men on Arnold's march, half-crazed from starvation and cold, cutting up Colonel Dearborn's dog. Fremont sat up and peered down at something she could not see. He picked up his gun, feeling for the bullets in his pocket, and crept out of the blind.

Carefully treading, he made his way along the ridge and down through the trees without a sound. She followed in each of his footsteps in the snow, ducking below the tattletale branches, until the whitetail buck came into view surrounded by a cluster of birch trees below them. She held her breath as the six-point buck lifted his nose to the scents in the revealing wind, flicked his tail. Fremont slid his slug into the shotgun when, from the brush, in tumbled another deer, a small doe, hobbling with a wounded leg. He cocked the hammer to shoot straight through the thicket of tree branches in the path of the wounded doe, which launched into the air before landing a few yards away, the buck now gone from the thick woodland, the recollection of his hulking form but a hunter's dream.

They followed the path of the bullet to the doe lying peacefully on the bank of a stream, the icy moss like a pillow for her head. "You let that buck get away," she said, staring at the doe he had struck in the left shoulder, directly through the heart, its wounded leg hanging in the icy stream, disjointed, a loose appendage.

"Only thing I could do." He bowed his head, the same way his grandfather and Longtoe had done to thank the Creator, the giver of life.

EVEN IN HIS EIGHTIES, Fremont refused help hauling the deer down off the base of the ridge to the truck. With the drag rope across his chest and over his shoulder, he pulled, aided by the slick snow but still with difficulty, over the thickets and blowdown. At his truck, she helped him hoist the beautiful body of the doe into the bed, her fallow pelt still warm, her broken leg dangling by a ligament, black glassy eyes. "Too bad she's so young," he said. "I wish hunters would be more careful." He pushed her legs in, her dark pointed hooves stiff, and shut the gate, the smell of her blood like copper and iron hanging in the air. "Let's go over to camp to get warm."

They traveled over the gravel road, passing by Otter Pond on the left, the snow coming down now in the low light. Pennie had no idea what time it was and didn't care. Out here, time stood still, and her mind wandered more into the nature of things, the way the air grew heavy with snow, the sweep of little timeless funnels, the way the pale sun filtered through the clouds and through the flakes. She thought of Bri, and something inside her ached with a certain knowing.

On Middle Carry, his cabin came into view, quiet and solemn, surrounded by tall pines and birches and the dancing flakes of a delicate snowfall. She remembered standing next to the big woodpile with Uncle Alfie waiting for the appraiser to finish and knew they would hear more from the power company soon. Fremont hung the doe under the big pine tree beside the woodpile, the same place where she had seen the shadow of his grandfather in her picture.

Inside the log cabin, the stale smell of mouse droppings, must, and mildew filled the air. Fremont shuffled, bent over to sit in the wooden Adirondak near the woodstove. Only then did she realize how worn out he was and offered to bring in wood for a fire. He waved and smiled, lighting a cigarette.

Soon she had a fire going. He propped his stiff feet in wool socks up on a stool to feel the warmth, to work the circulation back into his toes. She joined him, sitting in the matching Adirondack, and thanked him for taking her along. He blew a long stream of smoke, saying he was sorry she had to see him shoot the young doe.

"You did a good thing." The fire glowed between them, and he asked her to get his pack. There was leftover coffee in the thermos. They ate fried egg and bacon sandwiches, the best tasting sandwich she'd ever had, scarfing them down and chewing on roasted peanuts and cashews while he told her about the moose his grandfather used to bring home with Longtoe, how they cherished every part of that massive animal, from the neck to the tongue to the liver. "When you eat the food the land offers you, you become a part of it. I can't imagine living anywhere else. This place is a part of me as much as I am a part of this place."

"I can feel their souls here still, even the souls of the Revolutionary soldiers marching through this place," she whispered.

"My grandfather found lots of artifacts from the march. Musket balls, nails, pewter buttons, an English half-penny, even a polling ax."

"I wish that were enough to keep this place from development."

"He was always looking for that chest of gold coins or Arnold's artillery that was rumored to be buried around here." With the memories of his grandfather still on his tongue, he fell fast asleep, his head drifting to one side, the paper skin of his lids covering his sharp hunter's eyes.

The fire roared in the potbellied stove, and she let herself drift off into the dream of the sachem Jacataqua once again, at the Chain of Ponds...

THROUGH HER WOLF'S EYES, she stared at the butt end of a pistol, the deranged man cocking his gun. Jacataqua yelled to her, "Rabbit!" and she took off, racing toward the wooded hills where the rabbit glens hid, away from the smell of the blood and guts of Colonel Dearborn's black dog. Minutes later, she came back with a large brown hare, and Jacataqua offered it to the emaciated men on the condition they leave her alone, to which they greedily yanked the rabbit from her clenched teeth in the bargain.

Only after a single night on the bank of the freezing pond, tiny fires keeping the camp alive, they hefted their canoe from the banks to begin their long carry over the Height of Land, their trail leading to a gap in the Appalachian Mountains, ledges and cliffs testing their grit and will. The strongest riflemen hefted the seven remaining bateaux on their backs for the steep and treacherous climb over an agonizing five-mile wall of granite, shoulders ground raw over the terrible carrying place. Ascending the mountain, the embittered, battered men trudged over fallen trees and brush and rocks and debris, tripping, until finally making the descent. Men falling on men, trying desperately to give each other a hand, grasping at whiplike branches to stay on this side of the dirt, soldiers fell to their death, one after another, crying out for their brothers not to leave them there to die on the granite rock face.

The wolves' ghastly howls closing in, the remaining men trudged through the bogs and thickets of Seven-Mile Stream, around birch trees and scrubby brush, wading through the muck and mire until finally coming upon the promising sight of Lake Megantic, where Commander Arnold sat encamped inside a bark house built by the Natives of St. Francis. Here, she and Jacataqua waited outside while Aaron met with the commander, who railed against the young soldier over the lack of food, the traitorous Enos and his men who had turned their back on them, the faithless Native spies who had taken his messages to alert Quebec of their approach.

When he finally came outside, Aaron led Jacataqua away from the bark house to say that Arnold was sending him on a mission to get a message to General Montgomery in Montreal. "I have no choice, my dear." Jacataqua scowled at him, but he insisted it was his duty. "Besides, these men need you to make sure they get to Quebec. Only you know the way through the inlet on the other side of Megantic." And with that, he went away, his frame lean but still strong, promising to return to her in Quebec, leaving the mother of his child to help guide Arnold's men through the maze of swamps and bogs to hunt for any food they could scavenge in the ice-cold winter wind coming down from the St. Lawrence.

She sat in the canoe with Jacataqua who paddled down Lake Megantic with the five hundred remaining men and two women in the expedition in the shallow, bone-chilling water, the soldiers sinking up to their thighs in the bogs, carrying the last of the bateaux and the few food stores they had left, most barefoot, tattered and scratched over every inch of their bodies, breaking the ice with the butts of their rusted muskets, scrambling over cedar roots, knee-deep in the frigid mire and snow. Here, Jacataqua met Natanis in the tangle of the swamps where he helped the starving men by driving moose in their path, building fires, and roasting bear with Jacataqua on higher ground, but always out of the sight of the men who did not trust any Native warrior. Invisible Natanis and quick-footed Jacataqua led the men out of the maze of freezing swamps where they otherwise would surely have perished.

At the Chaudière, they again set in their canoes and bateaux for a ride over dangerous falls and rapids, this time around jagged ledges and boulders at every turn. Even as a lone canoer with her husky by her side, Jacataqua managed to expertly handle the twists and turns and ledges of the rapid river while the men were battered on rocks, the heavy boats in splinters, overturned in the raging falls, some drowning before they reached the rocky basin of the rapids. The survivors lived on roasted leather hides, many walking the final, frigid forty miles to Sartigan, leaving their bloody tracks in the icy snow behind them with their frozen comrades who had collapsed on the final march to reach civilization and sustenance.

At the French village with little whitewashed houses and wigwams in the fertile valley, Jacataqua, of half-French blood, conversed with the Natives of St. Francis and the villagers who supported the soldiers' fight for independence from the British. Here, men filled their bellies on rice and corn, many gorging themselves and succumbing to death by fever after the long and tortuous march through the primeval wilderness. Here, Natanis and his brother Sabattis, alongside forty Native braves dressed in full regalia, faces painted, demanded to know the intentions of Arnold and his men. The colonel spoke of his plans to fight the British, asking the Natives to join them in their attack of Quebec, to which they agreed, calling Arnold "Dark Eagle."

The Natives put in their twenty canoes, joining forces with the battered men who hefted their pine log dugouts on their shoulders to march the last thirty miles to St. Mary's plains of Canada, to the immense St. Lawrence River, under a blanketing snowfall. They finally came upon Point Levi, across the river from the grim, foreboding buildings of Quebec, the gates closed atop the immense walls of stone, the high precipice they called "The Gibraltar of America." The ragged bearded men, sick from near starvation and dysentery, limped and coughed as they set up camp. And here Jacataqua waited for Aaron, the great stone walls of Quebec reflected in her dusky, expectant eyes.

BESIDE HER, FREMONT WAS still sound asleep, snoring lightly. Jacataqua's dark eyes lingered in her mind, just like the intense eyes of Bri. She pulled out her phone to text her, staring at the glowing fire. After ten or fifteen minutes, a text came back from Bri saying she had had a fall, but she was doing fine. *A fall? What kind of fall?* No matter how many ways she asked, Bri only texted back she was doing fine, not to worry, she was a little drowsy, just needed to sleep.

Thoughts circled around Pennie's mind, and she finally nudged Fremont. With a snort, he woke up and ran his sleeve over his dry mouth. "What's going on?"

"Something is wrong with Bri. She had a fall."

"What kind of fall?"

"I don't know, but something is wrong. I can feel it."

He didn't fight her on it but stood up to straighten his creaky back, saying he had to take a leak. She shut down the woodstove to let it burn down before they grabbed their things to head out, leaving the dead doe hanging from the tree, her marble eyes reflecting the giving woods.

THE LONG DIRT DRIVEWAY seemed to go on for a mile before they finally reached the huge log cabin, the game hoist sitting empty, the ghost of the sow still lingering. The only car in the driveway was Betsy's Volvo. They sat in the truck, stalled in some kind of limbo, assessing the situation. An instant of foreboding passed unspoken between them until Fremont said, "Well, what are we waiting for?" At the door beside the garage bays, she knocked. No sound from inside. Knocking harder, they peered inside to see Betsy at the top of the long, steep stairway to the apartment. Pennie pounded again until she came down.

Her pinched face greeted them when she opened the door. "What do you want?"

Pennie said, "We're here to see Bri."

Her bucket face grew red, impatient, avoiding eye contact. "She's taking a nap."

"She texted me and said she'd had a fall."

The matron seemed to be mulling things over, her eyes flitting, before shaking her head, adamant. "Don't know what in hell you're talking about. She's just resting. This pregnancy is taking a round out of her. Baby must be growing like stinkweed."

Fremont moved in closer, only a few inches from Betsy's face. "Then you don't mind if we come in and check on her."

She puffed herself up. "You've got no right to come into my house." When she tried to shut the door, Fremont grabbed the doorknob and pushed back until she gave way, stumbling backward.

He stepped on the threshold. "Move aside before I break your god-damn neck."

Fear and indignation crossed her face, red and bulging. "Get the fuck out of my house."

This time he lost all courtesy, pushing her, knocking her against the wall. Pennie followed him up the stairway. At the top, they opened the door to the apartment with the small kitchen, the long table with the picture window looking over the woods in the back, the living room with the fireplace and large screen TV, JD's bear mount now hanging from the opposite wall, its glassy eyes dead and gone. A weak noise, almost a moan, came from one of the rooms, and Fremont followed the sound to a door where Bri lay inside on a large king-sized bed, covered by a red comforter, her eyes frightened, blinking.

Fremont grabbed the footboard as if to steady himself, his knuckles lined with black gun grease. "What's going on Bri? You okay?"

Betsy was behind them, standing in the doorway, her fat chin in the air. "She's fine. I didn't want you to wake her. She's not feeling well, *are you, dear?*"

Fremont turned and pushed her backward until she was well out of the room. "I've heard just about enough out of you." He slammed the door on her indignant face.

Bri blinked again, her skin sallow. "I fell." Her voice came out weak, tired. "I just need to sleep." She closed her eyes, her body a lifeless lump under the covers. Tentatively, Pennie grasped the comforter and pulled it up to look underneath. Bri was completely dressed in a white sweatshirt and blue jeans, her long legs unmoving. A cold awareness moved over her. "Can you get out of bed?" Bri's head moved back and forth on her pillow as if she were trying to wish away any negative thoughts that crept around. "I'm too tired."

Pennie held back her sadness and creeping fear, avoiding Fremont's eyes to keep up her mask of brightness. "Can you move your legs?"

Bri looked down at her body, as if willing her legs to move. "I hurt all over."

Fremont stepped up to the bedside. "Here, we can help you." He smiled, assuring her things would be alright. She flopped her head side to side again, drowsy, as he carefully scooped his arm under her shoulders to lift her up. Bri let out a piercing scream, a primal cry that cut through them to the quick. A look of fear mixed with hate crossed Fremont's face.

Pennie picked up her phone, trying to control her hands from shaking to call 911 for an ambulance. Fremont spoke low, masking his anger. "What happened?"

"It was just an accident. My baby. I know my baby is okay." The gold cross chain twisted around her thin neck. They looked out the bedroom window in desperation for the ambulance to appear, only to see Betsy in the driveway talking on the phone. Fremont's expression grew darker, grim. Pennie sat delicately on the bed and caressed the bruises on Bri's strong wrist, the wrist of a fisherwoman, and held back tears.

Bri's breathing grew heavy, labored, filling them with dread while they stared out the window for what seemed like an hour until the red lights showed up. Two men made their way up to the apartment and the bedroom to take her vitals, give her a shot for the pain. They carefully placed her on a stretcher as she cried and groaned for her baby, wanting to know if her baby was okay.

With slow deliberation, the strong young men moved Bri down the steep stairway and loaded her into the waiting ambulance under a cold gray sky. Before they closed the doors, Betsy piped up, "Don't worry, JD's going to meet you at the hospital. That baby is just fine. Don't you worry, dear."

Chapter 15
Treasure Hunt

IN THE WAITING ROOM, the intense smell of antiseptic and lemon wafted in the air with specks of dust. A shaft of sunlight cast on the floor. Betsy and JD sat opposite them, whispering conspiratorially. Anxiety crept over Pennie like an insidious vine. Fremont stood to look out the windows, away from JD and Betsy and their false empathy. Betsy said, "Bri was in bed sleeping until *they* showed up, barging in to *my* house."

The doctor, a middle-aged Indian woman, came out of Bri's room and walked down the corridor to greet them. Somberly, she shared that Bri had fractured her pelvis but that her chances of a full recovery were excellent. Since the pregnancy was "nonviable," only about twelve weeks along, aborting the fetus was the best option for Bri's full recovery without complications.

JD was the first to speak up. "Is there any harm to the baby?"

"Not as far as I can tell, but I would not recommend taking this pregnancy to term. It's too dangerous. She's young and healthy and should have no problem having another baby. It's the best thing for her long-term health and well-being. I'll explain this to Brianna when she's awake and alert."

Betsy sat up and puffed out her chest. "Can we talk to her as soon as she wakes up? I think this is really up to the mother *and father*."

The doctor remained placid. "Of course. The nurse will come for you when she's awake. In the meantime, please wait out here." She walked away brusquely, leaving them in the deafening silence of the waiting room. The low vibrations began humming inside Pennie, a slow insistent march of awareness, the truth of the matter. When Fremont stepped out for a smoke, she followed him.

Outside in the back parking lot, he lit up, blowing out a long stream of smoke and a sigh of sadness. "We'll tell Bri to follow the doctor's recommendation. That'll be that. If that prick tries to talk her into carrying this thing to term, I think I may kill him."

"Don't let anyone else ever hear you say that."

Her phone buzzed. Alfie. When she heard his voice, she knew it was not good news and put him on speaker. He explained how the Land Use Planning Commission had voted to approve the power line through all the unorganized territories to the north of Flagstaff Lake, down through the Carrying Place.

"It was a split vote, seven to five. Skelton voted in favor. I believe your property is the only thing in the way of the corridor, Fremont. Now that we have the prelitigation offer, I've responded with your refusal to sell. All we can do now is wait to see how they answer."

"Will we have to go to court over this thing?"

"Most likely. We'll cross that bridge when it comes. The power company will come after us with everything they have."

Fremont stared into space. She told her uncle about Bri's fall, saying, "She'll be fine, we just have to deal with her fiancé and his mother."

They hung up, and Pennie took Fremont's arm to walk back to the empty waiting room. Standing outside Bri's room, number 33, Pennie felt a high vibration, remembering when Uncle Alfie was in the hospital, how he'd recovered after his heart attack. Inside, JD and Betsy stood at her bedside, talking in hushed tones, stopping abruptly when they saw Fremont and Pennie in the doorway. Fremont smiled at his granddaughter, asking her how she was feeling. A glow came across her pale face. "Better, thanks. Especially knowing the baby is okay."

He gripped the plastic footboard, his thick knuckles still lined with gun grease. "Now, Bri, you listen to the doctor. She made it clear your best option was not keeping this baby, for your full recovery."

She sighed. "I know, I know, but this is so important to JD and me, and like Betsy says, this is in God's hands now." JD squeezed her hand, the hand with the bruised wrist. Her neck was now bare, free from the gold cross.

Fremont clenched his jaw. "You know how you've always talked about being a Guide, Bri, from the time you were old enough to pick up a fishing rod. You're putting all that at risk for no good reason. The doctor says you're young and perfectly able to have children once you fully recover. Let's be reasonable, honey."

Her jaw trembled and she began to cry, her hands covering her face, the hospital band slipping from her bruised wrist.

Betsy said, "Now look what you've done, you old bastard. Why don't you mind your own business and leave this poor girl alone to make up her own mind? Don't you think she's been through enough already?"

He looked as if he wanted to thrash the haughty red-faced woman, but instead he left the room. Pennie reached for Bri to tell her it was going to be alright before she followed Fremont out.

They found Bri's nurse at her station down the hall. Fremont explained to her, in plain unvarnished language, that Bri's fall was no accident. "And I'm also damn sure JD is responsible for the bruise on her wrist. Are you going to allow that wife beater to influence her to keep his child?" The nurse moved them to a small, empty private room and asked them to sit down so that she could get a social worker. Fremont's hands shook, the same ones that had so assuredly handled a shotgun earlier that day, shooting an injured deer instead of a prized buck. He grabbed his knees, looking at the polished linoleum floor.

It wasn't long before a social worker showed up, young, twenty-something, with a carefully groomed beard and wire glasses, soft-spoken and kind. He asked Fremont to explain what had happened, taking careful notes on his laptop. Unfortunately, they did not have any proof of the domestic violence, and Bri had never complained about JD. Pennie and Fremont both insisted that everything in their gut told them he was abusing her, and what course could they take? He carefully explained that these kinds of cases came up all the time. All he could do was consult with the doctor and counsel Bri.

THE NEXT DAY, FREMONT and Pennie drove to the hospital early, hoping to talk to Bri without JD or Betsy around. When they arrived, she was up in bed eating her breakfast of scrambled eggs, lime Jello, hash browns, and orange juice. The color had returned to her face, and she looked almost back to her own cheerful self. Fremont gave her a kiss on the cheek. Beaming, she said, "I slept all night long because I have this nice private room, not sure how that all worked out, but sometimes things work out in our favor, right Grandpa?" He nodded, just happy to have his granddaughter feeling good again. She went on. "The food's not as bad as I thought it was going to be, either." She scooped Jell-O into her mouth, smacking her lips. "Since I'll be here for a few days, JD promised to bring me magazines from home to keep me from going completely bonkers. The doctor said I'll be in for at least four days to stabilize the fracture and get fit for the pelvic brace."

"Did the social worker come and talk to you?" he asked lightly, hopeful.

She nodded with a mouthful. "Yeah, real nice guy, although he and the doctor asked me some uncomfortable questions about JD. Did you talk to them?" Her eyes moved from Pennie to Fremont and back again.

Pennie leaned against the bed. "We told the social worker we were concerned. What did the doctor say?"

She flipped her hair back. "She asked how the fall happened, and I explained that it was an accident. JD can have a temper. Sometimes he just can't help himself. And when he does overreact, he's the first one to say he's sorry. You know how important that is in a relationship, for someone, especially a man, to say they're sorry?" They both nodded, waiting for her to come to her senses. She took another spoonful of Jello. "Anyway, he and I are square now, and he promised to control his temper more. He just doesn't know his own strength. This whole thing was just an accident."

Fremont leaned toward her. "Accident or not, I hope you've come to your senses about the baby after talking to the doc."

"She's such a nice lady. Did you know she's from Calcutta? Grew up in a one-room hut with a dirt floor, and her parents sacrificed everything to send her to our country to become a doctor. Her family sacrificed so much so she could pursue her dream. She asked me about my dreams, too, and, I don't know, I felt so good after talking to her. I'm thinking the best option would be for me to not keep the baby at this point. And I already talked to JD about it. Of course he isn't happy, but he knows this is my decision, nobody else's."

They breathed a small sigh of relief. A smile took over Fremont's face, relief that had not graced his friendly, lined profile since he'd seen his granddaughter lying in the bed in that apartment. "I'm proud of you."

A noise came from behind them, and they turned to see a reedy woman, all skin and bones, peeking through greasy brown hair at Bri, grinning, her teeth brown with rot. A meek sound came from this stranger. "Hey there, sweetie."

Fremont's brow furrowed. Bri looked aghast, choking on her juice. "Mom? What are you doing here?" The frail, lanky woman crept up like a cat beside the bed, eyeing Fremont, and put her hand on Bri's arm. "I heard you was here recovering from a fall. You okay, my little tootsie roll?"

Bri began to cry, her face puckered. "Mom, I've been trying to reach you for months. You never return my calls. I thought you were, you were—"

"Hush, hush, now dear. There's nothing to be worried about. I was just getting my new career going. I'm working at the library over in Farmington, in the children's room."

Fremont interrupted her. "Nell, what kind of hogwash are you dishing out to her now?"

"Oh quiet, old man. You're not a part of this conversation. I'm talking to my daughter here." She glared at him. Without a word, he turned to leave the room.

"My dear Brianna, I hear you're expecting a baby. Wow, what big news—I'm going to be a grandmother." She clapped her hands to the sides of her gaunt face.

Bri started to cry again, and she reached out her hand to her mother. Pennie thought the fragile woman may have weighed ninety pounds soaking wet with ankle weights.

"Shh, dear. Now, you should be happy about this. You'll recover from your fall and have a baby in what, six months' time? Why, that's May, a spring baby. Do you know if it's a boy or a girl?"

She sniffed and reached for a tissue to blow her nose. "I don't know yet, but I think it's a boy. I can feel it."

The raspy-voiced woman had a gleam in her rheumy eyes. "A boy! How exciting, just like your brothers. They'll be so happy to hear they're gonna be uncles."

Pennie was thinking about ways she could shut up this anorexic interloper, but on second thought, decided it was best to leave them alone. In the hallway, she looked for Fremont. He had probably gone outside to have a smoke after seeing his wayward daughter in such a bad state. Was she living on the streets? Alcoholic? Drug addict? Then she spotted Betsy in the waiting area and wondered why she wasn't in Bri's room.

Pennie made a quick pit stop to the restroom. When she came back out, she watched Nell approach Betsy in the waiting area. The matron handed Bri's mother a stuffed manila envelope, thanking her with pursed lips. Nell kept walking toward the elevator, her affected happiness for her daughter now morphed into the grim anticipation of another fix.

OVER TUNA FISH SANDWICHES at Fremont's house, Pennie told him about Betsy giving Nell the envelope of cash. He flicked his long ash in the coffee can. "I expected as much from my daughter. She's been at the point of no return for a long, long time." His gaze went somewhere far away, perhaps thinking of happier times when Nell was just a little girl and Lena was still alive. "I only hope when I tell Bri, she can accept the truth. We've got to get back to the hospital soon." There was a knock at the door, and he opened it to the sheriff. "Afternoon, Fremont. Sorry about this, but you've been served again."

He accepted the letter and thanked the sheriff for his service. They both knew this was from the lawyers for the power company. The letter was notice of a petition filed in court for Eminent Domain and Declaration of Taking. Uncertain what this exactly meant, they called Alfie's office. Tita answered the phone. "He's on a call, but hold on, I'll let him know you're on the line."

She patched them through, and Alfie explained the declaration was a way to rush the process through the court system. He recommended Fremont request a hearing to challenge the declaration and the appraisal value. Lighting a cigarette, Fremont said, "I don't care if they offer me a million dollars. It's not for sale. Period."

Alfie explained it would be an uphill battle against the legal machine of the power company. "Pennie, I need you down here in Portland to help prepare. How much notice do you need to give that restaurant?"

She smiled. "None, I already quit." Her gaze turned to Fremont as she considered the situation with Bri. "I hate to leave with Bri still in the hospital, though."

"You get down there and help your uncle, Pennie. I'll keep an eye on Bri. She's in good hands with those nurses and doctors. There's nothing more to do but hope she makes the right decision."

After Fremont called the hospital to check on Bri, Pennie talked him into taking her over to the Eustis cemetery where the Dead River graves had been moved. The empty chapel stood quiet and still, a replica the power company had built in 1949 in New Flagstaff to replace the original built by Charles T. Rand for the King's Daughters of Flagstaff in 1902. Her dream came to her, of the windows piled in the back of the flatbed with the church bell, preparing for the flooding of Flagstaff and Dead River. Those beautiful stained-glass windows from the original church now graced this new church, and Pennie could hear the old hymn, "O God of Earth and Alter," coming through the glass as if a holy choir stood just inside and sang for her, for the people of this land.

O God of earth and altar, bow down and hear our cry,
our earthly rulers falter, our people drift and die; the
walls of gold entomb us, the swords of scorn divide,
take not thy thunder from us, but take away our pride.

Fremont came up behind her and said, "Jothan Sewell, an evangelist from Chesterville, was the first reverend of the church in old Flagstaff." Pennie followed him to the cemetery beside the church, where the 180 bodies were reinterred from the cemetery on Jim Eaton Hill. Fragments of her dream came to her again: the small boxes of bones, the old man buried with his wool socks, the child with her doll. On the ground, grass grew around the edges of the tiny memorials, engraved stepping stones of the *Dead River Unknown*, numbered from one to fourteen, tiny memorials sinking into the earth. Around them stood gravestones of all sizes, like slanting sunrays, markers for Stephen B. Wyman, 1851, and Samual Wyman, Jr., 1840; Caroline L. Wing, 1888; FUD and Jeanie (no date); Flora I., Wife of Warren Wing, 1902; Asa Green, 1883; Edw'd Thompson, 1895; William Butler, 1882; George W. and Ida M. Standish, 1897; Myles, Son of George and Ida Standish (13 years), 1897; Miles Standish, 1882; and on and on and on.

They stopped at every headstone, at every grave. A biting wind swept under their coats, the ground vibrating underneath their footsteps with a beautiful melody that sang of happiness and loss, of joy and sadness, of desperation and despair, of sacrifice for independence.

That night, she fell into a deep sleep...

THE FIRES OF THE Dead River sifted through her consciousness behind the eyes of the husky, riding in the back of the old pickup truck that Mama drove on their way across the bridge and out of the valley. Blazes ignited up both sides of the river, the charred landscape all around them under the sky, black as ink, a war zone of destruction of their woods and wagons, pastures and fences, barns and homes, hopes and dreams. Instinctively, she jumped from the truck to run in the thick smoke toward a small shack near the millstream.

Inside the hovel, she made her way between stacks of newspapers and magazines, cans of oil and paint, an assortment of knives and rifles, bear skins and lynx hides, until reaching the back, where she found an old, bearded man lying in his bed, fast asleep, wheezing in the smoke-filled room. She barked and barked until he awoke, sputtering and choking, points of moonlight coming through tiny bullet holes in his roof that pierced the clouds of smoke. He followed her out through the opening between piles of newspapers to the black night, where he caught his breath, blinking at the menacing fires closing in on them, his gray hair sticking out every which way, a deep scar on his cheek that seemed to pull one eye open. Bear claws and teeth around his neck jangled. "Saved by the she-wolf! You're really my grandmother come back to save me, ain't you?" Overcome with a coughing fit, he scratched her between the ears. "Okay, okay, let's go get that buried treasure before it's too late."

He jumped into an old Bush Roundabout with wooden-spoke tires, the single-cylinder engine in the open front sputtering and coughing, the canvas roof flapping, and she hopped on the seat beside him before he took off down the road, heading back east toward the Dead River plantation, passing the town green where the flagstaff still stood, its tattered American flag rippling in the smoky breeze, passing the little windowless shell of the chapel, the unearthed cemetery with the tall white pine that Wing had planted, Perley's farm on Jim Eaton Hill. They rode over the Big Bridge that had been blown down or flooded, rebuilt several times over, passing the place where Peter Wahl's barn once stood, where they had the dances, now burned to the ground. Passing by the old Ferry Farm, where fires jumped all around, changing direction with the fickleness of the breeze, passing Papa and the others digging the dirt firewall, the Rand farm and the big round barn, the Safford and Whitham farms and then Fud Taylor's where old Bert stopped the car, the flames of the fires behind them burning orange inside the valley.

"Well, what are you waiting for?" He grabbed his shovel and pistol with his three-fingered hand, cursing the bear that took his middle digits. "It's buried over here, right? On the other side of Roundtop?" She led the way, traversing the dark countryside, wading through brooks and over a rocky outcropping to the base of the mountain where a small stream flowed. He spotted an enormous boulder, where he began to dig with everything he had left, shoveling the soft silt of the bank. She jumped in the swift stream and dug with her claws, right beside him, until they hit something solid. He clanked it with his shovel. "Hallelujah to the Lord on highest!" Then shock filled his eyes and, paralyzed, he fell face forward into the little stream, dead as a doornail, his shovel still resting in the hole, three feet deep, the water rushing over his weathered hide.

SHE AWOKE WITH A jolt, the vision of old Bert Horton dead in the streambed pulsing in her mind, her whole body quaking. She knew that stream, that boulder; it was the same place where Fremont had shot the deer.

OVER A BREAKFAST OF coffee and plain donuts, Pennie told Fremont about her dream. He seemed skeptical. "No one's ever given those stories of Arnold's munitions buried around here much weight. Everyone thought old Bert was crazy as a coot, you know." Bartholomew sat on his lap, curling his tail around his waist, hugging him. "I guess it wouldn't hurt to look around, though." On a small napkin, she drew a picture of the stream as she remembered it, the large birch tree where Bert had dug the hole and yelled out as if he had found gold. Then she told him about the dream she had of his grandfather hunting with Longtoe, how she wondered if any other artifacts were buried on his property.

He took a long drag. "I guess you never know."

She thanked him and hugged him, saying that she'd call later to check on Bri. Driving toward Stratton, passing the silent Greedy Gullet, the little schoolhouse where the medium lived came into view and, on a whim, she pulled in to the small dirt driveway. Up on the covered porch, the little bird's nest in the eaves of the porch twittered with life. Despite the early winter, the miracle of new life still emerges. The small woman appeared in the doorway before Pennie even knocked. "I've been expecting you," she said, and opened the door. The smell of old books and lavender filled Pennie's senses, and an overwhelming sense of relief flooded her as she told the old woman about Bri, her "accidental fall," and her child.

A glassy look clouded Greta's eyes. She seemed to float off to a different space and time. "I can feel her sadness. She is conflicted because there are evil forces working against her, against her ability to make the best decision for herself and her child."

Pennie nodded. "I just, I don't know how to help her."

"Keep sending her your energy. Remember, Pennie, vibrations speak louder than words."

They sat together in meditation, their hands locked. As the old woman chanted, visions of Bri conjured up in both their minds, of lifting her spirit above the physical realm and into a place where peace enveloped it. "Sending you vibrations of clear thought and energy, of harmony," she whispered. Pulling out her deck of cards from the oaken box, she asked Pennie to shuffle them and think of a question.

"I want to know what I can do to help Bri, to help her see the light." When she was done, she divided the deck into three piles.

The medium said, "What should Pennie do?" She turned over 19, Grace. They stared at one another, and a chill went up Pennie's spine. "You are being sent a blessing, Pennie. Grace will provide you with the answers you seek." She whispered the question again and flipped over the card in the middle pile to see 49, The White Owl. "The magic of the owl is a sign that you can expect the unexpected." Again, the message sent a shudder through Pennie, the symbol of the owl seeming to follow her wherever she went. With a steady hand, Greta turned over a final card from the third pile, repeating the question, and 61, The Golden Rule, appeared. "You are striking the right balance, Pennie. The scales of justice are on your side."

They sat still and let the message of the cards, their powerful energy, move them through space and time. "Be true to yourself," whispered the medium, letting it float in tranquility, to flow through them. Pennie absorbed the numbers on the three cards: 19 plus 49 plus 61...or 129. Or 12. Or 3.

OUTSIDE THE LITTLE SCHOOLHOUSE, Pennie ran into the dowser, Mr. Snodgrass, who was holding the Y-shaped birch rod in his hand.

He looked so much like the wine seller in Portland, Pennie felt she was talking to the same person. "Leaving town so soon?" he said.

"How did you know I was leaving?"

"Oh, just a feeling, but I'm sure you'll be back."

She thought about Fremont and his camp, her dream of old Bert Horton. "Bri's grandfather, Fremont, is looking for artifacts over at West Carry and on his land over at Middle Carry. Any chance you could help him?"

He nodded. "I'll have to look him up." With that, he left to walk behind Greta's house in search of pure spring water.

Chapter 16
Conjuring an Apport

DRIVING SOUTH ON THE interstate, the luminous fall foliage now replaced by skeleton trees of early winter along the highway, her mind filled with images of the cemetery, the graves of the Malaga Island settlement and the Marks family where she had felt her first vibrations. She wondered if Stan and his girlfriend, Roxanne, were still together, living in the little white Cape next to the cemetery, now protected from development. A few exits later, she passed Falmouth and pondered Mrs. McCarthy, alone in her large white mansion on the ocean with her son-in-law building a home next door, the one who was friends with Ward. The mystery of Chloe still haunted Pennie. Again, an image of a child's jewelry box flashed in her mind. What could that mean? She had the inclination to take the exit but remained steadfast in her journey, too eager to get back to the downtown Portland office.

When she finally arrived, everything at Alfred Goode, Esq., was exactly as she remembered it: the retro desks and chairs in the main office, Uncle Afie's private office still paneled in brown, his large wooden desk covered with maps and legal documents. At her own desk in the spacious room lined with file cabinets overlooking Exchange Street, she found maps of the Dead River Valley that Uncle Alfie had found, the snaking river running down from the Chain of Ponds through the valley, with Bigelow watching over the homesteads of the old Flagstaff and Dead River and Bigelow plantations, Bryant's mill and Dutchie Leavitt's general store, the two-story school and pretty little steepled church and cemetery on Jim Eaton Hill, the working farms and drying sheds, vast pastures and clear, running streams.

Out the second-floor office window, she could see her uncle with Cassie, Teddy, Fella, and Daisy. The yellow lab, Cassie, led the way, wagging her tail. From her backpack, Pennie took out the picture of her mother and her husky, Togo, and placed it on her desk. When they came through the office door, Cassie ran to her and jumped on her lap to smother her with kisses. It was so good to be home.

"Morning, Lucky Pennie. We've missed you around here." He put his coat and hat on the standalone rack in the corner. "Your Aunt Aggie has a big dinner planned."

"Wouldn't miss it." She gave the other hounds her full attention, each looking for a scratch and words of love.

He pulled on the cuffs of his plaid wool button-down. "Where's your cousin?"

"I was about to ask you the same thing."

He harumphed. "Things haven't changed much, as you can see. Let's talk in my office."

He opened a letter and handed it over with a flourish. To her surprise, it was a date with the Maine Supreme Court for a hearing on the power company's Declaration of Taking. "Wow, that was fast. One week?"

"Oh, believe me, these guys aren't messing around, Fremont's property being the last one in the way of their grand swath through western Maine. I also got names of the biggest investors in the power corridor, and one of them is the Freedom Hedge Fund."

A little chime went off inside her head. "Let me guess, that's the hedge fund of the United Freedom Church."

He nodded, smiling at his pupil for doing her homework. She added, "I overheard Betsy talking to JD about it."

"They've invested $50 million in the corridor."

Pennie leaned forward. "Sounds like they might go to any lengths, like bribing a commissioner, for the deal to go through."

"I'm thinking maybe."

"Can we file suit before our meeting with the Supreme Court?"

"Right now, the only hard evidence we have is that JD's employer donated an SUV to the church, and that was probably just to sweeten the pot a little. Seems like JD has something to gain personally from this."

"Betsy and Bri have talked about some big church board position JD is up for. From the megachurch's website, it looks like there are regional boards, one for north, south, east, and west. I'm betting JD is up for the northern position."

"I'm sure those church board seats offer some good financial incentives, especially to young disciples who are willing to engage in bribery in the name of lining the coffers and spreading the gospel."

"And, at the commission hearing in Farmington, one of JD's buddies testified in favor of the corridor. Turns out he owns the local white-water rafting outfit, and the power company has promised significant investments in ATV trails and other 'tourist-friendly' improvements."

He nodded, scratching Fella, who had hopped on his lap. "For now, we have to concentrate on the hearing and how to convince the court that Fremont's property is worth saving, that maybe the power company can find another route."

Pennie shared the history she'd read about the Dead River plantations, how the crews had come in with their trucks and machinery, saws and axes, to clear the forest and land all around the valley, burning everything to make way for the flowage, forcing the families from their homes.

"Fremont already lived through this once. Such a tragic history repeating itself. And he says this is just the beginning. Once they start cutting a path through that wilderness, the door is open for more and more development."

A slamming door interrupted them. Tita breezed into the office looking like she had better things to do than be inside answering phones at a desk. He said, "Write up your notes about the history of the Dead River Valley, how the families like Fremont's were kicked out of their homes. We'll also focus on the historic preservation of the Arnold Trail. Can you call Rachel at the preservation commission and ask her to send you any details she has on that?"

"I'll call her today."

Out in the office, Pennie smiled to herself, happy to sit down opposite Tita again. "About time you showed up."

"Don't give me any grief, Pennie. I've had a long night." When she took off her sunglasses, the dark circles under her eyes revealed her exhaustion.

"Everything okay?"

With a great huff, Tita dropped her Italian leather shoulder bag on her desk. "Lars is selling the rights to our documentary to a producer who wants to expand it, to make it the *complete* history of women's freeskiing, from the early days to today. Can you believe this bullshit? This was supposed to be *my* movie, and he sold it right out from under me."

"How can he? It's your footage, your story, your *image*."

"Before he left to go out to California, he convinced me to sign some documents, giving him rights to market and sell the film. Obviously, I didn't read the fine print."

Tita's predicament gave Pennie a sinking feeling, how some people would go to such lows to get their own way, no matter what the cost, even if it's a relationship. "What can you do?"

"He just told me last night over the phone. Of course, I told him I would fight it and bring him to court. He's supposed to meet me here so we can go to lunch and *discuss* it." She glanced over at her father's office. "Whatever you do, *do not* tell pop. I'll work this out."

Tita's phone chirped, and she retrieved it from her bag. "He's downstairs. Tell Pop I'll be back." In a whirl, she grabbed her coat and sunglasses and walked out as fast as she'd come in. Pennie looked down from the second floor and watched as Lars, looming large over her, tried to greet her with open arms, only to receive the wrath of Tita, who swung her designer leather bag with all her force at his ear. When he held up his hands to protect his head, she swung it around to punch the other ear, screaming something Pennie could only imagine.

LATER THAT AFTERNOON, SHE walked over to Dani and Mali's studio on Congress Street to catch up and find out how their project was going. As usual, Dani answered the door of their walk-up studio with her black apron on, white paint in her hair. She barely wiped her hands before giving Pennie a big hug. "About time you're back! I didn't think you were ever coming home."

The prints hanging from every available studio space grabbed her attention, the intense cyan blue electrifying the air. "Looks like I've missed some amazing work here." Dani's husband, Max, appeared from the darkroom, blinking in the light.

He waved and dropped some negative film on the worktable. "You're back in town. Good thing. My wife needs other things to do than creating more of these." He motioned toward the charged blue artwork hanging by clothespins from wires all around the studio. "We're running out of room."

Dani rolled her eyes as he ducked back inside the darkroom. Arms outstretched, she described what she was working on, jumping right into the process of cyanotype. "It was developed by an astronomer, Sir John Herschel, back in the nineteenth century, using only two chemicals, sunlight and water." The intense blue hues, a little different in every image—water rushing over falls, fish with silvery white scales, underwater plants and algae, stones, clusters of leaves and rippling pools—gave the impression, the feeling, of a free-flowing river.

"I used the river water and the sunlight from the actual places on the Kennebec where the dams are located." She pointed to an image of grayish blue algae. "This was made with the water at the Wyman Dam." Then she pointed to the bright cyan silhouette of a great blue heron, "And this was created with the water and sunlight downstream, free of the dam. Don't you just love it? I'm trying to show how the living river is present in these images."

They were indeed mesmerizing, almost magical, leaping from the paper. Pennie pointed to a print of a brown trout hooked on a line. "Where did you take this?"

"Oh, that was when Bri caught the fish at the Round Barn site, remember? I snapped it with my phone."

The moment came alive in her mind, a cyan-hued movie in time, her dream of the river receding and Bri's image changing into Papa fishing on the Dead. Pennie's attention moved to the next image, of the mother bear with her cubs. Sadness moved her, remembering the bear mount in JD's apartment, the terror of seeing Bri in bed, unable to move. "Unfortunately, she's had a tough time since then."

Dani took off her apron and put on some hot water for tea. They sat down on the couch and ottoman with their steaming cups, and Pennie filled her in on what had happened to the bear and her cubs, how things had unraveled for Bri, and how she was still in the hospital recovering. Dani wanted to know what she could do, but Pennie knew that Fremont was there for her. Sitting back, relishing the red clover tea, she listened to Dani talk about their plans for the art show, absorbing the dramatic wash of the cyan prints that enveloped them like a vibrant river, so like the imprint left on her soul from the Dead River Valley.

AT THE BRICK TOWNHOUSE on Pine Street, she stopped at the front gate to grasp the homesickness of being there, her childhood home. A realization came to her that she had not dreamed of her mother on the bridge once while she'd been away, so caught up in the emerging history of the valley. A motion caught her attention in the window next door: old lady Payson and her cat spying on the comings and goings of the Goode household. Pennie missed Bartholomew and Fremont already.

Inside the house, the smell of roast duck filled the hallway leading to the kitchen. She knew Uncle Alfie and the dogs must still be at the office, otherwise she'd have a greeting committee. In the blue kitchen, Aunt Aggie stood at the stove stirring something and looked up in surprise. "Well, well, well...look who finally came home!" Pennie reached for her with a warm hug, and Aunt Aggie allowed a quick embrace before saying, "You couldn't spare me one obligatory phone call? Not one?"

She had expected this from her stoic aunt, and explained how busy she'd been working as a line cook. They settled into the wooden captain's chairs around the kitchen table, Pennie telling her all about her trials and tribulations working for Shep, learning the art of plating food in a fast-paced restaurant for an ornery cook with a penchant for whiskey. Her aunt said she didn't know a decent cook who didn't drink, making her way to the counter to mix a martini. Pennie joined her, and they were deep into the "talk soup" when Aunt Maude arrived, ecstatic to hear all about her adventures. The two aunts tsked about the bucket-faced matron who ran the dining room and said they knew a few of those women up north, the kind who liked to throw their weight around and usually latched onto the nearest man with deep pockets.

Tita showed up, breezing into the kitchen, her brown, curly hair exploding like a mushroom after a warm rain. "I see Pennie's catching you up on her time up in the woods with those hicks."

"They aren't all backwards, Tita. Fremont and Bri are great people." Pennie wanted to ask her about Lars but held her tongue.

Tita poured herself a glass of red wine. "Well, Bri was stupid enough to get involved with that pompous redneck who rides around on his ATV all day and night. Not sure what she was thinking there." It was clear she was projecting about her own romantic woes.

"She's young and just figuring things out. The pregnancy has clouded her judgment." Now Pennie had to tell her aunts all about Bri and her relationship with JD, the baby and the engagement, the bruises on her wrists and the "accidental" fall down the stairs.

Aunt Maude thumped her fist on the table. "I hope she's using this opportunity to get rid of his demonic seed."

"The doctor is trying to convince her it's the best thing for her long-term health, but of course, JD and his meddling mother are trying to talk her into keeping it. They don't care about Bri."

Aunt Aggie said, "Poor thing. I heard her mother's been useless for years now, gone to pot with drugs and alcohol. I don't suppose she's been around."

"She made a brief appearance," said Pennie. "But it was short-lived, and very apparent she wasn't there for her daughter."

HOURS LATER, PENNIE SAT with Aunt Maude in her little kitchen on the other side of town. Luckily, she and Uncle Charlie repeated they didn't mind her staying in their basement for as long as she wanted, and he gave her a kiss on the head before he went to bed. She ran her hands along the grooves of the same oak table where her aunt had made countless apple pies. Moonlight hung outside the window, streaming into the kitchen and catching the glint of her aunt's cairngorm brooch, the round pin that looked just like the one Pennie's mother wore in the photo with Togo. "Did you know my mother had a brooch just like that?"

Maude touched it lovingly, her fingers outlining the points of the gemstones. "Why, yes, used to belong to Grammy Goode, and I thought it was lost, but it miraculously surfaced in my garden last spring. Funny how things we truly miss, even yearn for, surface when we obsess about them."

Pennie fiddled with her necklace, the triskelion the husky had dug up in her dream so many months ago. The image of a child's jewelry box flashed in her mind again as she worried her triskelion. "Have you ever heard of objects appearing, seemingly out of nowhere, for no apparent reason?"

"Why, of course, Pennie. It's called 'conjuring an apport.' Family legend has it that Grammy Goode's mother was quite talented at that, you know. Scottish myth passed down over generations." The brooch glimmered with magic in the dim light, as if sending them a sign from another realm. "Your mother just loved this brooch. We thought it had disappeared after Grammy Goode died, too, but she found it in the ground out by the carriage house. Don't ask me how she found it. Must be some kind of spell attached to it."

Pennie wondered about the ability to conjure an apport, to psychically manifest items from the past. About whether objects carried a message, or a clue, from the spiritual realm.

Downstairs in the basement cave, she tossed and turned until finally sinking into a dream...

Jacataqua waited for Aaron on the shores of the St. Lawrence, outside the walled citadel of Quebec. The sachem's eyes lit with fire when she spied General Montgomery's army sailing in on schooners loaded with food, ammunition, clothing, troops...and Aaron Burr. On four legs, she raced with Jacataqua through the crusty snow to his open arms—arms robust again, strengthened with food, a fine silver saber at his waist. They walked together toward the woods to be alone, and he relayed stories about his journey from Montreal while caressing her belly growing with child.

A bellowing voice came from behind. Arnold called to them: "Burr, where do you think you're going? I need you and Jacataqua on a scouting mission to find alternative ways into Quebec." Resigned to his marching orders, they found their way again to her birchbark canoe, the same one that had carried them on their long, treacherous journey up the Kennebec rapids, over the Great Carrying Place to the winding Dead River, and up the Chaudière. Now they paddled together on the St. Lawrence River, around ice floes, to Port aux Trembles, where they disembarked on the snowy bank.

They came upon a free-flowing brook, where Aaron used his hat to scoop water for expectant Jacataqua. From the other side, a British officer appeared and waved to them, friendly, holding up a tin cup. He began to cross the brook in the bitter-cold current, and Aaron met him in the middle to shake hands, accept the cup, and engage in an amicable, yet somewhat surreptitious, conversation. Her ears pricked at attention, she barked, watching both men turn toward Jacataqua in good humor and cross back together.

Sensing danger from this redcoat, she guarded her sachem, but Aaron took her by the scruff of the neck as the British officer grabbed Jacataqua by the wrists and tied them behind her back. Aaron yelled, "Down, Adiak!" and forced her snout down, but she wrangled around to jump on the officer, biting and tearing at his arm until a shot rang out and a pain surged through her tailbone. Barking, she ran in circles around and around and around as Jacataqua was carried off, her face blanched white with betrayal, a face that turned from love to hatred toward the father of her child, who had finally come back to join her, only to help the enemy take her away.

The tortured face of the Swan Island sachem morphed into the distorted face of Bri, crying, alone.

PENNIE JOLTED AWAKE AND felt her backside for the bullet that had pierced her tail. She sat up to slow her breathing and peered at her phone: 5:52 a.m. Outside her little shoebox windows glowed the blue light of morning. She pictured Fremont in his kitchen having coffee with Bartholomew on his lap and instinctively pressed his number, hoping it was not too early. Her heartbeat settled as his gruff voice picked up on the third ring. "Yeah?"

"Oh, I just knew you'd be awake, Fremont. It's Pennie."

She heard him blow out a long stream of smoke. "What's got you up so early this morning?"

"I just had a nightmare and, well, I have this terrible feeling about Bri. I don't know, but something's wrong."

He coughed. "Yes, something is terribly wrong alright." She heard his rifle cock. "I went to the hospital yesterday and found him there in Bri's room with his mother and that preacher Laurel, Bible in hand, along with my daughter, looking like something the cat dragged in. The four conspirators had already wrapped up their ceremony by the time I got there."

"You're saying Bri and JD got married? Right there in the hospital room?"

"That's what I'm saying." He coughed again, hacking up half a lung. "I thought we were talking some sense into her, but that family has got their claws in deep."

Her thoughts went to her uncle. "Alfie found out that their church is a big investor in the power company corridor."

"Oh, I know what he's after. He thinks as soon as I kick off, my property on Middle Carry that's willed to my granddaughter will be his. That property means as much to him as my granddaughter does. They're both just pawns in his game."

She could picture him preparing his pack, the sounds of shuffling and the tinkling of bullets into a pouch. "Fremont, you're not doing anything rash, are you?"

"Just going out hunting. That little doe won't hold me all winter. A man's got to protect himself. Besides, I've got to look around for any signs of that treasure you dreamt about. Don't worry about me, pretty Pennie. I've been through worse."

The phone went silent, and she thought about Fremont tromping through the snow out to his blind, hopefully hunting for a deer, perhaps a buried treasure, and nothing more.

WHEN PENNIE ARRIVED AT the office of Alfred Goode, Esq., Jeannette McCarthy was sitting with her uncle inside his office. The last time Pennie had seen her was at Tita's documentary premiere, when she had given her Chloe's triskelion necklace. The aging southern belle smiled at Pennie when she knocked on the open office door, and they welcomed her in to join them. Chloe's charm bracelet hung loosely around her thin wrist. "Dear Pennie. I was just sharing something with your uncle, something I found in Chloe's jewelry box."

Her uncle held up a wrinkled sheet of paper, saying to Jeannette, "This may be enough to bring your stepson to court over the property."

Jeannette smiled at Pennie, the creases in her eyes soft, stretching to her temples. "I may have told you that I never touched Chloe's room after she died. It's been too painful. But the other day, something came over me and I told myself to go inside." She pointed to the triskelion around Pennie's neck and then to her own bracelet. "Because her jewelry had been unearthed from the ground where they were building the foundation for my stepson's house, I thought to look in her jewelry box to see if there was anything else in there." She pointed to the wrinkled sheet of paper. "This was inside, crumpled in a ball."

The image of the jewelry box flashed again in Pennie's mind, just like it had the night before, sitting in Maude's kitchen. Uncle Alfie handed the wrinkled sheet to Pennie. "It's a legal form signing over the rights of Chloe's property inheritance to Edmond, Jeannette's stepson." At the bottom of the form was Chloe's small loopy signature.

"But I don't understand. Why would she sign this?"

He pointed to the lawyer's signature at the bottom: Leadbetter. Her mind hiccupped, letting it sink in; this was the same lawyer who had defended Ward in court. "Oh my god." She looked at her uncle. "Do you think Ward was coercing Chloe to sign her property over to Edmond?"

"I'm not sure," he said. "If Ward was in debt with Edmond, it could very well be. And they forward dated the document to make it legal."

Jeannette pointed to the date on the contract. "That's Chloe's birthday, the day she would have turned eighteen."

Chapter 17
The White Owl

RESTLESS, SITTING IN HER pink swivel office chair, Pennie thought about the cards from the seer's deck: Grace, The White Owl, and The Golden Rule—guiding forces in the universe. She picked up her cell phone and called Bri's number. After three rings, she picked up the phone, sounding very weak. "I was just thinking about you."

Pennie took a deep breath. "I heard you got married yesterday." Bri began to cry very quietly, and Pennie's heart physically ached. "Bri, I'm happy for you...if that's what you want."

The cloudless winter sky over Exchange Street shimmered against the ice hanging from the eaves, the slow drip of a warm sun. "I don't know *what* I want, to tell you the truth." A quiet space spread between them. "Yesterday, when my mother showed up with JD and the preacher and Betsy, it seemed like, well, it seemed like getting married was the right thing to do, but when I woke up this morning, everything was different."

"What do you mean?

"I had the most vivid dream last night, Pennie. You and I were out at my grandfather's camp on Middle Carry, standing by the pond, when JD came across the water toward us in a small fishing boat with a loud outboard. You told me to come into the camp with you, but my feet were frozen to the ground; I couldn't move. You even grabbed me, but I couldn't move a muscle. JD landed on shore, jumped out, and grabbed me by the wrists, tying my hands behind me with a rope. You started hitting him with a long board before he reached into his vest for a pistol and shot you. You fell to the ground as he dragged me, kicking and screaming, into the camp and tied me to a chair. He was so full of hate. He said, 'Now you can stay in this lousy camp forever.' I watched him go back outside to the boat, stepping over your lifeless body to grab a gas can. Then he dumped gas around the camp to light it on fire." She sucked in. "I could feel the heat of the flames engulfing me before I heard you say to me, inside my head, 'Don't worry, Bri, this is only a nightmare. It's only a nightmare.' Then I woke up. It was so real, Pennie. It was so fucking real."

Pennie's own vision surfaced in her mind. "I had a similar dream, Bri. About the Native American sachem, Jacataqua, the one from Swan Island, being kidnapped by a British officer in Quebec. Aaron Burr was there. He helped the officer bind her and take her away. Burr set the whole thing up, to take her child from her."

Bri sniffed and coughed through her tears. "What do you think it means?"

Outside Pennie's window, a snowy owl soared by in the clear blue sky over the buildings on Exchange Street, perching on a flagpole in a park nearby. Fremont's words echoed inside her mind: *This country has a short-term memory problem. We've forgotten those Revolutionary soldiers who fought and died for our freedom from the English despots who used the power of wealth to diminish any individual rights we had. It's a simple concept. Individual rights. That's what's at stake here.* "I think it means you are fighting for your freedom, Bri. Fighting for your independence, your autonomy to make your own decisions. What is best for you."

UNCLE ALFIE CAME INTO the office with the dogs and checked the messages on Tita's vacant desk. Pennie thought about Fremont with his gun, vengeance on his mind. "Have you talked to Fremont?"

"As a matter of fact, he called me about an hour ago."

Cassie nudged her hand for a scratch. "What did he say?"

"That that dream you had was damn near accurate."

Her mind whirled. "What dream?"

"The one about the munitions buried deep inside the bank of that stream, close to where you thought it would be. Luckily, that dowser showed up with his rod. Took them right to it."

Pennie's emotions swung from apprehension to hopeful expectation. "Are you saying he found some infantry weapons? Like maybe from the Revolutionary War—Arnold's march?"

"That's exactly what I'm saying. Looks like the stars may be aligning in our favor."

Again, Pennie thought about the Grace card and The White Owl. She looked out her window at the American flag flying in the distant park, the owl now gone. "Should I call Rachel at the preservation commission?"

"Already taken care of. She's putting together her team to go over there and assess the artifacts. I gave her the exact coordinates, according to Fremont."

She pictured him cleaning his gun, getting ready to head out, the tone of his voice assured but melancholy. "Did he get a deer?"

"No mention of it. Why?"

"He said he was going hunting when I talked to him early this morning. And I know he's worried about Bri."

"He never mentioned it." Alfie walked into his office and sat at his desk, picked up his newspaper. From the other side of the office, Tita breezed in, pep in her step, smiling as wide as a sunburst.

"Morning, Tita. You and Lars have some things worked out, do you?"

"Now, let's not get ahead of ourselves. We're still *working* on things, but he is certainly making an effort." Tita pointed out the window for Pennie to look down. From the second-floor vantage, she glanced below to see the usual snow-cleared street, cars lining each side. "Yeah, what am I looking at?"

She held up a new car key fob. "The silver one is mine, directly underneath you." On second glance, a shiny new silver Range Rover stood out amongst the drab sedans and mini vans.

"Wow, that's yours?"

"That's mine. The Jan Van is now officially retired."

Images of the ski van played wistfully inside her mind, all their ski trips together, their trip to the Round Barn site, huddling inside the VW bus with Dani and Mali after hearing the gunshot in the dark, their headlamps lighting up their terrified faces. "Can I have it?"

"Are you kidding?" She scoffed. "I'll never give her up. She's just going into retirement."

"You'll be fighting for space in the driveway."

Tita acted like she didn't have time to chitchat, getting up to file some papers in the cabinets. "Maybe not. Lars and I are looking at condos to buy."

Pennie pictured his current housing in the sketchy apartment building with peeling paint off Forest Avenue. "Wow, he must have done pretty well on the sale of the rights."

With flourish, her cousin slammed the file cabinet shut and pretended like she was annoyed with their conversation, blowing a curl off her cheek. "Let's just say we're in good shape to move forward on our next project." Tita was obviously not in the mood to share, so Pennie would wait to see how things shook out. This was Lars, after all, and things could change on a dime.

The conversation with Bri fresh in her mind, Pennie knocked on her uncle's office door and opened it to find him working on a crossword. He looked up. "I need a six-letter word for the constellation Orion."

"No idea," she said. "I'm so worried about Bri. Do you think I should drive up there to check on her?"

"You have to let people make their own decisions, Pennie. You've done what you can, just by being her friend and offering your support." He jotted down his answer in the crossword: *hunter.*

THAT NIGHT, LYING ON the quicksand mattress in the dark, she texted Bri. *How are you doing? Still at the hospital?* Desperately, she wanted to ask her if she had decided to keep the baby or not. But this was a personal decision that Bri had to make. A half hour had gone by when her phone chirped with a text coming in. It was Owen.

What's up?

She chuckled to herself in the dark. *Not much, you?*

Did you hear about the nuptials at the hospital?

I did indeed. That's some fast maneuvering.

Too bad about the baby.

She hesitated. Did he know something?

What happened?

Bri had the D&C today. JD doesn't know about it yet.

She shook all over at the thought of Bri alone in the hospital, explosive JD showing up…*Is she okay? I'm so worried about her.*

I saw her today. She seemed fine. JD went on a weekend hunting trip with his buddies. Not expected back for a few days.

She sighed with relief. *Will you keep a close eye on her?*

Absolutely. Don't worry.

What about your mother?

She doesn't know either. Bri hasn't told anyone other than me, and maybe Fremont, but I haven't seen him.

Thank you. (heart emoji)

She tried calling and texting Bri again, but it was late and she was probably sleeping, hopefully peacefully, without nightmares.

Chapter 18
Preservation

THE NEXT MORNING, SHE got a call back from Bri, who sounded exhausted but relieved after having the operation. "Thank you, Pennie."

"Thank me for what?"

"For being here for me, and helping me see the light, to do what is the best for me and my situation, my future."

She knew this was not the best time to ask her about JD, so she let things lie where they were, offering Bri words of support and comfort. The nurses had moved her to another room while she recovered, and she hadn't heard from JD since he'd left on his weekend trip.

Meanwhile, Pennie waited impatiently to hear about the cache of infantry weapons, spending her free time bothering Dani and Mali in their studio, watching their storytelling masterpiece about the Kennebec River unfolding in a free-flowing current, charged with inspiration.

DAYS PASSED BEFORE SHE finally received a call from Rachel at the preservation commission. She had good news. Calling straight from her trip to West Carry with the state archaeologists, she said they believed the cache of about eleven rifles, muskets, and sabers dated from the Revolutionary War period, and quite possibly was left there by Arnold and his men during their famous march and portage through the Great Carrying Place. Everything had to be confirmed through archeological testing in the lab, but they were almost certain that the weapons came from that period. They guessed the soldiers probably either lost them in the march through the bogs or left them there, hoping to come back and retrieve them. "We found a silver hilt to a sword that was popular among the officers of the Revolutionary War, and we even unearthed a hull we think may have come from a bateau." The dream of the men sinking in the deep, black mud with their weapons, of the soldiers trying to save the bateaux swept up in the rushing waters of the Dead River flood, surfaced in her mind. She could see Colonel Arnold sitting at his desk in the tent, sword with the silver hilt and ivory handle at his elbow, soaking his feet in rosemary water.

Her pulse quickened. "Are these artifacts significant enough to preserve the area?"

"The entire Great Carrying Place will most likely become a national archeological research site."

ON THEIR DRIVE TO Augusta for Fremont's hearing, it snowed like a banshee, the wind blowing a gale. Her uncle insisted on driving his Packard through the storm, saying it was only supposed to last an hour or so. When they finally made it to Gardiner, which happened to be in the region where the Arnold Expedition started, and where Jacataqua had first met Aaron Burr and hunted the bear for the banquet, the snow stopped. The dream came back to Pennie of Burr standing aside as the British soldier banded Jacataqua's wrists and then shot at Pennie inside the husky, Adiak. The imaginary pain still lingered on her tailbone, and she shifted in her seat, again picturing Fremont with the gun, vengeance on his mind.

At the statehouse, they entered the chamber of the Supreme Judicial Court, black baluster railings dividing the room, the long bench for the justices at the front, the seats for witnesses and jurors on either side. Fremont had not shown up yet. She followed her uncle to sit in the back of the room on the long wooden pews. The room began to fill with other lawyers and power company heads. The outcome would hold significant weight, not only for the future of the corridor but for eminent domain cases in general.

The five justices dressed in black robes filed in, Chief Justice Ruth Moore taking a seat in the center of the bench. Fremont was nowhere in sight, and when the judge asked them to enter the hearing area, Uncle Alfie had to explain that the defendant had not shown up yet, but they could proceed. The lawyers for the power company looked pleased that he wasn't there for his own hearing to protect his property. When the judge asked the lawyer for the power company to explain to the court the entire process that had transpired leading up to the hearing, a gray-haired attorney with a mustache, wearing a plaid suit and red bow tie, outlined the steps the company had taken, from serving Fremont the Taking of Property Notice to mailing the Notice of Intent to Acquire and the prelitigation offer, to serving the Declaration of Taking, and finally, the defendant's request for the hearing today.

The spruced-up lawyer grasped the outside corners of the podium, his arms outstretched, in full command of his oratory. "Your honors, the power company is requesting to take possession and title of the property owned by Fremont Safford between West and Middle Carry Pond in the Carrying Place Township by depositing a good-faith estimate of the value of the property, which will be determined at a later trial and final judgment. By granting this Order of Taking request, the power company will be able to meet the time-sensitive requirements of the construction schedule. As the court is aware, the power company has weighed the alternative routes, costs, long-range area planning, and environmental, safety, and other concerns to develop the corridor plan. The Public Utilities Commission found the current transmission line route is the most reasonable choice to serve the public interest in the delivery of safe, reliable, and economic electric energy. This PUC approval includes obtaining property by eminent domain." He sniffed and pushed up his glasses. "To gain immediate possession of the defendant's property title, the power company is ready to deposit a good-faith estimate of value with the court today. Thank you, your honors."

When the well-trimmed lawyer sat down, Chief Justice Moore welcomed Alfred Goode to read his remarks. "Your honors, my client, Fremont Safford, is a descendant of the settlers of the Dead River Valley, and he is also my cousin. His father and his grandfather were woodsmen whose blood, sweat, and tears settled the Dead River Valley, a region rich in vast forests and fertile pastureland and rivers winding from the hills and valleys to the great Kennebec River. They were loggers, lumbermen, and river drivers. His mother and grandmother were everything from hunters and gatherers to gardeners and homesteaders, feeding their families and sustaining the livestock through the harsh Maine winters when their husbands were away for months on end. They did all this to forge lives and homes in the Dead River Valley, before the power company decided to impound the river, their homes and farmland, their community, their hopes and dreams, for the sake of more electrical power.

Today, we have the same forces at work, threatening to take his family property and hunting camp on Middle Carry Pond that has been in Fremont's family for over a hundred years, the same property where Benedict Arnold marched his men, 1,100 men who sacrificed their lives in the Revolutionary War for our freedom, the same freedom Fremont is fighting for today. With the court's permission, I would like to call a witness to document a discovery found near the property that has recently come to light."

The chief justice welcomed Dr. Rachel Goff from the Maine Historic Preservation Commission to enter the chambers and read the letter that had just arrived from the National Preservation Commission the day before. Rachel took the podium and thanked the justices before unfolding the official letterhead. "In light of the recent artifacts unearthed on the Arnold Expedition Trail, including a preliminary assessment of the arsenal of Revolutionary War infantry weapons, the silver hilt of a sword, and the hull of a bateaux built specifically for this epic march, the Commission intends to designate the Great Carrying Place, from Wyman Lake on the Kennebec River to Flagstaff Lake, under the protection of the National Register of Historic Places in the National Historic Preservation Act, Section 106. This area of the Arnold Expedition is a rare undeveloped route and can prove integral to our understanding of this important period in our nation's history."

The justices had many questions for Dr. Goff about the recent discovery of the weapons and musket balls, the accuracy of the preliminary findings by the archeologists, and how the hull of a wooden vessel could survive underwater for 250 years. For what seemed like an hour, she patiently answered all their questions, including explaining how vessels buried in the sediment of a stream could survive for hundreds of years.

After what seemed like an eternity, the court overwhelmingly, with a vote of five to zero, overturned the taking by order of eminent domain in favor of the defendant, Fremont Safford.

ON THE DRIVE HOME, the sky and roads now clear, she thought about Bri recovering in the hospital where the nurses had moved her to another room. Her phone buzzed with an incoming text. It was Owen.

What's up?

She laughed, texting back. *Not much, you?*

JD is dead.

For a moment, the topsy-turvy day stood still. The road underneath her disappeared. She texted back a caring emoji, not knowing how else to respond without being cruel. She asked him what had happened, but no text came back.

She called Bri, who picked up, sobbing into the phone. "Oh, Pennie, it's so awful."

"What happened?"

"He had a stroke and died. All alone, out there in the woods."

None of it made any sense. *A stroke?* "But...he's so young."

"It's Fremont, Pennie. Another hunter found him."

Pennie's heart sank deep down, an aching sadness. She tried to keep her voice from shaking. "Oh my god...I'm so sorry, but I, I thought it was JD."

"JD was shot in a hunting accident." Her tone was dead, flat. "Owen texted me early this morning. Then the police came to see me."

Pennie pictured her sitting in her hospital bed with a brace around her pelvis. "Do they think the two are somehow connected?"

"Fremont didn't have a gun on him. I guess he was just out walking in the woods and, boom, he had a stroke. No one else was around."

She pictured the old hunter among the birches, alders, and tall spruce trees, the place where he was at home. Pennie took a deep breath to reassure her young cousin, her friend. "He was where he loved to be, Bri, and even though he's gone, he left you his family legacy. He won the case against the power company."

It took a moment for the news to sink in. Her voice cracked. "I just wish he were alive to hear the news."

Chapter 19
Long Water Place

THE CHILL OF DECEMBER made her tailbone ache as she stood outside the Portland Museum of Art. It had been a month since Fremont's stroke. When Bri was ready to come home from the hospital, Pennie and Uncle Alfie had driven up to Eustis to bring her home. At Bri's grandfather's house on Flagstaff Lake, his will and testament papers sat on the kitchen table beside the Hills Bros. can. He'd left them there, knowing he wasn't coming home that day. He deeded everything to Bri. They found dusty old Bartholomew on Fremont's couch, lying dead on the memory quilt, waiting for his best friend to come home. The 12-gauge shotgun sat stoic in its locked case, waiting for the next hunt.

Uncle Alfie had helped Bri file and sign everything at the local attorney's office before they talked her into coming with them back to Portland to stay for a few weeks while she healed.

Pennie searched the busy, sleety intersection of Congress and High Streets for any signs of Tita and Bri, when she spotted the figure of large Lars walking toward her, loping, smoking a cigarette, dressed in a long, orange fisherman's raincoat. He seemed pleased to see her.

"Hey, Pennie. Heard you won your uncle's case up on Dead River."

Now that he was close-up, she could see faint bruises around his temples where Tita had boxed him in the ears, but maybe it was her imagination. "We were lucky on that one."

He squinted with one eye. "Sounds like quite a story. Between Malaga Island and the Dead River Valley, you've got some great material for a book, maybe even a documentary."

"Looking for a new project, now that you've sold Tita's film?"

He flicked his burning butt on the ground, squished it with his big black leather boot and chuckled. "Tita's getting used to the idea. The money we made is well worth it. She's coming around to it."

The figures of small Tita and lanky Bri came toward them. A few yards behind, Uncle Alfie and Aunt Aggie rounded a corner. "I'm happy you two are working it out," said Pennie.

Bri walked without crutches now, though she was stiff-legged in her pelvic brace. They all exchanged hugs. Tita, her head held high, took Lars's outstretched hand before they all walked inside, the crowd already mingling in the upper hallway. Down one flight, the larger gallery and meeting room in the lower level hummed with a high vibration where the luminous cyanotype river prints glowed along one wall, backlit in the low light of the open space. Mali's design installation gave Pennie the feeling of riding along the dips and turns of the Kennebec River, starting from the Atlantic Ocean, leading into Merrymeeting Bay, past Swan Island and Pittston, through Vassalboro and Ticonic Falls, past Skowhegan Island, Norridgewock Falls, and Caratunk Falls to Wyman Lake, the dammed impoundment where the Great Carrying Place began. In her mind's eye, Pennie could again see the rugged men in their fringed shirts and moccasins battling their heavy bateaux around the waterfalls and rapids, crashing into the unforgiving ledge and jutting rocks in the fierce cataracts of the Kennebec.

Dani had painted stark images of the five concrete dams along the river: the Lockwood and Hydro Kennebec Dams at Waterville, the Shawmut Dam at Fairfield, the Weston Dam at Skowhegan, the Abenaki and

Anson Dams at Anson, and finally, the Wyman Dam at Bingham. By operating levers in the installation, viewers could recess the 3D dams on the installation to make them virtually disappear, replaced by the free-flowing river, illustrating what the Kennebec looked like before the dams—alive with the movement of the cyan blue plants and fish stirring effortlessly on the connected canvases. The intense blue of the cyanotype, using sunlight to expose the images of algae, seaweed, and fish, washed with the river water, created immersive collages, springing with life.

After Wyman Lake, north to the Forks at the confluence of the Dead, the river meandered south through the rapids, the place where she and Bri had stood that day, their senses alive with the breathtaking falls of the young guide's favorite fishing spot, the same place where the power company corridor was passing over the river, where white-water rafting entertained thousands of thrill seekers every spring and summer. At the Long Falls Dam impoundment of Flagstaff, Dani had drawn in the meandering path of the long-ago Dead River, now flooded, lost to the hands of progress.

A few hundred people crowded the gallery. Donations for the river restoration project surged. Pennie stood between Mali and Dani, gushing over the installation. "I didn't realize so many of our towns and rivers were given Native American names."

"Our ancestors relied on the waterways," said Mali.

"And most of the names describe something about the rivers," said Dani. "Like, *Kennebec* from the Norridgewock tribe, meaning 'long water place.'"

"Fremont told me that hundreds of men in the Arnold Expedition would have died without the help of guides like Natanis and Jacataqua, Natives who knew these waterways intimately. I've had such vivid dreams about her, pregnant with Burr's child. I wonder whatever happened to her and her baby."

Another patron took Dani's attention away, but Mali leaned toward her. "When the men made it to Quebec, Jacataqua was taken to a nunnery. Burr sent her there to have his child, a daughter she named Chestnutiana, after the toast she made to him at the banquet at Fort Western." Pennie pictured the young couple coming from the woods after the hunt. Mali said, "But the British soldier who took her to the nunnery also took the baby from her and sailed off to England. After all she had done for Burr and Arnold and the expedition, they still betrayed her."

"What a sad story," Pennie said, watching leggy Bri admiring the artwork, a young man sparking up a conversation with her.

"Using force has always been the white man's way," said Mali. "The need to contain and harness life, any natural energy, for their own gain." This was the crux of it all. Sacrificing people and land in pursuit of the almighty dollar, in the name of progress. At least Uncle Alfie had won one small victory in court to protect Fremont's property and the Great Carrying Place, to try to make some peace with the past.

THEY ALL DROVE BACK to Eustis for Fremont's funeral in the spring-time, after the ground had thawed for his burial, the bright green leaves unfurling, the streams running free after the early melt. Pennie and Bri, Tita, and Mali and Dani took another hike out to the Round Barn site on Flagstaff Lake, but this time they brought along overnight packs to sleep on the porch under the stars, beneath the pull of the constellations.

Bri, now brace-free and back to her own winsome self, pointed out Orion, the Hunter, and Andromeda, the chained princess in the sky. She pointed out Ursa Major, the Great Bear, seven of its stars making the Big Dipper pointing to Polaris, the North Star. Nearby was Ursa Minor, the Little Bear, sharing her tail with the handle of the Little Dipper. "The Big Dipper always points to the North Star, the tip of the Little Bear's tail," she said.

Dani added, "The Big Bear is called Awasos or Muwin."

Mali finished her thought. "He is chased at night by three hunters who kill him every fall, turning the leaves brown, until he is revived in the springtime, turning right side up in the sky."

Pennie lay cocooned in her sleeping bag, looking up into the darkest of skies, at the brightest of stars, and fell into another dream of the Dead River Valley...

ALONGSIDE THE RIVER WITH Papa and Mama, Fremont and Fannie, she barked at Captain Wing, who motored by in the Grey Gosling, *towing the old, longstanding white flagstaff behind him. The oldest man of the valley spoke to them, keeping an eye on the floating staff, a ripple hugging its long outline in the winding, storied river of generations of settlers. "I had a feeling of shame, and it seemed to me that I could hear it saying, 'Captain, how could you do this, how could you leave me behind? Forty-five years ago, you helped to cut and bring me from the woods and erected me to stand for that which has been the backbone of Flagstaff history, part of the great expedition of Benedict Arnold and the men who passed this way.'"*

Afterword

Writing historical fiction is no small feat. I know because I've tried. It requires a tremendous amount of research. Then bringing to life stories of relationships, hardships, complex kinships like those of Jacataqua and Burr, Natanis and Arnold. Fleshing out historical knowledge and stories, layers deep, like forest-floor strata. That is true craftsmanship. How many have learned of Benedict Arnold's march to Quebec? How many know of the Abenaki woman who accompanied his men and the vast ecological knowledge she had to possess to see them through the wilderness of her homeland? She undoubtedly lived a life aligned to the rhythms of the earth, wild foods, traditional medicines, and ancient travel routes.

It has been said that every river has a tribe associated with it. Traditional Abenaki homelands were situated along both the Dead and the Kennebec Rivers. The Penobscot River is the river to which I belong. The waterways were ancient highways central in connecting lives. They were used to visit relatives, trade goods, reach hunting grounds, or to wage war. St. Francis, on the banks of the Arsikantegouk, established itself as a Catholic mission town in the 1700s. It had well-traveled routes to its shores by Abenaki and other tribes seeking refuge and safety from colonial violence such as the exodus following the Norridgewock Massacre of 1724.

For me, as a Penobscot and a tribal historian, the Native thread woven throughout this story set in the western mountains of Maine really anchors the story. It contributes thoughts and knowledge that recovers western Maine as Native space. It whispers memories of vibrant Indigenous presence that once existed in all areas of present-day "Maine"—in physical places on the land, around virtually every bend in the river, and in all the spaces that Native people hold within our collective histories: roles played in shaping the Nation, forging alliances, helping win wars, and keeping people alive.

A note regarding native languages. The tribal nations within this geographic region share similar languages all based in an Algonquin dialect. While some words are shared and used widely amongst the tribes, other words differ quite a bit from tribe to tribe. Only in the last century were alphabets and written words created for communicating Indigenous languages. Up until then they were strictly oral languages. Because native languages in this region are more descriptive than noun-based, how things were described from region to region could vary greatly. With the advent of the written word there were those who learned and adopted the written alphabet, and there were others that spelled out words phonetically, creating the possibility of even more variation in the stylistic presentation of Native words.

There is a saying in Penobscot,

N'kwe'ta'pekat—"It is all one story; it is an endless story."

The story is that of the interconnectedness of life, spirit, and the will to survive.

—Maria Girouard, M.A. in history, University of Maine, Orono;
Penobscot tribal member and tribal historian

Acknowledgements

A heartfelt thank-you to Flagstaff village descendent Kenny Wing, grandson of Captain Cliff Wing, and to Benedict Arnold expedition historian and author, Norman Kalloch, Jr. You both have been more than generous with your contributions, advice, and guidance.

In my early research, I came across *There Was a Land*: a collection of stories and essays from family and friends of the Flagstaff, Dead River, and Bigelow plantations. A special thanks goes to the late Ruey Stevens Baldwin for compiling and preserving these memories.

Thank you, Mary Henderson at the Dead River Area Historical Society, for sharing your story, and introducing me to the lives of the villagers and preserving their history.

For editorial direction and review, thank you Mark Athitakas, Kellyn Eaddy, and Amy Chamberlain—the same team who edited the first book of this series. Skilled editors are hard to find, and I am lucky to have your combined expertise.

Thank you, Maria Girouard, MA, Penobscot tribal member and tribal historian, for your careful review and Native American sensitivity edits. Your generous spirit and historical knowledge leave a lasting imprint of truth and reconciliation.

For the beautiful and bold cover design, thank you Mi'kmaq artist Marissa Joly. Your Indigenous spirit comes through with each cover in the series, and for this I am grateful and full of joy.

Thank you, Dorette Amell, the artist and visionary who beautifully illustrated the map of the Kennebec Valley and Dead River Valley region, and whose set of divination cards, *The Maine Oracle*, became an inspiration in the telling of this story.

For the Maine State Library and Maine Historical Society, thank you for your depth of resources, rich with hidden treasures of the great Pine Tree State. Special thanks to friend and fellow writer Kristin Rieff for reading and reviewing an early draft.

And finally, thank you to my husband, Jonathan Safford. You have been with me every step of the way, from trudging through the rain-soaked wilderness at the Great Carrying Place to climbing the Safford Brook Trail. Our journey always leads us to new discoveries. Because of you, Isaac and Ana, Claire and Sam, my feet are on the ground, and my head is in the stars.

Bibliography

Amell, Dorette. (2022). *The Maine Oracle Fortune Telling Cards: A Divination System.* Self-published.

Ames, Alfred. (Director). (1986). *From Stump to Ship: A logging Film* [1930 film]. Department of Agriculture, Forest Service, Division of State and Private Forestry, Fire and Aviation Management Staff. https://youtu.be/cIKCjQdxtO0?si=ksylnkhiH7zFX7fa.

Arnold Expedition Historical Society. (2009). *Arnold's Wilderness March map and guide* [Map and pamphlet].

Arnold Expedition Historical Society. (2021). *The Great Carrying Place Portage Trail.* AEHS. https://arnoldsmarch.org/wp-content/uploads/2021/06/AEHS-The-Great-Carrying-Place-Portage-Guide-2021.pdf.

Bacheldor, Eva D. (1949, July 5). All But One Flagstaff Resident Resigned To Approaching Flood. *Portland Press Herald.*

Burnell, Alan L., and Wing, Kenny R. (2010). *Lost Villages of Flagstaff Lake.* Arcadia Publishing.

Chenoweth, James H. (1988). *Hunting for Jacataqua.* Maine Historical Society typescript.

Chesterton, Gilbert K. (1906). O God of Earth and Alter [Hymn]. https://hymnary.org/text/o_god_of_earth_and_altar.

Coburn, Louise Helen. (2016). *The Passage of the Arnold Expedition through Skowhegan* [originally published 1922]. Creative Media Partners. https://www.google.com/books/edition/The_Passage_of_t he_Arnold_Expedition_Thr/qwwwvgAACAAJ?hl=en.

Codman, John. (1901). *Arnold's Expedition to Quebec*. The Macmillan Company.

Coffin, Robert P. Tristram. (1937). *Kennebec: Cradle of Americans*. Farrar & Rinehart.

Dead River Area Historical Society, Eustis, Maine. Various newspaper articles and *History of Flagstaff* [Poster]. Dead River Area Historical Society, Eustis, Maine.

Dingley, Theda Cary. (1916). When Arnold was Major Colburn's Guest. In Maine Federation of Women's Clubs, *The Trail of the Maine Pioneer* (2nd ed., pp. 293–298). Lewison Journal Company.

Eckstrom, Fannie Hardy. (1907). *David Libby: Penobscot Woodsman and River-Driver*. American Unitarian Association.

Fairbanks, Henry Nathaniel. (n.d.). Arnold's Expedition up the Kennebec to Quebec, in 1775 [Typescript of article]. Personal account dictated by John J. Henry, Bangor, Maine. Maine Historical Society Special Collection (Coll. S-4045).

Flagstaff Plantation High School Report. (1949). Flagstaff, Maine.

Franzmann, A. W., and Schwartz, C. C. (2007). *Ecology and Management of the North American Moose*. University Press of Colorado.

Hallee, Roland, and Rogers, Marilyn. (June 2019–August 2020). The Burial of Flagstaff, part 1–4. *The Town Line Newspaper*, 16(30–33).

Haskell, Jessica J. (1916). A Man and a Maid. In Maine Federation of Women's Clubs, *The Trail of the Maine Pioneer* (2nd ed., pp. 311–317). Lewison Journal Company.

Meigs, Jonathon. (circa 1929). *Journal of Major Return Jonathon Meigs of the Continental Army Expedition from Boston to Quebec, Septem-*

ber 17, 1775–January 1, 1776 [Typescript]. Maine Historical Society Stacks (Coll. S-8970).

Judd, Richard. *Walter Wyman and River Power.* Maine Memory Network, a Maine Historical Society website. Retrieved Dec. 3, 2024, from https://www.mainememory.net/sitebuilder/site/815/page/12 25/display?use_mmn=1.

Flagstaff Area Business Association. (2024). *The Valley Below: The Story of Flagstaff Lake* [Map and pamphlet].

Kalloch Jr., Norman R. (2018). *A Long Way to Walk.* Maine Authors Publishing

Leland, Charles G. *The Algonquin legends of New England* [1884]. Retrieved Jan. 24, 2025, from Sacred-text.com, https://sacred-texts.com/nam/ne/al/al74.htm.

MacDonald, Thomas L. (1974). *Scenes of Flagstaff and the Dead River.* Flagstaff Cemetery Association.

Merrill, Daphne Winslow. (1973). *The lakes of Maine: A compilation of fact and legend.* Courier- Gazette.

New England Historical Society. *Jacataqua, the Indian Sachem who bore Aaron Burr's love child.* Retrieved Jan. 29, 2025, from https://newenglandhistoricalsociety.com/jacataqua-the-india n-sachem-who-bore-aaron-burrs-love-child.

Posewitz, Jim. (1994). *Beyond Fair Chase*: *The Ethic and Tradition of Hunting.* Rowman & Littlefield.

Roberts, Kenneth. (1985). *Arundel* [facsimile of 1930 1st ed., 1st state]. Kenneth Roberts Centennial Commission commemorative limited ed. Gannett Books.

Various former residents and friends of the Dead River Valley. (1999). *There Was a land: Memories of Flagstaff, Dead River, and Bigelow.* Flagstaff Memorial Chapel association.